# The Queen's Painter

*Also by Wendy Holden*

The Governess
The Duchess
The Princess

Honeymoon Suite
Wild and Free
Gifted and Talented
Marrying Up
Gallery Girl
Filthy Rich
Beautiful People
The School for Husbands
The Wives of Bath
Pastures Nouveaux
Azur Like It
Fame Fatale
Bad Heir Day
Simply Divine

# The QUEEN'S PAINTER

A novel of Hans Holbein and Anne Boleyn

WENDY HOLDEN

MLP

First published in 2026 by Mountain Leopard Press
An imprint of Headline Publishing Group Limited

1



Cataloguing in Publication Data is available from the British Library

Hardback ISBN 978 1 0354 1920 3
Trade Paperback ISBN 978 1 0354 1921 0

Typeset in 13/16.3pt Garamond 3 LT Std by Six Red Marbles UK, Thetford, Norfolk

Printed and bound in Great Britain by Clays Ltd, Elcograf S.p.A.

MIX
Paper | Supporting responsible forestry
FSC® C104740

Headline's policy is to use papers that are natural, renewable and recyclable products and made from wood grown in well-managed forests and other controlled sources. The logging and manufacturing processes are expected to conform to the environmental regulations of the country of origin.

Headline Publishing Group Limited
An Hachette UK Company
Carmelite House
50 Victoria Embankment
London EC4Y 0DZ

The authorised representative in the EEA is Hachette Ireland,
8 Castlecourt Centre, Dublin 15, D15 XTP3, Ireland (email: info@hbgi.ie)

www.headline.co.uk
www.hachette.co.uk

To Noj, Andrew and Isabella

# *Prologue*

The Tower of London
19 May 1536, morning

He stands at the back of the big, expectant crowd. Everyone's talking about the scaffold; how there is no block, no coffin. People are saying it can't possibly happen. That there'll be a reprieve.

Will there? There are reasons to hope. Hans can see, from where he is standing, the gangling figure of the king's illegitimate son. Fitzroy is known to be delicate; he's never recovered from witnessing a hanging, drawing and quartering. Would his father really make him watch a beheading?

And above, on the turrets of the White Tower, are the domes the king put there for Anne's coronation. Henry changed the skyline of London for her, the whole shape of the nation, and beyond it, the known world. That was only three years ago.

To the left of the scaffold, out of the shadow of the keep, St Peter ad Vincula's new stone shines brightly. The chapel was restored only recently, and Henry had the roof inside made of Spanish chestnut so Katherine of Aragon could pray under the trees of her homeland. Domes for one wife, a ceiling for another. He was a loving husband once.

Above, white clouds sail in a warm blue sky. Apple trees foam sweetly with blossom, birds sing their hearts out, and beyond the thick grey Tower walls the Thames flows smooth as silk. It's inconceivable that on a day this glorious Anne can step out onto the bright green grass, feel the sun on her face and walk to her death.

He has no idea where in the Tower she is, from which direction she will come. Perhaps she will not come. They will be told to disperse, to go home. There is no coffin after all, no block.

But now the birds in the blossom trees cease their chirping. And now she appears, and suddenly it's all real and he knows, with a hard, cold, sure knowledge that gathers in his stomach and throat, that it will happen.

# *Chapter One*

Whitehall Palace, London
19 May 1536, evening

A bag over his shoulder, a lantern in one hand, Hans sidles along the courtyard wall. He doubts anyone will notice. After the vigilance of the last weeks, the soldiers are off their guard. It's all over now.

And anyway, the soldiers know him. Hans has lived in the gatehouse above them for years; it's where he works. *The Kraut painter*, they call him, in that affectionately xenophobic way typical of the English. So now, as he disappears through an archway, none of them bat an eyelid.

As expected, no one is guarding her apartments. What's to guard? The queen who lived here is executed for treason, bundled away in an arrow chest, shoved in the chapel floor.

The carved double doors are locked, but no matter, there'll be a window open somewhere. Outside, in the garden, he passes flowers that glow in the moonlight, exude faint scents. Nature, just carrying on. Being beautiful despite everything.

He's right, a window is open. He climbs easily over the sill with his long legs. These rooms were always so full of light and laughter. But now he jumps down into blackness, silence.

His lantern glow finds her falcon symbol carved above the fireplace. The stained-glass windows bearing her coat of arms. On the ceiling are her initials, entwined with the king's. The *HA HA* that courtiers laughed at behind her back. That the common crowd had shouted along her coronation procession. 'Ha ha! Ha ha!'

Damn them all, he thinks with a hot jab of fury. In this sense, at least, she's still here.

And, most gloriously of all, in the picture corridor. The king built it to connect his rooms to Anne's and provide a gallery for Hans's paintings of her. He had damask drapes put over them, to be pulled aside for dramatic effect. *Ta-da! My beautiful Anne!*

Hans parts the curtains, sees the images he created. He can remember the exact circumstances of each one: where it was painted, what she said, who came in and out as he worked. There are so many portraits she had laughed about it. 'You must be bored to death of painting me!'

It was a joke, nothing more, and so he had smiled back. For him to declare, *Never, not for a moment, you are the only subject* might have sounded a little dramatic. But it was what he'd felt; what he still felt.

Besides, she was never the same. Here she is, merry in a red dress and a pearl-trimmed hood. Here she is in a white dress with green sleeves. 'Henry's favourite, the Tudor colours,' she had said at the time. 'Makes me feel like I'm wearing a flag.'

And here she is in her favourite black, her gold B pendant at her long white throat. Hans had designed it for her and she wore it all the time. Three tear-shaped pearls hang from it; the same number as the years of her reign. As if he'd known all along how much time she had.

It is hard to look, but he can't tear his eyes away. Crushed and hollow with grief as he is, the sight of her draws him upwards, straightens his spine, pushes his shoulders back. He gazes and gazes, thinks what is lost, what can never be replaced. What you can only see here now, in his portraits.

Her eyes, so dark you can't see the pupils, sparkling with intelligence. Those witty red lips, the swirling energy of that shining black hair. That pale oval face that constantly changed expression, thoughts flying across it like clouds across the moon. That excited brush of pink high on her lovely cheekbones. Like strawberry juice mixed in cream. The energy and excitement that flowed from her. You can feel it all, see it all.

Hans bids each picture a silent goodbye before drawing the curtains for a final time. He is leaving and won't see them again. Only in his heart. But it's a comfort to know they're here, that there's somewhere in the world she still exists as she was.

And now he must do what he came to do. He goes to the portrait at the end, the biggest one of all. Drawing back the curtains, he pulls in a long breath. It always surprises him, this work. The power of it, the beauty of it, the success with which he realised it. Of all his portraits, it's the best, and certainly the greatest of his ones of Anne.

Except, of course, that she's not in it. Not physically, anyway. It's of two men, not a woman in sight. Two French ambassadors: Jean de Dinteville, envoy from the court of François I, and his associate, Georges de Selve.

As Hans works, he thinks of how this picture began. Anne's swift foot on the stairs, her tap on the door. She loved to come to his workroom, always under a cloak so the guards didn't know it was her. She liked to watch him paint, even sometimes joining in, grinding up the colours for him.

A long and boring job, that, he'd always thought. But she seemed to find it satisfying, pounding pieces of vermilion or lapis lazuli more finely even than he did himself. Or holding a piece of precious gold leaf on the tip of her tapering white finger. He knew, because she told him so, that his workroom was a haven for her. High up above the gate arch, away from the eyes of the court, free from being constantly on show.

Here she could take off her hood. 'It's so tight,' she would say, easing off the pearl-edged clamp around her hair. 'That feels better,' she would add, slipping off narrow brocade shoes and flexing long, elegant toes.

But on that day, that particular day, it was more than just a normal visit. She had had an idea. Her coronation was imminent and she wanted to mark it with a portrait. But not the usual type, a face, head and shoulders. 'Something different,' she said, dark eyes dancing with mischief.

As she explained, he listened indulgently, wiping oil paint from his hands with a rag. 'A portrait of you,' he repeated.

'Yes.'

'But you're not in it.'

'No.'

She stood with her hands on her aching back. Beneath a loose gown of black damask, the baby was growing. Her hair hung down, dark and glossy, and her bare toes peeped out from the hem of her dress. She was peering at the sketches pinned round the walls, a great many of which were of her. The paintings were long finished, but he kept the drawings up.

'You've done so many of me already,' she said. 'Henry's got a whole corridor of them. Me in a black dress, me in a red dress, me in a green dress.'

*Greensleeves was all my joy*, trilled someone in the background, to the strum of a lute. The singer Mark Smeaton had come with her; he seemed to follow her everywhere.

*Greensleeves was my delight*, he went on.

It was a song Henry claimed to have written himself. But Hans knew it was Mark's, as, no doubt, did Anne.

*Greensleeves was my heart of gold.*

Anne rolled her black eyes. 'I get so sick of that song,' she murmured. She looked over, smiled, shook her hair. 'Mark,' she said sweetly, 'can you leave us?'

Slowly, and with obvious reluctance, the boy got up and went. 'His voice is wonderful, but he's far too familiar,' Anne admitted. 'I shouldn't let him trail after me like he does.'

It was true that he was talented, but also far too forward. He needed to be careful, Smeaton.

'And I can't talk freely in front of him. Or say what I feel, as I can with you.' She smiled, and Hans felt the usual hopeless tug in his heart.

He knew all about not being able to talk freely. Or saying what he felt. He had never been able to do either since he met her. It had been years ago, and in another country. They had both been young and struggling. Both far from home, both trying, in their different ways, to succeed.

Since then, things had changed beyond the wildest dreams of either. Anne had risen to dizzying heights and taken Hans with her. He was, as she often said, not just her favourite painter but one of her oldest, most trusted friends. It went no further than that, not for her.

That was why, unlike Smeaton, he had never presumed. Why he'd buried his passion, given it rein only in his art. Anything beyond friendship, beyond artist and patron, was out of the question. And would have been even if Anne had returned his feelings. Their positions were too far apart. He was an artisan, she was an aristocrat. And about to become a queen.

Respectfully, he took off his paint-smeared smock. 'So how will it work?' he asked. 'This picture of you, without you in it?'

She picked up his overall from the floor and slipped it on. The rough linen, smeared with every conceivable colour, was incongruous. And yet she looked beautiful in it. She laughed and flipped her hair over the grubby collar. 'I would make a good painter, no?'

'You would,' he agreed. 'I've told you enough of my trade secrets over the years.'

She had picked up a brush and was walking round his easel. He saw that her ever-active mind had moved on, the portrait that wasn't a portrait left behind.

She must have been joking about it, he thought. She was merry all the time these days, joyously anticipating both the crowning and the birth of the son who would make her position inviolable. These days, Anne was riding high.

'Who's this?' she asked of the painting he was working on.

A German merchant, he told her. From the Hanseatic League at the Steelyard. Wealthy and regular clients, his countrymen, too, they commissioned portraits to send back to their families, joking that their wives thought his pictures more real than them.

'What's his name?'

'Herr Hermann Hildebrandt von Wedigh, since you ask.'

'A complicated character, evidently.'

'How so?' But he knew she had worked it out; she always did. She knew exactly what to look for.

'If you look at his right eye and the left side of his mouth, he's friendly,' she said. 'But if you look at his left eye and the right side of his mouth, he's serious.'

'My paintings are no mystery to you.'

'But you missed a bit here.' She dipped her brush into the mixed black paint by the easel, bent towards Herr von Wedigh.

He moved swiftly to stop her. 'No!'

'Do let me! Just the tiniest mark!' Her black eyes were mock-pleading, with just a sparkle of a tease.

'Not even you.' Gently but firmly, he took the brush from her fingers.

She gave a petulant toss of her hair, went to the window seat, shoved aside the pile of material he used for props and patted the space next to her. 'Sit here. Let's talk about my picture.'

So the portrait-that-was-not-a-portrait was not forgotten after all.

Far from it. 'You, Hans, are going to make the most extraordinary work that has ever been!'

## *Chapter Two*

Sitting right against her, he held his breath. Watched her lovely profile as she eagerly described her idea. 'I want it to be a discussion, a debate, a game. A map that if you follow, you get the answer. People will have to work out the meaning. Do you see?'

'Not really. Meaning of what, exactly?'

'Lots of different things.' She felt in her pocket. 'Here's the list.'

Her writing was famously slapdash, but he was used to it. A long list, he saw. Item One: Jean de Dinteville. Item Two: Georges de Selve.

'The new French ambassador?' He had seen Item One about the court. But Item Two, who was he?

'The Bishop of Lavaur. He's only just got here.' Anne tapped her delicate nose conspiratorially. 'On embassy from Amboise, with a very special secret message from François!'

The French royal court at Amboise was where Hans had first met Anne. 'Why didn't the king send it in a letter to de Dinteville? He's his ambassador in London, isn't he?'

Anne's eyes sparkled. 'Yes, but it was so secret it could only be delivered in person! A message of support. For my marriage to Henry. For my coronation.'

'Why does that have to be secret, though?'

'Oh, you know what François is like.' Anne shrugged her elegant shoulders. 'Nothing written down. Sits on every fence going whilst riding two horses in different directions at once.'

Actually, Hans didn't have a clue what François of France was like, any more than he really knew what Henry of England was like. To people like him, kings were distant figures. To people like Anne, they were friends and husbands. It was the difference between them in a nutshell.

'Will they mind just being things on a list?' he asked, of the ambassadors. He didn't know de Selve but thought de Dinteville looked arrogant. One of those wealthy, disdainful young men there seemed a superabundance of at court.

'They don't know. As far as they're concerned, it's a portrait of them. Commissioned by me as a friend of France.'

'Are they to stand, looking out at the viewer? Or sit facing each other?'

Anne thought for a moment. 'They are my supporters, so position them like the supporters on a coat of arms. Like the lion and the unicorn. One either side, with everything else in the middle.'

He nodded, made a quick sketch and showed her.

'That's it! Oh, and the picture must be enormous. The biggest it can possibly be.' She raised a slender arm to suggest the height of a door.

Life-size then. At least. Only Baltic oak would be big enough. He needed to order it from the Steelyard.

She grinned. 'Perhaps Herr Hermann Hildebrandt von Wedigh could help.'

'No doubt.' Hans looked down at the other objects Anne wanted in the picture. A lute and some flutes, a small crucifix, a globe. A hymn book, a sphere. And 'instruments that measure time and date'. If there was a connection, he wasn't getting it.

He looked at her. 'I give up.'

She laughed, then explained, and then he got it. And she was right, it was going to be extraordinary.

Hans's friend Kratzer, the king's astronomer, arrived a few days later with a box. Beneath his badly cut fringe his round eyes shone as he produced his beloved gadgets. The torquetum, the polyhedral dial, the shepherd's dial, all fiendishly tricky to paint with their many sides, angles and numbers. It was, Hans thought, lucky that he liked a challenge.

'You need to set the dials,' he told Kratzer.

'You said. Dates and times of significance to the queen. The picture is all about her, everything in it relates to her, and yet she is nowhere to be seen.' Kratzer had grasped the idea immediately and was practically rubbing his hands in glee. He loved the idea of a portrait that wasn't a portrait and yet was. It appealed to his love of the ingenious and the innovative, of pushing an idea as far as it would go.

'One date needs to be the eleventh of April. The day she was proclaimed queen.'

'Let me make a note.' Kratzer reached for a scrap of paper, snatched up one of Hans's charcoals. No one else – well, perhaps one other person – would get away with this. 'The eleventh of April,' he repeated. 'Know the exact time? I can put that on too.'

'No, but I can ask.'

'And remind me when the coronation is?'

The thirty-first of May, Hans said, but he had that date covered. He was proud of his moment of inspiration in Westminster Abbey. Marvelling at the mosaic pavement before the altar, the colourful beauty of it, the skill of those who had designed and laid it, he had also seen it was the answer to a problem. What to put on the painting's floor. 'Not one of your usual boring carpets, please, Hans,' Anne had teased.

He had been considering stone steps, or a map of France. But this pavement in the Abbey was the very spot where she would be crowned. Like the dials, like the French king's message, it represented another part of her story. Another moment in time. The ultimate moment, in which she became queen.

Kratzer was looking at the musical instruments assembled on the table. 'And what are all these flutes about? Lutes?'

'Harmony, in a word. She wants to make England a better place.'

'Good luck to her with that. And these people at each side?' He was examining Hans' sketch.

'They're French ambassadors; they represent France.'

'What's so great about France?'

'She lived there for a long time, before she came here.'

'So what? I lived a long time in Munich. Doesn't mean I'd want it in a painting.' Kratzer was looking at him closely. 'Weren't you there too, Holbein? In France? Didn't you meet her there?'

'Might have done.' Hans spoke casually, as if it was something he hardly remembered. Rather than the one thing he thought of all the time.

Now, three years later, he gently pushes the memories aside. There's a job to do. He sets down his lantern, produces candles from his bag, lights them from the flame. Drips wax onto the floorboards and sets them in it, until there is enough light to work by. He gets out the sketch he has drawn of the object he plans to add. It's complicated, a trick of perspective. He must get it exactly right.

It's positioned low down in the picture; he'll have to crouch or kneel to do it. And he'll have to paint quickly, more speedily even than usual. For if someone sees the light, comes in and discovers him, how will he explain himself? Even the inattentive soldiers would think it suspicious.

Kneeling on the floorboards, he glances up at de Selve and de Dinteville. They look at him down their noses, Kratzer's instruments stretching between them.

Hans recalls the ambassadors without affection. Arrogant buggers, the pair of them. Entitled in that rich-boy way. Superior, difficult and unreliable. Pinning them down for a sitting had been near-impossible. They were busy, they were in meetings, they were away from court. They were far too important; they could not be bothered. Any and all of the above applied.

And when finally they agreed – when finally they granted him a few hours in Bridewell Palace, which Anne had refurbished for de Dinteville's sole enjoyment – the ambassador did nothing but complain. Having to buy a new outfit for the coronation was a particular source of annoyance

'This,' he said to de Selve, shaking his pink sleeves. 'You would not believe the price.'

'But what a fine figure you cut, *mon ami*,' de Selve had replied drily. 'Who knew that the English can make clothes? To look at them, you would hardly think so.'

'They can't cook either,' de Dinteville returned. 'The food here, *oh la la*. It pains my stomach. Gives me the indigestion.'

An unmistakable smell underlined the truth of his words. Sketching in de Selve's expression of disgust, Hans grinned to himself. De Dinteville, meanwhile, banged on about the inconvenience and expense of having to find, feed and house twelve French cavalrymen. 'As well as dress them in blue sarcenet from head to foot. And that's just the horses.'

'But why?' asked de Selve.

'For this procession of the coronation,' was the exasperated reply. 'La Boulain wants them to ride at the front. Because of her marvellous French connections, you know?' De Dinteville rolled his eyes.

'But *mon ami*, where in London would you find twelve French cavalrymen?'

'Nowhere, obviously. I have to bring them over from Calais. *More* expense. All of which I have to bear myself.' The ambassador snorted in irritation.

'But our sovereign lord François will reimburse you, *non?*'

A harsh bark of laughter was the answer to this. '*And* I'll be here all summer,' de Dinteville added crossly. 'Waiting for La Boulain's baby. By this stinking river, in the boiling heat.'

'Unlikely to be boiling,' said de Selve. 'This is England, after all. When does the baby arrive?'

'Well, it *should* be nine months after the wedding. But I'm not sure when that is officially supposed to have been. It actually happened in January, but now it is March and Henri has only just announced it to his *parlement*. Someone needs to tell the boy not to arrive until Christmas.'

De Selve raised one of his long eyebrows. 'It will be a boy? For sure?'

De Dinteville shrugged his pink shoulders. 'It needs to be. Henri got rid of Katherine because she only had a girl. La Boulain must produce a dauphin. A princess would be bad news for her.'

He'd been partly right, of course. But Princess Elizabeth would have been fine news, had she been followed by brothers. The bad news for Anne had been the lack of boys.

Hans pushes the thought from his mind and gets out his brushes. Some have full bristles, while others are so thin they're just a couple of hairs. Next come the dishes he mixes his paints in, tapered like glasses and heavy-based so they won't tip over. Finally the colours. Finely ground white lead, black powder for the grey tints, ground ochre for the creamier tints, a flask of water for mixing.

His work now must be perfect, to blend in with the superbly skilful job he did for Anne. Those shining sleeves of de Dinteville's are especially excellent. White lead and vermilion had proved the exact right combination to capture the effect of light on pink satin.

De Selve's damask robe had required a different approach. It had taken ages to find that rich chestnut colour. He'd searched woods and fields for it, walked around with his eyes on the ground until he spotted exactly the right shade, to be picked out with a penknife and mixed with water. The elaborate tasselled dagger dangling casually from the ambassador's hand had been another challenge. He had built it up with adhesive before adding the gold. The effect was dazzlingly realistic.

Hans leans forward, makes the first stroke. Hours pass. By the time he is finished, the candles are down to their stubs and the pinking in the sky announces dawn.

*What are you doing to our picture, Hans? Our great portrait, the one we devised together?* A low, husky voice with a faint French accent breathes in his ear. He starts in shock, looks round.

'Anne?' He can't see her, but he can feel her near him. Smell her spicy lavender scent.

*Our painting!* she chides. *You have added this . . . thing without asking me! What is it anyway?*

Many people in the years to come will ask this question. Some will think it a fishbone, this white and slanting object, and viewed from the front perhaps it does look like one. Viewed from the side, however, the stretching slant shrinks and comes into focus. You can see what it is then all right.

'A skull.' In other words, death.

*Ugh!*

It's hard to say, but he forces it out. 'The painting was your story. And that was the way the story ended. But I wanted to make it a puzzle, like the rest.'

More soft laughter in the darkness. *Ah, I see now. Ingenious, Hans. However, you are wrong.*

'Wrong?' he echoes, in the familiar way. He's still repeating what she says, and she's not even alive.

*Because my story hasn't ended. Not by a long way. You're going to make certain of that.*

He's not sure what she means. That she lives on in his paintings? But he can't ask; she's no longer there. Perhaps she never was; perhaps grief has sent him mad. The sooner he leaves, the better. Now that she's gone, there's no reason on earth to stay.

# *Chapter Three*

Hans closes up his Whitehall gatehouse. He takes a wherry to the Steelyard, from where his ship will sail.

The Thames boatman is full of Anne-spite, how she deserved to die: adulteress, whore, witch, traitor. Admittedly, she'd never been popular with the people, but Hans had always been certain that, given time, they would come to love her. That the time might not be given had never occurred to him.

It's hard not to smash the man into the water, but Hans's aim is to leave this city, not languish in one of its jails. With a mighty effort of will he ignores him. Eventually he gets the hint, starts insulting other boatmen instead.

As London Bridge looms, Hans recalls his awe on first seeing it. How it had seemed less a river crossing, more an entire town stretched across the water, every inch crowded with buildings. It's so familiar now; he's seen it almost every day since. Incredible to think this will be the last time.

Going through the arches beneath is a famously dangerous undertaking. *Shooting the bridge* had been one of the first English phrases he learnt, along with *cupshotten* (drunk), *beldam* (old woman), *jakes* (where you shit) and *swive* or *fuck*, which means fornicate. The sailors on the boat over had taught him these. Strange words, he had thought, what on earth could the people be like?

''Old on to yer 'at!' the boatman alerts him in the London twang he has become so used to. Anne had loved to imitate it. He can hear her now, her accent mixing cockney and French. *'Old on to yer 'at, yer Majestay!*

As they bowl towards the bridge, gripped by the swirling water, Hans hopes they'll smash into the walls of the mighty arches. Be dragged down by the hungry current to the oblivion of death. *Take me*, he urges silently. *Spare me from the misery of the rest of my life.*

The noise of water roars in his ears. He is hurled from side to side, sees buildings fly upside down. Then, suddenly, all is calm and right again. The rows of small houses, tightly packed with sharply pitched roofs, are back where they should be, stretched along the riverbanks, interspersed with towers and spires. He's been spared, dammit.

The massive, high-walled Steelyard compound approaches. He arrived here thirteen years ago; it's where his English adventure began. A ship of the Hanseatic League has just docked, very likely the same he'll take to Antwerp in the morning. Ropes are being flung at the broad quay and a gang of burly stevedores are starting to unload the vessel.

On the ship itself, sailors clamber like monkeys up and down the rigging, or edge like acrobats along the yards. Sails are being furled, roped chests fly through the air on pulleys. A chain of sailors pass sacks up from the hold. Goods from all over the known world are emerging; everything the Steelyard merchants import into London. Furs and timber from the Baltic, glass and mirrors from Italy, wine and silk from France, wax and iron from Russia, beer and pepper from Poland. Packed in chests and barrels stamped with the double-headed eagle of the Hanseatic League, they roll like thunder down the gangplank.

He gets off, pays. *Thanks for the tip*, snarls the boatman, because there isn't one. As Hans walks away, he's followed by the wherryman's curses. Up the passage beside the huge wall. 'Bread and butter,' he mutters at the guarded gate. They might deal in luxury, but the Hansa's passwords are as practical as the merchants themselves. Nothing fancy.

Inside the Steelyard, the action from outside continues, barrows being shoved endlessly between the warehouses and the ship. Like a community of ants at work, but Hans turns his back. Such vigour and industry, such capable positivity, ill suits his mood. Instead, he trudges purposefully to the winehouse. He has done with England and now wants only oblivion until the ship sails. Blessed relief from thought, from memory, from everything.

It's sunny late afternoon and the atmosphere is convivial. Groups of drinkers stand about the garden. The Rhenish Winehouse has an excellent reputation, with Londoners in general as well as the Hansa and their sailors. You can spot the latter easily; the merchants in dark gowns, the sailors black-bearded and with huge booted feet. And while the merchants have a close gaze from peering at documents, the sailors' blue eyes have that faraway look from scanning distant horizons.

Inside the winehouse, beneath the low-beamed ceiling, Hans spots a poky corner. He slides himself in behind the tiny table, dumps his possessions next to him and waves at the potboys hurrying about with jugs and tankards. Shortly afterwards, something in a brown stone bottle arrives. Hans takes a swig and feels the familiar fire blaze down his throat. Takes another and waits for that blessed blur to seize his brain, for the noisy hubbub of the winehouse to wash over him like a warm sea.

But the blur does not come. The noise, meanwhile, takes the form of a drawling, sardonic voice.

'Holbein!'

He looks up from his tankard and finds himself staring into the lean, handsome face of Thomas Wyatt. Poet, dandy, diplomat. Traitor of the first water.

'You're a hard man to find,' Wyatt informs him. 'I've been looking everywh—' He doesn't finish the sentence. A moment later, he's sprawled on the ground, all six elegant feet of him, elegant outfit covered in sawdust, elegant fingers touching an elegant nose streaming inelegantly with blood.

The winehouse has gone quiet. Mine host, broad-shouldered and black-bearded, comes barrelling over. 'What's going on?' he demands. 'You know the rules. No fighting in the winehouse.' He glares at Hans. 'I'm putting you in the lock-up, you can cool your heels there.'

Alarm flashes through Hans. If he's locked up, he'll miss his morning boat.

'Should've thought of that before, sunshine,' retorts the landlord. He glances behind him, beckons a couple of muscly sidekicks.

A stirring from the floor. 'No need for that,' Wyatt assures them in perfect German. 'My friend Hans and I were just practising our act.'

The landlord turns to Hans, vast meaty hands planted on solid sides. 'Act? What act?'

Wyatt rises gracefully to his feet, smiling as persuasively as is possible given the damage to his face. 'Wrestling friars,' he says brightly. 'We dress up in habits and throw each other around. Don't we, Hans? We're very popular, we've often performed at the royal palace at Greenwich. Haven't we, Hans?'

Hans has no option but to agree that they have.

One of the landlord's sidekicks now steps forward, examines Wyatt's long, thin, now rather battered nose. 'That doesn't look like wrestling.'

'Ah, but we're diversifying into boxing.' Wyatt flashes his teeth winningly. He can even drawl in German, Hans notices crossly. 'Only we haven't quite got the hang of it yet.'

The landlord stares at them sceptically. 'Well, get the hang of it somewhere else,' he growls, throwing his wiping cloth over his shoulder and moving off.

'You can thank me if you want.' Wyatt remains standing by the table, his expression one of laconic amusement.

Hans stares at him incredulously. 'Thank *you*?'

'Well, you know the Steelyard.' Wyatt is lowering his tall, dark figure onto the opposite seat. 'Famous for its discipline. Without me, you'd have been looking at several days in the slammer. Plus a serious fine.'

Hans stares at him coldly. No, he is not grateful. He hates Wyatt with every fibre in his body. But he says nothing, in the hope he'll go away.

But Wyatt does not go away. Instead, he nods at the jug. 'Going to offer me some?'

Hans would rather bash his head in with it. But as violence will get him nowhere, he must make do with insults. 'Ponce like you doesn't have the stomach for it,' he snarls.

'I'm sure you're right,' Wyatt drawls loftily. 'But I don't want to drink it, I want to put it on my face. Looks like just the stuff.' He fishes out a handkerchief, picks up the jug, tips some of its contents on the linen and applies it to his nose. Winces. With his other hand he waves at a serving girl, who scuttles over at the double.

'Same again, my beauty.' With another flashing smile, Wyatt gestures at Hans's jug. Even in the gloom it's possible to see the girl's blush. 'And some of your excellent smoked meats, if you will.'

The smoked meats arrive in double-quick time, evidently fast-tracked and accompanied by pickles and a hunk of bread. Hans's stomach twists with hunger. He can't remember when he last ate. Like sleeping and feeling normal, food is something from another life.

And so is Thomas Wyatt.

The court's star poet, cynosure of every eye. Object of universal fascination, drawing all the attention without ever seeming to try. And who, because his father is a rich and powerful courtier, has never had to struggle as Hans has, never had to lift one of his elegant white fingers.

Hans has never been convinced by Wyatt. Or his verse, come to that. How is one to tell, with words? With painting, with what he does, merit is immediately evident. It either looks like the subject or it doesn't. But whether it's true, as people claim, that Wyatt's verse slips daringly between the conventions of courtly love and real passion, or combines dangerous ambiguity with dazzling wordplay, Hans has no idea. And cares less.

He'd known this was partly jealousy. Anne had been fond of Wyatt, and vice versa. As Wyatt never hesitated to inform everyone, she was his muse and his lady love. Which meant precisely nothing, as things turned out.

'Want some?' The munching Wyatt gestures at the platter.

'All I want is that you get out of my sight.'

Wyatt sighs and puts down his bread. Dabs his lips delicately with his handkerchief. 'Look, I understand. You think I betrayed her.'

'I *saw* you betray her.'

'I didn't mean to,' Wyatt protests. 'It was the last thing on earth I intended. She was my muse, and I worshipped her. She was the person I loved most in the world.'

Hans surveys Wyatt steadily. His contempt for this man is so great he can't even feel it any more. 'Yes,' he says flatly. 'It looked like it.'

Not a week ago, but it feels like centuries. The trial of the queen and her brother in the great hall of the Tower. Two thousand people crammed into the hastily built galleries. Under his cloth of estate, holding his wands of office, the bloodless, heartless, ruthless Duke of Norfolk. As England's premier aristocrat, the Boleyns' own uncle would preside over their interrogation. His expression of heavy sorrow was risibly unconvincing. By contrast, Anne and George's father, Thomas Boleyn, revealed no feelings at all. But when had he ever?

George Boleyn swaggered in first and performed with disastrous bravado. Handed a note with his own alleged remarks about the king, he was expected to peruse it in silence. Instead, as he read it aloud, two thousand people heard what he almost certainly never said about Henry's tiny penis and poor performance in bed.

Hans had listened in horror. But George had always been an idiot. Charming if you liked that sort of thing; good-looking, certainly. But fatally addicted to stupid risks. Gambling and male lovers, in the main. His courtroom recklessness sealed his fate, but he had obviously judged it sealed already.

The only question was whether it sealed Anne's too. Poised and beautiful in a black gown and red silk underskirt, a courageous white feather in her bonnet, she listened patiently and carefully to the charges. Like anyone standing trial, she was hearing them for the first time. But if they shocked her, she did not show it.

They were shocking, though. So shocking that Hans could not absorb them. They were so entirely unreal, so utterly unbelievable, that they refused to lodge in his mind. His head was a void, but a void full of noise, like a howl or a scream.

But Anne remained calm. When her accusers fell silent, her voice rose firm and clear. She pointed out that at instance after instance she wasn't even in the same place as her alleged lover or treasonous co-conspirator. Her interrogation over, there was palpable awe in the court. Who, after this, could condemn her?

But then the next witness was called, and it was Wyatt.

# *Chapter Four*

Now, in this gloomy corner of the winehouse, this same Wyatt is spearing a slice of smoked pork and pickles with his penknife. Hans's fingers creep to his waist, find his own blade. He imagines plunging it into Wyatt's skinny neck.

'Don't even think about it, Holbein. You'd end up hanged, which would be a shame.'

'You'd know about shame, of course,' Hans answers bitterly.

Wyatt slumps forward and claws through his thick dark hair. His nails are bitten to the quick, sore and bloody around the cuticles. 'Yes,' he says quietly. 'I am ashamed.'

Hans is surprised, but unconvinced. He does not believe this, not for a second. He neither knows nor cares why Wyatt is saying it, what he's doing here at all. But he's not prepared to forgive and he'll never be able to forget.

Wyatt entering the court with his escort of soldiers, the shock of it. And then, in his capacity as crafter of verses, Wyatt telling the trial that Anne had found her husband's attempts at poetry inferior. 'Queen Anne did laugh at certain verses written for her by the king.'

'I think of nothing else,' that same Wyatt now says wretchedly. 'It's before me all day long, every day, and it will be until I die. Of all the stupid things I've done in my pathetic excuse for a life, it's the one I regret the most.'

Hans curls his lip. He's not going to bend. At least Wyatt has a life, however pathetic. But Anne doesn't, and now Hans doesn't either. He slops more jenever into his tankard.

Wyatt raises his head. The daylight is fading and the gathering shadows cling to the bags under his eyes. 'They tricked me,' he pleads.

Really, it's pathetic. Is he going round everyone making this speech? Must be, if he's bothering to come here. Too late to develop a conscience now, though.

Hans says nothing, just swigs yet more jenever. Wyatt swigs some from his own jar, then chokes. 'Jesus Christ, what *is* this?'

Despite everything, Hans feels a snort rise. 'Jenever. Gin, basically. They drink it in Antwerp.'

'They must have hard heads,' gasps Wyatt. 'And there was I thinking grappa was strong. They drink it in Italy,' he adds, dabbing his streaming eyes.

'I know, I've been there. Just what the hell do you want, Wyatt?'

Wyatt pours himself more jenever. 'Not bad, this stuff, once you get past the first shock.'

'What do you want?' Hans repeats.

Wyatt plays with his penknife, holds the length of it between both forefingers, watches the point press into a tip, the dim light flash on the blade. Then he looks up. 'Vengeance.'

Hans bites back an instinctive burst of laughter. It's not pathetic, it's ridiculous.

'Well?' asks Wyatt.

'Well what?'

'I just said I wanted vengeance.'

'I heard you. Sounds even sillier the second time.'

'Don't you want it?'

'Vengeance?' Hans is incredulous. 'Me? Vengeance for what?'

'Would have thought that was obvious.' The poet's dark eyes are intent. 'For Anne.'

This is too much. Hans stands up abruptly, so abruptly that the stool clatters over. The noise attracts attention. Heads turn, mine host looks up. Wyatt grins round, raises a hand, *It's all right. Nothing to see here.*

Hans glares at him. How dare Wyatt assume the spirit of calm and reason? Even more, how dare he talk about vengeance? He who betrayed Anne, who stood against her in court, helped bring about her death.

It's hard to think straight through the tiredness and anger. Not to mention the gin. Before he hits Wyatt again, he's leaving. He's rented a room here for the night; time to get some sleep. Or, as is the way these days, to lie down and await the dawn. But as he takes a final swig, a set of long fingers, ink-stained and with badly bitten nails, grip his. Wyatt squints up through his floppy hair.

'Where're you going?'

'Bed,' Hans answers curtly. 'And tomorrow I'm leaving England.'

He tries to walk off, but the other man has his wrist. Those long, poetic fingers are surprisingly strong. 'You can't,' Wyatt pleads. 'You have to help me. We both loved her, after all.'

The violent fury now tearing through Hans makes him sway on his feet. How much more of this can he endure? Or is that the point? In the midst of his churning, burning thoughts, the possibility that he's being provoked now occurs to him. This is dangerous talk and these are dangerous times. Five men charged with loving Anne just went to the block. Is this a trap?

As hot anger gives way to cold fear, he struggles for calm. 'She was my patron,' he says levelly.

'She was much more than your patron!'

Hans clamps his teeth hard together. He must not speak. He imagines listening ears, soldiers outside to take him away.

'You have to help me avenge her,' Wyatt urges hotly. 'Defend her memory. You're the only other person left who cares.'

Hans is certain now that the poet is trying to trap him. 'A painter does not care,' he replies steadily. 'He does not take sides. He merely paints what's there.'

'Oh, come on, Holbein!' Wyatt exclaims in frustration. 'I've seen your drawings. Your paintings. The way you look – looked – at her. You cared all right.'

Hans feels his restraint unravel. He can't help himself. 'You talk about caring?' he snarls, putting his face close to Wyatt's. 'You cared so much you betrayed her in court.'

He braces himself to be seized and taken away, but no one appears. A sigh from Wyatt is all that happens. 'Yes,' he says. 'I did. And as I told you, I think of it all day, dream of it at night. I will get no peace until I revenge myself. My entire life is about that now, and nothing else.'

'Revenge yourself on who?' Hans demands, exasperated.

'The person who killed her, of course.'

'And that would be who? Apart from you, of course. And the king. And the headsman. And all those people who accused her. And the so-called jury at the so-called trial. Thousands, in other words. Going to revenge yourself on all of them, are you?'

He must be so beside himself with anger as to start hearing things, have drunk so much he has lost his mind, because now Hans hears, or thinks he hears, Wyatt say, 'No. Just Cromwell.'

'*Cromwell?*' He thumps back down in his seat in sheer shock. Cromwell as in Thomas Cromwell? As in the principal royal secretary? As in the king's chief minister? As in Hans's own very generous patron? As in Anne's *friend*?

Wyatt is glancing frantically around. 'Keep your voice down,' he hisses. 'This is the Steelyard. The walls here have ears.'

Don't they just, Hans thinks, as his earlier suspicions sweep back. Cromwell, though. Wyatt has got to be joking. Hans owes his career to Master Secretary, what part of it he doesn't owe to Anne.

'Don't be stupid,' he says loudly, so whoever's listening can hear.

Wyatt flicks him a weary glance. 'I am stupid,' he assures him. 'I'm a complete fucking moron in about a million different ways. But I'm telling you the truth about this. Cromwell killed Anne. There's absolutely no doubt about it.'

He must really want to get me, Hans thinks wildly. To say things this crazy, he really must. He can't think why; perhaps his own undisguised contempt.

His every instinct is telling him to leave, but what if there are men outside the winehouse? A blow to the head, a quick push in the river. Wyatt suddenly seems capable of anything. He must stay, try and talk his way out of it.

'Cromwell can't have,' he says. 'He was trying to help her. Right to the end, he was trying.'

'Trying?' Wyatt repeats acidly. 'Is that what you call it?'

Hans nods hard, forces his mind back. He'd been away when Anne was arrested, painting the wife of a new client in Norfolk. He was sketching her and her squirming pet squirrel when a servant with news rushed into the room. 'The queen is taken to the Tower.'

He'd galloped back to London, but could get no sense out of anyone. No one at Greenwich knew what was happening. There were crazy rumours about lovers, adultery, treason. The palace had been wild with fear, people rushing about with white, tense faces.

Hans had gone straight to Cromwell, the rags still round his hands to protect them, the mud still clumped on his boots. If anyone knew what was going on, Cromwell would. Hans had known him for years, had painted many works for him. Cromwell had become extremely powerful and many were afraid of him.

But between himself and Hans, a trust and ease existed. Cromwell would explain it all.

Cromwell, as ever, was busy. Behind his desk, in his discreetly rich gown, signing a pile of papers. Hans blurted out his confusion, related some of the rumours he'd heard about Anne, asked what was happening.

'Arrested, yes,' said Cromwell, imperturbably.

The world around Hans swayed. 'On what charge?'

'Various charges. Let me see. Adultery. Witchcraft. Treason. Quite the collection.'

Hans could hardly speak, so great was the shock. 'She can't be guilty,' he forced out, in the end.

Cromwell looked up and smiled. 'Of course not,' he said pleasantly.

The urge to burst into tears of relief was almost overwhelming. But Cromwell had not finished. 'And there is to be a trial, so the truth will out then.'

*'Trial?'* Hans's spine froze. He twisted his hat hard in his hands.

'Trials. The Boleyns, being aristocrats, will be tried by their peers at the Tower. The others at Westminster Hall.'

This was terrifying. More than one Boleyn? And the others? Who were they?

'In answer to the first question, Lord Rochford. As for the others, from the Privy Chamber, Norris, Brereton and Weston. From the queen's own rooms, Smeaton.'

Crazy laughter filled the room. It was a few seconds before Hans realised it was his own.

Cromwell was writing again. 'All somewhat unexpected, I agree.'

*Unexpected?* It was completely fucking insane. Smeaton was a poor foreign musician, young and obscure. Anne would never, ever, not in a million billion years. As for the rest, where did he start? 'Norris,' Hans blurted. 'He's like, he's the king's *best friend.*'

'I know. Surprising, isn't it?' Cromwell said genially. 'And your surprise does you credit, Hans. You were never especially fond of him.'

Hans was about to say that not being especially fond of someone didn't mean you wanted them dead. But there was something in Cromwell's eyes that made him decide not to. He swallowed, blinked, frowned. 'And Rochford, that's her *brother*.'

'Yes, shocking.'

'Can't something be done?' By which he meant, *Can't you do something?* Cromwell and Anne had been so close once. They had risen together, each helping the other.

'Doing what I can, dear boy,' was the breezy reply. 'Doing my best.'

Hans had felt his panic subside. Cromwell's best, after all, was the best of anyone's. He was all-powerful. 'So she can be helped?'

An indulgent chuckle. 'Dear boy, we can all be helped.'

He's back in the winehouse now, and Wyatt is watching him. 'Cromwell didn't want to help her,' he says. 'He wanted to kill her.'

Hans's chest feels tight and he's short of breath. His voice comes out as a squeak. 'That's impossible. He made her queen.'

The dark head opposite nods vigorously. 'Oh, did he ever. Changed the entire legal system, outwitted the bishops, masterminded the break with Rome, blah blah. Rose to the top with her, yadda yadda.' Wyatt drums his long fingers on the table. 'But when they fell out, he jumped ship and destroyed her.'

'You mean the monasteries?' Recently, Anne and Cromwell had disagreed over the money from the Dissolution. She had wanted it for good causes, he'd wanted it for the king. But that couldn't have been the reason. *A little tiff about some monks* was how Cromwell had described the disagreement to Hans.

Wyatt sighs. 'The monasteries, her lack of a son, the furious rows with Henry, you name it. Her power was waning, which was no use to Cromwell.'

Hans swallows. Some of this has the uncomfortable ring of truth. 'But Cromwell didn't sign the death warrant,' he points out.

Wyatt swats away the argument with long, bitten fingers. 'No, Henry did. But he wasn't the driving force. He'd sign anything if it meant he could get back to his hunting. His women.'

Hans draws a long breath. He's heard about this too. The hunting and the women were what the furious rows had been about.

'He'd had enough of Anne and wanted to marry someone else. He was, as usual, happy to leave the work to Cromwell. And dirty work it was too.' Wyatt pauses. His tone, as he goes on, is one of mild incredulity. 'You do know what happened, Holbein? What Cromwell did?'

This has gone far enough. He's being tricked, set up. 'Cromwell was trying to help her,' Hans insists, sufficiently loudly for any eavesdropper to hear. 'He tried, right up to the last minute.'

Wyatt lounges backwards, as much as is possible in the confined space. 'And yet,' he drawls, 'somehow he failed. The all-powerful Master Secretary. In charge of absolutely everything. But he couldn't manage to save one entirely powerless woman.'

Fear jumps in Hans. 'It wasn't his fault,' he blusters. 'Probably impossible to do anything, given the confusion, the speed . . .'

'Oh, for Christ's sake!' Wyatt spits. 'It's just not possible that's really what you think.'

If this is a bluff, it's a very extended one. Wyatt sounds increasingly as if he's in earnest. And yet he can't be.

'Look,' Hans says, 'I was away when she was arrested. I went to Cromwell as soon as I got back. He said—'

Wyatt holds up a hand. 'Let me guess. He said he was doing his best.'

Hans sits back. 'How . . .?'

'Do I know? Because he said the exact same thing to me.

Actually, he went further. He told me she would be spared. He used me,' Wyatt goes on, 'in exactly the same way he used you.'

'*Used* me?'

'As a spy, yes.'

'A sp—?' Oh God, this is truly crazy. He can't get the words out, so absolute is his amazement, so complete his confusion. Whatever it is Wyatt is trying to do, he's lost track of it.

His companion's worn, lean face reflects the same bewilderment. 'Come on, Holbein,' Wyatt says, uncertainly. 'You can't seriously mean that you didn't know?'

## *Chapter Five*

As Hans sits there, dumb and stunned, Wyatt waves for the potboy. 'We need more jenever. I can't go on without a drink. You neither.'

Once the boy delivers it and goes away, the poet sits back, stretches his long arms out and cracks his knuckles. 'Look, Holbein,' he says. 'I can see it's difficult to grasp. So he didn't tell you. But that doesn't mean he didn't use you.'

Hans shakes his head, face set and obdurate. He's gathered himself now, and this is definitely a lie. Another. 'Cromwell has been a generous patron,' he says firmly. 'He supported me from the start. I owe him a lot.'

'Not half so much as he owes you,' Wyatt snorts. 'You must have been a positive fucking mine of intel over the years. And that will have been useful, believe me. That's how he's got where he has. Knowing everything. Having spies everywhere.'

'But I wasn't one of them,' Hans protests. 'I'm a painter, in case you haven't noticed.'

'Yes, and a fucking amazing one, if I may say so.'

Hans does not react, tells himself it's just flattery. But it's hard not to be flattered. Wyatt is meant to be a fucking amazing poet. Praise is praise, whatever the circumstances.

'A painter, yes,' the poet goes on. 'With access for long periods to everyone who's anyone. In politics, religion, diplomacy, the royal family. Sitting sketching in the background while they hold private conversations with every other possible type of power player.'

Hans's wide eyes widen further with alarm. 'I have no interest in politics, in religion, in any of it. Nor have I, ever. I've made a point of keeping out of all that.'

'That's what you think,' Wyatt returns. 'But guess what? You've been right in the middle of it all along. Think about some of your commissions from Cromwell. Did you really never wonder why you were painting those people just at that time? The Archbishop of Canterbury at the height of the struggle with Rome? Thomas More, hopelessly divided between his God and his king? Did it really never occur to you?'

'The paintings are what I thought about,' Hans snarls back. 'I wasn't interested in anything else.'

'And that's precisely why you were so useful. You didn't take sides. Just told Cromwell what you heard.'

'I didn't even understand English! Not at first.'

'Which made it even easier for him to confuse you and take advantage. You were flattered. You were grateful. You suspected nothing. And you were buried in your paintings, as you say. Doing your artist thing.'

Despite himself, Hans feels doubtful. Could Wyatt be right? His focus really had always been his work, on rendering his subjects with perfect realism. Not just outside, but in. Their souls as much as their faces. If he had listened to what they were saying, it was only to inform his impression of them. The truth of what they were as people.

And the resulting portraits had been superb. Thomas More's rough-chopped hair and unshaven chin contrasting with his gold chain and crimson velvet robes. Archbishop Warham's red hang-dog face against a pearl-studded crucifix, a silver mitre rising behind like the open jaws of a huge fish, complete with gold-set jewel for the eye.

True, though, he had heard things while he worked. More arguing that the Catholic Church should not be cast aside because a temporal prince couldn't get a divorce. Warham, in Lambeth Palace, hammer and tongs with Cardinal Wolsey over the best way forward with the Pope.

Wyatt is watching him closely. 'Do you see now? How you were Cromwell's useful idiot?'

Hans's fists clench. Wyatt's cheek, it's breathtaking.

'Calm down,' the poet hisses. 'I'm not saying you *meant* to be an idiot. Just that you've painted a lot of people Cromwell's interested in. I daresay he liked to chat to you about them afterwards.'

Cromwell had, for certain. The two ambassadors come back into Hans's mind. Their conversation had amused Master Secretary a lot.

'And that was useful to him. You didn't know it, but you gave him valuable information.'

Hans says nothing. He hadn't thought it possible for things to get any worse. Another hideous revelation, on top of all the others. Cromwell using him. Cromwell destroying Anne. Can it really be true?

The tinkle of pouring gin reaches his ears. Followed by the sound of a tankard being pushed towards him. 'Drink,' says Wyatt. 'It's a lot to take in. It's tougher for you than it was for me. I knew that I was spying from the start.'

Hans says nothing.

The poet fiddles with his tankard. 'Let me tell you what happened to me.' He smiles. 'To understand is to forgive.'

Hans has no intention of doing either. 'I don't want to know,' he mutters.

'It might help. Show you weren't the only one taken in.'

'Who says I was taken in?'

Wyatt sighs. 'Look, I know you think I'm just a privileged wanker.'

Hans does not deny it.

'And you're not wrong. I'm certainly privileged and I'm definitely a wanker. But there's more to me than that. When I tell you I loved Anne, I mean it. I always have. I grew up with her. Hever Castle was the next estate to ours and we used to climb trees together. Anne would always climb highest, but you'd expect that.'

His reminiscent smile receives a hostile look in return. Hans doesn't care about him climbing trees with Anne. That he betrayed her in court is what counts. But Wyatt goes on regardless.

'I didn't realise that I'd fallen in love with her until she'd gone. I turned up at Hever one day as usual and knew she'd left even before they told me. The place felt empty, somehow. Something essential was missing. She'd been sent abroad. I didn't see her again for ten years.'

Hans knows this is true. He remembers Anne telling him about it. That sunny Amboise terrace, before any of this had happened. But he's not interested in Wyatt's love. He's seen it in action, the poet's passion. It ended with Anne on the scaffold.

'You'll be wondering what all this has to do with Cromwell.' Wyatt's light drawl reaches his ears. 'Well, our connection came through poetry. He lent me a volume of Petrarch's sonnets, hot off the press from Venice. I'd never seen a sonnet before, believe it or not.' He stops, looks expectant.

'So?' Hans says coldly.

'So, sonnets are my thing now, they're what I do? I'm, um, quite well known for them.'

Hans shrugs. He wouldn't know a sonnet from a bonnet. He's a painter. He doesn't care.

He expects – hopes – this will offend Wyatt, but instead the poet laughs. 'Fair enough. I don't know much about painting either. Anyway, I started writing sonnets and Cromwell encouraged me. And in return, I was happy to spy for him. I thought it was interesting work, nothing too dastardly, and I turned out to be a natural at surveillance. Which is probably no surprise given the poetry I was writing, full of hidden messages. So code, which I used for Cromwell, wasn't much of a stretch. He told me that when he was in charge of the foreign service, I could be ambassador anywhere I wanted. Music to my ears. I was desperate to go abroad and find Anne. But then the unexpected happened: she came back from France.'

Hans stares stonily into his tankard. The mention of Anne on Wyatt's lips makes his insides twist every time. How much more of this can he stand?

'In the ten years since I'd seen her, she'd changed out of all recognition. The wild-haired country girl had become a sophisticated Frenchwoman. An instant success, the talk of the court. Everything I'd felt for her before was multiplied by ten. But then the king got interested.'

Wyatt's tone is so contemptuous, Hans looks up in surprise. 'I tried my best to warn her,' the poet goes on. 'Verse poured out of me, almost all of it addressed to her. I was sailing increasingly close to the wind, and sooner or later I was going to get into trouble. Which I did. Big time.'

Hans doesn't ask. He knows he's about to be told.

'I was playing bowls with the king. I realised he was showing me his ring, which I recognised as Anne's. So I pulled out a necklace of hers that I had and measured the distance between bowls. Henry hit the roof, but before I could be sent to the Tower, Cromwell interceded and hey presto, my first posting as a diplomat. Mostly to get me out of the country. And then it all happened: Anne became pregnant, married, became queen. I arrived back in England just in time to pour scented water over her hands at her coronation.' Wyatt pauses, sighs. 'Afterwards, I went off the rails, getting in fights, even ending up in prison. And then, eventually, Anne did too.'

He frowns into the guttering light, says nothing for several minutes. When he speaks again, his voice is so low Hans can barely hear it.

'Her arrest was so quick, as you know. And like you, I went straight to Cromwell. Begged him to help her. He said he would if I appeared at the trial, told that story about the king's verse.'

Hans looks at him in disgust. So this is what it's all about. Making excuses for his treachery. Wyatt expects him to believe this, seriously?

'I refused, obviously. Said he had to be joking. But Cromwell promised that if I testified against her, she would be saved.'

'And you believed him?' Hans's voice drips with scorn.

Wyatt rubs both hands over his face. 'Of course not. Even for Cromwell it sounded far-fetched. I refused, and he was fine about it. Completely unruffled. Told me that he quite understood. Then he added that these were dangerous times and he was putting me in the Tower as well. Just for my own safety. Which is how I found myself in the Bell Tower, where Thomas More had been held before his execution. It didn't feel all that safe.'

It hadn't felt safe for Thomas More either. Hans knew this because he'd visited him there. But unlike Wyatt, More had held his ground. And paid with his life. 'So you suddenly found yourself on the witness stand?' he prompts, sarcastically.

Wyatt's dark head twists from side to side. 'No. Not even then. Not until after my father came to see me. He told me I was in danger and begged me to give evidence at the trial. Said if I didn't I would be executed, and if I did I would be released. He was very old and ill by this time and besides was in tears.' Wyatt's face is anguished, his voice pleading. 'It was impossible to refuse him, and so I agreed. I was on the edge already, mad with worry, ready to clutch at any straw. And of course, I had Cromwell's promise that nothing would happen to Anne.'

'But,' Hans says flatly, 'it did.'

Wyatt has covered his face. 'I was bound and gagged in the Bell Tower that morning,' he says through his fingers. 'Otherwise I would have screamed through the bars.'

## *Chapter Six*

At some stage the potboy must have come. A fresh rushlight flickers on the table, though, in the way of rushlights, emitting more smell than illumination.

'So there you have it,' Wyatt says.

'Have what?'

'My story. What happened.'

Hans folds his arms. 'Why should I believe you?' He's no longer so sure it's a trap. But that might be part of the trap. 'Why should I believe that's what happened?'

Wyatt rubs the heels of his hands into his eyes. 'Well, if you don't, I can't see how I can convince you.'

He's admitting defeat. Good, thinks Hans. Now, at last, he can go. He rises to his feet, his mind on his room, picturing the neat little bed. Although in truth he's so tired he could sleep on the winehouse floor. It would hardly be the first time. He'd slept on many floors when he first came to London.

Wyatt has remained seated, and now looks up. There's a desperate expression on his face. 'You say you have no idea what happened.'

Hans shakes his head, makes as if to move off. 'It was all very fast.'

'You do see that was part of the plan? Cromwell's plan.'

Got to hand it to the man, he doesn't give up easily. 'How do you mean?' Hans leans against a wooden post, waits.

'Confusion was the whole point,' Wyatt says. 'Speed too. Three weeks before her execution, Anne hadn't even been arrested. No one could work out what was going on. They still can't. It was over before most people knew it had started. There'll be places in England where they still don't know that it has.' He pauses, knits his dark brows. 'But when they do, they'll think she deserved it. That's part of the plan too.'

'How do you mean?'

'Because,' says Wyatt, 'her death makes people sure she was guilty. What else explains it? A queen of England, beheaded. Nothing like that has ever happened in our entire history. And so rumour has become fact. Lies have become the truth. Anne was an adulteress, a witch, a traitor. She must have been. And yet she wasn't. She was completely innocent. Her only crime was not having a son.'

Something is wrong with Hans's knees. They don't seem able to support him any more. He sinks back down, slowly, into his seat, rubs his mouth. 'So how . . .?' he mumbles.

'Did it happen?' Wyatt leaps in. 'Now you're asking, Holbein. How did it happen? Where did these lies start?'

They're back to square one, Hans recognises. 'I'm guessing you're about to say Cromwell.'

Wyatt's eyes blaze darkly into his. 'No, I'm not. I'm about to say Smeaton.'

The shock is like a blow to the throat. '*Smeaton?*' Hans gasps. 'Smeaton the *musician*? But he adored Anne. Followed her everywhere.'

'Exactly. That was his big mistake. It's why Cromwell tortured him.'

Hans's mouth drops open. *Tortured* him?

'There were five arrested, but Smeaton was the only one who could be tortured.'

That fragile, petulant boy? Hans shakes his head, can't believe it. Won't believe it.

'It's true,' Wyatt says wearily. 'Cromwell asked him to dinner, and before Mark knew it, he was in the basement. There's a rack down there, apparently, but they didn't start with that. They put a rope round his head and twisted it with a stick. Poor sod would have thought his skull was about to crack. Would have said anything about anyone; sounds like he did. Admitted to an affair with Anne, anyway. And on the basis of that, they rounded up the others. Including me, of course.'

Hans feels utterly sick. He can hear Cromwell's voice listing those arrested. *Lord Rochford. As for the others, from the Privy Chamber, Norris, Brereton and Weston. From the queen's own rooms, Smeaton.*

He finds his voice, finally. 'That's impossible. Torture wouldn't be allowed.'

'Actually, it was allowed. Mark could be tortured as a commoner and a foreigner.'

*A commoner. A foreigner.* Hans swallows.

'Yes. Like you, Holbein. But you were too useful, so Cromwell sent you away.'

'He didn't. The painting in Norfolk was a private commission.'

Wyatt's lean shoulders shrug. 'If you say so. But I'm betting it had something to do with Cromwell.'

It had. The lady with the squirrel had known the chief minister well. Hans feels panicked. 'That proves nothing,' he begins.

'Oh, come on, Holbein. Of course it does. You were being protected. You were a more likely candidate for adultery than, say, Brereton, who was not only ancient but hardly ever at court. And look at the others. Norris was her husband's best friend, Weston was about twelve, her brother was a sodomite and Smeaton was a penniless minstrel. But you, Holbein, you're young and good-looking. And you've been friends with her for years.'

Hans is feeling trapped. 'It was my paintings Cromwell valued,' he mutters stubbornly.

'Oh yes,' Wyatt drawls. 'I saw exactly how much he valued them on the bonfire today.'

Years ago, in a village in the Alps, an avalanche had approached. Hans had felt it in his body exactly as he now feels this. A sort of distant rumble, presaging something of unbelievable violence.

'Your paintings of Anne,' his companion goes on matter-of-factly. 'From the king's gallery at Whitehall. Cromwell's destroyed them all.'

'No he hasn't.' Hans's voice is sharp with panic. Wyatt will say anything to provoke a reaction. He's desperate. He's bluffing. He's lying. Again.

It's dark now, both inside and out. The rushlight digs into Wyatt's hollow cheekbones, licks up and down his bloodied, battered nose. He doesn't look as if he has the energy to lie. Like Hans, he appears utterly spent. He doesn't reply, just empties the last of the jenever into his cup.

'I only saw them a few days ago,' Hans insists. 'They were all fine then.'

Wyatt shrugs his lean shoulders. 'Well, they aren't now. They aren't anything, they don't exist. But don't take my word for it. Go and see for yourself.'

As Hans gets up, starts to push his way through the crowds to the exit, Wyatt calls after him, 'And when you have, you'll find me at Greenwich.'

Finding a boatman this time of night is tricky. Once found, he wants premium rates.

'Where to, guv?'

'Whitehall.'

They push off from the bank. The boat-lamp's dim glimmer

spins and swirls on the waves. Watching it, Hans feels his churning, tossing mind start to slow. Exhaustion steals through him, and he either tips into sleep or slips off into some other consciousness. The light on the water seems to broaden and brighten. The river stops moving, spreads out into a wide, white-gravelled terrace.

He knows it instantly. Amboise. His heart tightens. He's about to meet Anne for the first time.

## *Chapter Seven*

### The chateau of Amboise, Loire Valley, France
### Fourteen years earlier

Hans's journey to the French court had been a ruinously expensive failure. He had gone there on a false premise, with the wrong information. Told there was a position as painter to King François, he had arrived to find there wasn't. Someone else had got the job.

Now, his only option was to go back to Basel. A city with no prospects, which he'd only just left, and with such high hopes too. All now dashed, ground into the white dust of the chateau's terrace, high above the town.

Crossing the gardens, past box hedges persuaded into shapes of hearts and knives, he paused at the parapet and looked down. The height was dizzying, the river distant. Why not jump, just end it all? His career was a disaster. He had made a catastrophic mistake. Yes, he was only in his mid twenties, but what was the point of going on? Life seemed an impoverished burden, stretching ahead without hope or purpose.

He put down his bags and portfolio of work – fat lot of use that had been – and placed both hands on the carved white stone. Warm from the morning sun, it felt soft beneath his fingers, welcoming almost. He swung a leg over.

'I wouldn't,' someone said from behind him. 'And believe me, I've thought about it. I decided it might hurt. On the whole, living seems the better option.'

Sheer surprise unbalanced him, almost sending him to his death by accident rather than design. He righted himself, turned to look.

It was like being shot in the chest with an arrow whilst having a trumpet scream in his ears. Bright sunlight blasted his eyes.

Against the chateau's white stone she was like a sketch in charcoal. Everything black, from her dress to her large dark eyes. Her hair too, long and thick. The red of her lips in her white oval face was the only colour.

He had never previously seen her, but there was something about her he recognised. He felt something inside him roar into life, something that had long been waiting. '*You* thought about it?' he asked, astounded. Why would a dazzling creature like this want to end her charmed existence?

'I did, yes.' Her low, husky voice is attractive in itself.

'But why?'

She tossed her black hair so it swirled about her. 'Because my wretched father is selling me.'

'*Selling* you?'

The black eyes rolled in exasperation. 'Must you repeat everything I say? Is that a German thing?'

She'd recognised his accent, he realised in surprise. Most people didn't.

'Yes, well, I'm good at languages,' she said with another toss of the head.

Hans had never met a woman good at languages before. He hadn't known they existed. Basel, with its publishing, was a reasonably sophisticated place, but he'd never encountered anyone like her there. She was about his age, he thought, perhaps a little younger.

He wondered why she was bothering to talk to him. He was a foreigner, a nobody, while she was obviously a lady of the court.

'Come talk to me, German person, whatever you're called, wherever you're from.' As he told her, she headed for the shade where, sitting on the low wall beneath a tree, she returned the favour. Her name was Anne Boleyn and she was the daughter of England's ambassador to France. That she was English was another surprise. He'd thought her French; she spoke it perfectly, unlike his own clumsy efforts.

'So, your father selling you,' Hans said. 'Is that an English thing?'

She snorted, amused. 'It's a father thing,' she said. 'Fathers like mine, anyway, for whom daughters are goods to be traded. There's a disputed family will and he gets money if the wedding goes ahead.' Her lean face suddenly filled with sadness and anger. 'But I don't want to go back to England.'

'Is it that bad?' He'd never been to England, or met anyone from there.

'I don't know. I'd forgotten about it. I was sent away at the age of eleven. My father, again. All my life he's sent me from pillar to post, entirely for his own advantage. I've lived in France for the last ten years, I've become French. I don't just speak it, I think it, dress it, dance, sing and play it. Eat and drink it. I never imagined being anywhere else.' She sighed heavily.

He tried to cheer her up. 'But surely London isn't so terrible?'

'I wouldn't know. I've never been there. My family live in the absolute middle of nowhere. In Kent, where the apples come from. And the ale. The ale being the one thing they have to drink in England. To go with the one cheese.' She groaned. 'Now you see why I was thinking of throwing myself over the wall as well.'

'Bit extreme,' Hans observed, 'to kill yourself over cheese.'

She glared at him. 'It's not just cheese, although plenty of French people would kill themselves for less. I've never even met this Earl of Ormonde I'm supposed to marry. I hate feeling so powerless, having to do what my father says.' She bit her lip and her eyes glittered.

He suddenly wanted to capture that ever-moving face. Reaching for his bag, he took out charcoals, paper.

'You're an artist?' The tears vanished and her voice bounced with excitement.

'Not a very successful one. The painting business is pretty hopeless at the moment.'

Anne grinned ruefully. 'We have a lot in common, it would seem.' She raised her small chin and looked him challengingly in the eye. 'So Master Hans Holbein, painter of Basel, Switzerland, but born in Augsburg, Germany, explain how you came here and what went so terribly wrong.'

She listened carefully as he answered, looking, to his amazement, interested. She laughed in some places, bit her lip in sympathy in others. Her faint lavender scent ebbed round his nostrils. She was endlessly curious, wanting to know the details of absolutely everything.

'I can't talk and draw,' he said eventually. He could, but was sick of talking about himself. His tale, he felt, was not just miserable but made him look like an idiot. 'Tell me more about you.'

This made her laugh. 'There speaks an excellent conversationalist.'

He looked at her in surprise. He'd been called many things, but never that. He was awkward and taciturn, completely lacking wit and polish. Perhaps she was joking.

'It's one of the things you learn at court in France,' she went on. 'That the best conversationalists ask the best questions. And do you know what the best question of all is?' She leant towards him confidingly.

He shook his head. She leant back, looking triumphant. Yet another expression. He rubbed out a line, adjusted his sketch.

'To ask someone about their childhood,' Anne said. 'When you know about that, you know everything.'

## *Chapter Eight*

Whitehall Palace, London

May 1536

Now off the boat and approaching the red-brick gatehouse of Whitehall Palace, Hans glances up. His old home, all dark. The memories swirl back, her foot on the stair. He pushes them away, nods at the guards.

They greet him cheerily. 'Well, if it isn't the Kraut painter! Thought you'd gone. Forget something, did you?'

'Something like that.'

They wave him through. He hurries, heart pounding, into the gardens, to the window. It's shut. Very well then, he'll break into her rooms. Anything rather than leave Wyatt's lies unproven.

It's not necessary. As he goes inside and up the corridor, he sees that the great carved doors, previously locked, are open, propped at careless angles.

Inside the apartment, the floor is glittering. It looks like scattered diamonds, but it's broken glass. Her windows are smashed out, all the beautiful coats of arms by Galyon Hone. She'd sought the great Dutchman out after seeing his work in the king's chapel at Cambridge.

Hans looks up to the ceiling, where great jagged holes in the plaster gape like open mouths. It's where the decorations were, her initials entwined with the king's. *HA HA.*

Sickened, he bends, pulls out from the rubble on the floor the smashed-off head of a bird. The falcon, Anne's device, its long white neck still bearing its golden crown. Where it stood over the fireplace amid its red and white roses is now just a broken space. Most of it lies in the hearth below, the once-proud bird reduced practically to powder.

He bows his head, feels the now-familiar hard ache in his throat, the well-known sting of pressing tears. No time to weep, though. He must face the picture corridor. But he already knows what he will find there. Or won't.

The paintings are gone, the curtains yanked aside on empty panelling. Even though he expected it, he can't take it in. The shock of it, the finality of it. The knowledge that no image now remains anywhere. He won't ever see her again and nor will anyone else. She's gone for good. He feels almost as desolate now as he did at the moment of her death.

He sinks to his knees in despair. 'Oh my God,' he repeats. 'Oh my God.'

A warm low voice in his ear. Sounding amused. *I'd leave Him out of it if I were you. That's only ever led to trouble round here.*

Anne? He swallows, looks round. Nothing. Is he imagining it?

*Don't despair. They haven't destroyed everything.*

Is she speaking in his head, or out loud in the room? He can't tell. Perhaps both.

*Hans. Look over there. Our great picture.*

Scrambling up, he now discovers that the curtains across de Selve and de Dinteville still have the ambassadors behind them. The two Frenchmen regard him smugly.

As well they might. It's a miracle. 'A picture of you without you in it,' he exclaims. 'Of course. They wouldn't have realised.'

*No. They didn't destroy it because they didn't know what it was. The idiots! We were too clever for them, Hans!*

'You were too clever always,' he tells her in a rush of feeling. 'And too beautiful, too merry, too witty, too—'

*Flatterer!* Anne cuts in, before he can make too much of a fool of himself. But he wants to. Why not? He's been silent all these years while the slimy likes of Wyatt paraded their so-called love, poured their faithless, feckless hearts out. 'It's not flattery,' he cries passionately. 'It's . . . I . . .' He stops, tongue-tied.

*Don't, Hans. There's no need.*

And then she's gone, just like that. He can no longer detect her lavender scent. He wonders if he's embarrassed her, driven her away with his clumsy fervency. He curses his clodhopping lack of tact.

The opportunity he has lost, too. She might have told him who really destroyed the pictures. He can't, he won't believe Wyatt's account. Cromwell, Mark . . . no, it's too much. The pictures could have been taken away for safe keeping, were in the care of some loyal friend. Not that any came to mind.

But the damage to her apartment, what about that? How could that happen, with guards all over the palace? He decides to ask them, pauses at the gatehouse, sticks his head through the door.

After enduring their German-based joking with gritted teeth, he asks them where the portraits of Her Majesty are. Their faces immediately freeze.

He's known Will and Pete for years; everything about them is familiar. But not this strange new furtive expression on their mottled red faces. Pete shifts from boot to boot, avoids his eyes. 'There is no Her Majesty,' says Will.

'Not any more,' Hans sadly acknowledges.

'Not *ever*,' Will emphasises. 'The person you're calling Her Majesty never existed.'

Hans stares in disbelief from one to the other. 'But of course she existed! You knew her! You saw her most days. She came through here and she made you laugh. She gave you presents at Christmas. You *liked* her!'

They don't reply, just raise their rough, stubbled chins, eyes averted, uncomfortable but obdurate.

And now a terrible suspicion begins to form. Hans feels again the rumble of the avalanche. It's closer now, louder. About to erupt.

'Who's told you to say this?' he demands.

'It's by order of Master Secretary,' Will says coldly, with a touch of pomposity.

The impact sends Hans reeling. The explosion inside him is all shattered glass and broken plaster. 'Did Master Secretary order that too?' he screams at the soldiers. 'To have her rooms broken up?'

Will yanks out his sword, but Pete restrains him. 'He did,' he tells Hans quietly.

# *Chapter Nine*

Back at the Steelyard, Hans lies on top of the blanket. Three in the morning now, and the boat leaves at dawn. He will be on it. It's the only way forward, not to look back. Not to allow himself to think. Not looking, not thinking. That is his life from now on.

If only he could sleep. But the night drags on. Slipping finally into unconsciousness, he dreams.

He's in the Tower, at the back of a crowd. The sky is blue and the birds are singing. It's a beautiful morning in May. In the front row is Cromwell, imperturbable in furs and gold chain. His thick-fingered hands are folded calmly together, the early sun sparking the jewels in his rings. Hans tries to catch his eye, but fails.

Six set-faced warders now appear from an archway. Then some set-faced women, none of whom Hans knows. Then one he does, all too well. He feels his heart twist in his chest and rip away. Feels pain flood him.

Anne is still a few steps from the archway, as yet in the protection of the passage behind. She looks tiny and delicate beside the tall Tower governor, to whom she's talking as companionably as if they're taking a pleasant walk. But Hans can see the strain in her smile, the worry in her fine black eyes, the fear in her narrow, rigid shoulders.

As she gains the door and sees the black-draped scaffold, shock flashes in her face. She reels slightly backwards, but rights herself so quickly it's almost unnoticeable. As she emerges, the crowd gasp. As ever, she's dressed for an occasion: a magnificent gown of pale grey damask, fur-trimmed on every edge, over rich red skirts.

Amid the sensation of her appearance, someone sidles into view. A tall, muscular man of foreign appearance hurries up the steps to the scaffold platform. More whispers in the crowd: he's come from Calais. The king in his infinite mercy has allowed Anne a skilful French swordsman rather than a clumsy Tower axeman.

Hans can hardly believe it, but what's believable about any of this? He does the calculation. She was convicted less than a week ago. To get here on time, the headsman must have been summoned before the trial even began. Is that possible?

But the man on the scaffold has no sword. And there is, of course, no block. Then, as those around him whisper that a blade is hidden in the straw, that a swordsman beheads his victim kneeling up, Hans feels a fist squeeze his ragged, bleeding heart and another violently clamp the base of his throat.

The sun is warm, but his teeth chatter and clatter in his head. He wills Anne to see him as she moves before the crowd, but she doesn't look his way. She can't, he knows. So great is her terror, it would undo her to see her old friend.

He watches her mount the scaffold, place into the headsman's large palm a small bag of coins. Hears her in her beloved French gently brush away his apologies, ask where he lives in Calais. *Ah yes, I know it, on the square. I've stayed there in happier days than this one!*

Now she turns and faces the silent crowd. Standing on her black-draped stage, she's like a parody of some great entertainer. Her audience listen raptly as she speaks, her voice not warm and low but thin and weak.

Nonetheless, it carries. Everyone hears her say she has come here to die because she's been judged to die and she will speak nothing against it. That Henry is a gentle and merciful prince.

There's a murmur at this. Someone in front of Hans nudges their neighbour, whispers that she's only said that for her little girl's sake. Princess Elizabeth, rising three, to whom there was no chance to say goodbye.

Hans's heart twists again as he remembers the serious little redhead whose plump, small hand he often guided, showing her how to add flourishes to her signature. Anne's agony at leaving her child behind is unimaginable.

He understands for the first time what it is to be beside yourself. To be out of your natural body, distanced by sheer horror. What he's witnessing is so terrible his mind can't take it in. Instead, it's clinging to the hope of a horseman with a pardon, or of the clouds parting and an angel descending from heaven. For Cromwell to do something. But none of these things happen.

She is still speaking. To speak is to live.

'And if any person will meddle of my cause, I require them to judge the best.' Her eyes suddenly meet his, as if she is addressing him alone, and something like fire rushes through him. They stare desperately at each other as she continues. 'And thus I take my leave of the world and of you all, and I heartily desire you all to pray for me.'

One of the set-faced women now steps forward. She takes off Anne's hood, briefly releasing the glossy black mane before bundling it into a cap. The last he will ever see of it, that hair he has painted so often.

As she sinks to her knees in a billow of red silk, every part of his body shakes violently. 'To Jesus Christ I commend my soul; Lord Jesu receive my soul.' She repeats it over and over, in a high, fast voice.

He cannot watch what happens next. He sees the headsman

start to move and hears, as he turns away, what might be a sword slither from beneath straw.

The whistle of a blade, the groan of the crowd, the thud of something falling. A brief, stunned silence, then earth-shattering thumps: the Tower cannons firing. Telling the world that Anne is dead. Telling Henry he is free.

The cannons blow Hans apart too. His heart and soul explode into a million billion pieces. Those that float back together will make someone different. He might look and act the same, but he will never recover from what has happened here today, never absorb it or come to terms with it.

The future stretches ahead, empty and full of pain. Too devastated to weep, more wretched than he had ever thought possible, he slides down the wall of the White Tower, crouches at its foot and puts his head in his hands. Gazes into the hot darkness behind his fingers. He doesn't want to see the world any more, the one without her in it.

But as a familiar chuckle catches his ear, he drops his hands from his face. There he is, Master Secretary, joking with a group of courtiers. Some distance away, Fitzroy is vomiting against a wall. As Cromwell goes off, surrounded by sycophants, he looks round, sees Hans, nods. His ruby ring flashes red as he waves his fat white fingers.

Slowly, Hans gets to his feet. He's not sure how long he's been sitting there. A while, obviously, because most people have left. The scaffold is empty and dripping with water, the black pall gone; Anne too. A couple of warders carry the dirty rope handles of a rough wooden box towards the chapel.

In the distance, the headsman is walking away, his sword in one hand and something shiny and grey in the other. With a rush to the throat, Hans remembers that the clothes of the dead are the executioner's perquisites. This is her damask dress.

He squints up at the sky; how can it be so blue? How can the sun shine so cheerfully? As if nothing has happened, when everything has happened. He thinks of her tiny, trembling figure on the scaffold. Her thin, high voice. Her desperate eyes. *And if any person will meddle of my cause, I require them to judge the best.*

The words are still there, hanging in the air. He realises what she was saying. *Avenge me, Hans. Obtain justice for me where there was none.*

He starts out of the dream, back to consciousness. Sits up on his bed at the Steelyard. His chest is heaving and his face is wet with tears. He thinks of his lost paintings. Of Will and Pete. Of Anne's wrecked rooms. Of her shaking on the scaffold. Of Cromwell's laugh, the flash of his blood-red ring.

He knows now there is no going back to Basel. There will be no forgetting and he will think of nothing else. He will have no peace until he brings to justice the pitiless tyrant who has caused it all.

Outside, the sky is lightening; it is dawn. Hans hitches his bag on his shoulder, walks out of the Steelyard. Down the passage and towards the jetty, in the opposite direction from the great Hansa ship bound for Antwerp.

At the bottom of the water stairs, a wherry bobs on the waves. He steps in. 'Greenwich,' he says.

The boatman looks pleased; it's a three-hour journey down the river. Hans sits as far in the back as possible and watches the colours of morning streak the waves. A morning she will never see. The sunrise is red, like blood. He stares into its reflection, retreats into himself, into memory.

## *Chapter Ten*

The chateau of Amboise

Fourteen years earlier

'Ask someone about their childhood,' Anne had said. 'When you know about that, you know everything.'

He'd asked about hers, obviously. She was one of three, the younger of two girls, with a little brother bringing up the rear. She was the cleverest, the focus of her father's attention. 'From the very beginning, it was my progress at French he was most interested in. He boasted he spoke the best French of anyone in England.'

'Modest, then,' Hans grinned.

'Yes, and completely ruthless. I thought he was educating me because he loved me. But then one day, when I was eleven, he took me aside and told me I was leaving. I was to go to Mechelen in the Low Countries and join the court of the Regent of the Netherlands.'

Hans nodded. He knew of the regent, Margaret of Austria. She was the daughter of the Holy Roman Emperor Maximilian, the most powerful man in Europe.

'I was only a child,' Anne said. 'I had never been further than the local town. And suddenly I was to be a *fille d'honneur*, one of a group of girls my age drawn from various royal families.' She paused. 'I'm not one of nature's weepers, but I greeted this news by bursting into tears. The prospect of leaving my home, my family and my country was as miserable as it was terrifying. I collapsed sobbing on the floor, and it was then my father hit me.'

Hans wondered if he had misheard. But clearly he hadn't. Anne was staring into the distance, her expression that of the shocked little girl she must have been. She was right about her father; what a bastard.

'I was so surprised that I stopped crying. While I had occasionally seen him rain blows on my sister, Mary, and very often on my brother, George, Father had never raised a hand to me before. And as I struggled with the dizziness and pain, he roared at me that I was an ungrateful idiot, that the regent's offer represented months of persuasion on his part.

'"But why me?" I asked, once the room stopped whirling. "Mary's the eldest. Shouldn't she be going?"

'"I've got other plans for Mary," my father said. "She's good-looking. Ugly girls like you are a different matter. This is a great opportunity."'

'Ugly!' Hans was surprised enough to stop sketching. He was rewarded with a smile.

'You're sweet,' Anne told him. 'But actually, I wasn't a beautiful child. I was tall, long-faced and skinny. But I had imagined that being witty made up for it. Clearly it didn't. Anyway, I told Father that I didn't want a great opportunity. I told him I wanted to stay at home.'

'And what happened?'

'*Whoomp.* A flash of bright light, then a sort of spinning darkness. When I came round, he was standing over me, his face twisted with fury. "The opportunity isn't for you," he spat. "It's for me."

'He explained that he had recently been made ambassador to

this very same court. "So when I'm obliged to be in London, it would be useful to have eyes and ears at Mechelen. Few people having sensitive conversations would suspect a twelve-year-old girl is listening. Especially if she's a foreign child who they might not think knows French."'

Hans whistled. 'He wanted you to spy for him.'

Anne nodded. 'That was why I'd been taught languages. I'd only ever been a tool to be used.'

She was describing the sea journey now. 'Hell, basically. I have never known such terror combined with such sickness. The sea threw us around like a toy. Great waves crashing over the deck. Men running everywhere, panicking and shouting. The smell of the heads – where people went to relieve themselves – was hideous beyond all description. And then, at Calais, I was carried through the water by some stinking sailor. Hanging on to his filthy neck, I could actually see the lice crawling in his hair.'

She had, Hans thought, an artist's eye for detail.

'Then I was dumped on a windswept beach. Not the finest introduction to the country I would come to love above all others. For now, though, I was not staying in France but bound for the Netherlands.'

She paused, and Hans looked up. 'Well, don't stop there. I want to know what happens next.'

A pair of cross black eyes fixed his. 'There isn't time. Did I mention I'm being sent to England? Literally now. Or first thing tomorrow, at any rate.' Anne clenched her fists, screwed up her face. 'I howl whenever I think about it. Why should I have to do what my father wants and have no choice at all? Here I'm insanely popular, everybody loves me. I sound boastful, don't I?' She looked at him ruefully.

'Not in the least,' he assured her. Of course everybody loved her. How could it be otherwise?

'But in England,' Anne said fiercely, 'I'll have nothing in

common with anyone. Everyone knows that the English are philistines.'

'Do they? Are they?'

She looked at him in disbelief. 'English food and clothes are famously terrible. As for the weather . . .' She carried on lamenting her fate, working herself into a frenzy of misery.

It was sad to see, and Hans wanted to help. 'Perhaps you're looking at it the wrong way,' he suggested, earning a harsh laugh for his pains.

'And what would the right way be?' Anne's eyes blazed and her hair hung messily over her face, but somehow she looked lovelier than ever.

'Well . . .' He hesitated. 'England might be an opportunity.'

'An *opportunity*?'

'If they're philistines, they'll need someone like you. To show them how to dress, how to dance, sing and talk.'

Anne's face straightened out as she considered this. Then it screwed up crossly again. 'But what about Ormonde? I'll never marry him. I want to be in charge of my own life.'

'Then don't marry him,' Hans said simply. 'Find someone you want to marry. Or don't marry anyone. Do what you like. If you're the most popular girl here, with all the competition, imagine what you could be in England, where there's no one to touch you.'

Anne looked at him thoughtfully. 'Hmm. You might be right.' He was pleased to see her brighten.

'Show me?' She was gesturing for his drawing. He passed it over and waited, coursing with sudden dread. He realised that he cared more for this girl's opinion than anyone's.

Finally she turned her face up to his. The wicked eyes were soft with awe. 'Hans, you have a rare talent.'

'Thank you.'

'No, I mean it,' she enthused, obviously genuine. 'A rare, rare talent. I have never seen anything like it. In fact . . .' Her excited expression became speculative.

'In fact what?'

'You really should come to England too. If they're as philistine as all that, they need you as much as they need me. And then . . .' She paused once more.

'And then?' He knew he was repeating her words again, but he didn't care. He was spellbound, rapt.

A chuckle. 'And then I'll tell you what happened to me next.'

# *Chapter Eleven*

Greenwich Palace, London

May 1536

Once through the palace checkpoint, Hans heads for the middle range, where he guesses Wyatt has rooms. Anne's old rooms were also here, left the day they took her to the Tower. Are they smashed up too? he wonders as he passes the closed doors. But then they open and a woman sails out.

'Hans. Well, this is a surprise.' The voice is nasal and familiar. Jane Boleyn, Viscountess Rochford, wife of Anne's brother.

She's been a client; he's painted her. A strange woman to look at. Tiny and skinny, with bug eyes in a big head, more like an insect than a person. *And has the bite of a particularly savage mosquito.* He can hear Anne so clearly, it's as if she's next to him. Perhaps she is.

He bows his head politely. 'My lady Rochford.'

'Parker,' she corrects swiftly. 'I've reverted to my maiden name.'

*Nosy Parker!* cackles Anne in his ear. *What George and I always used to call her. Because she listened behind doors.*

'And what might you be doing here?' Jane Parker asks archly. 'Casting a last sad eye over the once merry scene?'

'Something like that. And you're here for the same reason?' He's being ironic. He knows, as does everyone, how Jane had loathed George and Anne. How jealous she had been of their closeness.

'Not likely,' she snorts. 'Good riddance to bad rubbish. Both my ex – or should I say *executed* – husband and my sister-in-law despised me.'

*And who could blame us?* whispered Anne. *A woman who makes jokes like that.*

'And I returned the compliment, it has to be said,' Jane Parker sniffs. 'So no, I am not here to remember happy days. Rather, to anticipate them. I am looking over these apartments for Lady Jane Seymour. Or Queen Jane, as she will be soon.'

'The king is marrying again already?'

'Yes, they got engaged the day Anne died. You know our Henry. Likes to crack on.'

It's hard to know what to say.

'You know her, of course?' Jane Parker goes on. 'Queen Jane-to-be?'

Hans ransacks his usually excellent memory for Jane Seymour. Nothing much comes up. Some dull brown hen-bird of a lady-in-waiting is the best he can do.

'I can't quite picture her face,' he says.

Anne in his ear. *No one can. It's a face you forget even as you're looking at it.*

*Plain, then?* he silently asks her.

*As a pikestaff, but with the distinct advantage to the pikestaff.*

He suppresses a snort, and earns a suspicious look from Jane Parker. Attack being the best form of defence, he tells her it's interesting she's to serve the new queen. 'You being a Boleyn and all.'

'By marriage only, and for reasons everyone knows, hardly a marriage,' Parker snaps back. 'Swearing allegiance to the little Seymour was a positive pleasure in the circumstances. Most of the ladies have transferred along with me.'

*Heartless traitors one and all*, Anne growls. *I almost feel sorry for my successor, saddled with such a household.*

'This is the only drawback, horrid thing that it is.' Jane Parker taps her old-fashioned gable hood. In her time as queen, and considerably before it, Anne had popularised the pretty French hood, along with French fashion in general.

*After all I did to get rid of those things*, she huffs. *They look like house roofs. Humble brought them from Spain a million years ago.*

Humble, Hans remembers, was Anne's nickname for Katherine of Aragon, whose motto was Humble and Loyal. She had worn these unflattering hoods. Why is Jane Parker doing the same, especially if she doesn't want to?

'Because Queen Jane-to-be prefers it,' is the reply. 'She considers French fashion unseemly.'

*Which it would be, on her.*

Jane Parker is looking at him speculatively with her strange insect eyes. 'You know, Hans, Queen Jane-to-be will no doubt like a portrait. To mark her marriage. I can put in a good word for you, if you like.'

Hans does not dignify this with a reply.

Wyatt's corridor, where the favoured courtiers live, is unusually quiet. But of course it is. Five favoured courtiers are in pieces in the Tower, the five men accused of committing adultery with Anne. A mere few weeks ago, their laughter echoed down the palace corridors. And now they are broken bodies.

Hans had not been there, the day they were marched to Tower Hill. But he's heard plenty of talk about it. How George, the first to die because the highest in rank, had stood with the May sunshine glinting on his thick black hair and warned the crowd to 'Trust not in the vanity of the world and especially in the flattering of the court.' A brave Boleyn joke, as no courtier was ever likely to flatter the gap-toothed gogglers in attendance.

Norris's message had been the angry retraction of a confession he had been tricked into making, while bewilderment was all over Weston's pretty face, as if even now he could not believe what was about to happen. Brereton alone said that he deserved to die, but if he hoped a reprieve might result, he hoped in vain.

And then Mark, the last of all because the lowest in status, had been half carried, half dragged by an escort of soldiers. He had stared in amazement at the size of the crowd gathered to watch his last performance. On the scaffold, he had slithered through the blood of four men to grasp the block with shaking hands and await the fall of the axe.

And now they all lie beneath a mound of fresh-dug earth beside the chapel. Anne would have seen it as she stood on the scaffold herself. Had she known what it was? That Cromwell is responsible for all this makes Hans's veins course with hatred. He walks rapidly along the corridor, searching for Wyatt.

The doors are closed apart from one. He peers round it and sees Wyatt writing at a desk. He looks terrible. His hair is at all angles, he wears the same clothes as last night and his face is dark with exhaustion. He obviously hasn't slept at all. He looks up and spots Hans, and a joyful grin splits his face from ear to ear. 'Holbein! You came!'

'Evidently,' Hans says abruptly. He's trying not to be charmed, but it's hard given Wyatt's obvious delight. He walks over to the desk, frowns down at what Wyatt is writing in his sloping, spiky handwriting.

> The Bell Tower showed me such sight
> That in my head sticks day and night.
> There did I learn out of a grate,
> For all favour, glory, or might,
> That yet *circa regna tonat.*

No prizes for guessing to what this refers.

'My new poem,' Wyatt says, somewhat needlessly. '*Circa regna tonat* means—'

'Thunder rolls round thrones. Yes, I know,' Hans snaps.

Wyatt looks stunned. 'You have Latin, Holbein.'

'Would have been hard to work in the Basel book trade without it,' Hans replies shortly. 'All the texts are in Latin. But no fancy tutor taught it to me. I had to go to night school for years after working twelve-hour days in the publisher's.'

He sounds defensive, he knows, and he expects Wyatt to look derisive in response. Instead, he's excited. 'Did you know Erasmus?' he gasps, his face alight.

*Horribly well*, Hans wants to say, but instead he nods. 'He was our star author. I illustrated several of his books.'

Wyatt waves an eager hand at a shelf where the Dutch intellectual's volumes line up. 'I've got all his works.'

Hans crosses his arms. 'Look, I haven't come to talk about Erasmus.'

'Of course not.' The eagerness drains from Wyatt's face, along with the delight. He gets up, hurries across the room and closes the door. His finger to his lips, he draws Hans over to the window. 'You've come,' he says in a low voice, 'because you've been to her rooms.'

Hans shoves his hands in his pockets, sighs. 'You were right. Not just the pictures gone, but every coat of arms smashed. Every motto, every device, anything of her, anything referring to her, all completely destroyed. Glass, stone, carving, painting, tapestry, embroidery . . .' He stops, shakes his head.

'Even the coins are being collected up and melted down,' Wyatt concurs. 'I hear they've chiselled her initials off the chapel at Cambridge.'

'Jesus.'

'King's, actually.'

Hans ignores this. 'My pictures, though. Cromwell commissioned some of them. Why would he destroy them?'

'Well, you've just said it. Anything of her, anything referring to her. He wants to wipe her out completely.' Wyatt steps away, rattles and sloshes, and a familiar gin whiff fills the air. He returns with two tankards and thrusts one at Hans. 'Jennifer? I've got rather into it, as you see.'

'It's jen*ever*.' But Hans accepts the tankard. 'Anne is dead,' he says, but whether it's the words or the gin that tear his throat, he doesn't know. 'How much more wiped out could she be?'

'Oh, much more,' Wyatt assures him. 'Until no one remembers she ever existed. That's what Cromwell wants.'

Hans thinks of Will and Pete. *The person you're calling Her Majesty never existed.*

'But why? Why isn't her death enough?'

The windows look over the gardens and the river beyond. Wyatt contemplates the view for some minutes. 'Well,' he says eventually, 'it's really all about managing Henry's memory.'

'His *memory*?'

'Yes, it's extremely short. Well, of course it is; how else do you explain his wives? Already on to number three after imprisoning the first and . . . well. You'd have to be a fucking amnesiac to move on from what he did to Anne.'

Hans shakes his head slightly, not understanding at all.

Wyatt extends his hands before him, cracks his knuckles. 'As you know, Holbein, I've been on various diplomatic missions. You could say I've seen a thing or two. In particular, I've seen how in some other countries, in certain regimes, when someone falls from favour, their memory is wiped out too. They're not spoken of, all trace of them is erased.'

'Like Anne,' Hans says slowly.

'Now you get it.'

'So she's completely disgraced and shamed.' He knits his brows as fury sweeps him.

'Ah, this is the other thing. You might think that, that it's all about shaming someone. But it's never about them at all.'

Hans is confused again. He looks blankly at Wyatt.

'It's about protecting those who remain in power,' the poet goes on. 'Our dear Master Secretary, in this case. All traces of Anne have to go, because as long as they're around, there's a danger that Henry might remember.'

'Everything Cromwell did to make her queen,' Hans says, as understanding returns. 'How he was her friend, her supporter. Changing the law, breaking with Rome—'

'And the total disaster at the end,' Wyatt cuts in. 'Exactly. And if Henry remembers all that, Henry gets angry. Blames Cromwell. And then Cromwell is vulnerable.'

Hans stares at the river as he considers this. Then he looks at Wyatt. 'So when do we kill him, and where?'

Wyatt's reply is unexpected: laughter. 'Dear boy, this is not an assassination.'

Hans scowls at him. 'Less of the *dear boy*. It's what Cromwell used to call me.'

'Me too. Hard habit to break, dear boy. Sorry.'

He rolls his eyes. 'If it's not an assassination, what *is* it? Aren't we going to kill him?'

'Not like that. Cromwell's a street fighter. He's been a soldier, a mercenary, God knows what else. If we tried to kill him ourselves, we'd have no chance. Look at us, we're hardly tough nuts.'

'Speak for yourself,' says Hans, huffily. 'I was the hardest painting apprentice in Augsburg once.'

'Sorry, Holbein.' Wyatt sounds apologetic, but a grin is tugging at his mouth. 'You get my drift, though. He'd have us up against the wall in seconds. And then it would be the block for us, not him. Do you see?'

Hans sees.

'Besides,' Wyatt goes on, 'we want justice. Our revenge must involve the full process of the law. We want Cromwell to suffer as he made his victims suffer. To wait in terror in a prison cell, then walk to the scaffold shitting himself. To weep as he kneels and shake as he waits for the blow. Which will hopefully be many, considering how fat his neck is. Especially with one of those incompetent axemen who need about five goes to strike it off.'

The images are hideous, yet Hans can feel no pity for the Cromwell of this scenario. But he knows it will never happen. Not the way Wyatt wants it to. After the king, Master Secretary is the most powerful man in the land. Possibly even more powerful, as he's the one who runs things. The entire machinery of the state is in those pudgy hands. And he's devious, ruthless and very, very clever. How can a mere painter and poet bring down such a mighty enemy? Bring to justice the one who is in charge of the justice system?

Frustration sweeps him. He's missed his passage back to Antwerp for this? He thought Wyatt had a realistic plan. A feasible course of action.

'Which I do,' Wyatt brightly confirms.

Hans folds his arms sceptically. 'And it is?'

'We wait.'

'*Wait?*' Hans frowns. 'As in . . . do nothing?'

'Exactly. Wait for Cromwell to make a mistake. Or be responsible for someone else's. In the king's eyes it amounts to the same thing. Henry's wonderfully non-partisan in that way.'

Hans is furious now. 'That's never going to happen,' he snaps. 'Cromwell will never make a mistake. He's far too clever.'

'You'd be surprised,' is the answer to this. 'I've watched him play at cards. He almost always loses. He's clever, but he isn't lucky. And we have one great advantage.'

'Which is?'

'He doesn't know. He has absolutely no idea. And for

Cromwell, knowledge is power. Therefore, lack of knowledge is the opposite. Weakness.'

Hans impatiently waves away the rhetoric. 'Doesn't know what?'

'That we're against him. That we hate him and thirst for his blood. That we're watching and waiting.'

'What difference does that make?'

Wyatt stares at him, exasperated. 'Can you really not see?'

Hans shakes his head. 'Nope.'

'It makes all the difference,' Wyatt says patiently. 'It means he trusts us. Not absolutely; I'm not sure he even trusts himself that much. But probably more than he trusts most people. And he might well need us now the king's engaged to Jane Seymour, a mouse who worships him.'

'A worshipping mouse is a threat to Cromwell?'

'No need to sound so scornful, Holbein,' Wyatt chides genially. 'She's not the threat, her family are. The Seymours. Low-key lot, old-style aristocrats. Live in the country, religious but incline back to Rome. Hate Cromwell for breaking away but hate him even more for being low and common. Friendly with the Norfolk faction, who hate him too. They all pushed Jane forward, practically threw her onto the king's lap, from what I hear.' He pauses. 'See where I'm going with this, Holbein?'

'I think so. You're saying that Cromwell has enemies.'

'And enemies on the rise, which means he'll turn to the friends he imagines he has, not realising they are far more dangerous. Us, in other words. You and me. He thinks we owe him.'

'Owe him?' Hans gasps, incredulous.

'Calm down, Holbein.' Wyatt shakes his head, tutting. 'You've got to think as he does. He's entirely transactional. He thinks you're loyal because he's your patron and he thinks I'm loyal because I didn't get executed. Therefore he thinks he can trust us. This is where our opportunity lies, if we can but wait.'

Hans can see all this now. It's ingenious. All the same, what's being proposed could take years. It might never happen. Which is all very well for Wyatt, a rich boy with family money. Hans's own future is somewhat less certain.

'Don't worry,' Wyatt assures him. 'If my calculations are right, there'll be some immediate results. Cromwell will want to encourage our great loyalty, so I'll get some prestigious diplomatic posting. To Madrid, most likely, where I can keep an eye on those pesky pro-Rome Imperial powers. He won't want the emperor encouraging the Norfolks and the Seymours. As for you,' he shoots Hans a grin, 'Master Secretary's sure to have something up his sleeve. An offer too good to refuse. Expect a dinner invitation.'

As he returns to the Steelyard, where he'll stay for the moment, Hans muses on the puzzle that is Wyatt. He still doesn't trust him, or even like him much, but he's clever, no doubt about it. Behind that poetic posturing is a cool head and a sharp perception. Very, very sharp; infuriatingly sharp. Wyatt's insight into the human soul far exceeds his own. He, Hans Holbein, is supposed to be the expert at this. The painter of truth. The all-seeing eye.

And yet he didn't see Cromwell.

Instead, he fell for him completely. Allowed himself to be lured, tempted. Missed all the clues, all along the way. Right from the moment he met him. Ten years ago now.

# *Chapter Twelve*

## London
## Ten years earlier

It was freezing and raining on the journey down the river. Did England, Hans wondered, have any other sort of weather? But as they approached Greenwich, the downpour ceased and a weak sun lit the palace's long red-brick front. It picked out the gold tips of the weathervanes and bounced off the glass of the tall arched windows. A fresh-looking sky stretched blue behind a roofline bristling with domes and twisted chimneys.

Hans had felt his spirits rising too. Hopefully, finally, the promise of London might come good. He'd had nothing but bad luck so far.

He'd been here for some months, staying with Thomas More. An old friend of Erasmus, More was a wealthy and powerful courtier and close friend and adviser to the king. Before arriving, Hans had imagined a potentate in furs and velvets, owner of a large and luxurious mansion within easy reach of the palace. He'd seen himself following this mighty figure into a tapestried chamber where the King of England sat on a gilded throne. Then Henry would appoint him his painter, a position Hans understood was vacant, and which he had come to fill.

But as previously in France, the reality was somewhat different. Chelsea, where More lived, was miles upriver, at the opposite end of London from Greenwich. The boat journeys had cost the earth. And More himself, while kindly, was a hair-shirt-wearing religious who hated the court and rarely went there. Hans had been nowhere near the king, or made any court contacts whatsoever.

Nor had he seen Anne. Not for a second had he forgotten her. Back in Basel, in idle moments, he had found himself sketching her eyes. Then her hair and face. Her smile, her hands. Now he was in the same country, possibly even the same city, but had no idea if she was here, or even still alive. In the four years that had passed since their meeting at Amboise, anything could have happened.

Initially, he had been in despair. But finally, on the strength of his portraits of the More family, he had been summoned to show his portfolio at the palace. Not to the king, but to the Master of the Revels with a view to painting decorations for a diplomatic summit. It was less than he had hoped for, but better than nothing. And it was at Greenwich, where the court was based. If Anne was there, he might see her.

He got off at the Greenwich jetty and tried not to look too stunned at the fare. 'Wind was against us, guv,' the boatman claimed, somewhat disingenuously.

As Hans counted out the coins from his meagre store, something red flashed in his peripheral vision. Glancing up, he saw someone huge and scarlet processing towards the water stairs. His hat of office was borne before him on a tasselled cushion; other minions in red livery carried huge silver crosses. *TC* was embroidered in golden letters on their breasts.

'Who's TC?' Hans asked. Someone of tremendous consequence, clearly. The great red figure was now at the waterside, radiating splendour and self-satisfaction. He was helped into a magnificent barge whose gilded sides and cloth-of-gold canopy blazed in the sunshine. Great gold flags with the hat device rippled in the river breeze.

The boatman looked, sneered. 'Thomas Cardinalis, it stands for. Cardinal Wolsey. He'll have been to see the king.'

As he did every day, Hans now learnt, sometimes several times. Pleasure-loving Henry preferred to hand the tiresome business of running the country to the man he trusted more than any other, who also happened to be the papal representative in England – the Pope himself, effectively – combining church and state in one enormous, all-powerful red figure.

'Father was a butcher from Ipswich,' the boatman sniffed as the great barge put out into the river. 'But now they say he's richer than the king. And he's certainly prouder,' he added, with venom.

The cardinal might be successful, Hans deduced, but popular, no. Personally, he felt positive towards Wolsey for proving the monarch was in residence. The English king, whose court painter he wished to be. Perhaps now it would all happen.

A soldier stopped him at the palace gate. He wore white and green livery. Flowering on his breast was a golden rose, an H on one side, an R on the other. Hans looked at it excitedly. *HR*. Henricus Rex.

Greenwich was enormous, even bigger than it looked from the river. The size of a small town, in fact. Hans was soon lost. He went under several arches, through many doorways, down endless corridors that all looked the same: rush-strewn floor, wood-panelled walls, white plaster ceiling.

Eventually he rounded a corner to find an impressive entrance. On a shallow flight of broad steps stood two guards, both dressed in the white and green livery, each bearing a halberd.

He was about to address them when someone appeared in the doorway, a tall young man in black velvet. 'May I help you?'

Like the guards, he had the royal initials and rose on his breast. He was extremely good-looking and radiated the assurance of high position.

Hurriedly, Hans gave his name, stated his business.

'My-name-ist-Hans-Holbein-I-am-a-painter.' The youth lampooned a German accent. 'You are a foreigner, *nein*? A filthy foreigner!'

Hans was more bewildered than insulted. Why such hostility?

'A filthy foreigner,' continued the other. 'Coming towards His Majesty's chamber carrying a mysterious parcel under your arm.'

*His Majesty's chamber?* Hans tried to stammer that he'd had no idea, that he was lost.

'What's in it, hmm? A dagger? An axe?' The young man was clearly enjoying himself.

'Neither,' spluttered Hans. Dear God, he was suspected of being an assassin. In the midst of his terror, he felt his portfolio sliding out backwards from beneath his arm. Someone was tugging it.

He whirled round indignantly. Three others in black velvet had materialised from somewhere and stood threateningly in the passage, fingers on their daggers, eyes as sharp as their blades. He had no chance, Hans knew. He could swing a fist in the street with the best of them, but these were the elite, trained with swords from early infancy. They'd peel him like an apple with a few strokes.

The one holding his portfolio let it drop. It hit the ground with a thud. Now came the rip of a dagger through the sacking that covered it, and a black-velvet-shod foot flipped the board cover open. 'Ah, drawings. Not bad ones either.'

The desperate hope this ignited was instantly dashed. 'Who cares?' demanded one youth, who despite his angelic looks seemed the meanest of all. 'He's foreign. We can't have foreigners stealing jobs from under our English artists' noses.'

The cry went up. 'We can't!'

'Destroy the lot!'

'That'll show him!'

Hans's heart thundered with dread. Would they really ruin his work, right in front of his eyes? Just for fun, just because they could?

'Please,' he muttered. 'My work . . .' He hated to beg, but what else could he do? His humiliation and helplessness were total.

'Your work, is it?' taunted the pretty boy. 'Oh dear. What a shame. Never mind.' The hands on the paper tensed, about to tear. Hans closed his eyes, braced himself to hear the rip.

What he actually heard was a voice. Quiet, throaty, amused. 'Good day, my lords of the Privy Chamber.'

Hans's eyes flew open. Someone was coming towards them. He was short, barrel-like, and his walk was rolling, as if from an old injury.

'Oh look,' said one of the young men, voice dripping with scorn, 'it's the son of the Putney publican.'

A chorus of jeers followed this. 'A pint of good ale, please, Cromwell!'

The man Cromwell seemed to Hans to be not in the least offended. On the contrary, his plump, piggy face looked amused. 'Entertaining yourselves, I see, gentlemen.' His tone was light, apparently uncritical, but the lords of the Privy Chamber clearly heard something else in it.

'We are permitted to play cards or chess whenever His Grace is away,' retorted the man Hans had first encountered.

'You are, Norris. Provided voices are not raised and you abandon your game when the sovereign returns,' Cromwell replied pleasantly. 'Don't forget, I helped my lord cardinal draw up the household rules.'

He looked at the pretty boy, who was still holding Hans's drawing. Sheepishly he flicked out his fingers and let the paper fall to the floor, where it slid down the steps.

'Careless of you, Weston,' tutted Cromwell, bending to pick up the drawing and put it back with the others in the open portfolio. He paused, studied it, lifted out a couple more from the folder, scanned them briefly.

'We were just having a little joke with Herr Holbein,' Norris said defensively.

Cromwell looked up from the drawings. His eyes were very small, Hans noticed, but very sharp and bright. 'Of course you were. And very amusing it was. But now you can leave Herr Holbein with me. I'll take him to wherever he needs to go.'

Hans, hurriedly collecting together his portfolio, glanced up just in time to see the youths eyeing each other with a mixture of defiance and unease. Norris was the first to speak. 'Horrid common little man,' he said, well within Cromwell's earshot, as he walked away.

'No need, no need.' Cromwell waved away Hans's stammered thanks. To his surprise, in German. 'I know many languages,' he explained breezily. 'I'm widely travelled, as you are yourself. No, it was a pleasure to help you, such a talented artist. Actually, now I come to think of it, there might be something you can help me with. In return, as it were. You will? Good, good. Well, let's sit here and we'll talk about it.'

Here was a roomy window seat. A smoky sun was setting over the river. Cromwell settled himself in, smoothed his robes. His large head, Hans noticed, seemed to be plonked directly on his broad shoulders. 'Let me introduce myself properly,' he said. 'Thomas Cromwell. Secretary to Cardinal Wolsey.'

'I saw him,' Hans said. 'Just now, at the water stairs. The boatman said he'd just been to the king, that he does all his work.'

He shut his mouth hurriedly. Oh, why had he said that? There was something about Cromwell that just brought it out; perhaps the wish to imitate his volubility, or to amuse him as a thank-you for his help. And he did look amused, the small eyes twinkling.

'Indeed, is that what he said? I wonder who does all the cardinal's work, in that case?' The small mouth twitched conspiratorially. 'Tell me, Hans, how is dear Basel? I know it well, but it's been many years since I was there.'

Hans felt his jaw go slack. He'd mentioned neither Basel nor that his name was Hans. 'How . . .?'

'How do I know you come from Basel?' Cromwell chuckled. 'Your drawings, of course. Meyer's boys, am I right?'

Hans was stunned. It was true that he'd travelled from Basel to Lyon with a mercenary army. Jakob Meyer, whose army it was, had converted payment for a portrait into passage for Hans into France with his gang of hired thugs. It was the safest option. A lone artist might be vulnerable, but no one would attack a mob of massive Swiss bearing their famously deadly pikestaffs.

'I'd know them anywhere,' Cromwell chuckled. 'Rough to look at, but hearts of gold.'

While Hans doubted he'd go this far, it was true that, fearsome though they looked, the mercenaries were friendly enough. For him, the breakthrough was sketching a skirmish they were involved in. That he only need glance at someone to reproduce them on paper filled them with simple amazement. They traded their rations for his drawings: sausages, beer, sometimes even money.

'But how do you know them?' he asked.

'Did my time in the wars,' was the reply. But no other details were forthcoming and Hans didn't like to ask. He thought of the rolling walk, those fat hands with their sausage-like fingers. Easy to imagine them gripping a halberd.

'And I also saw your fine drawing of Erasmus, who of course

has been in Basel for many years. So I put two and two together. I am a lawyer, you see. It is what we do.' Cromwell was smiling broadly, drumming the tips of his plump fingers together. 'Now tell me, how is our dear Sir Thomas?'

'Sir Thomas?'

'You look so shocked, dear boy.' Cromwell hooted with laughter. 'Thomas More, of course. Still flogging himself and wearing that hair shirt, is he?'

Of course, Hans thought. There were sketches of More in the portfolio too. He'd made them for the big family portrait.

He darted a glance at Cromwell. That plump, homely face with its snub nose and piggy little eyes. He didn't look clever, but he was.

'Fine drawing you've done of the family,' Cromwell went on, not missing a beat. 'The Mores to the life. Those brainiac daughters, all swotting away. And Alice, of course. How is the dear woman? Formidable as ever?'

Hans sighed. More's wife, Lady Alice, had found him an exasperating house guest. The relationship had not survived her discovering his drawing charcoals roasting in her dishes. He found himself telling Cromwell this, and was gratified when he roared with laughter. 'Indeed! The travails of the artistic genius!'

'Well, I don't know about that . . .' All the same, Hans now found himself describing his frustration at the Mores' house. How he had doubted he would ever meet the king, let alone paint for him, which was what he had come to London to do.

Cromwell picked up on this immediately. 'Paint for the king, eh?' He looked speculatively at Hans with his sharp eyes.

Hans felt cold horror swirl through him. He had not meant to reveal so much about himself. 'It probably sounds ridiculous,' he muttered.

'Not at all, not at all. Why not, dear boy? As you say, there is no court painter. And you are a sublimely talented artist. We'll have to see what we can do,' Cromwell finished, sending Hans's hopes soaring and the rest of him determined to do anything possible to ingratiate himself with this obliging gentleman who spoke his own language and knew everything and everyone – including Erasmus, it seemed.

'Having been so critical of the Church, our dear Erasmus rather sits on the fence these days,' Cromwell mused. 'Doesn't seem to want to come down on one side or the other. Do you have a side, Hans? Are you Pope, or are you Luther?'

Hans paused. Back in Basel, this question could mean life or death. He had learnt long ago to be circumspect. He drew out his stock answer like a protective sword. 'I am a mere painter,' he said hurriedly. 'I have no part in such disputes. I try to keep out of them.'

Cromwell slapped his plump knee in its dark hose. 'And who can blame you! If more people kept out of these disputes, how much happier a country we would be! How much happier a world!' He shook his head, still chuckling. 'And now to business. I wish to commission a portrait.'

Hans nodded, delighted. Now he could prove his worth to this person, who might show his work to the king. 'Profile? Three-quarter view?'

'Not of me, dear boy.'

'You don't want a portrait?' Hans was disappointed. He would love to paint Cromwell, and not just because of his obviously good connections. That blunt and thuggish aspect disguised such subtlety. He was so different from how he looked, the sort of subject Hans liked most.

'Of course, dear boy,' Cromwell assured him. 'Just not yet. I'm not quite where I aim to be. But when I am, you will paint me. For now, however, the subject is a certain young woman.'

Hans smiled. Ah, so Cromwell had a love life. Well, why not? He was obviously on the rise. Going places. A good bet.

'No need to look like that, dear boy. There's nothing romantic going on. Not with me, anyway. Far too busy for that.' He explained that this girl had caught the king's eye. 'It won't last, they never do. But I like to be thorough. Call it due diligence.'

'The king's eye?' Hans felt his heart beat faster.

Cromwell looked at him. 'Yes,' he said casually. 'I'll be showing the drawing to him.'

Hans wanted to jump out of the window seat with excitement and cartwheel down the corridor. He could hardly believe his luck. After all the false starts, setbacks and disappointments, something was finally going his way. Cromwell was a miracle. Hans blessed the day he'd met him.

# *Chapter Thirteen*

The girl who'd caught the king's eye wasn't exactly living in splendour. Her room was at the far end of the palace, down by the kitchens and the jakes. As Hans walked down the little passage, drawing materials under his arm, a blend of cooking fat and sewage ebbed around his nostrils.

He could hear something; voices, shouting. He slowed down. A row was in full swing. An older woman and a younger. And the room it was happening in was the one he had been sent to. He paused outside the door, waiting for a break in proceedings.

'This is your great opportunity!' the older woman yelled furiously. 'His Grace has favoured you with his interest!'

'But Mother, His Grace also favoured my sister and has now abandoned her.'

'You will do as you are bid. Encourage the king, as he wishes. You're lucky to be here. The queen has been very kind, inviting you back to court.'

'And I should reward her by having an affair with her husband?'

The mother took in a deep, rasping breath. 'Once again you're being given a chance! Once again you throw it away! I really don't see what you want out of life. Or what you've learnt from anything.'

'Freedom, Mother. That's what I want out of life. That's what I've learnt.'

A suppressed scream of fury, and the door, evidently swollen with damp, now rattled violently open. Hans backed into a corner as a woman with an angry, disappointed face swept out and stormed off down the corridor.

Hans waited a few moments before approaching the door, which remained ajar. The girl was sitting in the window, looking out at the view of the river.

'Master Cromwell has sent me,' he began, before she turned her head and the whole world juddered to a halt.

She was the same but lovelier; her beauty had gained a new depth. There were shadows in her eyes now, and her cheekbones were more pronounced. She flew to embrace him. 'Oh my God, Hans! Is it really you?'

His nose was buried in her hair, his helpless tears soaking into it. He hoped it was too thick for her to notice. He breathed in her lavender scent. It was like a dream, her being in his arms. But it was real, and the most wonderful thing that had ever happened.

It couldn't last, though. She drew back, and the world started again. She laughed and clapped her long-fingered hands. 'Oh, it's *so* good to see you. A friendly face from the good old days.'

He did his best to smile; was that really all he was?

'Oh, *Hans*. Last time I saw you, we thought our great talents would transform the English court!'

He nodded. 'We did.'

'I distinctly remember,' she said, sliding him an accusing look, 'you saying it would be a great opportunity.'

'You said it too,' he reminded her.

'Touché!' She raised her eyebrows and grinned. 'What were we thinking?'

'I think we were more hoping.'

Now her smile had faded. 'London has been utterly ghastly,' she said glumly. 'Even worse than I thought. No one asks me to sing, or play the lute, or make amusing conversation. It's such a *waste*!' She paused, gave a frustrated sigh. 'I can be witty in three languages. I can talk to anyone about anything. I can dance the latest dances, sing the latest songs, and I have fabulous clothes, not that anyone here realises.'

He'd been so dazzled by her face, he hadn't even looked at what she was wearing. But she was right, it was fabulous. Her black gown hugged her ribs, fitted close in the sleeve, had a lively swing to the skirt and was snug across the shoulder. Its deep, crisp black colour perfectly matched her shining hair and showed her whip-lithe figure to perfection. It was French, obviously, and no one else at court would have one remotely like it. No wonder she had caught the king's eye.

'Well,' he said, 'at least you're at court.' He gave her a short account of life stuck miles upriver in Chelsea. Her face lit up and she laughed loudly.

'Oh God, Hans, how hilarious. The Mores of all people. They're supposed to be terribly highbrow. Is it true his daughters are geniuses who only speak Ancient Greek?'

'Not quite. They learn Latin and Greek along with mathematics, music, philosophy, theology and about a hundred other ologies. They're very nice girls, only . . .'

'A bit dull?' she probed, eyes sparkling.

'Possibly slightly earnest. Everyone has to come to the dinner table with a point of view they're prepared to defend. Even the servants.'

She had her hands over her mouth, laughing. 'Oh dear. I feel rather trivial in comparison. But I have heard,' she added, looking suddenly wistful, 'that More is a loving father who is very close to his family.'

Hans nodded. 'That's definitely true.'

'In that case, I'd change places with them any time. Wait until I tell you what happened to me. I can talk while you draw, if you like.'

He nodded eagerly. Being with her was head-spinning. He never wanted the afternoon to end. He was famous for the speed with which he worked, but this would be the slowest drawing he had ever done.

'As you know,' Anne began, 'I was dragged back from France to marry Ormonde. My beloved father brought me here to Greenwich, which seemed so unbelievably damp and cold. I never took my fur off, even in bed.' She shuddered at the memory.

'James Butler, Earl of Ormonde, was cold and damp too. I was used to Frenchmen, who are witty and clever and love to talk and laugh. But Butler had no conversation at all and was as dull as the ditchwater in his misty Irish bogs.'

Hans paused. 'Irish?'

'Didn't I mention that? Oh yes, he was an Irish peer. I'd have to go and live in some bog. After beautiful Amboise! As you can imagine, I was at my wits' end. I played for time, dragged my feet, pretended to be ill, everything I could think of. And then, fortunately, something came along. Or, rather, someone.' She smiled, and her eyes softened.

'The king?' Hans guessed, heart sinking.

'No, *no*.' She searched his face. 'Oh God, you're judging me, Hans, aren't you? What have you heard?'

'Nothing,' he said.

'Well, nothing's what it is. I'm not encouraging Henry, I promise.'

'I never said you were.' And it certainly hadn't sounded like it, the other side of the door. But it was a relief to hear it from the horse's mouth, and that she cared what he thought made him warm with joy.

She sighed. 'It's just a way of getting away from Father. Out of his control. If he thinks the king is interested, he'll leave me alone.' She shook her hair. 'Now, where was I?'

'Someone had just come along.'

'Oh yes.' She raised her eyebrows ruefully. 'Harry Percy. His father is the Earl of Northumberland. I can see that doesn't mean anything to you.'

'I don't know much about English earls.'

'Well, he's a very powerful nobleman. And Harry, as his heir, was supposed to be marrying someone very important. But we collided in a corridor and he fell in love with me instead.'

Hans could imagine it, Anne moving quickly, long hair shining and rippling, dark eyes intent and preoccupied and then widening in surprise. A burst of infectious laughter. A dazzled young man.

'He was so sweet,' she said wistfully. 'Gentle and kind. And we were both in the same position, engaged to people we didn't want to marry. We began to meet in secret. And then Father found out.'

Hans paused his pen. 'And was angry?'

A snort. '*Au contraire*, he was thrilled. The son of the great Northumberland was a considerable improvement on a mere Irish earl.'

'So he didn't object?'

'Far from it. He encouraged it, even though it was all secret. When Harry proposed marriage, Father was beside himself with delight. And then Cardinal Wolsey got wind of it and was furious. He told Northumberland, who was furious. And then my father was furious too.'

Hans was confused. 'But you just said he was delighted.'

'He was.' Anne sighed. 'At first. But once all these powerful types got involved, he pretended he knew nothing about it. He blamed me, and so got off scot-free, while I was sent back to Hever in disgrace for three years.'

'What a shit.'

She flicked him an amused glance. 'You sound surprised. But that's the sort of man my father is. Just when you think he couldn't go any lower, he does. Can you blame me for wanting to do anything – absolutely anything – to get out of his power?'

He shook his head.

'Anything, that is, except be the king's mistress,' Anne went on, her brows drawn. 'I saw what happened to my sister. Thrown aside after a few years, her reputation ruined, married off to some yokel to save face. And she rather loved him, you know.' She was looking pensive now. 'I have to say, I do quite like him myself.'

Hans looked down at his drawing, said nothing. His insides felt tight.

'He's very handsome,' Anne went on dreamily. 'He came into Humble's rooms when I was there once.'

'Humble?'

Anne grinned. 'It's what I call the queen. Humble and Loyal's her motto.' She described how Henry had seemed to flood the place with light. How he had strode around, tall, broad, red-bearded, blazing gold and jewels, booming a constant stream of jokes and laughter. The sight of him had transformed his wife. 'She dropped her Bible and went all skittish.'

'And then he saw you?' Hans asked, trying not to sound as jealous as he felt, not as if his mouth was sour with it, his veins acid with it.

'God, no, no one could ever see me there. Humble always sticks me in the darkest corner. No, he saw me at a masque. One of those heavy-going, old-fashioned allegorical things.' She giggled. 'We court ladies were playing the part of Virtues. Which was a big joke, as my brother's completely evil wife was Kindness. I was Perseverance, which was actually appropriate, as I needed all the fortitude I had. I was stuck in a tower holding a burning flame, with Master Cornish of the Chapel Royal as Ardent Desire. He's over seventy, by the way.'

Hans did his best to smile.

'The tower was part of this model castle, painted green and called Le Chateau Vert.' She pronounced the French mockingly. 'It was on wheels and fell over as soon as they pushed it in. I laughed out loud, I could hardly help it, and the king saw me do it. Then he laughed as well, and after that, I could feel him watching me.'

The drawing finally completed, Hans took it to Cromwell's office. The room was small and plain, soberly wood-panelled, with hard chairs, a functional desk and a tiny fireplace.

In his black bonnet and dark robe, Cromwell too was sober and plain. He seemed aware that it was Hans without looking up, writing busily.

'Dear boy,' he said. 'Take a pew. I'm nearly done. Just writing out the *passe-partouts* for the cardinal. He's going to Avignon. Rome is rather out of bounds now.'

'Is it?'

'Mm. Just been overrun by rioting troops, sadly. Pope Clement is imprisoned in his own castle, more's the pity. Pity for us, that is. He's not going to be much use now.'

'Use for what?' Hans ventured, confused but also curious.

'The king's divorce, of course,' Cromwell, still writing, answered absently.

'The king's *divorce*?' Had he heard right?

Cromwell looked up, tapped his sharp little teeth with his quill feather. 'It's not widely known, dear boy, so keep it under your hat. But yes, the king wishes to part ways with the queen. Persuaded himself that he's in an incestuous marriage, believe it or not.'

If news of the divorce was astonishing, this was completely staggering. 'But . . . haven't they been married a long time?'

'Nearly twenty years, and yes, it could strike some as odd that he's only just noticed. Might have something to do with the fact that he doesn't fancy her any more and she's failed to give him a son.'

Cromwell's amused tone was almost as amazing as what it described. 'I see.' Hans stared down at the wooden floorboards, stunned.

'I'm glad to hear it. Few others do, His Holiness specifically. All the more so now he's imprisoned by the queen's nephew. That's the Holy Roman Emperor,' Cromwell added. 'Whose troops have just overrun Rome.'

'Right,' said Hans. He wasn't entirely sure he followed, but it sounded like a mess to him.

'Hence my lord cardinal's journey to Avignon. Might get some schismatic types to elect him pope, which would solve all our problems at a stroke. Failing that,' Cromwell concluded breezily, 'our dread sovereign lord might need to make himself head of the Church in England.'

Hans felt a twist of fear. He had known religious upheaval in Basel; Luther's revolution had been violent and frightening. He'd come here in part to escape it. Was the same thing going to happen in England?

Cromwell seemed entirely relaxed, however. 'You have to think big in these situations. Take control. If the king was in charge, he could divorce himself.'

'Divorce *himself*?'

The feather tapped the teeth again, the large head nodded. Cromwell seemed positively to relish the prospect of such chaos. 'And I'm doing my best to persuade him, goodness knows. Just dug up some laws that should help. Dear little things from King Arthur's time. About being in charge of our own kingdom, not pushed around by some foreign power. And not paying foreign taxes, Vatican ones in particular.'

'I didn't realise King Arthur was real.' Certainly not real enough to have laws.

'Oh, for these purposes he's as real as you or I,' Cromwell twinkled. 'But don't worry your pretty little head about that, dear boy. That's my job.'

He rang a bell and handed over the *passe-partouts* to the boy who immediately appeared. 'Now let's see this drawing of yours. That rackety Boleyn girl with her scandalous past.'

Hans felt defensive on Anne's behalf. 'She's actually not at all rackety.' He didn't know the word, but he could sense what it meant.

A snort from Cromwell. '*Not* rackety? Refused one suitable husband, had an affair with someone else? Exiled from court? What's rackety if not that?'

'There's a lot more to her,' Hans maintained loyally. 'She was educated with the royal families of Europe. Really, she was,' he insisted, as Cromwell rocked with laughter. 'It's true. When she was twelve, at the court of Margaret of Austria, at Mechelen in the Netherlands. She's just been telling me about it. She shared a classroom with Charles, Mary, Isabel and Eleanor von Hapsburg. Their tutor later became pope.'

Cromwell stopped laughing. 'Charles as in the current Holy Roman Emperor?'

Hans nodded.

'And Mary, Isabel and Eleanor as in the current queens of Portugal, Hungary and Sweden?'

'I think so.'

'And the tutor must have been Adrian of Utrecht? Who became Pope Adrian the Fourth?'

'I imagine he must have been.'

Cromwell leant forward. 'Go on, dear boy. Tell me exactly what she said. You interest me strangely.'

## *Chapter Fourteen*

'I thought I would hate Mechelen,' Anne had begun. 'But it was beautiful. Prosperous and spacious, with wide streets, elegant squares and canals, which I hadn't seen in a town before. The palace was exquisite; airy and light, with huge windows and tapestries. Paintings everywhere, too. There was one I particularly loved, of a couple getting married, the woman in a dress of beautiful deep green. Her husband had the most fabulous fur hat. There was a round mirror in the background, and a sweet little dog.'

'Van Eyck!' Hans exclaimed excitedly. He'd seen engravings, but never the real thing.

'That's the one. I used to look at it every day. And there was a huge library, which I was given the run of, could read whatever I liked, no holds barred. The Regent Margaret encouraged me to.' Anne's expression softened. 'She was such a lovely woman. She was in her early thirties then, with red lips and golden hair. She had the big eyes and heavy nose of the Hapsburgs, but thankfully only a muted version of their chin.' She grinned.

Hans knew the chin. He'd been in the crowd when it visited Augsburg a few years ago, attached to Charles V, who had just been elected Holy Roman Emperor. Charles had presented a magnificent spectacle, all horses, flags and cloth-of-gold. But even from a distance, there was no hiding that strange jawline.

'Margaret was not tall, but she was terribly dignified, and had a wonderful pale complexion. It looked its best in the black clothes she wore, always in the most beautiful, luxurious fabrics.'

'And now you imitate her.'

Anne smiled. 'I wanted to imitate her in everything. She was my pattern; I worshipped her. She was cultured, kind and wise and everyone admired and respected her. If ever I became a queen, I would think, I wanted to be like her.' She paused for a moment and looked wistful.

Then her vivid face became humorous as she described life as a *fille d'honneur*. 'I liked the Hapsburg girls, but they weren't what you'd call brilliant. Charles was much cleverer. Quite awkward and shy, but I got on with him.' She stopped again and sighed. 'But then suddenly it was all over. England switched sides from the Hapsburg Empire to France. My father was now ambassador to Paris, and I was moved to the other side of the diplomatic chessboard.'

Hans's drawing hand paused. 'That must have been difficult.'

Anne nodded. 'It was. I was still not yet thirteen. Margaret was almost like a mother to me, a much more interested and affectionate one than my own.' Her eyes glimmered. 'I never saw her again. And I miss her every day.'

'And then you went to France,' Hans prompted, after a silence.

'Yes, which was difficult at first. Starting again, among strange people in a strange land. But I grew to love the French, and they took me to their hearts. François and his sister, Marguerite, became my new friends. I replaced the Hapsburgs with the Valois. One royal family for another.'

'And now, in London, you can collect the set,' Hans joked. 'Become friends with the Tudors.'

'Not too friendly, though,' Anne frowned. 'I've told you, I want to be in charge of my own life. Be free. Have power.'

'But how do you become free? Have power?'

'As a woman? Wish I knew, Hans.'

She flopped back on the bed she sat on, put her hands behind her head and looked thoughtfully up at the ceiling. 'When you were at Amboise, did you meet Françoise de Foix? Otherwise known as the Comtesse de Châteaubriand?'

He shook his head.

'Well, François – as in the king – was mad about her and wanted her to be his mistress. She was extremely sexy, but she also appealed to his intellect. She was a very clever woman, a poet who spoke several languages. But the cleverest thing about her was how she handled the king. The entire court was in awe of her tactics.' Anne paused.

'Which were?' Hans prompted.

'Rejection, basically. She kept him at a distance for years and years. She would not surrender, which, as you may know, is correct form by the rules of courtly love.'

Ideal courtly love, when a man adored a woman from afar, knowing she would never give in? He didn't just know it, Hans thought. He lived it.

'But the comtesse,' Anne went on, 'turned the principles of courtly love into hard-headed advantage. She refused François' advances until her entire family as well as herself had been showered with lucrative favours. Clever, no?'

'Suppose so.' It sounded rather mercenary to him.

She grinned. 'I know what you're thinking. But extracting money from monarchs isn't what I really learnt from Françoise.'

He smiled back at her. 'So what did you really learn?'

She rolled over onto her front and gave him a wicked look. 'Deny a man and he'll give you anything. Continue to deny him and he'll give you everything.'

His report at an end, Hans waited for Cromwell's reaction. But Master Secretary said nothing; just stared thoughtfully at the sketch of Anne. 'You're quite right,' he said eventually. 'It sounds as if she's much maligned.'

Hans nodded, gratified. 'She is.'

'Interesting.' Cromwell sat back in his chair, tipped his chins up to the ceiling, twiddled his quill in his fat fingers. 'You know,' he said, musingly, 'I've been thinking about this a lot. Once the king gets his divorce, once he marries again, who will he actually marry?'

Hans shrugged. Presumably one of Anne's Hapsburg fellow-pupils. Someone like that at any rate.

'There's a vague idea of some French princess,' Cromwell went on, apparently confirming this. 'But there's no one particular in the frame. And now that we're thinking about breaking from Rome, now that we're thinking of ourselves as a sovereign power again, with our own national religion, well, how about our own queen?'

'Our own queen?'

An amused look from the sharp little eyes. 'Not *your* queen, dear boy. Not a foreigner. Someone English. An English queen on our English throne. An English consort for the head of our English Church.'

Hans's ears began to rush, his heart to thunder.

'Why not, after all? Why not her?' Cromwell's gaze swung suddenly to him. 'From what you say, she's done all the training. She's exceptionally well educated, speaks several languages and is personally acquainted with every monarch in Europe. And she's not bad-looking either.'

He laughed and slapped his desk. 'Really, she might just be our girl. I can't see her turning it down. I think it might suit her quite well. From what you say, she's never going to agree to be a mistress. Equally obviously, she loathes her father and is desperate to get out of his reach. And from what she said about our high and puissant prince, it's possible she might become fond of him.'

He got up, came round to the front of his desk and started pacing excitedly up and down. 'I never thought there was a woman like this in England. They all seemed such dull puddings. But she might just work. The people would love her. An English rose. One of them.'

The staring, gulping, staggered Hans was yet to find anything to say. But the words just poured out of Cromwell.

'Obviously it's not going to be easy. The king must get his divorce first, which means breaking with Rome. He'd prefer not to, he'll try to avoid it, but this might be the spur he needs. Depends how much he wants her. And how long she holds out. What was it she said? Deny a man and he'll give you anything. Continue to deny him and he'll give you everything?' Cromwell rubbed his hands excitedly together. 'Well then. Let's give her everything.'

## *Chapter Fifteen*

25 January 1533

A freezing dawn, the sun not yet risen. A secret occasion, so secret that the setting was not one of the many palace chapels. Nor even one of the city's two great churches.

Hans's chamber above the gatehouse at Whitehall Palace was usually full of painting clutter. Transformed by trusted servants, the small room was now lit with candles, hung with tapestries, padded underfoot with carpets. A small altar had been manoeuvred up the spiral staircase, hidden under sacking so the gatehouse guards wouldn't guess.

A tapping at the door. Outside, a tall man with a long, apprehensive face. Hans recognised him: Cranmer, freshly appointed primate of the new Church of England. His rise had been as sudden as it was great. One moment, obscure Cambridge theologian. Next, the first ever Archbishop of Canterbury with no allegiance to the Pope.

His first act was to declare the king's former marriage null and void. This despite anointed queen Katherine of Aragon's unwavering insistence that the union was lawful. Anne, meanwhile, following Françoise de Foix to the letter, had been equally stubborn about refusing Henry her favours. Six agonising years of deadlock had been the result. Two women frustrating the king in two entirely different ways.

But now, finally, the deadlock was broken. What had made the difference? The break with Rome, which had shocked the nation and the world? The harsh new laws upholding Henry's religious authority? The European universities that had supported the case for divorce?

None of these. Of all things, it had been the weather. Wind, rain and hail had succeeded where Pope, parliament and even Cromwell had failed.

Hans suspected, even so, that Cromwell was behind the decision, quite late in the day, for Anne to go with Henry on his royal visit to Calais. It was winter time, and Cromwell was easily ingenious enough, and experienced enough a traveller, to guess that bad weather in the Channel might delay their return home. 'And what else, dear boy, is there to do in Calais in December?' Hans could almost hear him saying it.

Even Anne, it seemed, couldn't keep up her resistance in the face of horizontal sleet in a northern French town. She was now pregnant as a result, and Henry was about to give her everything. Some said that he already had, that there had been an even more secret wedding in Calais as a condition of Anne's surrender. But if there had been, she wasn't telling anyone. Not even her old friend Hans.

He watched Cranmer fish a crumpled white surplice from his bag. Today's groundbreaking archiepiscopal act would be to make the king of England a bigamist, as Katherine was still resisting a divorce. But nothing was going to stop the birth of a legitimate Prince of Wales.

How the squeakily new archbishop squared all this with his conscience, Hans could not guess. But he seemed the slapdash type; the hem of his gown was soaking wet. He had been rowed over from Lambeth, of course. 'I haven't married anyone in an artist's workshop before,' Cranmer remarked lugubriously. 'Why did they pick it?'

Wasn't it obvious? 'On the outskirts of the palace so no one could see, of course,' Hans replied testily. Cranmer wasn't the brightest. Probably why they chose him.

Knocks at the door; tall, good-looking men in black velvet livery. George, Anne's brother, along with others of the Privy Chamber. If they remembered the way they'd treated Hans, they weren't letting on. But nor was he, all water under the bridge now.

With them was a tall, solid-set someone in a thick black cloak. Pushed back, the hood revealed a tired-looking Henry. His heavy face was reddened by the outside cold. He stumped across the floor, complaining about some pain in his leg. He ignored Hans completely.

Hans, fascinated, tried not to stare too obviously. Here he was, the king whose painter he'd once intended to become, although it had never happened. Far from it; he'd hardly even met Henry, had been this close to him only once before. Almost six years ago, at the time of the Greenwich diplomatic summit.

He'd been up checking the roof to ensure it could take the weight of his ceiling painting. The finished canvas, covered with stars, gods and symbols of the zodiac, was drying on the ground.

The cry had come through the hall. 'The king! The king is coming!'

And suddenly Henry was striding into the centre of things, a train of flunkeys hurrying behind. As he stopped right beneath his ladder, Hans could not see the king's face. But the faces around him looked dazzled, as if they were staring at the sun, and also terrified, as if the sun might explode at any moment.

He watched Henry walk round the perimeter of his canvas, studying the design. 'So here is the ceiling I have heard so much about.' The royal voice floated up to him, oddly light for someone so mighty. 'Scratcher, my astronomer, helped design it.'

Nicholas Kratzer had told Hans how Henry couldn't be bothered to pronounce his name properly. How kings were above courtesy.

Now, unexpectedly, Hans was called down to meet the monarch. He descended the ladder at the double. Looking up from the deepest bow he had ever done, his nose almost touching the broad royal feet in their square-toed velvet shoes, his first, overwhelming impression was of Henry's huge size. He was taller than anyone Hans had ever met. As high and wide as a red and gold cliff face. His clothes blazed with jewels, shone with gold, sucked towards them all available light. But for all the size and glitter, Hans had the impression not of substance, but of something empty, a big decorated box. Henry's face, meanwhile, looked like that of an old child. The little red mouth and tiny blue eyes too small for the big fleshy face. They gave him a petulant, self-indulgent appearance.

Henry nodded briefly at Hans before returning his attention to the painting. 'Here is Leo!' he exclaimed. 'The lion of England! With his lion's heart!'

As the sycophantic courtiers fawned in agreement, Hans remembered Kratzer saying what this constellation really was. A group of stars an impossible distance away. Not a heart at all.

And now, on the stairs, the light foot Hans knew so well. Anne appeared, radiant with excitement, a gown of flowing gold beneath her fur cloak. She swept Henry a curtsey before greeting each guest in turn. Coming to Hans last, her sparkling black eyes searched his. 'Can you believe it? When we met at Amboise, did any of this look remotely possible?'

He admitted that it didn't.

'The king has set me free, Hans,' Anne whispered. 'The king, and this little man here.' The white fingers lightly, happily, brushed the golden gown over her stomach. Hans thought of her slender body, Henry pawing it with his fat sausage fingers. He had a sudden urge to beg her to stop, implore her not to marry him.

'I have everything I ever wanted,' Anne told him. 'I am the most happy. That will be my motto, when I am queen.'

## The City of London
## 31 May 1533

The great procession. The sound of horses' hooves on specially laid gravel. The jingle of harness, the blare of trumpets.

Hans stood at the corner of Gracechurch Street. Here the merchants of the Steelyard had commissioned him to design a wine fountain, from which arched three red streams of imported Rhenish. Behind it stretched his great canvas of Parnassus, Apollo and Calliope. Real-life 'Muses' playing instruments sat at the foot of the painted mountain.

The hope of the Steelyard was that the new queen would pause here and greet them. The German merchants were gathered in their best black clothes, laughing as they practised their bows, occasionally glancing behind to see if the procession from the Tower had reached them.

The first they saw of the cavalcade were the twelve blue-clad Frenchmen de Dinteville had complained about having to supply. The French ambassador himself was further back in the procession, magnificent in his pink sleeves and expensive lynx-fur collar.

Anne herself was in the centre of the procession. Sitting on a throne in her open litter, the silver canopy above her fringed with tiny bells. The brilliant embodiment of a dream come true. She looked excited but composed in white cloth of tissue, tight-sleeved in the French manner and framed with white ermine. Dark hair flowing from beneath a circlet of gold, she seemed to Hans like a vision, a lady from a legend, not quite of this world. Everything around her shone, sparkled, shimmered.

She stopped at the fountain and the delighted merchants surged forward, yanking off their bonnets. Hans waited till they'd finished – they'd paid for it after all – then took off his own bonnet and bowed low. Anne beamed.

'Hans! I am on Mount Parnassus, I see!'

'Among the goddesses, as is apt, Your Grace.'

She laughed. 'Must you really call me that? I suppose you must. In public anyway.'

Her eyes danced with excitement. *I am to be queen, Hans*, they said. *Can you believe it?*

*Yes.* It was almost like flying, this dizzying sense of being at the very top of everything, the sun shining and the entire world spread below.

## *Chapter Sixteen*

May 1536

'Expect a dinner invitation,' Wyatt had said.

Hans doesn't have to wait long. *I pray you*, Cromwell writes, *come to supper at my house at the Austin Friars.*

He knows the area vaguely, behind Cornhill and Leadenhall. Tight-packed houses and narrow streets. But Cromwell's home is neither tight-packed nor narrow. On the contrary.

A great towered gateway announces the precinct of the former Augustinian monastery. In which, of course, the Austin Friars no longer live; the present inhabitant has seen to that. These days, the abbey buildings loom silently. No poor boys come here to be educated, no beggars come here for help. Thanks to Cromwell, the friars are now beggars themselves, desperate wanderers of the highways and byways.

As the familiar hatred surges, Hans yanks the entrance bell, reminds himself why he's here. Which isn't to indulge in loathing, but to appear Master Secretary's grateful friend. Cromwell mustn't suspect for a second that Hans knows his part in Anne's downfall. Still less that he and Wyatt are after his blood.

It's a tall order; he's never been much of an actor. His business is showing the truth, not pretending. He acted for years with

Anne, trying to hide what he felt. Now he wonders if she knew all along. Wyatt certainly seemed to. *I've seen your drawings. Your paintings. The way you look – looked – at her.*

But then Wyatt is cleverer than he is, cleverer than anyone he's ever met apart from Anne. As he predicted, he's just left to be England's ambassador to the Holy Roman Empire in Madrid. Cromwell has favoured Wyatt with the most prestigious foreign posting, and Hans guesses that he's been called here to be greatly favoured too. With an important portrait, probably.

And so, as he waits for the door to be opened, he practises his grateful smile, his most obsequious bow. 'Everyone loves flattery, Holbein,' Wyatt had said at their last meeting. 'But when it comes to Cromwell, lay it on with a trowel. He's quite ridiculously susceptible.'

Now, Hans rises from a particularly deep bow to see a servant in grey livery looking superciliously down at him. The great arched gates have swung open in a stealthy, oiled silence that seems typical of their new owner. Grey Livery smirks and invites Hans to follow him. They cross a great garden and approach a large house that looks recently built. By Cromwell, presumably.

It's so grand that even its garden side is decorated as elaborately as the street side would be normally. Hans recognises the modish Italian style of Vincent Volpe, a painter he has worked with on many occasions.

At the door of the house, Grey Livery hands him to someone in yellow. Yellow Livery leads him through a large, light entrance hall where awaits someone in green.

Like the exterior, the interior is in the fashionable new style, informed by the ancients, the revived interest in Greece and Rome. There are wide staircases, springing arches, huge rooms stretching away beneath coffered and gilded ceilings. Carved masks look down from vast doorways, mythical animals look up from mosaic floors. Pillars flutter with the golden wings of putti.

Statues stand everywhere: goddesses, emperors, great muscled heroes. No doubt about it, Hans thinks angrily, it's finely appointed, is Master Secretary's house of blood.

He remembers that he has to act. Look impressed. A pair of sharp eyes in a heavy, brutish face might be watching from somewhere.

And glancing up, he sees he's right. Cromwell's sharp eyes are indeed watching. Above the elaborate fireplace is his own recent portrait of Master Secretary. It's far from flattering, but his subject had been highly amused by its candour. 'You have certainly called a spade a spade, dear boy,' he had remarked, adding, with smooth, breathtaking hypocrisy, 'But you have told the truth, which I value above all things.'

As his gaze now meets the painted ceiling, Hans does a double-take. Swirling drapery barely covers plump thighs. Gods and goddesses cavort and wreak havoc. It's the map of the heavens he painted nine years ago for the Greenwich summit, soon after arriving in London. He'd always wondered what had happened to it.

And perhaps Cromwell really has been watching him all along. Because now a stocky figure appears at the end of the hall, a plump face approaches wreathed in smiles. 'Good to see you, dear boy!'

Hans absolutely must not look as if the only time it will be good to see Cromwell is in two pieces on the scaffold. He smiles and nods at the ceiling. 'So this is where it went.'

'Ah, yes. Well, that banqueting house was only temporary, as you know. After the summit, when they pulled it down, I thought I'd save it from destruction.'

The irony. 'I'm so glad you did,' Hans assures him with all the sincerity he can muster.

Cromwell shows him round, no costly detail going unremarked. In the dining room, the mirrors are Venetian. The candles come from the wax of Russian bees. The fine tapestries are from Flanders and hang on walls of Baltic oak. The silver plate on the sideboard is French and from Paris while the wine for dinner is French and from Gascony. One Italian has blown Cromwell's expensive glass goblets while another has delicately engraved them. The fire in the big brick hearth is of costly sea coal, not ordinary wood, which might smoke and interfere with the Turkish spice scenting the air. 'Yes, Hans,' Cromwell smilingly concludes. 'See what a man can gain in faithful service.'

The implication isn't lost on Hans. *Stick with me and all this can be yours.* Cromwell, he notes, bears little resemblance to the panicked creature Wyatt described, casting about for friends, feeling threatened. On the contrary, he seems content and assured.

Hans notices an item his host has not mentioned: a covered cup of gold in the centre of the table. It's decorated with red, blue and gold enamel and, in contrast to the brash newness of everything else, looks old.

'Ah,' beams Cromwell. 'I see you've spotted my hanaper.'

'Your . . .?'

'Or hanap, as I believe it's pronounced. A drinking cup, French, came over with some battle. Among the latest honours His Majesty has been good enough to bestow on me. As well as Keeper of the Privy Seal, Baron Cromwell of Oakham and Viceregent of the King in Spirituals, I'm Clerk of the Hanaper. Quite a thing, isn't it?'

He plucks the object from the table, proffers it to Hans to look at. The work is exceptionally fine. A woman seems to be in the middle of a fire.

'The martyrdom of St Agnes,' he chuckles. 'Not the jolliest of scenes.'

Anne's sentence at her trial had been burning or beheading. Henry and his famously infinite mercy had chosen execution over the stake. Hans feels jumpy, suddenly. Is Cromwell trying to flush him out? Threaten him? Say that he knows where his real loyalties lie?

Cromwell turns the cup in his coarse hands. 'The fire didn't work on Agnes,' he says fondly. 'So then they tried the axe.'

As they sit down at the long table, Hans realises he's trembling. He's entered the lion's den, and the lion might know why he's here. As Cromwell pours the Gascon wine from an engraved silver ewer, Hans sees it's engraved with Anne's falcon; something else he's 'saved', presumably. He swallows the wine in a nervous gulp.

Dinner is served, and it's delicious. There's capon in orange sauce, cheese and spinach tarts. Cromwell is a surprisingly delicate eater. He uses a sharp knife skilfully, slicing his capon into pieces to slip in the side of his little mouth. Hans pushes his food about his silver plate, his appetite completely gone.

Talk turns to Wyatt. Listening to Cromwell warmly praising him, Hans feels a fresh surge of doubt and fear. What if the poet is a double agent who has betrayed him?

*Before Mark knew it, he was in the basement. There's a rack down there, apparently, but they didn't start with that.*

The fine wine turns sour in his mouth. He imagines Mark arriving here, ringing the bell at the tower gate, being met by Grey Livery, handed to Yellow, led into the hall by Green, his dark eyes full of excitement at being somewhere so grand. Handed a glass of wine, smiled at, perhaps asked if he'd like to look around. Hans imagines a passage beyond the hall, a small doorway at the end, stairs behind it that twist tightly down to a chamber too deep for screams to be heard . . .

'I think I've persuaded His Majesty to make you King's Painter.' Cromwell cuts into these nightmarish visions.

Hans comes whirling back, stares.

'Being painter to the king is what you came to London to do, I seem to remember,' Cromwell smiles.

*Master Secretary's sure to have something up his sleeve. An offer too good to refuse.* It's all happening exactly as Wyatt had said.

Hans fights to present his violent relief as gratitude. 'Yes,' he says, nodding vigorously. 'Oh yes. Absolutely. It's what I came here to do.'

Cromwell chuckles. 'Good. You've had a few false starts, I know. But I think we're there now. I'm not saying it was easy; the king's a tapestry man at heart. Fortunately, I know how to persuade him.'

'And I'm truly grateful, sir. Truly.'

His new position, Cromwell says, brings him thirty pounds a year and rooms at Greenwich Palace with full *bouche de court*, the ration of firewood, food, wine and bread allotted only to favourites.

'Thank you, sir,' says Hans, humbly. 'I am in your debt for ever.'

'Dining hall rights, too, with the better class of menu,' Cromwell goes on. 'You even get your washing done!'

'I'm more grateful than I could ever say. You are far too generous and good to me,' Hans says, laying it on with a trowel as Wyatt advised.

'No problem at all, dear boy. Always a privilege to help the truly talented.'

Hans pushes away the thought of the sublimely talented Smeaton.

The servants place the next course on the table: trout on silver dishes under a cream sauce scattered with almonds. Cromwell picks up a fork, spears a fish. 'Let me tell you about your first painting.'

## *Chapter Seventeen*

'So,' says Cromwell. 'Jane Seymour.'

'The king's new wife.' Hans nods. He's still struggling to adjust to the speed of events. Two minutes ago, he thought his life was over.

'Not wife quite yet,' Cromwell corrects. He looks over at the big fireplace, above which hangs Hans's portrait of him. 'You are first and foremost the painter of truth,' he says. 'Your paintings are famous for their astonishing resemblance to their subject. No one else can achieve so brilliant a likeness.'

While Hans smiles and thanks him, he's aware that something's not quite right. Cromwell is never usually this indirect, or flattering. His earlier doubts crowd back. Is this a set-up after all?

'Lady Jane is possessed of what one might call a quiet sort of beauty,' Cromwell goes on in a musing way. 'In certain lights she can even appear . . . now how can I put this? Plain?'

Hans calms down a little. He sees where this is going. He's being asked to flatter the new queen with the forgettable face. 'You'd like me to be more complimentary? Make her look less plain?'

This might be difficult. His work is the only area of his life utterly without compromise. He paints the truth, as Cromwell has just said.

'Oh no, dear boy Not *complimentary*, no.' There's a note of theatrical horror in Master Secretary's voice. 'You are the nonpareil of verisimilitude.'

Hans nods, relieved.

'You must paint what you see, however unflattering. You must resist the temptation to present your subject in any light other than truth, and of the baldest, starkest, most fearless variety at that.'

Hans smiles uncertainly. It sounds almost as if Cromwell wants him to make Jane Seymour look worse. Which is ridiculous, obviously.

*Is that what you think?* Now, in his ear, comes a familiar soft laugh. *Can you really not see, Hans, what our dear Cromwell is doing?*

*No.*

*I'll give you a clue. The Seymours hate Cromwell. They all pushed Jane forward, practically threw her onto Henry's lap. Where I once found her, incidentally.*

*I'm still not getting it*, he tells her

*Oh really, Hans. Isn't it obvious? Cromwell wants to stop the wedding, and is using you to do it. He wants a painting of poor Jane that's so unflattering, Henry won't want to marry her after all. Why else do you think you've just been made King's Painter?*

'And how soon can you do it, dear boy?' Master Secretary is saying. 'Three days, four? I need it before the wedding, which is in a week's time.'

Hans's eyes widen. A week from now, and Anne hardly in her grave three days.

He feels a cold anger seize him, yet manages to smile at Cromwell.

'I'll be as fast as I can,' he promises.

That night, his last at the Steelyard before he moves to his new quarters, Hans dreams. He's in the Tower, approaching a building to the left of the chapel. Its broad, flat front is pale in the sunshine, but the inside is dark and cold. An evil-looking warder leads him up some stairs, brings him to an open door. 'No point locking it,' he cackles at Hans's surprise. 'He won't be walking anywhere.'

In the cell, darkness covers Hans's face like a hood. There's a waft of damp and a stink of shit. This is what terror smells like.

He lifts the lantern, throwing his own vast shadow across the stone walls. 'Mark?'

In the corner, something moves. He hurries over with his light.

Smeaton lies on his front in a way that suggests he was thrown there and has not moved since. His hands, those delicate musician's fingers, are bloody and twisted and his legs are at an awkward angle. He looks like a broken doll. His head is turned to the side and what can be seen of his face is covered by what looks like mud but Hans knows is blood.

The once-shining hair is matted with dirt and straw. Great tufts of it are missing, and bloody, scabby patches suggest terrible injuries. His ragged clothes are crusted with dirt, and worse. His eyes are blackened, swollen shut, and he emits a soft moan.

Hans bends over the wreck of a body. Jesus, the violence. Like stamping on a flower.

Mark stirs. 'Who . . . is it?'

Hard to sound normal, but Hans does his best, gives his name.

A silence. He knows the poor damaged brain is struggling desperately to place him.

'Ah, Hans,' Mark says at last. A brave attempt at a grin . . . oh, the smashed and broken teeth.

He mutters something, but Hans can't make it out. He bends down until the boy's sour breath is right in his ear. 'It hurt so much,' Mark whispers, with difficulty. 'I didn't know it would hurt so much.'

No need to ask what. Instead, gently, Hans touches the matted hair. Smeaton starts to sob, softly and hopelessly. 'Cromwell told me I'd be spared. That I could live. But I don't want to live. Not any more.'

Hans squats in the filthy straw, takes the broken hand that will never play a lute again.

'I want my mother.' Tears slide from beneath Mark's closed eyes, making white tracks through the dark blood.

Even in the dream, Hans feels the violence of the loathing that now grips him. Cromwell will pay for this too. He wakes with a start and sees he's in the Steelyard. But his fists are still clenched and his teeth grind together.

## *Chapter Eighteen*

Hans takes a wherry to the city. The day is hot and the river busy. The London streets are thronged with people. He enjoys coming here, joining the crowds in the narrow alleys beneath the jutting upper storeys of the buildings. All is noise, colour and movement.

He likes to look at the people, they're so various. To the left, a dark-skinned merchant from somewhere hot and distant. To the right, a fair-haired maid in a red dress with a white cap. And right in front of him, a frizzy-wigged harlot.

'Business, dear?' She flips up her dress and offers her services in the nearest alley. Smiling his no-thank-you, Hans jumps as a street hawker yells his wares right behind him.

He heads down the busy thoroughfare, his mind on the supplies he's come in search of.

Paper for the preliminary sketches, and wooden panels for the finished work. He's had to get used to English oak, light and slightly greenish, with a fine grain and a faint honey scent. But what really matters is how well the wood's glued together. No painting is any good if it falls apart.

He needs colours too. Lots of them. An apothecary on London Bridge sells malachite green, giallorino yellow, ultramarine blue and gold leaf, all of excellent quality. A plan is forming in his mind. A way round Cromwell's instructions without sacrificing his own principles.

He presses on. So many houses, so many shops, so many people. It's like being in a swirling river, but a river of humanity, colourful and noisy. He immerses himself in it, is swept along. Urchins surround him, jostling, asking for money. He shrugs at them kindly, raises his hands, explains as best he can in his halting English that he needs every penny he has.

They melt away and his fingers stray automatically to his waist, where his money bag is. Or was. No comforting pouch there now, only the frayed edges of leather strings. Someone has cut his purse off.

Sick panic tears through him. It's not just the humiliation and helplessness, it's the fact that without money he can't buy materials, meaning he can't make the painting. His career as King's Painter is over before it's begun.

He gives a howl of sheer frustrated fury. But such is the cacophony of the street, no one takes any notice. Even if they did, they'd probably just shrug. This is London. If you don't hang on to your money here, more fool you.

And then, a miracle. Two of the urchins are suddenly back before him, wide-eyed with terror. Between them, holding them hard by the scruffs of their necks, is someone in a white cap and a red dress. It's the fair-haired girl he saw earlier. She thrusts the drawstring money bag at him.

He takes it slowly, like someone spellbound. Stares at her, mouth open. Sees that she's pretty, extremely so. There's something clear and pure about her, something fresh; she makes him think of morning sunshine, or flowers after rain, or . . .

'Aren't you going to check it?' she snaps, nodding impatiently at the bag. 'That it's all there?'

'Oh . . . yes. Sorry.' Her accent's not a London one, he notes. There's a soft country burr; she's not from round here.

He wrenches the drawstring top apart, sees the gold glint of sovereigns inside, starts to stammer some sort of thanks. But there's no vocabulary for the gratitude he feels. Is that why his tongue is suddenly so tied?

The girl seems unmoved. 'You're welcome,' she says drily. She shakes the children. 'What do you want to do with them?'

Hans looks at them, dirty, scabby, ill-nourished creatures. He feels, despite everything, sorry for them. He's only just escaped penury himself.

'Turn them in to the constable?' suggests the soft country accent.

The children squeal and sob and plead. He shakes his head. 'No. Let them go.'

She says something to them, then releases them. They scamper into the crowds, gone in an instant. He glances after them, and when he looks back, she's gone too.

His new rooms at Greenwich aren't enormous, but they're in the prestigious central section, where the favoured courtiers live. Whoever they might be these days. He's in the midst of moving in when a knock sounds at the door.

A wiry old woman is standing there with a basket of linen. She introduces herself as Mistress Harris, the royal laundress. He stares at her uncomprehending before remembering Cromwell saying he gets his washing done. 'Oh. Yes.' He holds the door open. She comes in, closes it after her, hands over a folded note produced from the depths of the basket. 'Your laundry list.'

He's puzzled; he's sent nothing to be washed. And this doesn't look like a linen inventory. It looks like a letter, folded and sealed and bearing his name in a hand he immediately recognises.

*Wyatt!* He's about to exclaim, but Mistress Harris places her finger to her lips. Nods at the closed door. 'If it would please you to examine your list carefully,' she instructs.

Considerably confused, Hans turns the letter over to break the seal. Red wax, it bears a strange symbol: two blades with a hinge in the middle. He opens it, reads.

*My dear Holbein,*

*In normal circumstances I would reach you through the diplomatic bag. But as there is nothing normal about our circumstances and our enemy gets all diplomatic letters, I am instead sending you word through the washing bag.*

*Mistress Harris is an old friend; you can trust her absolutely. There is none better informed in the whole palace. Be careful otherwise. Walls have ears, doors have eyes.*

*As for me, I am arrived in Madrid after much difficulty. Life here is very expensive, especially after my entire wardrobe was impounded by the customs at Zaragoza. But on the positive side, the emperor, who is very sharp, thinks as we do. That a Queen Jane Seymour bodes ill for a certain native of Putney.*

*When you have read this, place it in the fire.*

*Your servant,*
*TW*

Hans reads it again, then drops the note in the flames. The paper is gone in seconds, and the wax seal with its strange little symbol. As he watches it, he wonders why this old lady is running messages for Wyatt. Why he's so sure he can trust her. The risk is huge.

Mistress Harris comes closer, and he sees her properly for the first time. Years bending over steaming vats have wrinkled and reddened her face, but her eyes remain quick and bright. 'Queen Anne was my friend,' she says rapidly, voice low. 'She loved to come to the laundry for the latest gossip. She knew that we see everything, that no man is a hero to his washerwoman. Certainly not a king who kills his innocent wife. And as for that stinking toad Cromwell . . .' She stops, eyes narrow with hatred.

Hans nods. He understands. And now he trusts her, not that he has much choice.

She raises her voice suddenly. 'Do you have any dirty washing for me, Master Holbein?'

He replies equally loudly. 'One moment, Mistress Harris.' Hurriedly he scribbles a note informing Wyatt of his new position and his first commission.

*Cromwell instructs me to paint Lady Jane as even plainer than she actually is. He wishes to dissuade the king against her and hopes to stop the wedding that way. I have devised a plan against this. I will make it a portrait of her clothes. That way her face doesn't matter; all anyone will see is splendour and colour. The king will be dazzled, Cromwell thwarted. Ingenious, is it not?*

He finishes, folds the letter, hands it over. Unlike Wyatt, he doesn't have a ring to seal it with. But he's happy for Mistress Harris to read it. From what she's said, she'll enjoy it.

## *Chapter Nineteen*

'Well, if it isn't the great artist!' Jane Parker, at the door of the rooms that used to be Anne's. Her manner, as usual, is all sardonic flirtation.

'You flatter me,' Hans says serenely.

'Not really. Great is what you need to be. You'll have your work cut out.'

'There is no one I would rather paint than the beautiful Lady Jane.'

'Beautiful?' An incredulous look. 'Seen her, have you?'

Jane Parker, Hans notes, is as disloyal to her new mistress as to her old.

'Beautiful,' he says firmly. *Certainly when I've finished with her.*

'I thought you were famously the painter of truth,' Parker returns snidely.

'And the truth is that there is beauty in everyone.' Then he pauses, looks her up and down. 'Well, almost everyone. Shall we?' He brandishes his bag of equipment.

Jane Parker, looking thunderous, leads him inside the apartment. That it looks so different is almost a relief. Anne had given careful thought to every aspect of her surroundings, from the masses of glowing candles to the music in the background.

But no one, it seems, has given any thought to this.

Everything's messy and badly arranged. A mirror hangs here, a tapestry there, all the wrong sizes and the wrong heights. Ugly furniture of unequal size is placed any old how. Boxes awaiting unpacking stand untidily about, and it's chilly – no fire in the fireplace. What has Jane Parker been doing? These are a lady-in-waiting's duties.

Hans looks more closely at the fireplace. Like that in Anne's Whitehall rooms, there once was a carved falcon over it. Unlike the smashed room upriver, there's still a bird here. It looks different, though.

'Repurposed.' From behind him – too close behind him – comes the acid Parker voice. 'It's a phoenix rising from the ashes now. Queen Jane-to-be's device. That's her motto beneath it, "Bound to Obey and Serve". Marvellously suitable. Had certain other queens adopted a similar modest attitude, they might be with us still.'

Hans does not dignify this with a response. All Anne's enemies, he reminds himself, will be brought down in the end. That's why he's here.

The phoenix herself is waiting in the inner chamber. He realises that if he's ever seen Jane Seymour before, he's forgotten it. Anne's right, she's completely unmemorable. Not only tiny, but nondescript to the point of near-invisibility. And yes, plain. She has a weak chin, a big nose, hardly any neck. Her eyes, of a washed-out blue, not only don't line up but contain no life whatsoever.

This much, of course, he has anticipated. It's why he has a plan. The problem is, it can't be put into action. He can't concentrate on Jane Seymour's clothes and make a feature of them for the simple reason that she's far too badly dressed.

He'd counted on colour and glitter; all court ladies go in for some of that. Except, it seems, for the one destined to be the head of them all. She makes, it has to be said, an extremely unlikely candidate. The gown she wears – or which perhaps wears her, given its size and thickness – is not only deeply unbecoming but practically shapeless. It's of a velvet the exact colour of mud. She's brown from head to foot, without a single jewel to cheer things up.

Desperately he searches for redeeming features. Does she have good hair? If so, it's completely hidden beneath that hideous gable hood. But given her scanty brows and lack of eyelashes, it's doubtful.

There are a few tricks of the trade he can call on, of course. Such as turning the face to three-quarters to minimise the nose. This would also straighten the eyes and possibly even give the illusion of cheekbones. But that really is about it. With a sinking heart Hans realises that Cromwell, after all, is going to get exactly the picture he wants.

Jane Seymour seems more than aware of her own shortcomings. She's unable to meet his eye and is holding something tightly; a small figure, it looks like. 'What is that?' he asks kindly.

Her nervous smile, full of apology, makes her thin lips thinner while exposing small, grey, inward-bending teeth. 'It's Arabella, Master Holbein,' she says in a near-inaudible monotone.

'I see. And who is Arabella?'

'My fashion doll,' is the somewhat unbelievable explanation. How old is this woman? She might look like a child, but his guess is late twenties. And that dumpy figure could easily pass for forty.

The subject of Arabella seems to have cheered her, however. 'I like to sit and sew outfits for her,' she goes on, a spark of eagerness now enlivening the monotone. 'Lady Parker,' she nods at the other Jane, 'has a fashion doll too, called Lettice. I gave it to you, didn't I, Lady Parker? Lettice and Arabella converse together, don't they?'

Behind her mistress's back, Jane Parker rolls her eyes at Hans. He blanks her.

His sympathy for Jane Seymour is increasing despite himself, despite the dolls, despite everything. She seems harmless, even vulnerable, especially with Parker circling her like a wolf around a lamb.

'What do you want us to do?' she asks in her tiny voice. 'How do you want us to sit?'

'Us? Oh, of course. You and Arabella.'

She nods, gives him a small, grateful smile. 'You must excuse me, Master Holbein. I have never had my portrait taken before.'

'You don't say,' he hears Jane Parker murmur.

'No one has ever thought me worth painting,' Jane Seymour rather touchingly explains. 'It was always assumed I'd be an old maid, my younger sisters all married before me. When I was a girl at Wolf Hall, I was briefly attached to the son of our neighbours. But his parents thought me of insufficient rank to marry into their family.'

'They must be kicking themselves now,' snorts her lady-in-waiting. 'You're about to be Queen of England.'

An expression of panic seizes the doughy Seymour features. She raises her weak chin. 'The king has done me a great honour.' Her voice is high and frightened. 'I pray that I'll be worthy of it.'

'Of course you will,' snaps Jane Parker. 'And a great deal worthier than your predecessor, adulterous traitor that she was.'

Hatred sweeps through Hans as he sets out his drawing equipment. He braces himself for Jane Seymour's reply.

'I was away from court when she was arrested on those terrible charges,' she says quietly. 'And if she was guilty then of course she deserved her sentence. But I can only speak of what I know, and Queen Anne was always kind to me.' She smiles faintly. 'She used to tease me about my shyness.'

'And yet,' Jane Parker puts in acidly, 'what a husband you have attracted with your modesty! As for shyness, had Anne Boleyn been more so, she might be alive today.'

As he spreads his paper over his board, Hans's fingers tighten round his silverpoint pen. No one, so far as he knows, has yet been murdered with one. But there's a first time for everything.

'Queen Anne always encouraged decorum in her ladies,' Jane Seymour murmurs.

'Pure hypocrisy!' Jane Parker snaps, making her mistress flinch. 'Talk about poacher-turned-gamekeeper! Giving us books of psalms to hang from our girdles! Making us sew for the poor for hours on end! And her in those tight French fashions and headdresses exposing her hair! The modest gable hood is infinitely preferable. And so much more comfortable.'

Hans throws her a look of disbelief. Who's the hypocrite now?

'I quite liked sewing for the poor,' Jane Seymour counters timidly. She smiles at her doll. 'I like sewing, don't I, Arabella? We've made you some fine clothes now you're to be the most important doll in all England!'

'But soon, madam, you will have something other than a doll to play with, God willing,' Parker tells her. 'You will have a son. Something else Anne Boleyn conspicuously failed to deliver.'

'Actually, she had many sons,' Jane Seymour says sadly. 'But only Princess Elizabeth living.'

'The Lady Elizabeth,' corrects Parker. 'Now that the little bastard has been disinherited, like her sister, the Lady Mary.'

Her vicious tone makes Jane Seymour flinch again. 'Those poor motherless girls.' She bites a thin and colourless lower lip. 'To reconcile the king to his daughters is my dearest wish. And to be what mother I can to them.'

'I would tread carefully with that,' is Parker's caustic reply. 'And I would concentrate on producing sons of my own. Did you know,' she adds, eyes gleaming with spite, 'that Anne Boleyn's last boy was stillborn on the very day of Katherine of Aragon's funeral? At the exact moment of the birth, the candles round her tomb suddenly lit themselves spontaneously.'

'Oh, surely no!' cries Jane.

'Oh, surely yes.' The glance Parker throws Jane falls somewhere between chiding and warning. 'For I was told this by none other than Master Cromwell, who organised the funeral and was present. But perhaps it is fanciful to believe in vengeance from beyond the grave.'

*Oh, I don't know.* The voice now breathing in Hans's ear is the one he's long expected.

*Where have you been?* he asks her silently. *I was waiting for you to defend yourself.*

*Oh, here. But I can't react to every last dig of Nosy's. I'd drive myself mad. And the little Seymour's loyalty is touching. Now come on, Hans. You've a painting to do.*

He positions a chair for Jane Seymour. 'If it would please you to sit here, madam.'

As she hurries to oblige, he gets a closer look at Arabella. The doll is infinitely better clad than her mistress. She wears a rich red velvet gown whose sleeves are worked with glinting gold thread, and beneath it a gleaming silver damask kirtle. At her wooden wrists are cuffs embroidered with unbelievable skill and delicacy. Unlike her owner, Arabella has jewels. They sparkle on her dress and glitter on her hood. Round her neck is a magnificent if tiny pendant from which a large single pearl descends.

'Did you make all this?' he asks, amazed.

Jane nods her little head but her pale eyes are apprehensive, evidently fearing his opinion. But he smiles at her warmly.

'I see there's more than one artist in the room.' He means it; her skill and attention to detail are extraordinary. Jane blushes with pleasure.

Jane Parker bustles up. 'I will take Arabella,' she says bossily, extending a skinny claw.

'Actually,' says Hans, seeing that Jane Seymour's face has fallen, 'I would rather she stays.'

'The future Queen of England can hardly be painted holding a toy.'

'Am I to take it that you are painting this portrait?'

As Jane Parker furiously turns away, the pale Seymour eye catches Hans's. There could be the glint of a smile in it. As she rises with her doll, a maternal determination comes into her face. It transforms it completely. Suddenly she looks more substantial. She has authority. One might almost call her queenly.

'Stay like that,' Hans instructs, an idea starting to bloom in his mind. 'Looking away, just like that. And holding Arabella.'

He begins to sketch. As he does, the idea continues to form. He can see now what to do. How to get round the clothes problem. How to make this woman, dull as she is, something to dazzle the eye after all.

As he draws, the familiar ease fills him. He loses all sense of self, becomes what he is seeing, disappears into his own genius, where no one can follow and no one can touch him.

Back in his workroom, he transfers his drawing to the oak board on which the final image will be painted. He uses the pouncing method: pricking all the drawn lines with a small bodkin, then pressing a bag of black powder to the tiny holes. Outlined in dots, the image appears on the board beneath. Jane, holding her doll.

Arabella herself is not part of the final portrait. It's true that a doll would be unsuitable in the circumstances. But Hans likes the shape Jane's hands made about her, the protective interlacing of her fingers, the angle of her thumb on top. Most of all, that quiet, proud confidence in her face. To which he will add a touch of defiance, a gentle hint of steel. Her lack of beauty will be truly conveyed, but so too will her integrity and generous nature.

Arabella's clothes, meanwhile, will become Jane's clothes. Just as the pouncing transfers the outline, Hans's skill with a brush will transfer the red dress with its thick silver sleeves from Arabella's wooden body to Jane's living one. In every detail, right down to a scaled-up version of the necklace.

*Clever boy*, says Anne. He can almost see her pacing around his easel, as so often she did in the Whitehall gatehouse days. Her lavender scent plays about his nostrils. *You've made the little Seymour almost beautiful.*

She's right. The contrast between plain face and gorgeous clothes gives the portrait a dynamic energy. The elaborate outfit distracts and enhances. Jane is an understated pearl in a magnificent setting. Dazzling all onlookers in the wardrobe she made for her favourite doll.

Perhaps now she is a doll herself. King's Doll. With her tiny stature and sumptuous wardrobe, she's the latest royal plaything. Henry's new toy now that he's broken all the others.

# *Chapter Twenty*

Standing before the easel, it's a few moments before Cromwell speaks. Hans waits, prepared to defend his work. It's not quite what was asked for, but nor is it anything else.

But when Master Secretary turns to him, it's with a cheery smile. 'Well done, dear boy. Our most high and puissant prince will be delighted with this.'

Pragmatic as ever, Cromwell seems to have decided that a portrait Henry likes is as good for him as one he doesn't. He'll get the credit for commissioning the artist. Perhaps he thinks this will offset any danger from the Norfolk and Seymour factions.

Perhaps he is over-optimistic.

Mere days later, after Henry marries Jane Seymour in the Queen's Cabinet at Whitehall, Wyatt writes to Hans with sensational news. After decades of fighting and scheming, it seems that King François of France and Charles V, Holy Roman Emperor and Hapsburg ruler of Spain and the Netherlands, are approaching an accord.

*The unimaginable has happened between them. Peace is breaking out. And with it, poor prospects for our friend Cromwell. François and Charles are loyal to Rome; they remember the deaths of Thomas More and Bishop Fisher, whose blood is on Cromwell's hands as well as*

*Henry's. They deplore the desecration of the shrines and the destruction of the abbeys. If they unite in earnest, imperial blockades on the trade routes could be the consequence. Even invasion of England. Which would be welcome news for the Seymours and the Norfolks, religious conservatives who might well rise with the invaders and see Henry overthrown.*

*When you have read this, place it in the fire.*

*Your servant,*
*TW*

'Your laundry this week is truly excellent, Mistress Harris!' Hans exclaims.

'I'm not Mistress Harris.'

Such was his hurry to read the message, he had failed to notice who had brought it in. Not the usual wrinkled washerwoman. A fresh-looking girl, about twenty. Last seen handing him his purse back in a city street.

'You!' He stares at her in astonishment.

'Me.'

A heat in his face; he's actually blushing. His tongue is heavy in his mouth, will only move slowly. 'I never thanked you properly,' he manages, awkwardly. 'If I can help you in return . . .'

'You could make out your laundry list.'

He hurries to oblige. All fingers and thumbs, all sixes and sevens, he scribbles Wyatt a reply. As she takes it, their fingertips connect, and it's like touching something hot. 'Why are you doing this?' he asks her, suddenly. Now he's over the shock, he wants to know who she is. Why she's taking this risk, making him take it too.

She nods, bends nearer. Her fair hair brushes his cheek. Her eyes are a clear, pale green, like water. 'Same reason as you,' she says softly.

He shrugs, not convinced. What does this mean?

'I was her maid. She brought me with her from Kent, when she came to court.'

No need to ask who. But he's racking his brains. He doesn't remember this girl, but then he rarely went to Anne's apartments. She preferred to come to him. And even if he was there, he still might not have noticed her. In a room with Anne in it, you saw no one else.

'And after she died . . .' The girl pauses, takes a breath. 'I was dismissed, along with the rest of her servants. I slept rough in the city. I didn't care what happened to me.'

He tries to imagine this blooming creature destitute on the streets. It must be why she spotted the thieves; a hastily developed instinct for self-preservation.

'But something kept me going.' She stops, looks away.

'What was it?' he prompts.

The clear eyes swing back, full of anger. 'Vengeance,' she hisses. 'To bring down those who destroyed her. And that meant staying alive. And that meant getting work.'

'So you went to Mistress Harris?'

A nod. 'I knew her, she was the head laundress. I often went to her with my mistress's dresses. She was shocked when she saw me, though.' The girl imitates the washerwoman's cockney tones. ' "Jennet, you look half dead! When was the last time you ate? Or slept?" '

Hans grins too; she's an excellent mimic. And her name is Jennet. Pretty name, makes him think of a bird.

That's his lot, though. She slips his note into her basket and leaves.

Next morning, he takes himself for a haircut. He's let himself go, he realises. As a youth he was considered handsome, but he's no one's idea of good-looking these days.

The finished result is a considerable improvement. The years haven't fallen away exactly, but the wide eyes showing beneath the shorter hair, the firm, clean-shaven chin and the broad, high cheekbones hint at the boy he used to be. And something has returned to his eyes. Life? Hope? Or something else?

The hope in Wyatt's letter proves unfounded, at least for now. If Cromwell has heard about François and Emperor Charles, he seems undaunted. He materialises in Hans's rooms. 'Great news, dear boy. The King's Painter is finally to paint the king!' He looks him up and down. 'Good thing you've had a haircut.'

# *Chapter Twenty-One*

In the royal apartments, Hans is shown to a bench to wait. He watches the Gentlemen of the King's Privy Chamber go about their business. There's an atmosphere of confusion; everyone at sixes and sevens. The timing seems to be off, everything a bit late.

The daytime ushers are only now reporting for duty, relieving the night guard at the door. The grooms are hurriedly sweeping the room, bumping into each other as they put down fresh straw. Inexpertly lighting the fire in the great hearth.

From his bench, Hans sees what the problem is. These men are all new to the inner sanctum, replacing those who lie dead in the Tower.

Does Henry regret their loss? he wonders. Norris, smooth, capable and with lifelong experience of the king's preferences, would never have tolerated the chaos he's now witnessing.

What seems like hours go by. The morning duties lurch to a haphazard close. The fire has finally been persuaded into life, the remains of candles and torches have been collected for reuse and the daily menus have arrived, disappeared into the bedchamber for perusal and emerged with choices made. But the king has still not emerged.

You have to wait for great folks, though. Hans learnt this at an early age with his father, the day he and Hans Senior went to

Maximilianstrasse, to the vast five-storey Fugger mansion every Augsburger knew for its colourful frescoes.

Walking beside his father into the Fuggers' inner courtyard, hearing the great gates behind him shut out the ordinary world, Hans felt a thrilling sense of privilege. He was about to meet the famous banker who had lent the Pope the money to build St Peter's. Jakob Fugger, it was said, was so rich he could loan you the money to buy an empire. Later, he did just that, lending Charles von Hapsburg the means to bribe the electors who chose the Holy Roman Emperor.

Today, though, Jakob Fugger wanted an altarpiece. And naturally he had turned to the Holbeins, whose speciality they were. The usual subject was agonising deaths, the main variant being the saint that the client had chosen. Whisper it soft, but Hans had long grown tired of painting them.

Young as he was, a mere teenager, he was fed up of the endless martyrs having their flesh ripped off. Or being stoned, or holding gouged-out eyes on plates. Waving enormous keys or models of Rome and always expressionless whatever their agonies, they stalked his dreams.

Recently, he'd been painting the martyrdom of Sebastian with his father. Although tied to a tree and pierced with arrows, the saint seemed only mildly perturbed.

This could not be the truth, Hans knew. Sebastian had to be in agony. People in real life felt pain; they had faces that expressed things: delight, fear, hope, love, happiness, excitement, misery. He couldn't recall a time when he didn't notice this, the way features revealed emotion, implied character.

'Do you believe Sebastian is a real saint, Father?' he had asked Hans Senior.

'What do you mean?'

'Do you believe he can talk to God for you?'

The clients thought the saints interceded with the Almighty on their behalf. But Hans struggled to believe this. He'd painted them himself, he knew how they were made, with pig-bristle brushes and spit. He could see every mistake and where it had been corrected. He knew there was nothing remotely holy about them.

Hans the Elder looked at him warily. 'Is this about that crazy Luther?'

'Who?'

Hans listened as his father explained about a monk in faraway Wittenberg who didn't think altarpieces talked to God either. And who also hated indulgences: forgiveness for sins in the form of mass-produced leaflets sold by the clergy to the poor. Martin Luther said this was wrong, and only enriched the Pope.

'I've never heard of him,' Hans assured his father. It was true; he wasn't interested in monks. Girls were what he cared about, and kicking an inflated pig's bladder about the streets.

'Well, let's hope Luther's views don't catch on,' Hans the Elder concluded. 'Because if they do, there'll be no altarpieces. And what will we Holbeins paint then?'

*Something else*, Hans thought with a bolt of rebellious excitement. Something other than flat-faced saints. Exactly what, he did not know. But what he did know, beyond all doubt, was that he was special, that a current of genius flowed through him and set him apart. Whenever he picked up a paintbrush or a drawing charcoal, he felt it run from his eyes to his brain. Down his left arm and along his left hand – yes, still his left hand, for all the painful, wrenching efforts to make him use his right. Then into the pen and onto the paper, or into the brush and onto the board. Everything one piece, one smooth working unit. Brain, arm, eyes, hand. And memory, of course. His was prodigious, the merest glance to remember every detail of something. Or someone.

The figure who eventually came to greet them in Fugger's courtyard was so magnificent, Hans thought it must be Fugger himself. But no, just a factotum, who told them to wait. And so they waited, his father and himself, on a polished bench in a slender-pillared arcade, backs against the sun-warmed marble wall. The jet from the courtyard fountain glittered like a plume of diamonds.

People came and went. At one point a young girl appeared, hair flowing beneath a cap whose jewels sparkled in the sunshine. Her heels clicked on the marble as she came along. 'Look down,' hissed his father, urging deferential respect. But Hans had looked up instead. He'd never known such goddesses existed; certainly, he'd never seen them in the street. This was their private world.

Finally they were ushered into the Presence. As Hans the Elder bowed, or cringed, so low it seemed he would never straighten up, Fugger took absolutely no notice. Hans was fascinated. Never had he met anyone who blazed with power quite like this. His hungry gaze harvested the potentate's every aspect: his quick glance, his square jaw, the big velvet hat over his gold skullcap, the way he crackled with impatient energy, how his velvet-shod foot beat the carpet, how he tapped an inlaid table with a beringed and testy finger. Fugger was not, Hans noticed, especially tall.

As, finally, his father began the sketch for the portrait that would appear in the altarpiece – perhaps Fugger kneeling at the feet of the Madonna, perhaps among the saints off to the side – a stream of clerks and assistants came and went. Some brought sealed documents, which were opened and read in seconds. Others proffered a quill for parchments to be signed with a decisive scratch. Not for a second was Fugger unoccupied. He asked questions abruptly, answered them shortly. Hans, straining to listen, felt his ears prick up when a clerk mentioned Martin Luther, the one with the controversial views. 'He intends,' the clerk added, 'to nail his pamphlet to the church door at Wittenberg.'

Fugger scoffed. 'Well, let him.'

The clerks and factotums laughed.

As Hans the Elder, conscious of his patron's lack of time, drew nervously and rapidly with his silverpoint pen, his son watched the image develop. The drawing was for a work where Fugger would be one of many figures. But it dawned on Hans that it could exist in its own right, a portrait of the financier as an individual.

This linked in his mind with something he had heard about, something they did in Italy and the Netherlands. Paintings of heads and shoulders, with no religious context. *Ritratti*, they called them. Portraits.

Were he drawing a *ritratto* of Fugger, Hans thought, he would do more with the clothes than just record them. He would pick out certain aspects – the gold cap, the great jewel on the finger – to convey character. He would broaden the shoulders to suggest power, make the body lounge slightly to suggest arrogance. The finished work would be ravishing in its splendour and astonishing in its realism. But to those who looked deeper, it would reveal what was hidden. The inner man behind the mask.

Excitement seized him. This was it, what he wanted to do. Not to paint altarpieces: stiff-faced figures for the faithful to worship in the hope they'd intercede with heaven. Instead, he wanted to paint the gods of earth. The Fuggers and their like, who determined the fortunes of nations.

And now here he is, waiting to see Henry of England. It's been many years since he's thought of that momentous day in Augsburg, which dictated his eventual direction in more ways than one. His father had been as right to fear Luther as Fugger had been wrong to dismiss him. Luther's views on the corruption of the Church had led to Europe-wide revolution. Basel had been engulfed in it, and the market for artists destroyed as a result. As Hans Senior had foreseen, the Holbeins had stopped painting altarpieces and scattered in all directions. It had been the original spur for Hans's wanderings; without Luther, he might still be in Augsburg. He would certainly not be sitting here in London.

Another hour drags by. Then another. Then Cromwell arrives, and suddenly it's all go.

## *Chapter Twenty-Two*

Hans's first impression of the inner sanctum is intense heat and a sweet, unpleasant smell. It's high summer, but a great fire roils in the royal bedchamber's huge brick hearth. A vast red and gold bed with the curtains drawn dominates the room's centre. The painful thought of Anne in there rushes in before he can stop it.

Fortunately, Cromwell's not looking at him. With what seems audacious familiarity, he's gone up to the bed and poked his head through the curtains. Hans can hear the king speaking, his voice low and fretful. 'This garter round my leg. Jane says I should loosen it.'

'Sire,' replies Cromwell. 'The doctors all say that it should be as tight as possible around the knee. Starve the wound of blood so it will heal.'

'Doesn't feel like it's healing,' Henry growls.

'Give it time, sire,' soothes Cromwell.

'And I'm so hot. Look how I sweat. Open a window, let some cool air in.'

'The doctors advise against, sire, lest pestilence enter the wound.'

Before the groaning, gasping monarch can muster a counter-argument, Cromwell draws back one of the drapes. Shocked by what he sees, Hans can't imagine why he's been summoned to see the king in this state, why it's so important to draw him now. The contrast between the Henry Hans saw last and this one is enormous. Literally.

He looks not just fatter, but much older and much iller. His head's like a boiled ham; red, sweaty and completely bald. A small, sparse beard fringes the lower regions. From between the open flaps of his red and gold doublet rises an enormous stomach in a white linen shift, below which, in white silk hose, stretch shapeless legs as big as tree trunks. Around one fat knee is a tight jewelled garter, and below it a huge, thick bandage. There's a bloodstain visible through both that and the hose. The bandage, Hans realises, is the source of the smell; like decay, as if Henry were rotting from the inside.

Imagining his feelings on seeing the king again, Hans has envisioned blind fury and bloody hatred. This, after all, is the man who signed Anne's death warrant. But beyond revulsion at the smell, the gross appearance, what he now feels is disappointment. That the man who destroyed such splendour is so pitifully unimpressive. Henry lies there like a decaying whale; huge, stinking and stranded. Looking at Hans with his nasty little blue eyes.

'Your Majesty,' Cromwell is saying. 'Here is Master Holbein. The King's Painter.'

The blue eyes look briefly confused, as if it's the first Henry's heard of this. Then they clear. The big face wobbles in a nod. 'Ah yes, the painter Holborn. You painted my darling Jane.'

*And your former darling Anne*, Hans starts to think, but has to stop. Has to bow and say, 'I had that pleasure, Your Majesty.'

'Cromwell tells me I need to have my portrait made.' Henry's voice is now more the one from before; strangely thin and high, like air forced through a small hole.

'Indeed you do, sire,' Cromwell confirms unctuously. 'So it can be copied and sent throughout the kingdom. Image is—'

'Power. Yes, yes, so you keep saying,' Henry cuts in forcibly, then winces in agony. Even speaking hurts, it seems. 'Just be quick, can you, Holborn? I'm expecting my astrologer.'

'Astrologer, sire?'

A testy blue eye glints in Cromwell's direction. 'To tell me when my son will be born, of course.'

Hans holds his breath. He knows from Wyatt that were Jane Seymour to bear a son, she and her family would be invincible. Until then, like all previous wives, she risks Henry suddenly tiring of her, something Cromwell is surely praying for.

You really wouldn't know it, though. Master Secretary's smile as he congratulates the king is broader than ever. He is truly the actor's actor. 'Sire! What wonderful news. Allow me to be the first—'

Henry scowls at him. 'Jane's not with child. Not yet, anyway. That's what I'm consulting him about. To find out when she will be. And . . . Ow! *OW!!*'

A great lion's roar of royal agony sends Hans's sketching pen skittering across the paper. Picking up the bread he uses to rub out mistakes, he glances at the jewelled garter around the king's knee. It's so tight you can barely see it, embedded as it is in surrounding flesh. Surely Jane is right and it would help to remove it. He watches covertly as the king winces, groans and, as the pain crests, yells again. Hard to imagine someone in this state fathering a child.

*That's the whole point*, a low voice says in his ear.

*What?!*

*To reduce Henry's capacities as much as possible, obviously.*

*Why?*

*I can't imagine*, is the sarcastic response. *In whose interests would it be to do that? Prevent the king fathering a son, something the whole nation is waiting for? Apart from one person, possibly.*

Hans turns his eyes to Cromwell, who is smiling his obsequious smile. 'And we all pray Her Majesty will be soon in that happy state, sire,' he's saying.

'And to find out the best day to get her crowned,' Henry gasps, when the attack subsides.

Almost imperceptibly, Cromwell's smile fades. 'Ah yes, sire. About that.'

'Oh?' The small eyes glint suspiciously. 'There's a problem?'

'Oh no, sire. Not a problem, not at all. Nothing that can't be dealt with.'

Henry's eyes narrow to slits. 'And this non-problem would be . . .?'

'Just those risings in the north, sire. Against the break-up of the monasteries. We need to show them who's in charge, keep them in their place.'

'Just a few grumbling peasants, isn't it?' the king says, dismissively. 'So round 'em up! Give 'em a traitor's death!'

'Yes, sire.' Master Secretary clasps his plump hands, then unclasps them again. 'It's just that . . . well, it may be rather more than a few.'

'How many?'

'Thousands, it seems,' Cromwell admits.

A blue vein throbs in Henry's temple. *'Thousands?'*

'Possibly tens of thousands. As many as forty thousand. It might not be possible to hang, draw and quarter them all, sire. More peaceful means might be advisable, a measure of persuasion. Hence the portraits of you. They will have a positive effect.'

'Portraits?' explodes the king. 'You want to put down a rebellion with *portraits*?'

Hans agrees. It's a ridiculous idea. Especially from the master strategist Master Secretary. What's he playing at?

'Your Majesty is too modest. You underestimate the power of your magnificence,' Cromwell tells him. 'The splendour and authority of your presence.'

So blatant is the flattery Hans would have thought it

laughable, had Henry not now nodded thoughtfully, his rage quite disappeared. 'Yes,' he says, musingly. 'I am rather magnificent, aren't I?'

'And the great degree to which your subjects love you.'

He rubs his thin beard. 'Hmm, yes. They do, don't they?'

'Utterly, sire. These rebellions are a cry for attention, as naughty children to distracted fathers. Distracted, in your case,' Cromwell smoothly adds, 'by the business of England.'

'Yes, yes, they should realise that. How I toil ceaselessly in their cause. My every waking thought devoted to them.'

He's serious, Hans sees. He really believes it.

'And such is Master Holbein's skill,' Cromwell oozes on, 'the portrait he makes of Your Majesty will be as if Your Majesty was in the room. No loyal subject could fail to be deeply affected.'

High praise, Hans knows. England's second most powerful person lauding him to the most powerful. It should feel like the height of his career, but instead it feels like he's being used. What are these pictures about, really? Cromwell is up to something here too, but what?

'So we will take these persuasive measures, sire. And until they take effect . . .' Master Secretary pauses, sighs, and adds with a sorrowful expression, 'the queen's coronation will sadly have to be postponed.'

Ah. Hans's fingers tighten round his pen. So that's it.

Cromwell doesn't want Jane Seymour crowned any more than he wants her to have a son. So he's making sure neither happens. By doing nothing about the rebels; pretending a few portraits will chasten them. By rendering Henry physically helpless; insisting on the garter and increasing his agony. It's breathtaking, the audacity of it, the way it's happening in plain sight under everyone's nose. Cromwell plays Henry like one of those new instruments Hans saw when he was in Italy. What are they called? Violins, that's it.

'Postponed?' Henry repeats in a hoarse, horrified whisper. 'My darling Jane's crowning? Postponed because of the *peasants*?'

'It is for the best, sire. Just until everything dies down—'

A strange, strangled noise now interrupts Cromwell. To Hans's astonishment, the great red face has crumpled and a tear is rolling slowly down the fleshy royal cheek. Henry is crying.

'Who would be a king?' he weeps. 'Never a moment's peace, never a moment's safety. It has been thus all my life. My first memory was being told that the pretender Perkin Warbeck was marching on London to seize my father's throne. And now, another rebellion.'

'Sire, sire,' Cromwell soothes, looking as upset as the king himself, though inside he's surely singing. 'Be assured, you are safe. I see to that, as you know.'

Henry dabs his streaming eyes, sniffs loudly. 'Yes,' he nods. 'It's true that I have you to depend on, Cromwell. I don't know what I'd do without you.'

## *Chapter Twenty-Three*

It takes Hans a long time to put all this in a message for Wyatt, especially in the mirror script he uses; legible only by putting the letter up to a looking glass. He's checking it in his own small mirror when something red glides across it. He looks up; Jennet has come in. She can't have seen him because she goes straight to his easel, on which the portrait of Henry leans.

He watches her in the mirror as she examines his work. She looks at it long and critically. What is she thinking?

That Henry looks like a king, possibly. Hans has been down to the royal wardrobe and chosen a suitably magnificent outfit: a silver doublet covered with jewels, a gold cloak trimmed with lynx, a black velvet feathered bonnet to cover the bald head. When they were sent up, he put them on the wooden dummy he keeps for the purpose and painted them from that. This is normal practice, even if his subjects don't have bad legs and can't sit up. Clothes are expensive, luxurious things, clients want every detail included, and this takes time. They send their outfits separately, after the first sitting when he sketches their faces.

She's really looking, staring hard. He rises quietly and, grinning, tiptoes up behind her.

She gasps, whirls round. Her face in disarray is beautiful, framed by flying flaxen hair.

He gestures at the painting. 'You were giving it quite an examination.'

She nods. 'It's very him.'

'Him?'

Hans had struggled with Henry's face. How to tell the truth about this man. All-powerful, but in Cromwell's complete control. Cruel, yet self-pitying. Magnificent, yet rotten. In the end, he'd painted a fantasy of his own. He'd imagined the moment Henry realised how Cromwell had manipulated him. The terrible, subtle moment before the lethal lashing-out. Brutality is gathering in the grey, fleshy face. The small eyes are cold, the small mouth tight.

'He looks frightening,' Jennet goes on. 'And he is. I always thought so, right from the start.'

'You knew him?'

She looks at him with her clear green eyes. 'Of course I did. He was in and out of my mistress's rooms all the time.'

She was there, Hans is thinking. This girl in the background saw the relationship develop; she was in the same place. He'd seen it mostly from afar, his only information court gossip and what little Anne chose to tell him.

'And he was frightening,' she repeats. 'But my mistress relished the drama and danger. She treated him like a lion, growling back, snapping, cracking her whip. But she loved him.'

He looks at her. 'You think so?'

'I know so,' is the calm reply. 'She would never have married him otherwise.'

Something like a hot knife twists in Hans. He'd convinced himself it was royal power that had ensnared Anne. The chance to escape her father, arrange her life as she wished. But no. *She loved him*, he thinks. *And he killed her.*

'She didn't think he was going to,' Jennet says, making Hans realise he's spoken out loud. 'When I went to see her in the Tower, she was sure he would save her.'

Hans is jolted from anguish to surprise. 'The *Tower*? You went there? How?'

A shrug. 'Asked Cromwell for a pass, of course.'

'You knew him too?'

'I'd seen him around. He often came to visit my mistress. But I didn't think he noticed me.'

'And he had?' Hans isn't sure why, but his heart is sinking slightly.

'You could say that.' She imitates Cromwell's emollient tone. ' "A pass? Of course, Jennet. How can I resist when you look at me with those big green eyes of yours?" ' She pauses, then describes how Master Secretary's own sharp eyes had rolled slowly over her body.

'No,' says Hans, cold with horror.

'It was over quickly, thank God. Don't look at me like that. How dare you judge me? What other means of persuasion did I have?'

Hans stares at the floor as anger and shame fight for dominance. She's right. How dare he judge her? But he can judge Cromwell, to whose crimes can now be added this latest revolting piece of opportunism.

Jennet is describing how she'd feared to find Anne in a bare stone cell. 'But instead she was in the grand apartments in which she'd slept before her coronation.'

Hans shakes his head. The unbearable cruelty of it.

'That's what I thought. But my mistress saw it as a good sign. "Henry would hardly have sent me here if he really meant to kill me," she said. "He put a crown on my head last time. So he's not going to cut it off this time. There's a plan, Jennet, you see."

' "A plan, madam?" I asked.

' "Yes! At the last minute, Henry will send me to a nunnery!"

'My mistress thought this a great joke. But any nunnery, I felt, should be honoured to have her. She was the most genuinely good person I have ever known. Generous, brave, loyal and kind. The Anne Boleyn they talked of at her trial – the witch, the adulteress, the incestuous fornicator – had as little connection to the truth as the lying witnesses.'

Jennet pauses, and pain floods her face. 'People told such wicked, *wicked* lies.'

'Wyatt,' says Hans bitterly.

She raises her eyebrows. 'Actually,' she says, 'of all the so-called evidence, his was the only account that was true.'

*'True?'*

Jennet nods firmly. She had been there, she explains, that carefree afternoon in Anne's apartment when the king's verses had arrived. Followed soon after by Wyatt. 'Tom, you have a rival!' Anne had cried merrily, before reading out Henry's poem.

'There was no malice intended, no mockery,' Jennet concludes. 'But at her trial they said she was laughing at the king.'

Hans is struggling to accept that Wyatt had not lied to save his own skin. He realises how he wants to believe it, to maintain his long-held grudge.

Jennet is talking again.

'I begged my mistress to let me stay and serve her. But she had some women already. Among them was a Mistress Stoner and, incredibly, a Mistress Coffin. My mistress giggled as she whispered their names. The king's idea of a joke, she was sure. A message to her, reminding her how the two of them had loved to laugh.

'And they had. I used to hear them. But Lady Kingston, the wife of the Tower's constable, did not look like a joke to me. The waiting women swigged the wine that had been sent for my mistress and which, with typical generosity, or perhaps hoping to stir their pity, she had pressed on them. But they did not look pitying.

'"No king of England has ever executed his wife, let alone an anointed queen," my mistress said to me. "It would break the most sacred of holy laws." Moreover, she pointed out, she had asserted her innocence to Cranmer, the Archbishop of Canterbury and her confessor. If she were lying, it would imperil her immortal soul. Would Henry, who took faith so seriously, disregard all this? Fly in the face of God himself?'

She looks at Hans, shrugs. 'What could I say to that? Did the king take faith seriously? He'd split with Rome and, for a brief period, been married to two women at once. Now he seemed to be contemplating his second divorce.'

She pauses before going on. 'She was sure he would save her. She said that she knew her husband, and he was not a murderer, although she now accepted that he wanted rid of her. And yes, perhaps this had been obvious for some time, and perhaps she had been reluctant to accept it. The reason was simple: she loved him still. She had given her heart to Henry, and it remained his despite everything.'

The hot knife in Hans twists again. It remained Henry's even then?

'But she recognised that he wanted to divorce her, and that this process could be slow and complicated, as disconnecting from Queen Katherine had shown. She believed that with Master Secretary's help, the king had decided to expedite things. Condemn her to death on trumped-up charges, then spare her at the last minute. That was the plot. That was what she thought would happen.'

The belief had been contagious. Hans remembers the rumours sweeping the crowd, the talk of reprieve.

'A clever way of satisfying her enemies, that's what she said. Bringing her to the edge of destruction before absolving her. No one could then claim that she had got off lightly. A pardon would arrive, she was sure of it. "I know the king. I know how he thinks." That's what she told me. "Don't forget, Jennet, I was at his side for three years. Every moment of every day. He consulted me on everything, he made no decision without me. He won't kill me. He loved me once." '

Jennet pauses again, and her eyes glitter with tears. 'Then she started talking about her daughter. Little Elizabeth, of whom she was so proud. Another reason, she was sure, why she would be spared. Her child would otherwise be left motherless, and this would be inconvenient for the king.'

She briefly covers her face, then gathers herself, carries on. ' "Who will plan Elizabeth's education, choose her tutors, check her progress, supervise her clothes and diet?" she asked me. "Not Henry. I always took care of everything." Then she talked, full of hope, about being freed to live with her daughter at the pretty manor at Hunsdon where Elizabeth has her household. Where she could teach her, play with her in the garden, ride with her in the fields. Her pale oval face, lovely still – lovelier than ever, it seemed to me – lit up. She leant over, clutched my hands. "The quiet life," she said wistfully. "How I'd love it, after all these noisy years at court." '

The last few words have been forced out between heaving breaths, and now Jennet is properly weeping. Her sobs are ragged and gasping. Hans edges over, puts an arm round her. Feels grief rack her narrow body. Hears her muffled voice below his chin. 'But now I wonder whether she really believed any of it. Or whether she was just saying it to make me feel better.'

He waits for the voice in his ear, but it does not come. On this point, it seems, Anne is keeping her own counsel. 'It's possible she believed it,' he says, as comfortingly as he can manage.

He was holding her gingerly to begin with, but now he's drawn her closer, and Jennet's sobs are calming. 'It hardly matters now,' she says. 'Revenge is the only thing that does.'

*That's the spirit*, says the low voice in Hans's ear.

## *Chapter Twenty-Four*

Hans's first commission as King's Painter is a success. Henry is delighted with his portrait. He sees none of the hidden meanings, only the power and magnificence. Hans had been worried he'd gone too far, far more than usual. Fortunately kings, far more than usual, see what they want to see.

Henry is back on his feet. The northern rebels are suppressed. The Duke of Norfolk took an army and dealt with them, brutally. The Seymour faction have taken matters into their own hands. Will they now take Cromwell?

But when Master Secretary appears in his workroom, he's whistling cheerfully. 'Dear boy. How are you on frescoes?'

Well, yes, obviously Hans knows how to paint on wet plaster. He's a trained artist, isn't he? But in England the climate is far from ideal. He thinks of Italy, Mantua, the great frescoes by Mantegna in the Gonzaga Palace. Greenwich Palace, by the damp riverside, is completely unsuitable.

'Well, it's going to have to be suitable,' Cromwell tells him. 'The king wants one.'

Turns out that it's for Whitehall, the finishing touch to the renovations. Henry wants to commemorate and immortalise his marriage to the woman he's confident will bear his son. 'A great painting of the royal family for the Presence Chamber,' Cromwell says.

'Royal family?' Does this mean that Anne's little Elizabeth and Katherine's big Mary have been welcomed back into the fold, as Jane intended they would be?

'Not exactly,' is Cromwell's crushing answer. The royal family in question are the king's parents, Henry VII and Elizabeth of York. Plus Henry and Jane, of course.

Hans frowns. He has no idea what the senior Tudors looked like. Cromwell thinks there might be paintings somewhere, old ones. He'll have them found and sent round for reference.

Hans goes up to Whitehall to check the site. The wall that Henry's chosen is absolutely enormous. He's going to need a lot of plaster. A lot of sand, a lot of lime. Plenty of buckets and trowels, a couple of plumb lines to get the level and plot the space out. He's busy taking measurements when, in that sudden way of his, Henry strides in, a train of flunkeys hurrying behind. While he grips a big gold stick, his leg is obviously much better.

'Ah, Holborn,' he says.

Rising from his bow, Hans sees that while the bandage is still there, the garter below the knee is considerably looser. Jane, it seems, has prevailed.

'I have the design,' Henry announces in his strange high voice, and proceeds to instruct Hans in a pedestrian arrangement of four people standing on a carpet. 'Around a central plinth, see,' he says excitedly. 'It's a competition.'

'A competition, sire?'

'Who is the best king, my father or myself.'

'Yourself, sire, clearly,' one of the flunkeys exclaims.

Henry smiles smugly. 'I am not a despot,' he says. 'I want people to make up their own minds. Put the evidence before them, let them reach their own conclusion.'

'Evidence, sire?' Hans ventures after he has squeezed all incredulity from his voice.

As the king describes the Latin inscription he wants on the

plinth, Hans's heart plummets. There are few things he dislikes painting more than letters. They're exacting but boring – careful spacing, super-straight lines, and mistakes are always horribly obvious. His only hope is that the inscription, which is apparently still in preparation, will be short.

'The background to the painting must be very fancy,' Henry instructs. 'Lots of pillars and carvings, shells and statues, that sort of thing.'

Hans doesn't like painting any of those much either, but prefers them to letters. Why can't this fresco be like the lovely informal portrait he did years ago of Thomas More's family, sitting and talking together? Or Mantegna's colourful crowd of Gonzagas, spread out behind a balustrade? What Henry's describing sounds like an enormous bookplate, stiff figures around a box of words.

He reminds himself that it's a means to an end, although when and how that end will come is less and less obvious. Even if Jane Seymour bears a son, it's hardly going to result in Cromwell's death. Master Secretary is too adept at keeping on the right side of Henry. Perhaps they should be thinking of murder after all, a hired assassin.

He writes wearily to Wyatt describing small gains and losses, positions changing slightly but not significantly. To make matters worse, it's not even Jennet who takes the letter, but Mistress Harris.

When he asks where Jennet is, he's rewarded with crossed arms, a hard stare. 'She's keeping out of trouble.'

'No trouble here,' says Hans, innocently. Apart from the plot to kill Cromwell, of course.

'So you say. But it's all very well for you men. You take a girl up, toy with her, tire of her. And then what's she supposed to do? I won't have her messed about with.' The old laundrywoman's lips press together.

Hans says nothing, but excitement flares in his insides. Jennet must have said something. Something hinting that she finds him attractive. Why else would Mistress Harris be saying this?

The laundrywoman has hardly gone when Master Secretary rolls in. 'Here,' he says, handing over a rolled scroll tied with a ribbon.

His spirits still buoyed, Hans risks a joke. 'What's this? My knighthood?'

'Ha ha, very funny.'

It's Henry's final text for the plinth in the centre of the painting. Cromwell's been up all night with it; the king kept changing his mind. 'Hope your Latin's up to it, Hans.'

'I was a friend of Erasmus, remember.'

'Oh yes,' chuckles Cromwell. 'There were a few of those, I understand.'

'Not that sort of friend,' Hans says firmly, although in fact there had been an incident. He'd just arrived in Basel from Augsburg and was working at Froben's, the publisher. Erasmus, their superstar author, was visiting and had glided up to him, smiling suggestively, and placed his hand somewhere completely unexpected. 'Tell me, young man,' he had murmured, 'why do you carry house bricks in the front of your hose?'

The incident was not repeated, and Hans has wondered since whether he had imagined it. Not so, it seems.

'An interesting man, no doubt about it,' Cromwell says breezily. 'Still, each to his own, I always say. Live and let live. What people do in private is their own affair. It doesn't bother me.'

Hans forces away the thought of what Anne and those accused with her were supposed to have done in private, and how very much that had bothered Cromwell. He unrolls the paper and his jaw almost drops to the floor. The script Henry wants on his plinth is as immodest as he is, and almost as enormous.

*If it pleases you to see the illustrious images of heroes, look on these, no picture ever bore greater. The great debate, competition and question is whether father or son is the victor . . .*

It continues for what Hans estimates will be seventeen densely packed lines in total. He scans it briefly; it seems to contrast the older Henry's military success with the younger one's restoration of the true religion.

'What military success?' he asks, and is astonished to be told about the Battle of Bosworth. How the dull old man in the bad painting he's been given to copy was once a young upstart who bided his time in France before invading England and seizing the crown, as bold as you like.

'And therein lies the problem,' says Cromwell.

Hans blinks. 'Problem? But he became king. Started the Tudor line.'

'Yes, but Henry the Seventh took the crown over the head of the old families. They think their claim is greater, which is why they cannot be trusted. People like the Norfolks, the Courtenays, the Poles.'

*And the Seymours*, Hans thinks, adding the name that Cromwell's left out.

It's Jennet who brings the next letter. The thought that she might be attracted to him, rather than just the cause they share, heats up his face, ties his insides in knots. But there's no encouragement in her expression as she hands Wyatt's note over. It's as if the emotional scenes of last time never happened.

He takes the letter. It's not encouraging either.

*Don't despair*, is the message from Madrid. *Keep the faith. Cromwell will make a mistake, I know it. Then we will have our chance.* Wyatt reports that he's getting on well with the emperor. *A clever and cultured man who favours me above all other envoys.*

He ends with a jolly description of life at the Hapsburg court, riding up front with his new imperial friend as they journey from palace to palace on what seems an endless holiday through Spain. It is, Hans concludes bitterly as he thinks of Henry's seventeen lines of self-praising Latin, all very well for some people.

'Bad news?' Jennet asks.

He looks into the clear green eyes. 'So-so.'

He scribbles a reply, hands it over. She remains, however. She's looking at him. Something's coming, he can feel it. His hopes rise again, his pulse quickens.

'I wanted to ask you something,' she says.

He nods. 'Go ahead.'

'You once said you'd help me.'

His pulse slows again. She just wants a favour, then. 'I did,' he agrees.

She's looking down and twisting her hands. If he didn't know better, he'd say she was nervous. 'You're the King's Painter,' she says.

'I am.'

She raises her chin, meets his eyes. 'Can you show me?'

'*Show* you?' He frowns. 'Show you what?'

She glances down again and mutters something he can't quite hear.

'Sorry?' he says.

She sighs, looks up. Her gaze is defensive, slightly wild. 'How to be an artist.'

His eyes widen. That's what he thought she'd said. He waits a moment or two, thinking. It's obviously cost her to say this; he wants to let her down gently. But perhaps it's best to be honest. 'Women aren't artists,' he says, regretfully. 'They never have been. I'm sorry, but there it is.'

But if he expects her to just accept this, he's quite wrong. She holds his gaze. 'What, no woman ever?' she demands.

'Well . . .' he says, doubtfully. Actually, he knows of one or two. Italians. Daughters of master painters mostly. No laundry-maids, though.

'So what?' she says. 'This laundrymaid just happens to be an artist.' She takes something from her pocket and shoves it at him.

It's a drawing of himself. 'Did you do this?' he asks.

She nods. Her eyes are defiant, but her face is full of fear. He looks back down at the sketch. She's talented, no doubt about it. Has a natural feel for space and perspective. A delicate line. And the likeness is excellent, especially given that she didn't do it from life. Meaning that she has that most crucial of artistic attributes, an accurate, retentive memory.

'Well?' she asks, as he's said nothing for some minutes.

'It's good,' he admits. He doesn't want to encourage her, but credit where it's due. 'All the more so as you have no training.'

'Yes, well, that's the bit you're helping me with. You can have apprentices now,' she goes on, in a rush. 'Now you are the King's Painter. You can have a workshop, hire assistants.' She's obviously practised this bit, done her research.

'I don't want an assistant,' Hans counters. He's never found one good enough, and it's too much of a risk anyway, given what he and Wyatt are planning. But now it occurs to him that Jennet probably is good enough, or will be. And she knows what they are planning; is part of the plan.

'I practise all the time,' she's saying now, her face shining with eagerness. 'I draw every day. I know that you have to, when you're an artist. I use old laundry lists, I even draw on stones sometimes. Sticks in the ashes, anything.'

He sees the fervour in her eyes, the authentic light of the driven.

It seems that he has an apprentice.

# *Chapter Twenty-Five*

The king wants four full-length portraits on the fresco. He's in the front of the picture obviously, his father behind him. The two queens, Elizabeth and Jane, are on the other side of that confounded plinth. It's necessarily enormous, to fit all the words in. It completely dominates the design and looks worse because there are only four figures.

Hans uses the sketches of Jane and Henry that he's already done as guides for the ones here. They're much smaller, but he can scale them up. Jane's original painting was only three-quarter-length, but making it full-length is merely a matter of extra skirt. Henry is more of a problem. His painting was only waist-length, and there's plenty to add below that. His legs, for instance. Though considerably improved from the first time Hans saw it, one nonetheless remains rotting and bandaged.

He produces a set of cartoons, drawing the figures on paper first in his workroom. Slightly bigger than life-size, they are cut out separately so he can move them about the composition at will, before transferring them onto the wall. He has already sketched in the background, and the plinth, of course.

As it's winter now, and gets dark early, he's working by candlelight. The Presence Chamber, on whose wall the fresco is, is huge. Despite the fact that he's stuck candles everywhere, the glow extends only a foot or two before plunging into darkness. The rest of the court is at Greenwich; apart from a skeleton staff, there's no one here but him.

Or so he thought. But quite suddenly, he feels her near him. The lavender scent, the low voice with its faint French accent. *Ah, Hans. When will you meddle of my cause?*

'I'm trying my best,' he pleads. 'But Cromwell holds all the cards, all the time. Wyatt says we should wait and he'll make a mistake. But I honestly can't see what. Or when.'

*A journey*, she says. *A long journey.*

'A journey where?' Is she telling him to give up and go home?

*Your arse of iron, Hans. Remember?*

Of course he remembers. It was a joke he once told her. Quite risqué for him, but Anne, with her French ease, loved rude jokes as much as clever ones.

They had been out on the Greenwich river terrace, listening to the wherrymen shouting insults at each other. Anne found these hilarious, the more obscene the better. 'That's a new one,' she would say, laughing. 'I thought I'd heard them all, but not that.'

Hans's joke was to make her guess which part of the body was most important to a painter. He remembers how she tipped her head on one side, put a long white finger to a full red lip, regarded him with thoughtful black eyes. 'A steady hand?'

He'd looked down, flexed his strong, square fingers. 'That matters, of course. Got to take care of your hands. Rub them with olive oil. Protect them from cuts and burns. Bind them in rags before any long journey . . .' He'd stopped then; he'd almost given her the clue. But not quite.

Anne tilted her small chin at him, shrugged a pretty French shrug.

'You give up?' he'd asked.

She nodded. Her black hair gleamed and slid over her narrow shoulders.

'An arse of iron! Thighs of steel.' He'd flexed his well-shaped legs in their hose, struck the solid muscle with his fists. 'If you can't ride seven miles an hour, eight hours a day, you can forget painting. You'd never make it to your next job.'

She'd hooted with laughter. Now, though, she's talking. *His parents*, she's saying. He's briefly confused before realising she's looking at the wall, where the big cut-out drawings of Henry VII and Elizabeth of York have now been positioned either side of the plinth.

*He adored his maman*, Anne muses. *Hated his father.*

Hans is interested. Drawing the elder Tudors without knowing anything about them has been difficult. He wonders what the king had against the older Henry.

*Well, well, Lady Jane*, Anne says. She's now obviously inspecting her successor, positioned in front of Elizabeth of York. *Who would have thought you'd be Queen of England? Not me, even when I caught you sitting on my husband's knee. Oh yes, Hans. Don't be fooled. Not quite as innocent as she looks, the poor thing.*

'Poor thing?' he echoes, doubtfully. Jane seems to him to have done all right. His queenly sympathies lie in another direction altogether.

*Yes, she'll have found out by now that being married to Henry isn't as much fun as it looks. Not if you don't bear him a son, which, as I understand it, she hasn't yet.*

Then a giggle, an exclamation. *Illustrious images of heroes!*

She is reading the plinth. Of course, she could read Latin as easily as English, as easily as French and Italian, come to that. *Whether father or son is the victor?* She snorts in disbelief.

'I know, it's ridiculous.'

*It's certainly terribly written*, she muses. *Personally, I wouldn't describe my former husband as either heroic or illustrious. Let alone great and virtuous, as I see he is describing himself down here . . .*

'He wants the viewer to put him on the plinth, though, as the greater king.'

*Out of the question, obviously*, she says crisply. *And you'll find a way to make that clear. To those who are looking.*

She says nothing more. He speaks her name, but his voice echoes emptily in the huge room.

He works all night. At some stage he must have fallen asleep, because when he comes round, it's light and he's slumped against the panelling, his neck stiff and his fingers clamped round his piece of charcoal. The candles have all burnt down, thankfully; lucky he didn't set the place on fire.

And what's woken him is evidently some sixth sense, because he can hear the thump of a royal walking stick.

He scrambles to his feet, startled. No one told him Henry was coming. But now in he stumps, and after him scurries Jane, great exhausted shadows under her pale little eyes. In her usual drab brown, she contrasts with the crowd of courtiers swarming in her husband's wake, peacock-bright in their rustling silks and velvets. Among them is Jane Parker in bilious green. And Cromwell, of course, in rich dark furs.

Wincing and irascible, Henry reaches the wall. 'Skinflint bastard,' he says, venomously.

'Your Majesty?' Hans shoots up in alarmed surprise from his deep obeisance.

An icy little blue eye meets his. 'My father, Holborn,' Henry growls. 'That tight-fisted old sod you've got up there. Mean as mouse shit. When he had to pay someone, he did it in pennies. Counted them out from a chest, one by one. It could take all morning. All day.'

Jane, now by his side, gives an uneasy titter. Her husband's cold gaze switches to her. 'It wasn't funny.'

'No, sire,' says Jane, and her eyes brim.

Henry looks back at the other Henry. 'He was a terrible father as well. When I was nine and my mother died, he didn't even tell me himself. Just sent a couple of courtiers to break the news. I remember going to my mother's room and weeping into the sheets of her empty bed.'

He's going to cry again, Hans thinks, seeing how the king's eyes are brimming. 'He took no notice of me whatsoever when I was a child,' Henry sniffs. 'He was only interested in my elder brother, Arthur. He was heir to the throne, and I was never as good as him. Never.' The white feather in his bonnet shudders as he shakes his head in despair, and the tears roll down his big face.

'Oh, Henry, I'm sure you were,' Jane soothes, placing a tiny hand on his huge embroidered arm.

'Well, of course I was!' Henry snaps, making her jump with panic. 'I was actually brilliant, but my father thought Arthur was even better. At sixteen, he knew twenty-four books by heart. All Greek and Roman authors.'

Cromwell steps forward from the crowd. 'Probably just his tutor boasting, Your Majesty. You know what these people are like.'

Henry glares at him. 'Are you saying my brother wasn't brilliant?'

'Of course not, sire . . .'

'Arthur was to be king,' Henry goes on, 'but all I had to look forward to, as second son, was being Archbishop of Canterbury. Which in view of subsequent events is quite amusing.' His laugh is sudden, like a burst of gunfire. After a second, the courtiers start laughing too.

But Henry is now looking angry again. 'Then Arthur died, right after he married Katherine. My father moved like greased lightning and made me marry her instead. Being the tight sod he was, he didn't want to see her dowry leave England. She swore she was a virgin and had never slept with my brother. And being an impressionable seventeen-year-old, I believed her. Only later did it strike me that Arthur died *five months* after the wedding. And what else is there to do in Ludlow? Hmm?' He looks round, his expression demanding.

Master Secretary, of course, is smiling. Jane Seymour's expression is inscrutable.

'So when I found that passage in Leviticus,' Henry goes on, 'the one that said I was in an incestuous marriage, and our lack of sons was God's judgement, it suddenly all made sense.'

There's an uncomfortable silence after this précis of the cataclysms of the last ten years. Some of the courtiers, Hans sees, are staring at the floor. These, presumably, are the old guard. The ones who deplore the break with Rome. The Courtenays, the Poles. The troublemakers. Cromwell's enemies.

Then Henry turns to his wife. 'But I will have sons now. Very many sons.' It sounds rather like a command. Jane smiles nervously. Poor thing indeed, Hans thinks.

'My father had three sons, but my brothers died. He was so terrified of losing me too that he practically locked me up when I was Prince of Wales.' Henry is sounding sorry for himself again. 'He never trained me in anything. Never said a word to me about Bosworth, even. Thanks to his lack of advice, I've had little military success. I also blame my poor captains, bad weather and untrustworthy foreign partners.'

With Henry, Hans notes, everything is always someone else's fault. His lack of sons, his lack of victories. His father had both, so one thing's for sure. Henry Senior is the winner of the competition. He should go on the plinth. Not his son.

*You'll find a way to make that clear.*

# *Chapter Twenty-Six*

Jennet's training has begun in earnest. By day she's in the laundry, but she comes to him every night. Her energy is inexhaustible, her commitment and concentration extraordinary. Within a day she can cut a quill, within a week, manufacture brushes.

She learns like lightning.

Hans, meanwhile, is feeling lightning of another kind. It flashes through him whenever he takes her hand to guide her use of the tools. But as he looks into her face as he explains things, all he sees is the intent wish to learn.

And so, with resigned patience, he shows her how to make charcoal. How willow twigs are gathered and cut to length, sharpened to a point and bound with wires before being put overnight in the hearth. And then are black sticks in the morning, ready to draw with.

He explains about egg yolks. 'An artist must know his hens.'

'Or *her* hens,' Jennet corrects sharply. She looks at him uncertainly. 'But seriously, *hens*? Are you making fun of me?'

'Far from it. Hens are crucial. When I was a boy in Augsburg, I was forever chasing our hens through the town. They were too expensive to lose.' A memory comes back: just-risen sun silvering sloping rooftops, narrow lanes ringing with the clatter of his clogs as he dashes, cursing, after the escaped bird. The housewives opening their window shutters all tutting in unison as they recognise the younger of the two wild Holbein boys from the painter's workshop.

'No painting without chickens,' he goes on. 'You use the yolks to mix colour. That of town hens is paler, so best for the flesh of young people. And country hens have redder yolks, so good for old people.'

He tells her about colours, the many reds. Porphyry, hematite, lac, dragonsblood, senaper. 'You use different reds to achieve different effects.' She nods, seriously.

He shows her how lampblack is made, holding a flame under a vessel and scraping off the resulting powder.

'Lampblack is one of the very best blacks,' he tells her, although Alice More with her ruined casseroles took a different, angrier view. She had been equally ferocious in her care of her husband, begging Thomas to submit to the king's will and swear that he was head of the Church. But Thomas hadn't, and wouldn't. Hatred twists in Hans's heart. Of the many axe blows it might take to get Cromwell's head off, one would be for More.

He shows Jennet how to prepare paper, the different background tints. He's taken to using a pink one, saves time on the flesh colours. Mastering silverpoint is trickier, but she's getting it, all the same.

She starts to help him prepare the boards for his portraits. The oak must be spread thinly with a mixture of ground bone and saliva. They need lots of bone, and he sends her hunting under the long dining tables in the great hall. 'Look for the wings of fowl,' he tells her. 'Bone from the second joint is best. Or a capon, the older the better.'

She looks at him, exasperated. 'How am I supposed to tell? When it's just a bone?'

You can't. It's an old apprentice joke, up there with asking for a long stand. But there are no flies on her; she spotted this immediately.

Nor is that all she spots.

He takes her, late at night, to the Presence Chamber, shows her the fresco. Explains the problem with the king, the plinth and the hole.

In order to fit in all Henry's self-praise, the plinth is almost as high as the top of the room. And so someone can stand on it, as there's otherwise no space, there's an aperture in the ceiling. A square hole, just above the plinth. Whoever's on the plinth will have to fit through this hole.

'Right,' says Jennet, nodding. 'Terrible design, though.'

'It's not mine,' Hans says quickly. 'It's the king's. And it's completely illogical, because the hole isn't big enough for him. Just for his father.'

Tall and thin, in his old-fashioned long coat, Henry VII will fit through it easily. But big fat Henry VIII, in his wide clothes, will have considerably more difficulty.

Jennet turns to him. 'So where's the problem?'

He frowns at her. 'Isn't it obvious? The king's too big for the hole.'

Her face is shadowy and dim in the candlelight. But her expression is amused, with a hint of triumph.

He looks back at the fresco. She's worked something out. But what?

'The king's too big for the hole,' she repeats, meaningfully. 'He might not fit in it. He. Won't. Fit. In. It.'

How could he not have realised? The answer was there all along. Henry is too broad to win the competition. But to really make the point, he can make him even broader.

He picks up his charcoal.

'Wider,' says Jennet, from over his shoulder. 'As wide as he will go. And then wider still.'

Hans reaches for his piece of bread, rubs out the lines, starts again. Makes Henry twice as wide as any normal man, three times as wide as his father. Far too wide to even stand on the plinth, let alone fit through the hole.

'Bigger,' urges Jennet, and Hans reaches for the bread again. She's right. Those great fur collars, those padded arms lend themselves to almost infinite expansion outwards. Before long, Henry is almost wider than he is tall. It's an overblown, impossible shape.

And yet it works. It's unbelievable, but also the truth. It represents how Henry wants to appear – vast and powerful – whilst also suggesting this is an illusion. That beneath the exaggerated carapace of his outfit, he is vulnerable, in every sense smaller, lesser. His dynasty is new and weak and he has no son to secure it. To make this point further, Hans adds, as a final touch, a comically enormous codpiece, broad, fat, jutting commandingly upwards and festooned with a decorative ribbon.

Nonetheless, this Henry has lost the competition. His father, with all his faults, was a better king than he will ever be.

But this isn't what Henry sees when he views the final design. He meets his own eyes, the only ones looking directly out of the picture. He sees himself as potency incarnate. He roars with approval and claps Hans on the back so hard it sends him reeling across the Presence Chamber. He orders a hundred portraits on the spot, to be sent to every corner of the land. God only knows who is to paint them all.

'Well done, dear boy,' murmurs Cromwell as he follows the delighted monarch out. 'You've created an icon.'

And Henry, it seems, has created something as well. The rumour at court is that Jane Seymour is finally pregnant. It will, of course, be a boy.

## *Chapter Twenty-Seven*

October 1537

The king is beside himself. The court is beside itself. After a lengthy and difficult labour – two days and three nights – Queen Jane has given birth. And yes, it's a son. The bells ring, the Tower guns boom, there are bonfires in the streets. At Hampton Court, where Edward was born, Hans crowds with the other courtiers beneath the gold-starred blue ceiling of the Chapel Royal and watches the baby being christened by the Archbishop of Canterbury.

Hans never sees Cranmer's long, lugubrious face without thinking that he's the one to whom Anne made her last confession during those final, desperate days. That he was much use or comfort seems unlikely.

When the prayers for Edward start, Hans closes his eyes. But he's not thinking of the baby, nor is his heart full of God's grace. It's full of guilt and frustration and the same black vengeance as it has been for a year and a half.

Nothing has changed since that May morning in the Tower. He's no nearer to destroying Cromwell than he was then. Will the chance ever come?

And even if it does, by the looks of it he will be taking it alone.

Wyatt remains in Madrid, doing God knows what. There has been little news for months. If France and Spain have indeed combined, they remain in no hurry to harry England in the ways Wyatt said they would. Still no sign of any blockades of the trade routes, and certainly no invasion.

As for weakening Cromwell, he seems stronger than ever. Even the birth of the Prince of Wales doesn't seem to bother him in the least. Master Secretary seems cock-a-hoop, despite the fact that Jane's position is assured and her brother has been made an earl. Perhaps because of the rumour that Cromwell himself is soon going to be an earl too.

The light falls through the high chapel windows onto the Tudor-red hair of four-year-old Elizabeth. Carefully carrying her new brother's golden robe up the aisle, she looks solemnly ahead with black Boleyn eyes. Anne would be so proud. *Is* proud, Hans amends. She is watching from somewhere, he can feel it.

Afterwards, he goes back to his workroom, pushing through the crowds of drunken courtiers. There's a fountain flowing with free wine, and everyone's taking full advantage. There are singers everywhere, wandering about with their lutes. The music and laughter annoys him. He feels about as much part of the celebrations as a creature from one of the distant stars he would look at with Kratzer from Thomas More's roof, just after he first arrived from Basel.

He'd learnt a bit about constellations from the sailors on the boat over. Andromeda was a favourite, chained to a rock and naked apart from her jewellery. The mariners had particularly appreciated that detail.

Hans sighs. He'd been a stranger in a strange land and struggling for work, but in retrospect it had been a golden time. The weight that these days drags down his heart from dawn till dusk had been blessedly absent.

It's late in the afternoon, and the torches have been lit in the palace corridors. The sky through the lattice windows is that flat dark blue just before it becomes night-black. The carousing is now a distant echo, and for a second he half thinks of turning back, of forcing himself to join in. Never has he felt quite so lonely and hopeless.

But there's a bottle of jenever in his room; he'll just drink himself to oblivion alone. Or maybe he'll work. There are a couple of court ladies on his easel at the moment, both slightly overdue.

He reaches his door and shoves it open. He doesn't remember leaving it this orderly, or with candles lit. A fire glows in the hearth and his bedlinen is no longer twisted on the floor. It's back on the bed.

And someone is in it. Smiling, fair hair spread against his pillows. 'I thought I'd surprise you.'

He's surprised, for sure. Delighted too, but also suspicious. 'I've been warned not to lead you astray,' he says. He wants to keep the mood light until he understands what's going on.

'But what if I led you astray?'

'What about Mistress Harris?'

Jennet laughs. 'What about her? Worried she'll drown you in one of her washing vats? Beat you to death with one of her paddles? It's none of her business; she doesn't own me. It's up to me what I do. And I want to do this.'

She tosses back the covers, swings her legs out, stands up and walks towards him. He has tried many times not to think what her body's like beneath her clothes, but the reality far exceeds his imaginings. Like a Greek statue, small-breasted, slim, long-legged. Her waist curves in and her stomach is gently rounded. The sudden urge to sketch her sweeps through him, but the urge to do something else is far stronger.

She stands close to him and traces the outline of his lips. Then, slowly, she kisses him. When they've finished, she smiles. 'I've wanted to do that ever since I saw you.'

'Really?'

She twists her mouth. 'I didn't want you to know. After what I told you about Cromwell, I didn't want you to think I'd sleep with just anyone. So I waited.'

'For what?'

She regards him boldly. 'For you to take me on. Realise I'm good.' She tips her chin up. 'Respect me.'

As her lips meet his again, he's almost knocked sideways by the strength of his need. It's been so long.

'That was nice,' she grins, when the world slows down again. She looks at him. 'What's the matter?'

Hans has no idea what to say. He clamps his hands to his head as the guilt and blame crowd in. What was he thinking? Pursuing pleasure when his every thought should be bent on revenge.

Jennet sits up, sighs exasperatedly. 'It's her, isn't it? My mistress. Your Anne.'

He doesn't answer. But it is, of course. He waits for her to be angry, but instead feels her fingers stroking the back of his hand.

'I'm not the same,' she says. 'I know that.'

'It's not that at all.' He sighs heavily. 'You're lovely. It's just . . .'

'You feel guilty?' There's sympathy in the clear green eyes. 'Look,' she says gently. 'Our beloved lady is gone and nothing is going to bring her back. Nothing can replace her for either of us. And we are going to kill those responsible, but we ourselves are still alive.'

He nods. She's right, of course. But even so, the last hour is the first in eighteen months that he has not been thinking, either consciously or at some other level, of Anne. It feels like a betrayal, like being unfaithful.

'But you're not being,' Jennet says softly. 'You adored her, but she was never on your level. She was always out of reach.' She looks at his face in concern. 'Is it hurtful, me saying that?'

He shakes his head, no, it's true. His love for Anne had always been hopeless. Remote, impossible, unreal. And yet he had never wanted it any other way. Until now.

She's stroking his back; her hands slip round to his chest. And then lower. 'So why not enjoy it?' she urges softly. 'It's quite safe, you know.'

'Safe?' Safe is hardly what he's feeling now. Or what she's doing.

She laughs, but doesn't stop.

Afterwards, she props herself up on one elbow, gazes at him with her clear eyes.

'Safe as in I don't want to marry you. Or anyone else, come to that.'

'I thought all women did.'

'Then all women are pretty stupid.' Jennet rolls onto her back. 'They think marriage means security, but from what I can see, it's the opposite. Your husband has all the power. If you're poor, he might beat you. Or leave you. Or drink away his money, leaving you a beggar. And if you're rich, well. As my mistress has just shown, your fate can be much, much worse. Marriage,' she concludes lightly, 'is dangerous.'

He looks at her in wonder. And yes, respect. Those clear eyes see the world with a brutal honesty. There's a sharp brain behind that lovely face. She moves her head, and her hair glints gold in the glow of the candles. She kisses his nose. 'So stop worrying. My mistress of all people would want us to snatch some happiness while we can.'

## *Chapter Twenty-Eight*

Jane is dead. Everyone is stunned. Given the length of her labour, she had seemed to make a good recovery. Then she became ill again. Complications set in. As October drew to a close, a mere nine days after producing the Prince of Wales, the third of Henry's queens is no more. Although never crowned, and married to the king less than eighteen months.

The colour is still wet on Hans's painting of her on the fresco. He thinks of the young woman nervously clutching her doll. He notices that Jane's necklace in his original picture has one pearl for her single completed year.

And now, amid the uproar, Cromwell has summoned him to dine. As usual, it's not clear why. So also as usual, Hans is on his guard.

Besides, there have been rumours about Master Secretary and Queen Jane's death. According to Jennet, the laundry was alive with them. 'When she got worse, no one could find the royal doctor. He'd been sent into Kent, you can imagine by whom. By the time he was summoned back, the queen was dead.'

Tonight's food seems designed to flatter and seduce, even more sumptuous than Hans's last dinner at Austin Friars. Among the many dishes are quails stuffed with rose petals, but summer is long past, and with it the roses. Where on earth can they have come from? Perhaps Cromwell's a magician; that would explain a lot.

'I saw her just before the end.' Cromwell is talking about Jane. 'She was delirious. I blame her ladies for letting her eat all the wrong things. Letting her get cold.' He cuts into a quail. 'It's a good thing, Hans, try to see it as that.'

'The death of the queen? But she was only twenty-eight. And leaves behind a motherless baby.' Another one. There are three now. Mary, Elizabeth and Edward.

The glitter of jewels as a fat hand waves. 'Oh, the king would have tired of her. Bound to, he always does. Now he's been spared the problem of getting rid of her.' Cromwell dabs his chins with a napkin. 'Which, given that she was mother of the heir and saviour of the dynasty, might have been tricky.' He proffers the ewer. 'More wine? Yes?'

Master Secretary seems his usual blithe self, but Hans has the feeling he's less composed than he looks. He senses things moving and shifting, but in what direction he's not sure.

'So, on to wife number four,' Cromwell breezes.

Hans almost chokes on his Rhenish. 'The king is marrying again already?' With poor Jane not cold in her grave? Actually, not in her grave at all; they haven't even had the funeral yet.

'We need to find the next lucky lady. A smooth transition, that's what we want.'

*We?* Hans thinks. Who, exactly, is we?

'But who will he marry?'

'Ah, now that's the question.' Cromwell reaches for his wine goblet. 'And you,' he adds, looking brightly at Hans over the rim of it, 'are going to help me find the answer.'

*'Me?'*

'You, dear boy.' Cromwell, chewing, shoots him a merry look. 'This crazy experiment with English queens is over. We're back to the Valois or the Hapsburgs. A good old-fashioned European dynastic union. We've identified someone suitable and I want you to go there. Take her likeness.'

Hans sees who the *we* is now. Cromwell, moving to take the initiative. Relying on his tried and tested method: bewildering speed. 'Go where?'

'Oh, didn't I say? France.'

The name swings through him like a bell. France, where it all started. France, where he first met Anne. France, where he will finish off Cromwell for good.

It doesn't feel like it. If this is the long-awaited opportunity, he'll be taking it alone. He hasn't heard from Wyatt in weeks.

When Jennet comes later, he tells her what Cromwell said. 'He's blaming the ladies-in-waiting. Says they gave her the wrong food and didn't keep her warm enough.'

'Well, he would say that, wouldn't he?'

'He says the king would have tired of her and has been spared the problem of getting rid of her.'

Jennet's eyes narrow. 'And Master Secretary has been spared the problem of the Seymours, the Norfolks and the rest of them. Funny how these things work out.'

She's swinging her pale hair, gathering it back in both hands to tie it up. In preparation for work, otherwise it dangles in the paint. Oh, the lovely curve of her cheek, the graceful back of her neck. The now familiar fire goes through him. How he will miss her. 'He's sending me to France, to paint the new wife,' he tells Jennet, as their lips part briefly.

She looks startled, but there's no time for her to reply, because the door suddenly bursts open and slams against the wall. They spring apart, Hans's fingers flying from her breast to the dagger at his waist. He now realises that he's always expected this moment. The proof that Cromwell has suspected him all along, has been waiting to trap him.

The tall, dark newcomer lounges in the doorway, arms crossed over his travelling cloak. 'Sorry,' smirks Wyatt. 'Didn't realise I was interrupting something.'

He pushes himself from the door jamb, comes in. He's not embarrassed in the least; on the contrary, he seems amused. 'Well,' he says, flopping in a chair and pushing the hair from his face. 'I didn't realise you two were a couple.'

'I'm his apprentice,' Jennet challenges.

A bark of laughter. 'Is that what they call it now? And how are you these days, Jennet? Looking well, I see.'

'You know each other?' Hans had almost been pleased to see Wyatt. Now the old animosity is back, plus extra.

'You could say our paths have crossed,' the poet drawls.

'Years ago,' Jennet adds, firmly.

Hans fights for self-control. The idea of her with Wyatt makes his blood boil. He badly wants to know, and even more badly, he doesn't.

'But now you work for Mistress Harris,' Wyatt is saying. 'Strong arms and a still tongue, eh? What you need to work in the laundry. That's what she told me.'

'Stop flirting with her,' snaps Hans. Jennet's arms remain folded defensively, but she definitely looks amused.

Or did. Now she's glaring at *him*. 'Don't tell Tom what he can't do,' she says icily. 'You don't own me. No one does.'

*Tom.* Hans looks at the floor, resenting Wyatt more than ever. Damn the man. Everything was fine until he turned up. 'What are you doing here?' he growls. 'I thought you were in Madrid.'

'I've been recalled.'

Good, Hans thinks with bitter triumph. Diplomats only usually come back if they're incompetent. So Wyatt's been taken down a peg or two. Even if, typically, he doesn't look it.

'It's known as a secondment,' Wyatt goes on. 'My celebrated diplomatic skills are required elsewhere. For a highly sensitive mission.'

'Oh really?'

'Really,' is the drawling reply. Wyatt stretches out his long legs. 'Long story short, I'm coming with you to France.'

*What?* 'You can't be,' Hans says, with an assurance he doesn't quite feel. 'Cromwell said nothing about it.'

'Well, I've just come from him now and there's no question. You'll have the joy of my company as you go to paint Madame de Longueville.'

'Who?'

Wyatt puts his hands behind his head. 'Madame de Longueville. Daughter of the Duc de Guise. Young widow, supposed to be very beautiful. Her mother had thirteen children, so good breeding stock as well. Oh, and the King of Scots is after her. You know how our high and sovereign lord likes a bit of competition. Even from his own nephew.'

It's hateful having to find all this out from Wyatt, and in front of Jennet too. Makes him look so clueless, the second fiddle, the unimportant one.

'I say, Holbein, you don't have anything to drink, do you? Some of that jenever?'

Before Hans can say he hasn't, Jennet has hurried to get it. Wyatt knocks it back in one. Lets out a long, satisfied sigh. Holds out his cup for a refill.

The resentful Hans has had enough. 'But why are *you* coming?' he demands. 'I'm going to paint a portrait. I can do that by myself, I don't need a nursemaid. Least of all you.'

'Hans!' admonishes Jennet.

'It's all right, sweetheart, it's just his artistic temperament. Let me explain, Holbein,' Wyatt says. 'How shall I put this diplomatically? Being a diplomat, you'd think I'd know. In a nutshell, it's this King of Scots thing. James is quite a lot younger than his dear uncle Henry. Possibly quite a lot thinner as well, and it's not completely out of the question that he's ever so slightly better-looking.'

As Jennet giggles, Hans folds his arms. 'So?'

'So,' says Wyatt, patiently, 'our dread and sovereign lord has to be the first choice of any woman he deigns to favour with his interest. If such a woman were to turn him down, he would be very angry. So that's where I come in. Cromwell wants me to go with you to smooth the diplomatic path. Your job is to paint her, but mine is to persuade Madame de Longueville that Europe holds no finer marital prospect than Henry the Eighth of England. You see?'

'I suppose so,' Hans grumps.

'Only,' Wyatt adds ruefully, 'I have the sneaking suspicion that persuading her will not be easy. That it might even be impossible, and the king might be angry as a result.'

He pauses, for longer than might be expected. His dark eyes are bright with mischief, Hans sees.

'And that would be *such* a pity,' he goes on, mock-sorrowfully. 'Because if the king is angry, the person he's going to be angry with is the person in charge of finding him a new wife. Can you think who that person might be?'

Jennet's the first to get it. She squeals, claps her hands. 'Cromwell!'

*A journey. A long journey. Your arse of iron.*

'You're not going to persuade Madame de Longueville, are you?' Jennet asks breathlessly. 'You're going to completely fail.'

'Alas,' sighs Wyatt, 'I fear so.'

Jennet's now rocking back and forth in delight. Wyatt looks at her chidingly. 'I don't see why it's so amusing, my dear. It's very distressing to think how greatly Cromwell has overestimated my diplomatic powers.'

Hans steps forward, stretches out his hand. Wyatt clasps it and their eyes meet. They smile at each other, first hesitantly, then broadly.

Somewhere, dimly, Hans can hear a woman laughing. It might be Jennet, it might be Anne.

This is it. Finally the chance has come.

## *Chapter Twenty-Nine*

France

February 1538

It rained all the way down the river; Hans's last sight of England was a dim grey outline through a veil of hissing water. They were practically blown across the Narrow Sea by a spiteful lashing gale, but this meant a swift passage, kept the ship moving. Wyatt, who, unfortunately for an ambassador, suffered badly from seasickness, lay green-faced and groaning in his hammock most of the time.

Blowing on his hands, flexing his fingers to keep them if not exactly warm, then at least alive, Hans stood on deck in his great travelling cloak, companion on many a journey, soaked with linseed oil to make it waterproof. Cold as he was, he felt warm inside. Call it hope. Call it purpose. Best of all, call it revenge.

They're safely across to France now, but Madame de Longueville is still several days' ride away, at the de Guise family chateau in the north-eastern town of Joinville. Because of the time pressure they're under, the arse of iron is being seriously put through its paces with a target of fifty miles a day on hired horses. These range from the practically dead to the wild and unbroken. The wayside inns in which they sleep are of similar varying quality.

Hans minds this less than he expected, because Wyatt has proved a surprisingly engaging companion. He's cheerful, generous, sympathetic and, especially surprising given his slight build and foppish manner, tough and resilient. He's endearingly self-deprecating and endlessly curious. He gets on with everyone and has an infinite fund of amusing stories.

Tonight, as they face each other over the dim candle, sticky table, thin stew and vinegar-like wine – or maybe wine-like vinegar – of a particularly wretched establishment, Hans's eye catches the signet ring on his companion's little finger. Its symbol is the strange hinged object he saw on Wyatt's seal. 'What's that?' he asks.

Wyatt twists off the ring, passes it to him. It's warm and smooth in Hans's palm, but also terribly scratched and bashed about.

'You'll have to guess,' its owner says. 'Is it a) a metal clamp you put on a horse's mouth to make it behave? Or b) a Plantagenet instrument of torture?'

Neither sounds likely. 'B?'

'Wrong, I'm afraid.' Wyatt pours them both more of the terrible wine. 'Actually, it's both.'

'Both?'

'My father chose the right side at Bosworth, if you know what that is?'

Hans thinks of the Whitehall fresco. 'The battle where Henry the Seventh won the English crown.'

'Right,' Wyatt nods, wincing at the wine. 'My father had supported him from the start. Even while Richard the Third was still on the throne. Richard the Third?' He slides Hans a questioning look.

'The king before?' Hans hazards.

'Right again, Holbein. We'll make an Englishman of you yet. Well, Father had a hard time. Richard had him tortured with a horse barnacle. This thing here.' He takes the ring back, slips it on. 'His teeth are all broken as a result and the bottom of his face is loose and floppy.'

'The poor man.'

'Well, yes and no. Obviously it was awful at the time, but Father is delighted now with the way he looks. Really, Holbein, you should paint him. When this is all over, I'll arrange it.'

Hans nods. 'I'd like that.'

'Sir Henry Wyatt, the personification of loyalty to the Tudors,' Wyatt says, expansively. The wine, dreadful as it is, is starting to do its work. 'And Father's loyalty has been richly rewarded, which is why that blasted barnacle is now all over Allington, from the pattern in the curtains to the seal in the rings, as you see here.'

'What a story. You must be very proud of him.'

A rueful look crosses Wyatt's face. 'I am. But I can't say the same about him of me, sadly. I'm his eldest son and he wanted me to achieve even more than him in the service of the Tudors.' He sighs and fiddles with his wine cup. 'Only it hasn't really worked out that way.'

'But you're the ambassador to Madrid,' Hans points out, surprised.

Wyatt pulls his long face into a comic expression. 'Yes, but Father thinks diplomacy is a rackety new profession, not very respectable. He's a money man himself, managed the Tudors' finances and wanted me to follow him as a Treasury high-up. Unfortunately, I'm not interested in money, apart from spending it, ha ha.'

More awful wine slops into the cups. 'No, what I really wanted to do was write poetry. But Father thought that was even more out of the question than diplomacy. I was put in his department as a junior accountant and told to get on with it. I hated it.'

Hans feels the tug of a smile. Wyatt, dealing with accounts.

'I also hated having to marry a wealthy local landowner's

daughter. Elizabeth Cobham. I didn't like her, but I went along with it. George Boleyn was in the same boat. His father was making him marry another neighbour's daughter, Jane Parker.'

'I know her.' Hans winces.

'Famously poisonous, yes. We tried to buck each other up, George and I, even though his problem wasn't quite the same as mine. I realised this the day I saw him coming out of the stables with his shirt off, followed by one of the grooms.' Wyatt shakes his head.

'So now I was a reluctant husband and a completely useless accountant. But that still wasn't enough for Father. He wanted me to be the king's best friend as well. This mainly involved thundering up and down the tiltyard dressed from head to foot in steel. Otherwise it was hunting, chasing some poor animal through a forest whilst wielding a crossbow. I found it all insufferably boring. The king's other friends were especially boring. Idiotic oafs with huge teeth and braying laughs, competing to see who could drink the most, or bed the most women. And not a brain cell between them.'

Hans chuckles. He knows some of these people; he couldn't agree more.

'But I had to do it to please my father. Was your father like that, Hans?'

This is a way of Wyatt's, suddenly turning the tables, asking point-blank questions. A diplomat's trick, Hans assumes, and an effective one. 'Not really,' he answers.

'Well, what *was* he like?'

Hans searches for the word. 'Chaotic.'

'Chaotic how?'

'My mother died, so he brought us up alone, me and my brother, Ambrosius. Trained us both in his workshop.'

Wyatt pounces on this. 'Ambrosius, wow, quite the name. Do you get on with your brother?'

Hans sighs. 'He's dead. Died of plague in Basel. My family are all dead now.'

Wyatt nods sympathetically. 'That's why you left, and came to England to paint the king?'

'It wasn't quite like that. I went to France first and tried to paint their king.'

Oh, why had he said that? His companion's eyebrows have shot up, his eyes widened. They'll be here all night now.

Wyatt waves his hunk of teeth-breaking bread. 'So tell me about it. What happened?'

'Nothing happened,' Hans says shortly. 'The French king didn't need a painter, as it turned out. It was all a complete disaster.'

But Wyatt looks more interested than ever. 'I love disasters. Always more interesting than triumphs. Come on, Holbein. Stop being such an international man of mystery. I've told you all about myself, haven't I?'

Hans puts down his spoon and rubs his eyes. 'It's a long story.'

'So much the better. This is a long journey.'

'And a long time ago. Must be sixteen years at least. I was living in Basel—'

'You went all the way from Basel to Amboise for a job that didn't exist?' Wyatt interrupts, incredulous.

'Well, I didn't know that it didn't exist. Erasmus told me—'

'Erasmus? What did he have to do with it?'

'Everything,' Hans growls. 'Look, I'd rather not talk about it if you don't mind.'

But Wyatt has the bit between his teeth now. His eyes gleam with mischief. 'But I do mind. Very much. Come on, Holbein. Don't keep me in suspense.'

Hans looks around. It's not just that he really, really doesn't want to tell Wyatt what happened. He's also identified their lodging as the type they'll have to leave before dawn. A necessary precaution sometimes if mine host is the sort to alert his footpad friends to the presence of two prosperous-looking foreigners. Really they should go to bed.

Besides, the candle has burnt down almost to nothing. They've drunk the disgusting plonk to the last drop. They're the only people left in the inn now, and from the corner, beside a sulky fire and a nasty-looking dog, the villainous landlord is sending them hostile looks.

But Wyatt now cheerfully calls over and mine host shambles resentfully across. The nasty dog stands in the doorway that leads to the upper rooms, baring its teeth.

'Another jug of your absolutely excellent wine, please,' Wyatt says, so smoothly that even this old rogue is dazzled and goes off with what looks suspiciously like a spring in his step. Hans can only shake his head in ironic wonder.

When it arrives, the wine is accompanied by, miracle of miracles, a new rushlight. And a key the size of an iron bar. 'Lock up when you're done,' growls the landlord. 'I'm off to bed. Come along, *chérie*.' This is the dog, somewhat improbably.

'So come along, *chérie*,' Wyatt prompts Hans, after man and beast have disappeared into the dark. 'Tell me about France.'

## *Chapter Thirty*

### Fifteen years earlier

Hans had been highly flattered when Erasmus told him that the French king needed a new court artist. 'And why shouldn't it be you, Olpeius?' The great scholar liked to give his intimates Latinised versions of their names. 'The death of Leonardus is a tragedy, but for you it is also an opportunity.'

Leonardus was Leonardo da Vinci, who had been painter to François for some years. While it was never convenient to lose a genius, Erasmus went on, for Hans the timing could not be better. The chances of success were high.

'A rolling stone gathers no moss,' he had added.

It was one of his most famous aphorisms, along with calling a spade a spade. But the rolling stone that was the Dutch intellectual, suffering with gallstones and age and a hypochondriac into the bargain, was less keen than he had been to travel long distances on his small mule. Instead, he was trying to persuade Hans to undertake and underwrite the journey to Amboise, seat of the French court.

Hans was tempted. Basel, where he'd moved from Augsburg, was hard work and not very lucrative. And the portrait he had just completed of Erasmus was one of his best. The scholar wished to make François a gift of it and gradually persuaded Hans that because the king knew him well, he would see what a brilliant likeness it was. He would therefore give its painter the court artist job on the spot.

The journey was tough, but finally Hans reached the Loire and was amazed by its beauty. A mass of liquid silver flowing through soft green meadows to a horizon of misty blue. Eventually he saw Amboise in the distance, rising like a knightly dream. The white castle walls, the rounded barbican at one end, the graceful spires, arches and terraces at the other, the pointed towers, the gilded pinnacles, all shining in the sun.

It seemed the epitome of promise, the manifestation of all his hopes. Here he would make his fortune, become famous, work for a king.

Under the chateau's great entrance arch, two halberdiers appeared, crossed their weapons before him, asked him what his business was.

He explained that he was here to see King François, to deliver a painting. His French had improved throughout the journey, but the blank faces of the soldiers suggested that none of this was going in.

He was going to have to show them. Placing his bundle down carefully on the stone cobbles, he peeled off the sacking protecting the portrait. Beneath their steel helmets, the guards raised their eyebrows. 'He is who, this old man?'

'Erasmus of Rotterdam.' Hans looked at his work with pride. The resemblance was stunning, right down to the ink-stained fingers.

'Why's he got such filthy nails?' the soldiers wanted to know.

But they were sufficiently bored or sufficiently satisfied to nod him on through the arch. Crossing the sunny garden terrace with its view over town and river, Hans imagined da Vinci walking here. And now him, in Leonardo's footsteps.

He went down a passage brilliant with stained-glass windows and into a vast vaulted hall. Here he waited for the king and his hordes of fawning courtiers. To pass the time, he studied the detail on a carved overmantel: two crowned angels holding a pair of shields.

It was, he thought, strangely quiet. You might have expected more people around. They were all outside perhaps, watching a joust or a tennis match, or whatever it was courtiers did. According to Erasmus, they spent their time in elegant amusement. Hans had never spent the day in mere amusement, elegant or otherwise. He wouldn't know how. From his earliest boyhood, his entire life had been work.

The thought made him realise how tired he was; his journey had now caught up with him. He plonked himself down in a sunny window seat, slumped against the latticed pane and was all but asleep when something rustled next to him. His eyes snapped open and horror charged through him as he found himself staring into a handsome, long-nosed face.

He shot to his feet. His companion was tall and dressed simply but magnificently in black and white. His slim legs were endless in their black hose. He had narrow dark eyes, an elegant beard and silky black hair curling over a white lace collar. François the king, Hans knew, looked like this.

He swept a bow as deep as his aching limbs allowed.

'They tell me,' he was informed in nasal French, 'that you have brought a painting. And that you are Swiss.'

'Yes and no, Your Majesty. Yes, I have a painting, but no, I'm not Swiss.'

'Ah, a misunderstanding!'

'Yes, I'm German.'

The man covered his mouth with long white fingers and laughed a strange, shrill laugh. 'Not that. About the majesty. I'm not the king. The king is not at Amboise. *Le roi n'est pas ici.*'

*N'est pas ici* . . . not here. Hans's stomach dropped and his head swam. How was this possible? After all Erasmus's assurances?

'So,' the vision in black and white continued, 'you can show your painting to me, if you would like. Come, my little friend from the land of the bratwurst. Don't be shy.'

'Do you know Erasmus?' Hans asked stonily. No point showing him if he didn't.

His companion's screech of laughter startled him. 'I should say so. Oh yes, we all know Erasmus here. But he is the greatest thinker of the age, *non*? No one expects such people to be normal.'

Hans peeled the sacking off the portrait again.

'Aha!' His companion bent down, peered closely. 'Erasmus to the life! An excellent likeness. And with a little something else besides. As if you can see into the mind, yes?'

A faint ray of light now seeped into Hans's gloom. It strengthened and brightened when his companion went on, 'The man who painted this, he is exceptional.'

Hans raised his chin. 'That would be me.'

'You! But you look like a farmer. This hair . . . *oh la la*!' Long fingers flicked his blonde mop. 'But you are *sans doute* a very good painter. When I give this to Sa Majesté, he will be delighted.'

The relief that gripped Hans was so intense, it completely wiped the insult from his mind. Sa Majesté? So the king was here after all?

'*Pas ici exactement.* In his chateau of Blois, up the river. The queen, *la pauvre*, is ill and he is with her, as is the entire court.'

'I would like to see Sa Majesté,' Hans gabbled. 'I would like to be his court painter.'

'Ah! Unfortunately that is not possible.'

'But you said I was a very good painter.'

'Which you are. Excellent, in fact. But it is still not possible for you to be Sa Majesté's painter.'

'Why not?' Hans pressed. 'Leonardo is dead.'

'Ah *oui*.' The feather on the bonnet shook sorrowfully. 'And buried here at Amboise. In the little chapel, just outside.' White fingers waved in the direction of the doorway.

'So,' Hans pursued doggedly, 'there is a vacancy.'

'*Malheureusement, non*. Leonardo has been replaced. In as much as anyone can replace such immortal genius.'

'Replaced!' It came out as a yelp. 'By whom?'

A rustle of silks, a bonnet plucked from a head, a deep, courtly bow. 'By me. Jean Clouet *à votre service*.'

Wyatt is laughing, and Hans looks at him, offended. 'It's not that funny.'

'No. Sorry.' Wyatt dabs at his eyes with a handkerchief. 'It isn't. Not at all. It's just that . . .' His shoulders start shaking again.

'That what?' Hans demands.

'Clouet is hilarious. *My little friend from the land of the bratwurst . . .*' Wyatt dissolves into giggles again. 'You're a very good raconteur, Holbein, you know that?'

Coming from a storyteller with Wyatt's wit and flair, this is undoubtedly flattering. And Hans is flattered, for all he suspects this is flannel.

Wyatt pours some more wine. 'So come on,' he urges. 'What happened then?'

# *Chapter Thirty-One*

Seeing Hans's face, stunned with disappointment, Clouet was both sympathetic and apologetic. 'Come, *mon ami*. You have travelled far. You have suffered a shock. I will take you to my house and we will dine. And drink wine. Wine is the best thing for shock.' He laughed his high-pitched laugh again.

Hans felt a smile tug his grim expression. Clouet might be occupying the position he'd travelled halfway across Europe to gain, but it was difficult not to like him.

A page materialised, his jerkin quartered with the fleur-de-lis of France and two strange animals. One all spikes and the other like a large fire-breathing lizard.

'The salamander, it is the symbol of François,' Clouet explained. 'And Queen Claude, she is a porcupine. Don't ask me why. She is the least porcupine-like person imaginable.' He beckoned the page with a long white finger. 'Take it to Sa Majesté,' he ordered, gesturing at the portrait of Erasmus.

'Keep your hands on the frame,' Hans instructed. 'Don't touch the painting.'

Clouet laughed. 'The servants here handle paintings all the time. *Le roi*, he is always moving his collection, always buying new works. You would like to see? Yes? Then I will show you. This way, please.'

François' art collection covered the walls of the chateau's staterooms, magnificent chambers with tiled floors, large, light windows, high ceilings with painted beams and vast fireplaces with carved overmantels. But Hans had only the vaguest awareness of the surroundings. His entire attention was on the paintings. François owned pictures he had only heard about, or imagined, or seen bad reproductions of. Sa Majesté, Clouet explained, had agents everywhere and bought the best he could lay his elegant royal hands on.

The collection was extraordinary, every work astonishing. How had Piero della Francesca achieved those colours? That delicate, luminous effect? The work had a shimmering purity, a silvery grace not quite of this world.

Leonardo was an even greater mystery. Having never seen one of his works in the flesh before, Hans had never realised how they combined, apparently effortlessly, so much impossibly difficult technique. The handling of light and shade, the posing of figures, the depiction of drapery, water and trees. All achieved with a miraculous ease.

'What was Leonardo like?' he asked Clouet.

'Tough as the old boots, *mon ami*. Sixty-four and rode all the way from Italy on a mule. Over the Alps. Can you imagine? God knows how he did it, especially with all these paintings. Those three there, yes, St John the Baptist, St Anne. And that one there, the silk merchant's wife. He was a lucky silk merchant, *non*?'

Hans examined in wonder the flesh tones and shadows, the distant blue hills, the general dreamy atmosphere. The painting seemed to hover between the real and the imaginary.

'Her name is Lisa. She has a mysterious smile, no? Now, my friend. Dinner awaits.'

Clouet's house – once Leonardo's – was tall, large and beautiful. Almost a mini chateau itself, with carvings, balustrades and pointed gables of stone-faced red brick. They walked through a garden alive with evening birdsong and gilded with the setting sun. Flowers glowed in the last of the light.

They sat in cushioned chairs at a large oak dining table, warmed by a fireplace that stretched the width of the entire wall. The most delicate roast duck Hans had ever tasted was washed down by local wine as free-flowing as the Loire itself.

After supper, Clouet called for lanterns. 'Now I will show you *mon atelier*, my workshop.'

It was at the top of the house, a large room with big windows. It must be full of light in daytime. Clouet strode to an easel and whipped off the cloth covering it. 'My work in progress! Sa Majesté!'

The upper body of a man; dark-haired, long-nosed, narrow-eyed, magnificently haughty. And bearing a strong resemblance to Clouet. 'Do all Frenchmen look like you?' Hans asked, amused.

'Actually, I am from the Low Countries. A foreigner, like yourself. We outsiders make the best painters. We notice more.'

Clouet certainly noticed clothes. Hans had never seen any painted so brilliantly. The representation was so miraculously real, one could almost feel the thick, smooth coolness of the satin, the metallic threads in the gold embroidery. His sleeves seemed to billow and ripple into the room, every gorgeous detail captured with superb attention and given a heightened, even living reality.

By contrast, strangely, the king's features seemed dull, almost secondary. While light leapt and danced on the garments, the face and the red background behind it had the passive flatness of the altarpieces Hans had once so disliked painting. There was more life in François' clothes than in his eyes.

*'Eh bien?'* Clouet was looking at him expectantly. 'Well? You must tell me the truth, as one artist to another!'

Put like that, what could he do? Hans took a deep breath. 'It's magnificent. But Jean, this is a portrait of silks and velvets, not a person.'

Instead of being offended, Clouet looked delighted. 'Of course!'

'But should not painters of portraits show the truth about their subjects?'

Clouet raised surprised eyebrows. 'But I *am* showing the truth. The truth about King François is that he likes expensive clothes.'

Hans blinked. 'Isn't there more to him than that?'

'I don't think so.'

Clouet now showed Hans his materials. All plentiful, and all of the very best. Brushes of every thickness, neatly arranged in size order; shelves with blocks of wax and rosin, bottles of oil for mixing, mortars to mix them in, slabs on which to grind and pound. And, in special shallow boxes, a rainbow array of colours, all of superb quality. One contained precious ultramarine blue. In another, gold leaf gleamed in the light of his lantern. 'What it is to have a royal patron!' Hans groaned.

Clouet laughed. 'But *mon ami*, you could have one too. François is not the only one.'

'All the positions are filled,' Hans pointed out. 'The Pope has Michelangelo. The doge has Titian. The emperor has Dürer.'

Clouet's shriek of a laugh rang through the air. 'Yes, and poor Albrecht! Having to paint that Hapsburg chin! But,' he added, 'you've forgotten Henri.'

'Henri? Henri who?' Some French duke or other, Hans supposed.

'Henri d'Angleterre. He needs a painter.'

'Henri d'Angleterre . . . Henry of England.' Hans frowned. 'The *king*? The King of England has no court artist?'

'No, he has not.'

Hans looked hard at Clouet. He had bitter experience of being wrongly informed on this point. 'Really? Why not?'

'Because,' Clouet shrugged, 'the English are complete philistines. Can't paint to save their lives.'

'Haven't they got foreign artists?'

'No one in their right mind wants to go there. Cellini said he wouldn't live among such beasts as the English. Torrigiano went for a while, but he'd been working for the Borgias, so the Tudors were a step up.'

'You're really selling it to me, Jean.'

It was out of the question. He knew practically nothing about England, had barely given the place a thought. As for going there, getting to France had been expensive enough, and England was an entire sea away. He couldn't afford another journey, another risk, more wasted time. Especially with a pricey ocean crossing thrown in.

'*Voilà*, an opportunity!' Clouet was urging. 'A second chance!'

'Or a second disaster. It's a no, Jean.'

Clouet's silken black and white shoulders shrugged. '*Hélas*. As you like.'

'And yet,' Wyatt says, when Hans has finished, 'you did go to England. Something happened to change your mind.'

Hans meets his dark gaze. 'Yes, it did. The next morning, I met Anne.'

Remembering that day, how she had looked, what she had said, he's overwhelmed with sudden grief. He covers his face with his hands.

Wyatt's long, strong fingers close around his wrist. 'We're going to get him, Holbein. Never doubt it for a minute. We're going to destroy Cromwell. That's why we're here.'

## *Chapter Thirty-Two*

They're south-east of Calais now, in the Marne country. It's gently hilly, and no doubt lush and green in summer. But this is February, and it's freezing. Pretty, though; the frosted grass aglitter under their horses' hooves and milky morning mist rolling into the naked trees. But freezing all the same.

Hans's precious fingers are wrapped with layers of oiled bandage, but it's going to take time for them to thaw, if indeed they ever do. Plenty of time for Wyatt to do the talking when they get to the Château de Joinville, seat of the mighty Duc de Guise.

Wyatt's long, sharp nose is red with cold. He wears two bonnets and any number of cloaks and scarves but shivers violently all the same. He's not substantial enough for these weather conditions.

'If you ate as much as you drank, Wyatt, you'd feel better,' Hans says.

'I'll bear it in mind,' Wyatt drily returns, 'when we come across something worth eating. But I appreciate your solicitude.'

The sun is starting to sink as Joinville is reached. A small canal crossed with cheerful little bridges reflects a blazing pink and coral sky. A road of neat houses leads to the great chateau gates.

'What are you going to say to Madame de Longueville?' Hans asks, curiously.

Beneath his two hats, Wyatt rolls his eyes. 'Believe it or not, I've been told to make it sound as if Henry doesn't want to marry again at all. That he's really most reluctant. But that his Council are insisting he does it for the sake of the realm.'

Hans is astonished. 'Why's he saying that?'

'He thinks she's going to bite his hand off. He imagines that sounding reluctant will make her even keener.'

Hans shakes his head. 'The man's delusional.'

'And thank God for it,' says Wyatt, with a grin.

The Château de Joinville, its pale stone lit by the winter sunset, is huge, magnificent and very modern, with great windows and carving in the new classical style. On the roof, colossal chimneys promise enormous fireplaces. Hans imagines, with longing, great golden flames rolling up from huge logs. He and Wyatt trot across the courtyard cobbles full of anticipation. They're cold, tired and hungry, but any minute now, they'll be warm.

They tie up their horses, bound up the steps to the vast front door and pull on the bell chain. A distant interior jangling can be heard, but no one answers. Wyatt yanks it again, and after some minutes there's the sound of steady footsteps, the snap and slam of bolts sliding back. The door opens, but only slightly. Hans can see a pair of eyes.

'We're here to see Madame,' Wyatt informs the eyes in his best charming diplomatic manner. He adds that they have come from the court of the King of England and have important business.

The door opens wider. A lantern shows a gaunt black-clad figure with a bony, skull-like face. He says nothing, but stands aside to permit entry. The hall is dark, to their disappointment; what's worse, no fire is lit. As they follow the gaunt figure, his light skims the edges of tapestries, the corners of pictures, the details of carvings and drapes. Splendour in the dark.

Through a carved screen they follow, and along a dark passage. The gaunt figure moves rapidly; they're almost stumbling after him. Then he stops, so suddenly they nearly pile into him, and indicates a door. Then he disappears into the dark.

Wyatt turns the handle, pushes the door open. The room inside is wood-panelled, small and comfortable. There are tapestries, a mirror. And here, at last, a fire, with a grand carved mantel above it. Before it someone is sitting, back turned, figure silhouetted by the flames. It's a woman, as the wide skirts attest.

'Madame de Longueville?' says Wyatt, sweeping off his bonnets and bowing low. His hair is sticking up in clumps. Hans can't help grinning.

Now, at last, the figure turns. Her visitors brace themselves for her famous beauty, but what now falls on their sight is wrinkles and narrowed, glinting eyes. They stare in astonishment. It seems reports of Madame de Longueville's loveliness are exaggerated.

A snort. 'Most certainly I am not. I am Antoinette de Lorraine, Duchesse de Guise. Madame de Longueville is my daughter.' The crone surveys them stonily. 'And who might you be?'

'We come from the court of King Henry,' Wyatt says, with another sweeping bow.

The crone looks unimpressed. 'Oh. Him. Killed off another wife, I hear.'

Wyatt hastens to correct what is, officially at least, a misapprehension. 'His Majesty is devastated at the loss of Queen Jane. So much so that the thought of marrying again is anathema to him.'

'It should be,' sniffs the crone. 'Henry Tudor is a danger to women. A danger to the true religion as well. Breaking with Rome. Disgraceful.'

'It may be,' Wyatt says, 'that he's inclining back towards it now. Somewhat. Possibly.'

'After he's killed all those people?' the crone says in disgust. 'He's changed his mind?'

'His Majesty, as I mentioned, has no wish to take another wife,' Wyatt says. 'But his Council thinks differently. His people think differently. Henry needs to marry, for the good of England.'

'The good of England? What do I care about that? I'm French, in case you haven't noticed.'

'I've been asked to ascertain whether there might be any interest,' Wyatt says.

'Interest in what?' the crone snaps. 'Why are you talking in riddles?'

'In your daughter honouring our great and sovereign lord by becoming Queen of England.'

A sort of furious incredulity flashes over the old duchess's face. *'Marie?'* she thunders. 'Become *Queen of England*? Never! Not if Henry were the last monarch on earth. A daughter of Guise become the fourth wife of a man who has already murdered three?'

'Madame, really, I must object . . .' Wyatt murmurs.

But the duchess is in full flow. The hooded eyes either side of her beaky nose blaze with anger. 'Has that repulsive Tudor any idea of his reputation outside England?' she storms. 'How here in Europe we regard him as an abhorrence? An outrage? An Antichrist?'

'I'm guessing that's a no, then.' Wyatt backs towards the door, Hans edging after.

'It most certainly is. And even were that not the case, your great and sovereign lord, as you so misguidedly call him, is too late. Marie's not here. She left yesterday. For Scotland.'

*

'Wife-murderer. Abhorrence. Antichrist. What was the other one?' grins Wyatt, later. He's composing his report for Cromwell. The castle's hospitality not, in the end, being available to them, they have put up at a local inn. It's a vast improvement on those they have experienced lately.

'Outrage,' snorts Hans. 'Oh, and repulsive Tudor.'

'That's it!' Wyatt takes up his pen again, cackling as he writes.

They are both in excellent spirits for people who a mere couple of hours ago were practically hurled out of the gates of the Château de Joinville. 'I didn't even have to try to be incompetent,' Wyatt had crowed. 'Henry's done all the hard work for me, bless him.'

'What else are you telling him?' Hans wants to know.

'The regretful fact that our high and puissant prince would seem to have something of an international image problem.'

'You could say that,' Hans agrees. 'Hardly worth me bringing my charcoals really.'

'And sadder still,' Wyatt continues gleefully, 'if Henry's got an image problem, our dear Master Secretary's got a problem too. If no woman in Europe wants to marry the king, where does he find a wife?'

At dinner, the wine is excellent, the food too. Pork with prunes, delicious. As for warmth, they're so close to the fire they're practically sitting in it.

Wyatt is holding up his wine, examining its colour, smacking his lips as he drinks. 'Here's to the Antichrist, the abhorrence, the outrage. And Henry as well, of course.'

They clink glasses, chortle.

After a couple more well-fed days, Hans and Wyatt set off for England. No reply has come from Cromwell. Presumably he's trying to think of his next move. 'Going to have to try pretty hard to get out of this one,' says Wyatt.

They're in the highest good humour. Singing and joking, they're halfway to Calais when they spy the horse in the distance. They stop and wheel their own steeds about, suddenly wary. The last inn they stayed at was of the villainous type. And they're in lonely country. Is this the long-feared footpad, demanding money with menaces?

'I don't think so,' Hans says, as the rider gets closer. Of the two of them, he has the keener sight. 'It looks like a messenger.'

They expect him to pass them with a nod, a brief exchange at the most. Messengers are always in a hurry. They're surprised when he stops altogether. 'Sir Thomas Wyatt?' he asks Hans, who jerks his thumb at his companion.

The young postboy rummages in his saddlebag. 'For you,' he says, handing a letter over. Then he turns and gallops away in the other direction.

'How did he know it was us?' Hans muses, watching the figure diminish. 'But then there's only one road. He was bound to come across us sooner or later.'

Wyatt doesn't answer. He's reading the missive, cursing darkly under his breath. When he looks up, his sharp features are twisted in a scowl. 'It's from Cromwell. He's not giving up, blast him.'

'What do you mean?' Hans is blowing on his fingers, rubbing his nose. It's too cold to hang about like this.

'Turns out that Marie de Guise has two younger sisters. Louise and Renée. According to the French ambassador, they're even lovelier than Marie. We're to go back to Joinville.'

Hans stares at him in dismay. '*What?*'

Wyatt is furious, but mostly with the two of them, it seems. 'What were we thinking? Of course it was never going to be that easy. This is Cromwell we're dealing with. There was always going to be a countermove.'

Hans is more apprehensive about what lies ahead. 'There's no possibility that terrifying old termagant will let us in the door again. Let alone see her daughters.'

Wyatt eyes him mordantly. 'She's going to have to. And you're going to have to get out those charcoals. We don't have a choice. The king wants portraits of them both.'

## *Chapter Thirty-Three*

'Back already?' says the landlord of the Joinville inn.

'Couldn't keep away.' Wyatt smiles through gritted teeth.

Less of the sarcasm, Hans thinks. The innkeeper seems a reasonable sort; runs a decent place. And if he's curious, is that so surprising? They're in the back of beyond and his interest in two exotic visitors, origin unknown, appearing, disappearing and then reappearing is understandable. Perhaps they should take him into their confidence. To a certain extent, anyway.

As mine host goes off, whistling, to fetch their wine, Hans leans over to Wyatt. 'We could just ask him about the daughters. Straight out, what he knows about them. We're going to need some help from someone.'

'Stupid idea,' Wyatt says crushingly. 'What we're doing is a state secret. And if that old bat finds out, it could all go horribly wrong.'

'How much more horribly wrong could it go?' Hans retorts, stung.

Wyatt scowls, but brightens as the landlord returns, a jug of good Marne wine in one hand, a plate of sliced sausage in the other. 'On the house,' he says, putting the plate down. 'I like to reward repeat business.'

'Very civil of you.' Wyatt spears a piece of sausage with his dagger.

'From my own pigs.' Apron round his waist, cloth over his shoulder, the landlord lounges against a post. He seems inclined to talk. 'Back for long, are you?'

'That depends,' says Hans, then realises this is a mistake as the landlord seizes on it.

'Depends on what?' he grins. 'You getting thrown out of the chateau again?'

Wyatt puts his wine beaker down. 'Ah,' he says. 'So you know about that.'

'I should say the whole town knows,' chuckles the landlord. 'A character, ain't she? The old duchess.'

'That's one way of putting it.'

'You were lucky that's all that happened to you. She's burnt people at the stake before.'

Hans catches Wyatt's look. Its meaning is clear enough. *That's how much more horribly wrong it could go.*

'Some Lutheran, it was. Don't like the new religion, the old duchess,' the innkeeper adds fondly.

'Sit down, join us,' Wyatt urges him, indicating a nearby stool. 'You might be able to help us with some information. If you have time, that is.'

It's Hans's turn to stare meaningfully at Wyatt. *So, not such a stupid idea.*

The landlord's fetching the stool. He sits down, looks about the empty room, sighs. 'Oh, I've got time all right.'

'Not a busy time of year, then?'

'It's never a busy time of year. What would you like to know? Who are you, anyway?'

Hans holds his breath. But Wyatt smiles broadly. 'We're publishers,' he declares without missing a beat. 'Travelling around France for a book project.'

To hide his astonishment, Hans looks at the floor. What's Wyatt up to?

'Book project?' Mine host sounds disappointed. 'There's some in the town as thought you were spies.'

A burst of disbelieving laughter from Wyatt. 'Spies? Us? My dear fellow, I hardly think so.'

'No?' The landlord is looking from one to the other. He doesn't sound entirely convinced.

'Absolutely not. But you and your fellow eagle-eyed townsfolk are right about one thing. While we're certainly not spies – oh dear me no, the very thought . . .'

Hans tries to catch his eye. *Don't overdo it, Wyatt. There's such a thing as protesting too much.*

'. . . we are on a mission.'

'Mission?' The innkeeper sounds excited.

'Yes, to find the most beautiful noblewomen in France. We are compiling a book of them, for publication.'

Ah. He can see what Wyatt's doing now. He does his best to keep a straight face. Clever. Ingenious, in fact. A directory of beautiful women, it's the perfect pretext. Now they can ask what they like.

And actually, Wyatt's not even lying. 'I'm the writer,' he's explaining earnestly, 'while my friend here,' he gestures at Hans, 'draws them.'

The landlord has clearly fallen for it hook, line and sinker. 'Beautiful noblewomen of France!' he exclaims. 'Now there's a book I'd like to see.'

'I'll ensure you're sent a copy.'

Beneath the innkeeper's blunt fringe, his round eyes light up. 'Really?'

'Absolutely. But first we need a little help. A little . . . information.'

'Gladly,' says the landlord.

'Excellent. Well, we came here last time in search of Marie de Guise. She was not here, as you may be aware.'

'Gone to marry the King of Scotland!' Mine host sounds proud. 'Lovely woman. Big, if you know what I mean.' He makes a curved gesture with both hands. 'Perfect for that book of yours.'

'No doubt,' Wyatt concurs. 'But as you saw, her mother felt otherwise. The Duchesse de Guise,' he adds regretfully, 'considered that the inclusion of her daughter in such a volume was beneath her status and dignity.'

'Ah. So that's why she threw you out.'

'Regrettably, we were obliged to leave empty-handed,' Wyatt concedes. 'Then we discovered en route that Madame Marie is not alone; that the duchess has two more daughters, Mesdemoiselles Renée and Louise. We have returned,' he concludes brightly, 'in the hope that we can put *them* in our book. Even if we have missed their sister.'

There's a silence. Hans and Wyatt look expectantly at the innkeeper. He, however, remains silent.

'According to our sources, they are even more worthy of inclusion than their sister,' Wyatt presses eagerly.

Another silence.

'What's the problem?' asks Wyatt, at length.

It turns out that Renée de Guise has become the abbess of a convent. And while it's thought Louise is at home, no one has seen her lately. 'But if she'd died, I think we would have heard,' their host adds, helpfully.

Later, Hans is lying on the bed in their room, sleep tugging at his eyelids after an enormous and excellent rabbit-pie supper, accompanied by plenty of wine.

But Wyatt, who as ever has eaten little, is fizzing with nervous energy and pacing the floor. 'Can you believe it? Marie de Guise goes to Scotland, her sister goes to a nunnery. Bloody rotten luck.'

'At least Renée's not marrying one of the king's rivals,' Hans points out. 'She's entering the service of God.'

'Henry definitely sees Him as a rival,' Wyatt retorts. 'Albeit one of the less important ones.' He rakes both hands through his unkempt hair. 'We've got to get a picture of Louise,' he frets. 'If we go back to London empty-handed, Cromwell will think we're useless. He'll get someone else to do what we're doing. And that will be it. Our chance to get him gone.' He looks at Hans. 'You have to draw her, Holbein.'

'Yes, but how?' Hans wants to know. 'We can hardly force our way into the chateau.'

From where he's lying, he can see out of the room's small window. Not that there's much to see. No sunset tonight; darkness has fallen like the lid of a chest.

Wyatt now strides over and stares out himself, hands in his breeches pockets. His shoulders are slumped in despair, his whole mien one of frustration and defeat. Then, quite suddenly, he straightens. He turns, grinning.

Hans's heart sinks. Wyatt's had an idea.

'You're right,' the poet tells him excitedly. 'We can hardly go in and look. But we can look from outside.'

'Look in the chateau?' Hans thinks of how tired he is. Thinks of the cold night, the terrifying duchess, the burning at the stake. 'But what if she sees us?'

His reward is a withering look. 'She won't, *Dummkopf.* The windows will be lit so we can see in. But outside will be dark so they won't be able to see out. It's the perfect cover.'

'If you say so.' Hans closes his eyes, starts to drift off.

'I do, my dear Holbein, I do. Now get up.'

Hans's eyes fly open. 'Get up? *Now?*'

'It's the perfect time. It's night; if Louise is in there, chances are she'll be with her mother. Having dinner or something.'

Hans thinks miserably of the cold, dark walk. For all Wyatt's fighting talk, he's doubtful of success. The chateau wasn't well lit. The duchess's room apart, it had lacked a single light. Oh, must he really move? He's completely exhausted, warm and comfortable, and wants to do nothing more than sleep.

But Wyatt's obviously not going to let him. 'You only need to glance at her, isn't that right?' he demands. 'To be able to draw her? With that *amazing* memory of yours . . .'

'No need to smarm, Wyatt,' Hans says irritably.

Mere minutes later, he's hurrying down the twisting wooden stairs. In the main room, by the fire, the landlord is sitting with what is presumably a group of locals. All of them turn to stare.

'Going out, gentlemen?' The innkeeper sounds surprised, as well he might. It's past eleven.

'As you see,' returns Wyatt, pleasantly.

'In the dark?'

'An English custom. To aid digestion.'

The locals mutter at this. Hans can make out *les rosbifs* and *complètement fou.*

The main street is completely silent, every house with its wooden shutters closed. Cracks of glimmering light between them suggest cosy firesides within. Wyatt stalks ahead. Those long, thin legs can stride surprisingly fast.

They sidle through the chateau entrance and keep to the shadows of the wall. As Hans has feared, the front of the place is a solid dark mass, almost indistinguishable from the black sky. There is no moon.

'Round the back,' hisses Wyatt. 'That room was right at the end.'

'What about mantraps?' Hans hisses. If ever a woman looked like she bought them in bulk, that woman was Antoinette de Guise. The grounds were probably full of them.

'Trouble with you, Holbein, is that you only ever see problems.' But Wyatt slows down, starts to tread more carefully.

At first, the rear of the chateau looks as dark as the front. They've almost reached the far end when Wyatt stops. 'Look!'

The next window along, while not exactly illuminated, has a faint glow to it. They edge towards it, peer through the diamond-shaped panes.

It's the room they were in before; the tapestries, the mirror, the fireplace. Before it, her back to the window, is the familiar, formidable figure of the duchess. Facing her and the window is someone else: a dark-haired girl, much younger. Louise, presumably.

'There!' hisses an exultant Wyatt. 'Are you getting a good look, Holbein?'

The light's not the best, just a few candles and the fire. But it's enough, and Hans rapidly scans the sober face, the unflatteringly scraped-back hair, commits every detail to memory.

Now Wyatt too has looked more closely, and his early triumph has dissipated. 'Even lovelier than Marie?' he groans. 'Bloody ambassador's idea of a joke, obviously. I should have realised sooner. Marie de Guise away, her sister a nun. They're playing us, those bloody French. Been wasting our time all along.'

# *Chapter Thirty-Four*

They're woken next morning by a violent banging on the door.

'What the hell?' mutters Wyatt, swinging his lanky body out of bed and stumbling to open it.

Mine host bursts in, eyes bulging with fury. 'You've been recognised,' he cries, as Hans stares at him over the sheet edge.

'Recognised?'

'You're not publishers. You're courtiers from London. Imposters and liars!'

As is rarely the case, Wyatt is lost for words.

'The duchess saw you last night at the chateau! Sneaking around, trying to look at her daughter!'

She saw them, in the dark? The woman must have the eyes of a thousand cats. Then Hans remembers the mirror. Of course. She had seen their reflection at the window.

'Peeping Toms!' rants the landlord. 'I'd get out of town now if I were you. She'll have you horsewhipped! But only if you're lucky.'

They set off, the usually irrepressible Wyatt more dejected than Hans has ever seen him. He sets about raising his spirits. 'It's hardly our fault if the French have played us. We weren't to know, we were only—'

'Acting on orders,' Wyatt heatedly interrupts. 'Yes, but Cromwell will blame us all the same. You know how it works at court. Next one down carries the can.'

Hans considers this as they ride along. 'But if that's how it is, we're never going to destroy Cromwell,' he says eventually. 'No matter what happens, he'll always have the advantage.'

Wyatt now changes tack himself. Assumes a brisker demeanour, pulls up his horse, turns to Hans. 'Look, Holbein,' he says. 'I realise things look pretty bleak to you.'

'To me? They were looking pretty bleak to you five minutes ago.'

'Yes, yes. But we have to keep believing. I just know that we're going to get him.'

'How?'

'I've told you. He's going to make a catastrophic mistake. And that will be our chance.'

Not this again. 'Yes, but when? It could be years. It could be never.'

They've stopped on a ridge overlooking a wooded valley. There's the sharp scent of pine in the freezing air, and way below, the flash of a river. The horses move restively, uncertain why they've stopped. 'It might take a while,' Wyatt concedes. 'But this wife-hunting business just has to be an opportunity.'

'Really?' Hans looks at him doubtfully. 'I don't see how.'

'Because I'm the trusted envoy and you're the trusted artist. Trusted and great,' Wyatt adds cajolingly.

This obvious flattery annoys Hans, makes him feel patronised. 'You keep saying that,' he says in a burst of impatience. 'But I don't see why I'm needed, particularly.'

'What do you mean?' Wyatt looks astounded.

Hans's horse wheels about, disturbed by his unusually agitated tones. 'Cromwell told me that all they want is an old-fashioned dynastic marriage. So if the alliance is the point, it doesn't matter what she looks like. She could look like Louise de Guise, easily.' He pats his saddlebag, where the poor plain girl is safely rolled up. 'Any old dauber could do the painting. It doesn't have to be me.'

'No, no, Hans. You've got it wrong,' Wyatt insists. 'It has to be us.'

'You, possibly,' Hans concedes. 'They'll need someone competent to make the agreements and do the contract. That's what dynastic alliances are all about, I imagine.'

'Yes, but Henry doesn't want a dynastic marriage.'

'But Cromwell said—'

Wyatt's eyes are gleaming excitedly. 'He *thinks* that's what Henry wants. And Henry thinks it's what he wants as well. But they're both wrong. Henry doesn't want a soulless alliance with just anyone. He wants to be in love.' He chuckles. 'He *loves* to be in love. Believe it or not, Henry Tudor is a romantic.'

Hans wonders if the freezing temperature is affecting his hearing. Whether his cold red ears are playing tricks on him. Romantic? The man who abandoned his first wife, murdered his second and neglected his third?

'Oh, absolutely.' Wyatt is nodding. 'Believe me, he is. He's entirely led by his cock. Chose his last two wives because he fancied them. Married for love, as he sees it.'

'*Love?*' Hans gasps. He's bulge-eyed, incredulous. 'What can Henry Tudor possibly know about *love*?'

'Lust, then. Same thing in his book.'

Hans has had enough. He doesn't believe what Wyatt is saying, he doesn't think they'll bring Cromwell down and he doesn't want to hang about for an opportunity that may never come. The final straw is the thought of Henry in love.

'I'm not coming back with you,' he says flatly.

'What? Now hang on a minute, Hans. Hold your horses, literally. There's no need to be hasty.'

'I'm not being hasty. I've made up my mind.'

'But where are you going?'

'Home.' And why not? If they're not going to get Cromwell, he can at least attempt to find some peace. Two countries and a sea away from England, among people who've never heard of Anne, it might be possible.

'Home?' Wyatt's mouth opens and shuts. 'But you live in London.'

'Yes,' Hans agrees tersely, 'but as I've explained, I came from Basel, in the Swiss Confederacy. It's three days' ride from here. I'll never be this close again.'

Wyatt's so shocked, he's gabbling. 'You can't. Holbein, you just can't. We have to destroy Cromwell. We've agreed. We've—'

'He's indestructible,' Hans cuts in.

'He isn't. I know it. So long as he walks the earth, there's a chance we can bring him down. And we will. And so you can't leave, you can't, you can't.' Wyatt is wringing his hands, distraught. 'Please don't. I'm begging you, Holbein.'

Annoyed though he is, Hans is hating this. It's horrible and uncomfortable. He's come to like Wyatt, to enjoy his company, to respect his ingenuity and quick brain. He doesn't want to wound him. All the same, he raises his chin, looks his companion unflinchingly in the eye. 'I'm sorry,' he says. He means it, but it comes out more curtly than intended.

'Sorry?' Wyatt repeats, softly. He shakes his head in bewilderment, looks away. But when he looks back, the desperation has gone from his face. Something flat and hard has replaced it. 'You can keep your sorrow,' he says coldly. 'I'm sorry for *you*, Holbein.'

Hans is indignant. 'Sorry for *me*?'

'Yes,' says Wyatt derisively, 'because you can't see what's obvious.

What else do you think there is for us? What other purpose do our lives have but vengeance? What else is there in the world?'

Hans says nothing. He slides out of the saddle, starts to rummage in his bag, hands over Louise de Guise. 'Here.' *Give it to Cromwell with my love* is on the tip of his tongue. But Wyatt's face makes him think better of it.

'And what about Jennet?' his companion demands. 'What's she going to think?'

Hans heaves himself back on his horse. Just hearing her name makes him long for her. But there's no point, there's no future. He has always known this. 'What difference does it make?' he hears himself say.

'I thought,' Wyatt says scornfully, 'that you were sweet on her.'

'Since when was that any of your business?'

'Since she was in this with us.'

Hans thinks of the apprenticeship, how she's going to hate him. 'You mean you think she'll rat on us now?'

'She'd never do that. Unlike some people, she's loyal.'

Hans is pulling on his reins, steadying himself in the saddle. 'I'm not taking lectures on loyalty from you.'

'At least I'm not running away like a coward.'

The contempt in the other man's voice makes Hans furious. How dare Wyatt despise him? He's not the person who stood up in court and gave evidence. 'A *coward*?'

Wyatt looks at him steadily. 'You heard what I said. You should come back with me. Revenge Anne. Destroy Cromwell. And yes, marry Jennet. Why not?'

'Not possible.' Hans wheels round to face the south, starts cantering away.

Wyatt's response is a howl. 'WHY NOT?'

Hans's reply echoes down the valley. 'BECAUSE I'M MARRIED ALREADY.'

# *Chapter Thirty-Five*

The spires of Basel appear three days later. As he approaches, a sense of familiarity fuses with one of strangeness. He feels both that he's never lived here and that he's never lived anywhere else.

How tiny the city looks. It used to seem so big. But years amid the size and rush of London have changed his perspective. It all seems so small now, the massive central river excepted. Not even the mighty Thames can rival the wild, wide Rhine.

As he rides slowly along, he's aware of people staring. His clothes, he knows. As King's Painter, he dresses well these days. Fine wools, linens with embroidered collars. Velvets. And fur, of course, lots of it in this weather.

He reaches Gerbergasse, his old street. It looks the same as always; smells the same, more to the point. It's where the tanners live. The stink of the vats in which animal skins steep in urine, or worse, is overwhelming.

Tanning was Elspeth's business, or, rather, her first husband's. It was why Hans had married her. He'd been twenty-one, a penniless newcomer. And banned from joining the Basel painters' guild because he was single. He had found in the widow Schmidt the answer to several prayers.

Elspeth had been ten years older and with a small son, Franz. She was not good-looking, her eyes damaged by tanning chemicals, which made the lids swell and droop. He had felt tenderly towards her because of her hard life. He'd hoped to bring her some happiness in exchange for the security and status she gave him. Perhaps even grow to love her. Only later had he discovered her terrible temper.

Erasmus had joked about it. 'Sometimes I think of marrying, and then I think of your wife, Holbein.'

Hans ties his horse up in the yard, approaches the low, squat house. Places his hand on the door he last closed several years ago. Takes a deep breath, pushes, enters.

It's like going back in time. Everything looks as he left it. Perhaps he hasn't actually left, and London's all been a dream.

'Good evening, Elspeth.'

His wife looks exactly the same too; thick-bodied in a worn apron, even stirring the same round black cauldron in the hearth. He can tell from the smell that it's cabbage soup; she's still making that too. He thinks guiltily of what he's become used to: the petal-stuffed quails, the crisp trout pasties. The cheese tarts as light as air.

She turns her rough red face, looks this magnificent stranger up and down. 'What do *you* want?' she barks.

He laughs. 'Elspeth. Do you really not recognise me?'

'Yes, you're Hans. But what do you want?'

Admittedly, he hadn't expected much. Happy tears, rushing into each other's arms had never been on the cards. They were never that sort of couple and it was never that sort of marriage. But this is restrained even by Elspeth's undemonstrative standards.

'I've come back,' he says, rather plaintively.

'Why? There's nothing for you here. They still don't want painters. They've only just stopped smashing up the churches.'

The Lutheran revolution was well under way when he left. Mobs were stripping the altars and dragging out the paintings, including many he'd worked on himself. Piling them in the main square, setting them on fire. Meanwhile, the wealthy who commissioned portraits went to ground, fearful of being persecuted as members of a rich elite.

'I know.' He nods.

'You knew, and still you've come back?' Elspeth sounds disgusted. 'You should have stayed in London. Here, you're just another mouth to feed.'

His eyes stray to the cabbage soup and shrink away again. He rummages in his sack, produces a small bag. As he places it on the table there's a faint chinking. 'Hopefully this will help.'

Elspeth blanches in amazement. She opens the pouch, digs a rough red hand between the cool gold coins. They light her features, soften them. She looks up, glowing. 'All this, for me?'

'I promised you I'd bring you back riches.'

'You promised all sorts of things when you went to England. I thought it was just flannel, as it was when you went to France.'

Her voice is less harsh now, though. She stretches out a finger, strokes his sleeve. 'That velvet?'

'It is, yes,' he admits, awkward. As she was when he last saw her, Elspeth is wearing a cheap blue dress. Very likely the same dress.

'Bit different to what you used to wear at Froben's,' she remarks.

He nods, agrees, thinks of the publisher's where he worked from four in the morning until seven at night. His ancient, ink-smeared jerkin, the old wool hose soaked with sweat.

'And I can see you don't cut your hair round a bowl any more.' She is smiling, as she rarely does. 'You look good, Hans.'

He thanks her, and tells her she hasn't changed. But a feeling of dread has started in the soles of his feet. It's spreading upwards to his knees, jumping about in his stomach. Coming home was a bad decision. What had he been thinking? What has he done?

He had come out of guilt, because he knew he owed Elspeth.

And because he wanted to be anywhere but England. Peace of mind, that was what he'd been hoping for.

Now he sees how impossible this is, how wrong he was. He feels just as bad as he ever did; he might even feel worse. It's not Elspeth's fault, or Basel's. It's his. Geography has nothing to do with it; the problem is inside him. He'll take what happened wherever he goes, every minute of his life.

*What else do you think there is for us? What other purpose do our lives have but vengeance? What else is there in the world?*

Wyatt is right, there will never be any respite. And Wyatt is right about something else too. He, Hans, is a coward. He has tried to run away from his duty. Not just to Wyatt and Anne, but to Jennet too. He must go back. But first he'll have to extract himself here. He takes a breath, tries to think what to say.

Now the door opens and three children come in. Two boys and a girl barely more than a baby.

'Hello, Franz,' Hans says, assuming the eldest is his stepson.

'That's not Franz, it's Philipp,' says Elspeth sharply.

Philipp? Hans looks again at the boy, more carefully this time. Was Elspeth pregnant when he left? He doesn't think so. And this child is dark and thin with a pointy nose, while he himself is fair-haired, snub-nosed, stockily built.

He looks at the other children, none of whom resemble him either. They're an ill-favoured lot, he can't help seeing. He looks back at his wife. Whose children are these?

Elspeth shoos them all outside again, then turns to Hans. Her expression is defensive, her tone heated. 'What did you expect me to do? I had no idea when you were coming back, or if you were coming back at all.'

She expects him to be angry, he realises. Outraged, even. But he's none of those things. Life for Elspeth without him must have been hard, lonely and difficult. He doesn't blame her in the least for seeking comfort and company. 'Who's the father?' he asks gently.

'Lars. He's a tanner too. A widower. A good man.'

The relief in her voice echoes his own. There's no need to stay after all. Elspeth is clearly settled, can look after herself, especially with the money he has brought her. She and Lars, the good man, can buy a whole new house with that. He'll leave some of his clothes, too, for her to sell. And when he gets back to London, he'll send her what he can, when he can.

'Well, I wish you both happiness,' he says, meaning it. 'Do you want a divorce?'

She shakes her head. 'No need, we're fine as we are. Anyway,' she adds shyly, 'there's a certain status in being married to the famous Hans Holbein.'

'Famous?' He's astonished. They've heard of him here?

She smiles. 'We hear things even in Basel.' Then her face falls. 'I'm sorry,' she says.

'No need. As you say, what did I expect you to do?'

'Not that. About poor Queen Anne. We heard about that too. She was your friend, I know.'

He can say nothing. This has come out of nowhere, and hits him hard. He covers his face with his hands.

Elspeth strokes his shaking shoulders. 'The poor lady, and that little motherless child,' she says softly. 'What a terrible business.'

He peels his fingers from his face, wipes his eyes with the back of his hand. 'It's the reason I have to go back,' he tells her.

She nods. 'Go, with my blessing.' Then, unexpectedly, she kisses his cheek. 'And find what happiness you can.'

## *Chapter Thirty-Six*

Hans has only just got back when he's immediately summoned to Cromwell. Master Secretary's formidable intelligence network is clearly working as well as ever. He'd sidled into Greenwich the back way, but had been spotted nonetheless.

He had intended to find Wyatt first, mend fences. But before any of that could happen, someone had appeared at his door, wearing the familiar yellow Cromwell livery.

All the way down the corridors, his bowels churn with fear. Wyatt will by now have given his own account of the two of them parting at Joinville. Hans is going to need a good excuse. He'll have to explain his unauthorised abandonment of official government business.

But Master Secretary is all smiles when he's shown in. 'Dear boy. You see before you the Baron Cromwell!'

It's the latest instance of the king's favour. In the pockets of his breeches, Hans clenches his fists. Bloody Cromwell. Attracts honours as shit attracts flies.

'Of Wimbledon, no less,' the baron adds as Hans forces a congratulatory smile. 'An estate that not only used to belong to the archbishops of Canterbury but includes in its rolling acres the noble hamlet of Putney, in whose cradle I was rocked as a child. Who'd have thought it, eh?'

Hans knows this isn't why he's been summoned. But he's not going to be told yet, either. Baron Cromwell of Wimbledon, as usual, is going to make him wait.

'Take a pew,' he smiles. 'I won't be a minute.'

The pew is a grand seat by the fire, magnificently upholstered in gold damask and lavish fringing, more like a throne than a chair.

For a while, there is no sound but the busy scratching of a quill. Then the scatter of sand over ink, the thump of a seal on wax. 'Diplomatic bag to Madrid,' Master Secretary says, handing it to the attendant who scurries in at the ring of a bell. 'Attention of Sir Thomas Wyatt.'

'Wyatt's back in Madrid?' Hans is as disappointed as he's surprised. How's he going to mend fences now?

Cromwell's fleshy cheeks wobble as he nods. 'Slight change of plan on the king's marriage front.'

Hans holds his breath. Is Cromwell about to tell him that they've given up the wife hunt? That Wyatt has been stood down? And he's been summoned to be told that he has too?

'Sadly, it didn't quite work out with the French,' Master Secretary goes on.

Hans swallows. So, as Wyatt would have it, they've missed their chance. 'Were there no other suitable candidates?' If the hunt is off, their opportunity is gone.

'Oh, indeed. Quite a few. Our sovereign lord suggested they all gather at Calais for him to inspect. Unfortunately, that was the last straw for our Gallic cousins.'

Hans eyes widen. 'Why so?'

'You may well ask, dear boy. The king was only trying to be helpful, thinking that this would save time. But François took umbrage, saying that the noble ladies weren't to be paraded like ponies, and would Henry like to go further and mount them in turn, retaining for himself the best ride?'

'He said *that*?' Hans fights hard not to laugh.

'Typical French vulgarity,' Master Secretary tuts. 'After that, things fell apart rather.'

'So that's it?' Hans asks. 'The search for a bride is over?'

Cromwell's large head moves from side to side. 'Oh no, no, *no*. No, no, no, no, *no*. By no means. Negotiations with the French are ongoing. Very much so. We're just hedging our bets, that's all. Trying the Holy Roman Empire now as well. That's why Wyatt has gone back. To see if there's anyone suitable on the Hapsburg side.'

Hans slowly slides a hand behind his back, crosses his fingers hard. 'And . . . is there?'

'Oh yes. Quite a promising one. A certain Christina, Duchess of Milan. A widow.'

This doesn't sound at all promising to Hans. His recent experience with widows and duchesses has not been encouraging.

'Daughter of the King of Sweden and currently living with the Regent of the Netherlands, the Archduchess Mary, her mother's sister. And sister of the emperor of course,' Cromwell rattles off.

Out of this confusing list of places and titles, Hans focuses on the Netherlands bit. He's just been through them, for God's sake, on his return from Basel. Does he have to go all the way back?

It seems so. 'The Regent's court is at Brussels. Mechelen, to be specific.'

Mechelen. It rings a bell. Of course, Anne had been there as a child. At the court of a previous regent, Margaret. 'There's no possibility of the duchess coming here?' he asks, slightly desperately.

'I'm afraid the Imperial court aren't going to have her inspected like a horse either.' Cromwell produces a piece of paper. 'Anyway, this is what our man in Brussels says about her.' He clears his throat. '"She is not so pure white as Jane Seymour, but she hath a singular good countenance and when she chanceth to smile there appear two pits in her cheeks and one in her chin which becometh her right excellently well."'

'Dimples, he means?'

'I expect so. Hutton has a rather singular turn of phrase. It's certainly got the king going, though. He's in raptures. He's heard that she likes hunting, and in addition that she is young – sixteen.'

*Sixteen?* Henry must be well over forty. And that stinking leg.

'He's already thinking about the titles he's going to give their sons. He has a Prince of Wales already, of course, but York, Gloucester and Somerset have been mentioned.'

Hans pushes back his revulsion. That's not his business. His business is to destroy Cromwell, any way he can. And here, just when everything looked hopeless, is what could be a new opportunity. 'So, a drawing, as before?'

'A painting. A beautiful painting of a beautiful woman.'

Hans eyes Cromwell warily. 'You know I never flatter.'

'Of course you don't,' he is assured. 'You paint what you see. You are the painter of truth; it's why I value you so highly. Your likenesses are the most faithful it is possible to be. Which is why I know I can place my entire trust in you.'

Jennet had barely got through the door before they fell on each other ravenously. Lying with her afterwards, his heart hammering, her long, pale legs wound around him, Hans wondered how he could even have thought of staying away. And now he has to go once more. 'I'm going to miss you,' he says.

'Then take me with you.'

He laughs, then realises she is completely serious. She shrugs her lovely straight shoulders. 'As your assistant, why not? You've just been saying how hard it will be to paint something so quickly.'

'Well, yes, but—'

'But I could help you,' she cuts in. 'With the preparation, the colour-grinding, the pouncing, the charcoal-making, all that. Everything you've shown me,' she says eagerly, tucking a blonde curl behind one of her perfect ears.

'Well, yes,' he allows. 'There's no question of your abilities. But . . .'

'But what?' she challenges, her green eyes fierce.

'Isn't it obvious?' He looks at her hair, the flaxen mass of it, and her long, beautiful and very female body. 'You're a woman,' he says.

'So?'

He sighs. 'So, women can't be artists' assistants. Not out in the world where everyone can see. They can do it in secret, behind closed doors, as you do. Or, if they're married, they can help their husbands run workshops. But we're not . . .' He pauses. Oh, shit. He has tried to avoid this subject area.

'Married. No, we're not.' She pauses, before adding lightly, 'I understand you're already spoken for.'

A great jolt goes through him. He looks at her in terror. Her smile is gone and her expression is inscrutable. Her voice, too, gives little away; it is flat, steady.

'Wyatt told you,' he says. The bastard. On the other hand, can he blame him? Why would Wyatt have kept his secret?

Well, that's it. Humiliatingly, he feels the tears prick. He looks down, blinking.

'It doesn't matter,' he hears her say. 'I've already told you. I look after myself. I'm not interested in marriage to anyone.'

Relief thunders through him. He knows now how very painful

it would have been to lose her. He reaches for her, not trusting himself to speak.

She resists, though. 'You're not out of the woods yet. There's something else.'

'Tell me.'

Her gaze is challenging and direct. 'What will your wife think? I'm not some cheap whore to keep hidden. If you and I are to continue this, it must be above board, with her blessing.'

His words tumble over each other as he hastens to reassure her, tell her what Elspeth had said.

'That's all right then.' She smiles, and winds her arms about him.

'Oh,' she says afterwards, reaching from the bed to her clothes on the floor. 'From Wyatt.' She rolls gracefully back upwards, a sealed letter held between her fingers.

How did he know I'd come back? Hans wonders, as he unseals it.

*My dear Holbein,*

*You had no option but to return, that's how I knew. Our lives have no other purpose and there is nothing else for us in the world.*

*Now, regarding this match with the Duchess of Milan. The emperor is gaily encouraging the idea of our king marrying his niece. Fear not, though. I don't believe he's serious. It's very possible that Charles is playing with Henry, as François was. They are amusing themselves while they build their own alliance. Which, of course, would isolate England and make her vulnerable.*

*As you know, this is Cromwell's worst nightmare. He will therefore be desperate for the marriage between Henry and Christina. Not just because Milan is such a rich and powerful duchy, but because the king will be united to the emperor through his niece. A power in Europe once again.*

*And as Cromwell will make sure he gets all the credit for brokering it, our cause will be hopelessly lost. You must do everything to make sure it doesn't happen, Holbein, and I mean everything.*

*Finally, while I remain in Madrid supposedly protecting Master Secretary's interests, your diplomatic assistance on the Christina mission takes the handsome, plausible form of one Thomas Wriothesley. He's a Cromwell man, the slimiest ever born, and would sell his own grandmother. That aside, he's admirable.*

*When you have read this, place it in the fire.*

*Your servant,*
*TW*

Hans finishes the letter with a feeling almost of dread. The task ahead is daunting, and he must do it without Wyatt. He must handle a tricky situation, and a tricky person too by the sound of it.

But it's more even than that. He'd really wanted to make things right with Wyatt. They'd become a partnership. Their characters differ greatly, perhaps as different as it's possible to be. Wyatt's exuberance, Hans's taciturnity. Perhaps that's why they fit so well together. Whatever it is, Wyatt is now someone he's fond of, perhaps the closest thing to a friend he's ever had.

'Wyatt's not coming,' he says dully, handing Jennet the paper. 'Someone else is. Called,' he frowns, consults the letter, 'Writhingsley.'

She's reading the note. Rapidly, confidently. He wonders for the first time how a former maid can do that. Mostly they're illiterate. But now is not the time to ask. She drops the note in the fire and turns to him. 'Risley is evil.'

'That's how you pronounce it? Ridiculous, these old English surnames.'

'It's not old. It's new. He made it up. Pretentious, yes?' She narrows her eyes. 'He's a nasty piece of work; we all hate him in the laundry. Sly, mean, a liar.'

Oh God, thinks Hans. He'll have to spend months with this person. At the closest of quarters, too. He'll be alone with one of Cromwell's men, doing the exact opposite of what Cromwell has requested.

Jennet's obviously thinking the same thing. 'You need someone to look out for you,' she says decisively. 'He might guess what you're about, otherwise.'

He looks at her wryly. 'You, you mean? You don't give up easily, do you?'

'I'd have been dead in the street long ago if I had. But no, I don't, since you ask.'

Curiosity flares; he wants to know more about the street. But like the reading, now is not the time. And there's no possibility of her coming. If he'd been travelling with Wyatt, it might have been managed somehow. But with this Risley, never.

In reply, she twists her fair hair up, reaches for his black bonnet. She pushes the hair inside it, then picks up the doublet he cast aside some hours ago. Slips her arms in, pulls it tight across her chest. 'No tits, see,' she grins. 'No hips either.'

Then she picks up his breeches. It's true that they hang off her, but she does look like a boy, albeit a very pretty, delicate one. She strikes a pose. 'Look! I'm your German assistant. Let's call me Lars.'

As in Elspeth's new man. 'Not Lars,' he says quickly.

'Well, whatever I'm called, you brought me back from Basel

just now. I don't speak a word of English. I understand it, though.'

'But . . .' says Hans, then stops, no longer sure what he's objecting to. It has to be more complicated than this, surely. 'What about Mistress Harris? Won't she miss you in the laundry?'

Jennet shrugs her slim shoulders in his broad doublet. 'Yes, but I have two jobs there, as you know. I work for her, and I work for my mistress. This is for my mistress.'

## *Chapter Thirty-Seven*

They're on the boat now, travelling over the Narrow Sea yet again. Amongst Jennet's many impressive gifts, Hans has discovered, are her talents as a thespian. She is completely convincing as his assistant, who they have decided to call Jan. It is similar to her real name, as well as being that of the great van Eyck.

The illusion has been greatly helped by Mistress Harris's help with Jennet's wardrobe. Apprised of the plan, she not only gave it her full support, but even supplied a couple of suits altered to Jennet's size. They have apparently been some years in the laundry's lost property and are starkly different in style; one a plain blue serge, one a magnificent green velvet affair with gold embroidery. It's rather more splendid than Hans's own best suit.

'Who on earth would leave that abandoned in the laundry?' he wondered.

'Best not ask,' was Jennet's response. 'It probably came in for mending and then something happened to the owner that meant they were unable to collect it. On a permanent basis, possibly. These are bloody times.'

Wriothesley has, from what they can tell, completely accepted the artist and assistant story. He doesn't seem to see anything amiss. But then he isn't looking at much apart from himself. He's astonishingly vain about his admittedly good looks, his large, glassy light blue eyes checking his appearance in every reflection going. He's also overweeningly self-important, as much of a pretentious show-off as the reinvention of his name suggests. He refers to himself as 'one'.

Hans and Jennet, meanwhile, refer to him as 'Grisley'. Strictly between themselves, of course.

'Don't you think he's handsome, though?' he asks her.

'I don't go for pretty boys. I prefer the more experienced look.' She runs a finger affectionately down his cheek, kisses his nose.

'I was a pretty boy once,' Hans grumbles.

All the same, it's obvious to them both that beneath Grisley's silken-haired glamour is someone hard-hearted and self-serving. 'But trying to pass himself off as a nobleman, even so,' Jennet says witheringly. 'Have you seen his signet ring? Huge, new and completely invented.'

Hans thinks of Wyatt with his barnacle, and a pang goes through him. It's wonderful to have Jennet, but he still misses his old companion.

'And he's wearing it on the wrong finger.' Jennet is still talking about the signet ring.

He slides her a look; how does she know that?

Nothing seems to escape her notice. She knows that details are all-revealing, that they are everything and the devil is in them, certainly in Grisley's case. She has an artist's sharp insight to go with her artist's eye and increasingly skilled artist's hand. At the rate she's going, she really might be able to help him paint Christina, the less demanding sections anyway.

Grisley is too much of an opportunist to pass up the chance to have Hans capture his own likeness, although he baulks at paying for it.

'I wonder you even mention a fee, Master Holbein! Surely it's all included in the huge sum Master Secretary is paying you!' He stretches his strange light eyes wide in genteel surprise.

Hans does not press the point. Cromwell's actually not paying him much beyond what's fair. But there's nothing to be gained in arguing.

'And you've made one's nose too large.' Grisley is looking critically at the drawing. 'Reduce its size, will you?'

Hans nods at Jennet, who passes him a piece of bread to rub out the offending line. He makes a great play of doing this, and of making fresh marks with his pen. But in reality he has changed nothing, and when he turns the drawing back to Grisley, it's exactly the same. Grisley nods in satisfaction nonetheless. 'You see? One was right, it is much improved.'

The voyage is a stormy one, but Grisley, Hans notes, seems unaffected by seasickness. Perhaps because he does not drink. 'Not in one's profession,' he says, when Hans comments on this. 'One needs one's wits about one. To make sure no one is pulling the wool over one's eyes.'

Hans thinks of Wyatt, who was rarely sober but who had the wool pulled over his eyes by one person alone, a person due to pay a heavy price. But not yet, obviously. With Grisley watching like a hawk, it's going to be tricky not to give Master Secretary exactly the portrait he wants. Especially as the rumours are intensifying that the emperor and the King of France are to be formally allied by and with the Pope. In Nice, soon, the story goes. If England is not to be completely alone, and correspondingly completely vulnerable, marrying Henry to a Hapsburg is becoming a matter of urgency.

Under a clear blue spring sky, after a few days' hard riding, Mechelen approaches. Hans thinks of Anne taking this road as an eleven-year-old, to the court of the Regent Margaret. Nearly a quarter of a century later, here he is himself, heading for the court of the Regent Mary, Margaret's niece. Whose own niece, Christina, is a prospective bride for Anne's ex-husband. It's crazy, all so tightly connected.

Jennet paces beside him, in superb control of her horse. How come she's such an excellent, elegant rider? Another question for another time, like so much about Jennet. He wonders what her story is, whether he'll ever find it out.

As they enter the city, Anne's description of it comes back to him: the spacious wide streets, the elegant buildings, the squares and canals. All is exactly as she said. Jennet looks about her, exclaiming and admiring. Even Grisley looks impressed.

In the centre is the regent's palace; patterned red brick with steep stepped gables. The guards at the gates are expecting them and wave them through. They ride into a grand courtyard. Walls pierced with arches give views of lovely gardens.

Through one of the arches a young woman in a rose-coloured gown is playing with a child. It's roughly clad – a servant's child, probably – while the woman is very obviously of the court. Her magnificent dress is so heavily jewelled Hans can see the glitter from here. He can't see her face, only her tall, elegant figure, but he guesses she's beautiful. And high-spirited; there's delight in her laughter as she throws a ball. The child whoops as it hurries after it.

It's a lovely picture and Hans's fingers itch for his charcoal.

'Holbein!' Grisley bawls, breaking rudely into his thoughts. He's on the steps at the palace entrance. Off his horse and glaring impatiently. Jennet, meanwhile, is handing her mount to the groom. Time to go in.

The palace interior is cool and shady and has an orderly air. They follow liveried servants down a series of corridors.

A gasp from Jennet, who has paused by a doorway. Mounted against the gold silk damask on the wall is the van Eyck that Anne mentioned. The couple standing together, the woman in the green gown, the man in the large fur hat. The round mirror in the background, the small dog. It's a moment of intense connection. He pictures her looking at it, the small girl with great curious black eyes.

'Ridiculous hat.' Grisley has come up behind him and is looking at the picture too. He's a fine one to talk, given what he is wearing. Dressed to the nines in his best slashed silk, and on his bonnet an ostrich feather of improbable proportions. He stalks off, gesturing imperiously for them to follow.

They wait in a magnificent hall for the Archduchess Mary. It has great windows and a curved roof like the lid of a chest. At the far end, pillars in black marble flank an elaborate black throne above which spread the black wings of the Hapsburg double eagle.

Hans stares at this famous symbol, more powerful by far than either the red Tudor dragon or the blue and gold Valois lilies. He hopes desperately that Wyatt is right and the emperor is not serious about marrying his niece to Henry. Perhaps the Regent Mary will take a leaf out of the Duchesse de Guise's book and send them away with a flea in their collective ear. Or threaten to have them horsewhipped. He'd particularly like to see Grisley horsewhipped.

But the woman who now enters the room does not look the horsewhipping type. She is middle-aged, dignified and obviously sad. Her eyes have red rims, as if she has been weeping. She takes her place on the great black throne of the Hapsburgs with an air of gloomy resignation. 'So,' she intones listlessly, 'you come from the court of Henry of England.'

'What did she say?' asks Grisley.

Hans looks at him; is it possible he has no French? A diplomat coming to handle a delicate negotiation at a European court? When it's the language of diplomacy?

He translates, and Grisley bows, so deeply his nose almost touches the floor. 'One has the inestimable honour of serving that great prince,' he declares in English as he rises back up.

The regent looks at him wearily. 'My brother the emperor tells me that your king wishes to marry my niece. You are here to make a portrait of her.'

'Not One,' exclaims Grisley when this is translated. 'One is here to discuss the terms of the marriage agreement.' He waves his outsized signet ring at Hans. 'Holbein here is doing the painting.'

Something jumps in the archduchess's face at this. The dark eyes seem to brighten as they look at him. 'You are the famous painter Hans Holbein?'

Hans bows and admits that he is. Grisley, meanwhile, looks affronted. He's the celebrity here.

'You are famous for the truth of your pictures,' the regent remarks.

'It has been my life's work,' Hans assures her, gratified.

She says something then, in French, that he only just catches. But he must have heard it wrong, because it sounds like *Yes, that's what I was afraid of.*

'When can we meet your niece?' Grisley demands. 'We need to obtain her likeness and conclude the business.'

Mary raises her head. Hans senses, for the first time, a slight rallying of the spirit. 'A good question,' she says. 'Christina is missing.'

'Missing?' echoes Grisley, his light blue eyes bulging. '*Missing?*'

'For the moment at least,' the regent returns calmly. 'But don't worry, we'll find her. She can't have gone far.'

## *Chapter Thirty-Eight*

'Wyatt was wrong then,' Hans says to Jennet as they wander through the gardens. Christina has still not been found, and while Grisley paces and growls inside the palace, they've gone outside and are killing time among the fountains and flower beds.

Jennet has stooped to examine a flower. 'Wrong about what?' she asks, burying her shapely nose in the scented petals.

'He said the emperor wasn't serious about the king and Christina. Didn't support the marriage.'

It may only be March, but the sun is warm, and they're sufficiently far from the palace for Jennet to pull off her black apprentice's bonnet. Her golden curls cascade over the shoulders of her blue woollen doublet. Hans would like to paint her like this. Sometime. For now, however, there are more pressing matters. He feels disappointed. Angry. Irritated with Wyatt.

'Poncing about in Madrid, sending inaccurate information.'

'It might not be inaccurate; it might be some sort of double bluff,' counters Jennet. 'Or even triple. You never know.'

He looks at her. 'What's a triple bluff?'

A shrug of the blue shoulders. 'No idea. But Wyatt would know.'

Hans stares glumly up at the sky. If he's annoyed with Wyatt, he's even more annoyed with Jennet for defending him. He can't help it; there's still some jealousy there. All the same, he wishes he were here. Unlike Grisley, very unlike Grisley in fact, Wyatt is clever. He would think of something.

'There's one possibility,' Jennet muses. 'Probably only one, but it could save us.'

He looks at her, startled. 'What?'

She lifts her golden hair with both hands, shakes it out, lets it flop on her shoulders. 'Well, if Christina's not Henry's type, he won't be interested.'

Wyatt had said the same thing, Hans remembers. How Henry wasn't really interested in dynastic marriages at all. How he was entirely led by his cock. Chose his last two wives because he fancied them. Married for love.

'If she's ugly, you mean?' he asks Jennet.

It's the wrong thing to say. She looks at him angrily. 'Ugly,' she says hotly, 'is a horrible word to use. Especially about a woman. Oversimplifies it, too. You of all people know that what someone looks like is only part of the story. *Not his type* is what I said.'

Duly chastised, and not a little ashamed, Hans nods. 'Not his type,' he repeats obediently. He's not entirely sure what she means.

They've walked right to the end of the grounds now, reaching the kitchen garden: pleached fruit trees blossoming on red-brick walls, salad lettuces in plump green rows, herbs in profusion. The palace buildings are small in the distance. Hans glances over; perhaps, he says, they should go back, see what, if anything, is happening.

'But it's so beautiful here,' sighs Jennet. 'And we get so little time alone.'

They sit on the lush grass. Then they lie in it. He draws her to him, lifts her hair, buries his face in her neck. Lust roars to life within him. But Jennet has drawn away, sat up.

'What's the matter?' he asks.

'Can't you hear it?'

Birdsong? His own racing, thumping, excited heart?

'Crying.'

Now that she mentions it, he can. A low sobbing, coming from somewhere quite close. They scramble to their feet, start to look around.

'There?' Jennet points to a small hut built into the angle of the wall. The sort gardeners keep their tools in, or shelter in on rainy days.

As they get closer, the tears sound more like frustration than sorrow. A dismissed gardener? A wronged maid? They approach with trepidation.

It's shadowy inside, but they can see someone there. Sitting on a pile of sacks, hands over her face, magnificent pink satin dress spread about her, is the young woman Hans spotted through the archway. Hours ago, when they arrived. Has she lost the child? he's wondering vaguely, when she leaps to her feet and stares at them in alarm.

Jennet works it out first. 'You're Duchess Christina!'

Up close, she's younger than she looked from a distance. And yes, beautiful. A high, bright colour, unusual almond-shaped eyes. Rich, loose brown hair. Her dress, tight-bodiced to show her tall, supple figure, is absolutely covered in pearls, embroidery and elaborate trimmings. A full-length painting is going to take years.

Nor is that the only problem. Christina is Henry's type, no doubt about it. There isn't a man on the planet whose type she wouldn't be. There's no question that the king will want to marry her. Cromwell's position will consequently be unassailable.

One hope alone remains. The possibility that Christina is mad flits across Hans's mind. Insanity runs in the Hapsburg family; one of Katherine of Aragon's sisters, he seems to remember. Madness, now that would help. Henry wouldn't want a lunatic; he's enough of one himself.

'What are you doing here?' he asks her gently.

'What does it look like?' she snaps. 'Hiding.'

'From whom?'

'You.'

'*Us?*'

'I saw you arrive earlier. You've come from England to arrange my marriage to . . .' she screws up her face in disgust, 'that *king* of yours.'

Hans blinks. 'We're not doing the arranging. We've come to paint you.'

'So you *are* doing the arranging,' Christina retorts, bitterly triumphant.

'No, I just explained. We're painters.'

'Yes, but whether the marriage goes ahead depends on what you paint. Your king will make his mind up on the strength of this portrait.'

This is unarguable, so Hans doesn't argue. He can see where this is going now.

'And it will be a beautiful picture, won't it?' Christina demands, fiercely.

Reluctantly Hans admits that yes, he wishes it were otherwise, but what else can it be? She's a beautiful girl in what he guesses is her best court dress.

Christina's eyes glitter with angry tears. 'But I don't want to look beautiful. I don't want to marry the King of England.'

And we don't want you to marry him either, Hans is thinking. But with Grisley on the one hand and your appearance on the other, what can we do?

The duchess's hands cover her face again. 'I know all about him,' she says through her fingers. 'Katherine of Aragon was my great-aunt. And my mother and Aunt Mary shared a classroom with Anne Boleyn when they were all girls here at the court of Margaret of Austria. Anne was very clever and my aunt liked her very much. She couldn't believe what happened to her.' She peels her fingers away, looks up challengingly. 'My aunt thinks the charges against Anne were made up. Because Henry had tired of her and wanted to get rid of her. Is that true?'

There's a silence as Hans searches for what to say. Then Jennet, who he's assumed has understood nothing of this French exchange, says quietly, and in French, 'Yes, it is.' He glances at her in astonishment.

'Thank you for your honesty.' The duchess gives them both a faint, rueful smile. 'And now I will be honest with you. I have no wish to end up on the block at the Tower of London. Or die of cancer and neglect – and I have also heard rumours of poison – in some remote and rotting fortress. I don't want to leave Aunt Mary either. We're very close. She's been like a mother to me, the nearest to one I've ever known.' She's holding high her proud Hapsburg head, but her bottom lip is definitely trembling. She's so young, of course.

'Can't your aunt object to the marriage?' Hans asks. The Duchesse de Guise did, after all. And she was much less powerful than the Regent of the Netherlands.

'She's tried. She's in complete despair about it. She doesn't want to lose me and she thinks Henry is a monster. But my uncle Charles – the Holy Roman Emperor, as you know – wants this match and she has to do what he says. As do I,' Christina sighs. 'As I have done all my life.'

It's so like Anne. The powerless girl, the ruthless family, with the emperor playing the Thomas Boleyn role. The dangers of high-status marriages. Jennet was completely right about them. And it's sickening, the thought of having to help the process along. 'I wish there was something I could do,' Hans says.

Christina's eyebrows lift a little. 'Perhaps there is.'

Hans shrugs. 'Like what?'

The almond eyes have a bold, speculative look. 'This painting you're doing of me. You could always make it unflattering.'

'Unflattering?'

Christina smooths her satin skirts. 'People are kind enough to say I am beautiful,' she says. 'Lively, clever. All manner of agreeable things. But such qualities, even if it were true that I possessed them, are dangerous in a situation like mine. I do not want to attract Henry of England. On the contrary, I want to *repel* him.'

There's what sounds like a snort from Jennet.

'I see that,' Hans says. 'But—'

'So make me look horrible.' Christina's leaning forward, a pleading look in her brown eyes. 'You can do it, I know. My father was painted by Lucas Cranach, who made him look absolutely hideous.'

'Cranach made everyone look absolutely hideous,' Hans remarks. 'Him and Quentin Metsys both.'

This makes Christina smile. And here at last are the famous dimples; it's no exaggeration to say that they become her right excellently well. 'So take a leaf from their books! Or, rather, a strand from their brushes.'

Hans shakes his head sadly. 'If I could,' he says, 'I would.'

The dimples vanish. Christina frowns imperiously. 'You can't?'

'I'm sorry.'

'Because I'm really that amazingly beautiful?' Her tone is sarcastic.

'No. I mean, yes. You are very beautiful. But it's not that.'

'What is it, then?'

He takes a deep breath. 'To make you look ugly wouldn't be

true. And my entire life as an artist has been dedicated to representing the truth.' Even to his own ears he sounds pompous, but what can he do?

Christina doesn't argue. 'Oh,' she says. 'Of course. I see. Yes, well, you must uphold your artistic ideals. And I must obey the emperor. And end up on the block at the Tower of London.' She rises to her feet in a rustle of pink satin. 'I'm going outside. I need fresh air.'

She sweeps out, and Jennet hurtles over. 'For God's sake, Hans. Why can't you make her look terrible in the picture?'

His hands are over his face. He doesn't want to meet her accusing gaze. 'I can't.'

'You have to!' she hisses. 'That poor girl. She'll be a lamb to the slaughter otherwise.'

'I can't help that.'

'Because you're the painter of truth?' Jennet demands. 'Do you want Cromwell to get away with everything? I thought we were here for revenge.'

'We are, it's just—'

'What if Henry does send her to the block in a couple of years?' she cuts in furiously. 'How would you feel then? Can't you drop your precious principles just for once? Paint something other than exactly what you see?'

He turns away, miserable, exasperated, frustrated. There's no point arguing; she'll never understand. No one can who doesn't happen to be him. It's not a question of being callous, or self-indulgent, or not caring, or any of the other things Jennet clearly thinks it is. It's that he really can't do anything else. Over a lifetime of work, his art and his principles have become so deeply intertwined that he can't paint anything but the truth, not even to save his life. Or anyone else's, come to that.

'The only way it would work,' he grinds through his teeth, 'is to paint her with a black bag on her head.'

Outside, Christina is standing in the sunshine. Hans braces himself for another angry appeal, another attempt to talk him round. But she's lifting her face to the warmth and looks quite calm. 'They say there's no sunshine in England,' she remarks.

'There's a bit,' he offers.

'About noon on the third Wednesday in July,' says Jennet.

## *Chapter Thirty-Nine*

The three of them walk slowly together. For their different reasons, none are in a hurry to return to the palace.

They drift into a small ornamental garden. Its central fountain features a chubby little statue of Cupid. Christina walks to it, arranges her shining dress on the stone edge of its large, shallow bowl. 'Do you know what I would really like?' she muses. 'If I could have anything I wanted?'

Is she talking to them, or to Cupid? Unsure, they say nothing as Cupid smiles back at her, his dimpled cheeks not unlike her own.

Independence, Hans expects her to say, as Anne so often had. To escape from the power of others.

'To marry for love and be happy. That's all.'

She's changed tack. Opened another flank on his sense of guilt. It's such a simple, ordinary wish.

'People imagine it's magnificent to be a Hapsburg, and the daughter of a king,' Christina goes on. She's still addressing Cupid, but obviously she's talking to them too. 'Yet I have not found it so. When I was three, my father lost his throne of Denmark. He probably deserved to; he didn't behave very well. He had a mistress, the daughter of a merchant, who he refused to give up when he married my mother, Isabella of Austria. Eventually the mistress was poisoned and someone who actually might not have been responsible was executed. This led to unrest and eventually the uprising against my father.'

She stares down into the water and stirs it with her hand. 'After that, I roamed, a small child of three, with my family from country to country. My father was trying to raise support from his fellow monarchs to regain his throne. None were terribly sympathetic; they felt he'd caused his own problems. But they were all very sorry for my mother, a Hapsburg princess put in such a humiliating position. She died on our travels, aged only twenty-four, having caught a cold in a storm.'

As Jennet murmurs her sympathies, Hans wonders how much worse he could possibly feel. Poor Christina. Her short life has been so difficult. And about to get more so, because of him.

The duchess shrugs. 'I was too young to really remember her. But with my mother dead, my Hapsburg relatives swung into action. I became the ward of the emperor, who lost no time launching me as a pawn on the political marriage market. The offers soon started to come in. Francesco Sforza, Duke of Milan, was the chosen groom. I was only just twelve, and he thirty-nine.'

*Twelve!* Jennet puts her hand to her mouth. Christina chuckles, showing the dimples again. 'Being a Hapsburg isn't for the squeamish,' she says. 'And I was fortunate really.'

'Fortunate?' Hans echoes.

'Yes,' the young duchess says brightly. 'I liked Francesco. His health wasn't the best, admittedly. He had survived a poisoning attempt, but only just. He had paralysed hands, used a cane to walk, and there was concern he would never have heirs, if you get my meaning. He was a bit serious and religious, possibly, but he was kind to me. He did his best to make me feel welcome. He decorated the palace and there were hunting parties and music, both of which I love. And the Milanese people took me to their hearts. For the eighteen months our marriage lasted, I was the nearest to happy I'd ever been.' She pauses, bites her lip. 'Then Francesco died, and I was a widow at thirteen.'

'A widow at thirteen,' Jennet repeats.

'Yes, which is when I came to Aunt Mary in Brussels. Where I am happy and safe and can consider my future. There have been various suggestions of new husbands; the Prince of Savoy was one until he died. Then the Pope's nephew floated past, then the son of the King of France. And of course, now, the King of England. But I am tired of being a piece on the international marital chess-board. I feel that I have done my Hapsburg duty. After all I have been through, I should like to marry for love. I am only young, after all.'

Jennet looks at her thoughtfully. 'Do you,' she asks, 'by any chance still have your widow's weeds? Your black mourning clothes?'

'In a chest somewhere, yes. Why do you ask?'

'Are they very heavy and concealing?'

'I should say so,' the young duchess snorts. 'The Italians take mourning very seriously. I had to wear solid black for two years, not a strand of hair showing, no jewels apart from the ruby Francesco gave me on our wedding day.' She extends white fingers to display the red stone among many others.

'Two years?' Jennet repeats.

'Yes, the minimum period,' Christina explains. 'Some people are in mourning far longer. For ever in some cases. But I looked so completely awful I stopped wearing it as soon as possible. It was like a huge black bag.'

'A huge black bag,' Jennet muses. 'Just imagine that.' She's looking straight at Hans.

The last hour has been all frantic activity, but you wouldn't know it to look at Hans and Jennet, now standing calmly before the regent's throne. Archduchess Mary, too, is composed, her previous gloomy manner completely gone. Her eyes no longer look red; there is, in fact, a subdued sparkle to them.

Grisley is all agitation, having been told that Christina is found and expected any moment. He's pacing before the Hapsburg double eagle, singing Henry's praises. 'If your niece was matched to my master, she would be matched with the gentlest gentleman that ever lived,' he asserts. 'His is a nature so benign that few have ever heard an angry word from him.'

As Jennet tries to suppress a sudden coughing fit, the regent nods politely. Her red lips are faintly smiling; it's not impossible that she's amused.

Light heels on marble. A figure appears at the door. 'Ah,' Archduchess Mary says happily. 'Here she is at last. My niece Christina.'

As Grisley gazes, stunned, Hans and Jennet exchange triumphant glances. Together with the regent, they saw Christina less than an hour ago. Her appearance now is no surprise to them.

The young duchess glides in, hands folded, eyes downcast. And dressed completely in black. The dazzling duchess has become the mourning widow. The tight-bodiced court gown has given way to heavy black robes. What shape she has is completely concealed. Her pretty hair, too, hidden under a severe black cap that makes her seem much older. Her face, from which all colour seems drained, is expressionless, without a hint of a smile.

'*Jesu Christi*,' Grisley mutters through his silky beard. 'Thought she was supposed to be beautiful. What a frump.'

'What a rude man,' Christina remarks in Italian, another language Grisley does not speak. 'And such strange eyes, like glass balls.'

It's all Hans can do not to grin the broadest grin. He'll have no trouble depicting Christina exactly as she is now. To the truly discerning, those prepared to look closer and deeper, she will still seem beautiful. But to Henry and Cromwell, she'll be blank-faced in dreary robes. As if she's wearing a black bag.

Grisley rounds on him. 'You can't paint her like this, Holbein. She needs to put some proper clothes on. She was the former leading lady of the Milanese court. We need silks, satins. Embroidery, jewels.'

Hans shrugs. 'I can hardly tell her that. I'm just the painter.'

Grisley gives him a look of glassy exasperation, then clears his throat and raises his voice to Christina. 'Madam, pray return to your chamber and change.'

'Pray excuse me, I don't understand English,' Christina returns in demure Italian. She does understand, of course, perfectly well. It's just another way to tease Grisley.

Hans steps forward. 'I can translate. I have some Italian from when I was travelling there.'

'*Grazie*, Maestro Holbein,' Christina says soberly. 'Perhaps you could explain to this rude man with eyes like glass balls that I cannot change these clothes because I am a widow mourning my husband Francesco Sforza, the late Duke of Milan.'

It's to be hoped that Grisley doesn't notice there are creases in the skirt, exactly as if it's just been dragged from a storage chest. Or smell the camphor that hangs in the air.

He doesn't seem to. He is watching them both suspiciously. 'What's she saying?'

Hans translates, and Grisley slaps a hand to his face in frustration. He yelps as the oversized signet ring makes painful contact with his eyebrow. 'You are joking? Oh, for God's sake. Sforza died years ago.'

Hans repeats this in Italian, wincing at Grisley's lack of manners. He's a poor specimen of a diplomat. Wyatt would be appalled.

'I was very fond of my husband and regret his passing every day,' Christina replies with dignity.

'Fond of him!' Grisley snorts when Hans translates. 'She was twelve when she married him and he was nearly forty. Paralysed into the bargain. And couldn't get it up, or so I hear.'

Grisley is contemptible, thinks Hans as he explains, confining himself to the first two sentences, although Christina has obviously understood them all.

'Francesco was very kind to me,' she murmurs. 'Possibly I will never again find such a husband.'

Grisley sneers when this is translated for him. 'Not in that bloody awful outfit.' He folds his arms sulkily, not easy given his ridiculously elaborate sleeves. 'The king won't even look at her. Unless he has some kind of nun fixation. But he's just dissolved the monasteries, so I think we know how he feels about that.'

He looks Christina rudely up and down. 'Tell her,' he commands Hans, 'that once she's changed her clothes, she'll make a most suitable Queen of England.'

'Tell him,' Christina replies, with spirit, 'that court mourning at Milan can go on indefinitely. As for being Queen of England, I fear I'll be most unsuitable. Having just the one neck.'

Hans decides to translate only the first sentence.

# *Chapter Forty*

They're back in London; it's only taken five days. Grisley was in no hurry to return, keen to put off facing the music – or, rather, Cromwell – for as long as possible. He's obviously dreading showing him the portrait.

Christina gave them a three-hour sitting for the sketch that became the painting. A long time for a high-spirited girl not to smile. But Hans warned her that the appearance of the dimples could ruin everything. She must hood her eyes, look plain and sober.

The finished portrait might represent the wreck of Cromwell's hopes, but it's a step forward for Hans as an artist. He's never painted anything quite like this before, so austere and yet so magnificent. Christina's all in black, for sure, but the way he's caught the velvet of her coat, the soft brown fur trim at its edge, even for him it's extraordinary.

'Makes you want to touch it,' Jennet says. She's helped with the black brushstrokes, starting with the very bottom of the hem. But her contribution has been more than that.

Hans made the sketch in the regent's cabinet, an ornate room whose details would have taken an age to capture. When he began the painting, it was Jennet's idea to simplify the background and save time by making it all one shade of blue.

'Anything but that old green curtain,' she said with a smile.

Hans was indignant; what was wrong with his curtain? The same emerald drape had appeared behind Erasmus, Thomas More, William Warham and even the French ambassadors. It's one of his most reliable props, travelling with him from workroom to workroom, its purpose to add movement and the play of light as well as strong colour.

'A plain blue background might look too flat,' he said to her. 'Too stark.'

She accepted the point, thought about it and suggested adding shadow behind Christina. This worked much better. It looks dramatic, dynamic. An incredibly real Christina seems to be about to step forward, hold out her hand, open those gently red lips and say something. There's an air of possibility that is exactly appropriate given that this picture is intended to free her. Hans has painted her walking into her future, one she will hopefully choose herself, her face full of quiet authority. With possibly a touch of Hapsburg haughtiness.

He has also made her tall, slightly taller than she really is. She looks imposing, and the black cap makes her age hard to fathom. She has an eternal quality, untethered from the here and now. And all this is true to her. Nothing is hidden, disguised or distorted. Here is a beautiful princess, just shown in an unexpected way. Quiet luxury, as opposed to the ear-bursting splendour of the picture he did of Henry.

But he very much doubts Henry or Cromwell will see it that way.

They made excellent time on the return journey. The weather on the roads was good and the wind on the Narrow Sea perfect. The ship fairly shot back to Dover. Grisley kept mainly to his part of the vessel, avoiding their company, fretting, plotting. But all in vain, Hans is sure of that.

Spring in London is not as far advanced as in Brussels; what was flowering there is still in bud here. This tightness is reflected in Baron Cromwell of Wimbledon's plump face. There's a cat's-bum scrunch to his mouth as he looks at Christina.

'Well,' says the lord of Wimbledon, after scrutinising the portrait a while. 'I suppose she has a certain understated elegance.'

'A definite *je ne sais quoi*,' agrees Grisley nervously.

Hans and Jennet glance at each other. It's as much French as either has heard him manage before.

Master Secretary stares at him. 'You say,' he remarks, 'that you couldn't get her out of the weeds? Widow's weeds,' he adds irritably, as his man looks confused.

'Unfortunately, it wasn't possible, Master Secretary,' Grisley hastens to assure him. 'The court mourning at Milan can go on indefinitely.'

'Is that what they told you?'

Grisley's shining locks swirl round his head as he eagerly confirms this. 'Yes, Master Secretary.'

'Interesting.' Cromwell's small, sharp eyes skewer into him. 'The minimum period was two years when I lived in Milan. A young girl like Christina would have been out of it for almost a year by now. Times have changed, evidently.'

Grisley's Adam's apple bounces in panic.

The small, sharp eyes are on Hans now. 'It also seems,' Cromwell remarks, 'that reports of the duchess's great beauty were somewhat exaggerated.'

Hans meets his gaze steadily. 'As Gris . . . Risley says, it was a challenging situation.'

'That outfit is certainly challenging. Challenges one to guess her shape, her hair colour, whether she has teeth or ears.'

'I could only paint what I saw,' Hans says firmly. 'The truth.' He hesitates. 'Perhaps,' he begins tentatively, 'if you think the lady unsuitable . . .'

'Which I have to say I do.'

*Well, in that case don't send for her*, is on the tip of Hans's tongue. Then Grisley rushes in where angels fear to tread, defending himself and his recent mission.

'Of course she's going to be suitable!' He gestures at the portrait. 'This hints at inner strength, resilience, nobility. All the qualities necessary for a queen of England.'

Cromwell explodes with sardonic laughter. 'Including looking as if she's wearing a black bag? For your information,' he growls, 'the qualities necessary for a queen of England have changed somewhat. Strength, nobility and . . . what was the other one? Resilience, yes. Well, we're not looking for those any more. We've been down that road a couple of times already, not entirely successfully. These days we're more about complete unquestioning obedience and the wish above all to please. Which, to be frank, I rather doubt this picture will.'

Grisley now looks pointedly at Hans, but Master Secretary's eyes remain on the diplomat. Grisley has drawn the fire, Hans realises with relief. He is taking the blame.

Cromwell shifts beneath his furs, on which his great gold chain of office sits heavily. 'Well,' he says. 'Time to show the lovely lady to our high and puissant prince. See how she goes down. I'm not optimistic.'

Hans and Jennet begin to wrap Christina in her protective cloths, ready for the journey to the Privy Chamber, when the messenger hurries in, wild-eyed and sweating. He scrabbles in his bag and produces a letter. 'For you, Master Secretary.'

Cromwell takes it in his plump hands, examines the seal. Hans is close enough to recognise the Hapsburg double eagle. From the Regent Mary? The emperor? And presumably about Christina. Has she married someone else? Is she ill? God forbid, has she died? Cromwell's little eyes switch from side to side as he reads. But his expression gives nothing away.

Finally he looks up. His fat face is wreathed in smiles. Clearly the communication has been entirely positive so far as he is concerned.

Hans frowns. 'My lord?'

'The Regent of the Netherlands writes in her capacity as the guardian of Christina of Milan. She has heard from the emperor concerning the marriage between the duchess and the king.'

'What has he said?' asks Grisley.

Hans holds his breath. Is Uncle Charles sending Christina to England in her finest silks and jewels?

'The emperor, in his infinite wisdom, wishes for a papal dispensation before the wedding can take place,' Master Secretary informs them. He's smiling broadly.

Grisley gasps. 'On what grounds?'

'Not sure. Does it matter? Let me see.' Cromwell squints back at the letter. 'Oh, consanguinity. That old chestnut.'

'Consanguinity with whom?' Grisley presses.

'Not sure. Could be anyone. These royal families, they're all related. Henry was married to her aunt three wives ago; perhaps it's that. Who cares? I don't! A papal dispensation!' Cromwell slaps his knee. 'Who doesn't love one of those!'

Grisley is clearly wondering if his superior has gone mad. 'Do you think we'll get one?'

Master Secretary looks at him, incredulous. 'Are you joking? I spent seven years trying to get one last time. Changed the laws of England, the Church of all Europe, executed any amount of naysayers and still got nowhere. And there's even less chance of it happening this time, because in case anyone's noticed, the king has broken away from Rome. The Pope is so inclined to help him out there's even been talk of excommunication.'

Grisley's bulging eyes are full of confusion. He's trying and failing to work out the positives in this. 'One thought you wanted this marriage,' he says to Cromwell.

'One did!' his master explodes. 'I did! And so did the king! Until you brought back this nun.' He gestures at the portrait, then glances at its painter. 'No offence, dear boy.'

'None taken,' Hans shrugs.

'But now, thank God, I don't have to try and persuade him to marry her!' He pumps his fist, bares his teeth. 'Saved!'

Hans slides a glance at Jennet. It's a bittersweet moment. Christina has escaped, but so has their enemy. Cromwell has the luck of the devil, probably because he is the devil. What now? Master Secretary is looking at Hans, his fat face radiating delight.

'We don't need your picture any more,' he breezes, 'sorry about that, dear boy. But we'll be looking for another wife now, so don't put your paintbrushes away just yet.'

# *Chapter Forty-One*

*I was right,* Wyatt writes from Madrid. *The emperor never intended the wedding to take place. This papal dispensation is a complete red herring. Just part of the game he and François are playing with Henry, and with each other. He just wanted to scupper any possibility of Cromwell resuming negotiations with any French princesses.*

The Holy Roman Emperor, Hans thinks, must have a character as strange as his looks. Causing his family such misery over something that was never going to happen. It had been real enough to poor Christina and her aunt.

*But of course,* Wyatt goes on, *there's fat chance of that, as you and I know more than most. The Tudor name is mud all over France, and now the Netherlands too. Charles and François are doing an excellent job of making sure Henry never marries again. Every eligible woman on the continent of Europe now knows about England's murderous king and the way he treats his queens.*

As he throws this letter in the fire, Hans bites his lip. Wyatt had ended with the usual expressions of reassurance, but the possibility of bringing Cromwell down over the business of finding a wife seems more and more unlikely. What wife, where?

Perhaps Cromwell has drawn the same conclusion, because things on that front now go quiet. Hans takes the opportunity to move to a small house in the city. A home of his own, at last, after all these wandering years.

It's in Aldgate, ten minutes from the river and a boat to whatever court he's required at. Within the parish of St Katharine Cree, just along from where the great maypole gives the church of St Andrew Undershaft its name. A prosperous district where the air is fresh and the houses are new, with good-sized gardens, it's the perfect spot for the established painter of portraits to live with the woman who may be his mistress, may be his wife. But in the city no one asks; here we mind our own business.

And Hans's business is going well, no doubt about it. With Jennet to prepare the paper, fashion the brushes, ready the boards, make the charcoal, grind the paints (all except the dangerous white lead; Hans does that himself), the work is positively flying out. He's always been industrious, but now he's more productive than ever. There must be hardly anyone at court, servants included, who remains unpainted. Few of the provincial wealthy too. Even someone from Cornwall, the other day, a county apparently in England's far south-west and famous for its tin and cream.

Now that she works with him at home, Jennet rarely dresses in her apprentice clothes. But she puts them on to go with him on his latest commission from Cromwell, one in which the baron is putting great personal store. The portrait of Henry's infant heir will be Master Secretary's contribution at the New Year gift-giving, when the king receives presents from his courtiers, the more expensive the better. What he gives them in return is a brutally public indication of exactly where they stand in the pecking order. Something costly if you're in favour. And if you're not, then, well.

Cromwell is in favour; certainly nothing suggests that he isn't. He's more than survived the Christina affair, successfully persuading the king that the emperor was to blame. Even so, he's keen to protect his position. He wants Hans to paint Edward as a miniature Henry and has commissioned an elaborate suit of clothes for the baby prince to wear. It's a scaled-down replica of his father's outfits, in Henry's favourite red and gold, faithful in every detail right down to the ostrich-feather bonnet. Edward will even hold a gold rattle in the style of a sceptre and raise the other hand in kingly benediction.

'Really?' says Jennet when this is explained to her. 'He's a one-year-old child and won't sit still for a minute.'

Hans agrees. And normally he'd object to this level of direction, but it's not really worth making a fuss. He needs to keep Cromwell on side, just in case. *Keep Master Secretary thinking you're his loyal painter,* Wyatt writes, *while I stay here looking for opportunities to make mischief.*

As usual where Henry and his family are involved, there's text in this picture. Not content with flattering the father through his son with the image, Master Secretary is driving the message home with words. He's got one of his rising toadies to write a fawning Latin inscription.

*Little one, emulate your father and be the heir of his virtue, the world contains nothing greater. Heaven and earth could scarcely produce such a son whose glory would surpass that of such a father. Only equal the deeds of your parent and men can wish for no more.*

'Yeuch,' says Jennet. 'Surely even Henry will think that's a bit much.'

'If anything, he'll think it's an understatement.' Then Hans looks at her sharply. 'You can read Latin?'

'A little.'

'How come?'

Her eyes meet his, full of sad exasperation. 'How do you think? My mistress taught me, of course. To read, to speak French, to know some Latin, to ride.'

Hans bows his head, remembering how this was a point of

contention with Cromwell. Anne had wanted to school poor women with some of the money from the monasteries. That they should be educated whatever their background was one of her most passionate beliefs. Grief tears through him, not just for what he and Jennet have lost, but for what the country in general has. All the good she might have done.

Prince Edward turns out to be a winsome child. Presumably because, as yet, he has no idea of the dynasty he's been born into, the father he has and the mother he hasn't. He has a nurse, who seems kind, and a vast household of chamberlains and liveried servants, none of whom seem of any practical use.

The prince has a large head like his father, and something of Henry's impassiveness. But there's no trace of Jane Seymour. Not just in her son, but anywhere. Not because her devices have been smashed like Anne's, and all paintings destroyed. Rather, because she wasn't around long enough for any to be made in the first place.

Hans wonders again, with a clutch of panic, if this really is it for Henry's queens. There's been no more talk of a new wife, of someone to add a Duke of York and a Duke of Gloucester to the nursery in which, at the moment, Prince Edward plays alone.

And if that's the case, where and when will the next chance come from for him and Wyatt? Who is anyway not here while Cromwell very much is. Waxing more powerful, bold and successful with every passing day. And, to add insult to injury, using Hans to help him.

'It's more than two years since she died,' Jennet frets. 'And we're no nearer to avenging her than we were then.'

# *Chapter Forty-Two*

Easily moved like all bullies, the king is touched by Cromwell's gift. Hans's painting of his son and heir delights him; the great hall of the palace fairly shakes with his appreciation. But then something happens that has Henry roaring down the corridors for rather different reasons, Cromwell scurrying behind him.

Hans, putting the finishing touches to a courtier's portrait in his rooms near the Privy Chamber, can easily guess what the rumpus is about. Mistress Harris delivered the news earlier.

*This is it, Holbein.* Wyatt's handwriting is more than usually fast and shaky, his excitement coming off the page. *This is our chance. After all these years, after all the setbacks, we're going to get our man.*

*The impossible has really happened. The emperor and the King of France have signed a treaty in Nice. To make things even worse, it's brokered by the Pope. Cromwell's nightmare has come true. The Empire, France and the Papal States are now united. England is isolated.*

*Possibly even vulnerable to invasion, because any force led by these allies, either singly or united, may find support in England among the old families and religious conservatives who never accepted the break with Rome. The Tudor dynasty is planted in shallow soil and it has not yet put down roots. Henry could well be overthrown.*

*Cromwell is under the greatest pressure of his life. England needs a new alliance, and Henry needs a new wife to consolidate it. But he won't get one; he's tried them all and they've all said no. Cromwell is finally completely defeated.*

*Who is there left to stand with England against the three greatest powers in Europe, and have an eligible bride as well?*

'The Schmalkaldic League,' says Cromwell.

It's a few days later, three glorious Aldgate days celebrating Wyatt's news, but now Hans is back at Whitehall in Master Secretary's office. 'The what league?' he asks.

Cromwell repeats it. 'Not the easiest of names, I admit.'

'I'm German,' says Hans, 'and even I can't say it. The Small . . .'

'Schmalkaldic, Schmalkaldic, Schmalkaldic, Schmalkaldic!' Cromwell gets up from his desk and almost capers about the room. 'The Treaty of the Schmalkaldic Alliance, named after some town called Schmalkald. But you're right, dear boy. You'd think they could have done us all a favour and picked somewhere more pronounceable.'

Hans watches in amazement, and growing apprehension. It's possible that Cromwell has gone mad, sent over the edge by stress. But he does not look mad; on the contrary, he seems rational as well as delighted.

He shakes his head, uncomprehending. 'But . . . who are they?'

'A league of states in the German north!' Cromwell has danced over to the window and is looking out.

'There's a league of states in the German north?' It's the first Hans has heard of it. Then again, he's from the German south, has lived in the Swiss Confederacy and has only the vaguest idea of what happens beyond Cologne.

'Has been for a while, not that anyone particularly noticed. A union of Protestant princes headed by Saxony and Hesse. Seven princes of the new religion, unconnected to Rome.' Cromwell dances back to his desk, sits down and looks at Hans. 'You don't get it, do you?'

'I'm not sure that I do.' But it's more that he doesn't want to. Because if it's good for Cromwell, it must be bad for him, Jennet and Wyatt.

A great cracking sound makes him jump. Cromwell's hand has slapped the desktop in excitement. 'German Lutheran princes against the Hapsburgs, basically. The Holy Roman Empire almost completely surrounds them, so it's a safety-in-numbers thing.'

Oh God. If the Imperial–French uniting was the impossible happening, the even more impossible has now occurred, Hans realises. The ever-ingenious, ever-resourceful Cromwell has found an alliance. Incredibly, even in these circumstances, he has found a rock for England to cling to. This unpronounceable league.

But surely, *surely* he can't have found a bride too. That's completely beyond the impossible.

'We might have found a bride too,' says Cromwell. 'Ever heard of Cleves?'

Hans shakes his head.

'No one has, dear boy. It's in some clunge in north-west Germany. But a useful little spot, it turns out. The Duke of Cleves is also Duke of Guelders, which gives him access to the Zuyder seaboard. Meaning,' he adds as Hans looks blank, 'that Cleves controls a strategic portion of the Lower Rhineland. One of his sisters is married to the head of the league. It's his other sister we might be interested in.'

'Right,' Hans says, heavily.

'What was her name, though?' Cromwell frowns, trying to remember. 'I'm sure it was mentioned when poor dear Queen Jane died. I would have made a note. Hold on, dear boy. Let me find it.'

He rummages happily amid his papers, chatting merrily as he does so. 'I'm almost certain there was an idea, at some stage, about a double marriage between them and us. The Princess Mary to Duke William of Cleves, and the king to this unspecified sister. I think we all laughed at the time, but now, well, things have changed.'

After a few minutes' more rummaging, he produces the paper. 'Here we are. The Duke of Cleves' unmarried sister. Her name is Anne. Oh dear.' Cromwell pulls a comic face. 'Awkward. Let's call her Anna. We want to avoid any unfortunate associations.'

Later, even Mistress Harris looks tense when she delivers the laundry basket. That Wyatt is worried too is obvious.

*I hate to say it*, he writes from Madrid, *but this is a countermove of genius by Cromwell. No one saw it coming. The emperor is infuriated at the idea of the Cleves match. He's obsessed with the Zuyder seaboard and he's even talking about moving Christina back into play, but there's no way I'm telling Cromwell that. Don't worry, though. We'll think of something. Perhaps when he sends you to paint Anna.*

The commission is not long in coming. 'I've been doing some research,' Cromwell announces. 'The princess of Cleves sounds just the job.' He produces something from the folds of his robes. 'Just listen to this from our contact at the court of Saxony. "She excelleth as far the Duchess of Milan as the golden sun excelleth the silver moon. Every man praiseth the beauty of the said lady as well for the face as for the whole body above all other ladies excellent." '

He rolls up the paper. 'Why they all have to phrase things like that I'll never know. But you get the gist.'

Hans does. If she's better-looking than Christina, she must be stunning. He tries valiantly to look as if his heart's not sinking into his boots.

They discuss the logistics of the journey. Cromwell merely waves his hand at the suggestion of Hans's German apprentice. 'Take him by all means, dear boy, anything. Just bring back a true likeness as fast as you can. Accuracy and speed, that's all that matters. I know I can trust you.'

To his surprise, Jennet's face does not light up when he tells her. 'Don't you want to come with me?' he asks.

'There's nothing I'd like more.' Her face is soft, and her eyes have a message. 'But . . .' She strokes her belly.

He catches his breath. 'You're not . . .?'

She nods. 'I've missed my courses. Twice now. Do you mind?'

'Mind?' He falls to his knees, buries his face in her dress. A child, together. A family of his own. She strokes his hair, laughing gently.

He looks up at her. 'Will you manage while I'm away?'

'Splendidly. Mistress Harris will look after me.'

For the journey, Hans had feared having Grisley imposed on him again. To his relief, it's Richard Beard, an obliging young groom of the Privy Chamber. He's more intelligent and user-friendly than Grisley, and a great deal less arrogant. He's also straightforward, confessing to doubts about the bride.

'Master Secretary is determined to further the match,' he tells Hans as they ride to Dover. 'But I don't think this woman will please the king.'

'But why not? I thought every man praiseth her beauty.'

'Every man who thinks that's what Master Secretary and His Majesty want to hear,' Beard says. 'But it's not the real story.'

He now tells Hans what Cromwell hasn't. About the dispatch from Nicholas Wootton, head of the English delegation in the Rhineland, which struck a considerably less rapturous note about the prospective bride.

'He's actually met her,' Beard says. 'And it sounds very much as if Master Cromwell has allowed his desire for this marriage to cloud his judgement.'

Hans looks down at his hands on the reins. As usual on journeys, they're wrapped in layers of rags to protect them. Such an ordinary sight, such an ordinary moment, and yet he senses everything is about to change.

Is Wyatt's long-ago promise about to be proved right? Is Cromwell finally going to make a mistake?

The familiar journey to Antwerp by Hansa boat, then north to Düren, a wooded and secluded spot on the River Ruhr. The August heat makes the journey oppressive, but Hans shrugs off the discomfort and the difficulty. He's sweaty and thirsty, but his heart is light, his spirits high. Unlike Beard, who's more doleful by the day, he cannot wait to meet the princess of Cleves.

First, however, he has to meet Nicholas Wootton, who gives them a fine sauerkraut dinner and a gloomy description of Anna. 'Lumpy, talentless, homely. Can't play an instrument, can't speak any language but German, has no education and spends all her time sewing at her mother's knee. That's what the reports say. That's what I've heard.'

'But what have you *seen*?' Hans asks, trying to tamp down the excitement in his voice. 'Haven't you met her?'

'In theory,' says Wootton. 'But we never got near enough to look at her. She stayed at the other end of the room. When we tried to get closer, the court officials grew angry. Started accusing us of wanting to see her naked.'

'Bit of an overreaction,' frowns Beard.

'They're an odd bunch,' Wootton says. 'That brother of hers, the Duke of Cleves. Real piece of work, he is. He's got his own reasons for wanting this marriage. The emperor thinks Guelders and the Zuyder seaboard belong to the Hapsburgs, so Cleves is keen to ally himself with England to protect his assets.'

As Beard takes a swig of beer, his young face in the candlelight is miserably tense. Hans sympathises. His first proper mission as a diplomat is a tough one, no doubt about it. 'We need to stop this marriage in its tracks,' Beard says firmly. 'Before it goes any further.'

Hans's sympathy vanishes. That's the last thing they need to do, by the sound of it.

He's relieved when Wootton, the seasoned envoy, shakes his grey head. 'Out of the question. Too many people want it to happen. The king. Cleves. And most of all, Cromwell. There's nothing we can do.'

There's silence for some minutes, apart from the slurping of sauerkraut. Then Beard puts down his fork, looking more cheerful. 'Well, Anna must have heard about Henry's reputation. How could she not? And it certainly dissuaded the other candidates.'

Wootton strokes his beard. 'It's a possibility. We can but hope.'

Under the table, Hans crosses his fingers. He's certainly hoping, for the exact opposite.

The castle of Düren is on the other side of the river. They trot over a wide bridge towards the towered fortress. In the great arched stone entrance hall, someone awaits them. He is tall and imposing, with a foxy face and a pointed black beard. 'Welcome,' he says, his smile not reaching his eyes. 'I am William of Jülich-Cleves-Berg. Duke of Cleves, Berg and Jülich and Count of Ravensberg.'

It's the piece-of-work brother, thinks Hans, as Beard introduces them both.

The duke speaks over him. 'Yes, yes,' he says, waving an impatient hand. 'No need for formalities. We are pleased to accept the proposal from your king. My sister will make an excellent Queen of England.'

'We haven't quite got to that stage yet,' Beard says hurriedly.

'Indeed we have.' Cleves' teeth show in his beard as he smiles. 'It's all decided and agreed. Your king wants to marry my sister.'

'He wants to see a picture of her first,' Beard counters. 'That's why we've come. So Master Holbein here can paint her.'

Another careless wave of the hand. 'No need for that,' the duke says genially. 'We'll just firm up the final details between ourselves. Then you can take the signed contracts back to England.'

But Beard stands his ground, shakes his neat dark head. 'Impossible, I'm afraid. We're here to take Her Excellency's likeness.'

Cleves' smile has faded and his foxy eyes have hardened. 'This portrait, it's unnecessary.'

Beard raises his chin. 'We have our instructions.' He's tough, Hans thinks, for all he's young. Unlike Grisley, he has the makings of an excellent diplomat.

The Duke of Cleves sighs. 'Oh, very well. If you insist. But this is very inconvenient. My sister will have to change into her court clothes, and that will take a great deal of time.'

Beard crosses his arms. 'Your Excellency, we have all the time in the world.'

# *Chapter Forty-Three*

Shown into a gloomy waiting room, they wait. Hans sets out his equipment and positions a chair for his sitter. Hours pass. Nothing happens. He fiddles with his equipment. Beard stares out of the window at the river. Still nothing. Hans puts Beard in the chair and sketches him. More hours pass.

'Oh, really,' the young envoy says at last, even his calm tolerance stretched to the limit. 'How long does it take to put a dress on?'

His question is now answered by the arrival of something at the room's far end. It looks like a dress, perhaps with a woman inside, although it's so dark it's hard to tell. The dress and the woman remain where they are, however, and do not come towards them. 'Your Excellency?' calls Beard, hesitantly.

*'Ich bin Anna von Jülich-Cleves-Berg,'* is the reply.

They look at each other. Is this her? They start to walk in the figure's direction.

*'Halt!'* the woman says. She sounds alarmed. *'Aus England, ja? Mein Bruder sagt ich sollte die Engländer nicht zu nahe an mich heranlassen.'*

'What's she saying?' Beard hisses.

'Says her brother has told her not to let Englishmen get close to her.'

'Suits me,' says Beard.

Hans clears his throat, addresses her in his native tongue. 'Your Excellency, madam. I am here to paint you. I really do need to be able to see you.'

Anna, unexpectedly, accepts this immediately. '*Ach, ja.* I suppose so.'

There's a clacking of wood on tiles, and as she bustles out of the shadows, they see not just that the dress is strangely shaped, with a great, stiff, bell-like skirt, but that it stops at ankle level, exposing the fact that she is wearing a pair of big red-painted wooden clogs.

'Jesus,' breathes Beard.

The clogs are only part of the problem, however. Raising his eyes to her face, Hans sees immediately why Englishmen, envoys specifically, are not allowed close, why Wootton received the reports he did and why there is no possibility that the king will want to marry this woman.

Whilst Beard, beside him, mutters his disappointment, the joy sweeping Hans is so strong it almost knocks him over. This really is it. The chance they have been waiting for.

Anna von Jülich-Cleves-Berg is extremely plain, with a large nose and small eyes. Her skin looks muddy, and what hair she has is completely hidden under a hood of a shape he has never previously seen. With something of the helmet about it, perhaps. Thickly jewelled and tasselled, it sticks out either side of her head and is covered for good measure with a short transparent veil. Compared to this, even the dreaded English gable hood is positively dashing.

Her dress seems designed to conceal as much as possible. Neck and bosom are covered by a thick lace panel piled with necklaces. Great red velvet sleeves explode on either side, caught at the elbow by thick bands of gold before billowing out again. More thick gold bands and red velvet extend down the front of the dress. It's an intensely complicated outfit and he can well believe it's taken this long to put on.

But he can see the potential already, see how he can make it work. How to produce an image that looks like Anna but will also entice Henry. How he'll use the tricks learnt from painting Jane and Christina, from observing Clouet, from listening to Jennet, to make the most important painting of his life. It's as if everything he's ever done has been leading to this portrait, the image that will bring down Cromwell and finally avenge Anne.

A great energy sweeps him, obliterating the tiredness of the journey. He can't wait to start. He knows exactly how to do it. Anna's clothes, strange as they are, have a certain magnificence. All that velvet, all that decoration. He'll do what he did with Jane Seymour: use the dress, use the gold, use the red. They are Henry's favourite colours anyway. And behind her put one of Jennet's plain blue backgrounds, but not a subdued one, one as bright as the sky instead.

As he reaches for his charcoal, Beard leans over. 'You're not actually going to paint her?' he hisses. 'It's a waste of time. Wootton was right: there's no chance the king will want to marry her. Cromwell must be mad. If Henry sees this woman, he's finished.'

*Exactly.* But it's a tricky moment. Beard could easily insist they abandon the mission, then sweep them both out of the castle and away. Hans racks his brains for a reason to persuade him not to.

'Oh, we're here now, may as well go through the motions,' he says. 'Could be a diplomatic incident otherwise. Given the touchy brother and all.'

'Already is, if you ask me,' Beard mutters. Thankfully, though, he doesn't argue and goes off to find a seat in the corner.

Anna, meanwhile, plonks herself gracelessly down on the chair in front of Hans. 'Like this, yes?' She smiles broadly to reveal teeth that are brown and receding; some of them even missing.

He can hear Beard from across the room. *Oh God.*

He invites Anna to turn her head to the side. Her nose is absolutely enormous. 'Perhaps more towards me,' he suggests. 'Yes, straight on. Could you stand up, do you think? And look more serious?'

Oh yes. It's all coming together now. Front-on, that enormous nose is greatly reduced. Standing up, she's more imposing, there's scope for symmetry. Her face will be expressionless, a face on which Henry can project whatever he wants.

'Lovely. And clasp your hands? That's it,' he says, encouragingly.

The elaborate headdress crackles and wobbles as Anna earnestly nods her head. '*Ja*, my brother William says this is why King Henry wants to marry me.'

Hans pauses, looks at her, puzzled.

'Because I am lovely, *ja*? Because tales of my beauty and accomplishments have spread throughout Europe!'

When Hans translates this, Beard's mouth falls open.

Anna continues happily. 'My brother William assures me that Henry and I will be extremely well matched. He says that Henry is young and attractive . . .'

Turning for another stick of charcoal, Hans sees Beard's incredulous face. Buried in this German valley, cut off from the world, Anna obviously has no knowledge of Henry's marital history. My Brother William has made sure of that.

'. . . My brother William also says that England is a country with excellent weather . . . Are you all right, Herr Holbein? That sounds like a nasty cough.'

Hans recovers, and Anna goes on.

'. . . and that English people are very well disposed towards foreigners, Germans in particular. William says that most English people actually speak our language, so it doesn't matter that I don't know theirs. I have never been a particularly adept linguist, or an adept student at all. But in Cleves it is not appropriate for ladies to be educated.'

Beard leans forward in his chair. 'What's she saying?'

Hans translates as little as he can get away with, but Beard still looks stunned. 'We all speak German? Where on earth did she hear that? What utter rubbish. Not that it matters; she doesn't stand a chance. There's no possibility she's going to be Queen of England.'

'I am looking forward to being Queen of England,' Anna says cheerfully. 'I am very well suited to the role, being very aristocratic. Through my dear mother Maria, the Duchess of Jülich-Berg, our line stretches all the way back to Sophia of Saxony, Adelaide of Teck and Sybilla of Brandenburg, after whom my sister Sybilla is named. There have been counts of Cleves since the eleventh century, and a romantic legend tells of the knight who appeared to the heroes of Cleves in a boat guided by swans, hence our use of the swan device in our coat of arms. I am sure all this will interest King Henry very much.'

'Somehow,' says Beard, 'I rather doubt it.'

But Anna doesn't doubt it, or doubt anything. She has a cheerfully positive view of the future. 'I look forward to a long and happy marriage. My parents have always been devoted to each other and my sister Sybilla's marriage to the prince of Saxony is equally blessed. We ladies of Cleves seem very fortunate in our choice of husbands! But poor King Henry, it seems, has been less than lucky with his wives. He has been widowed three times.'

'Widowed three times!' chokes Beard. 'Well, it's one way of putting it.'

'I have no information about them because my brother William, try as he might, has been unable to find much out. But he has warned me it is insensitive to pry, and that I should not. I think that what happened is that English ladies are delicate and do not enjoy the good health of we German women.'

Hans's fingers, initially so swift and enthusiastic, are slowing over his sketch. His initial euphoria is ebbing. Despite himself, he's feeling slightly sorry for her. Ignorant and delusional though she is, she is obviously a good-natured creature with a kind heart.

'Poor King Henry.' Her small eyes are bright with sympathetic tears. 'I feel so sorry for him. It is terribly tragic. To lose one wife is bad enough, but three! I will do my best to comfort him and be a good mother to his children. I am sure his daughters will enjoy learning needlework in the Cleves style.'

'It's actually cruel to let this go any further,' says Beard, when Hans translates. Hans pauses his pen. He agrees. Suddenly, it's hard to carry on.

Anna happily continues, however. 'And I look forward one day to having children of my own. Once, that is, my husband has instructed me in the procreative acts, about which I am entirely ignorant.'

*Ew. Possibly too much information there.* The familiar voice curls in his ear. His heart jumps; it's been months. He never thought to hear it again.

*Anne!*

*Why've you stopped drawing?*

*I can't do this,* he tells her silently. *She's as vulnerable as a child. They'll eat her alive in London. Henry. Cromwell.*

*So? Don't you think they did the same to me?*

*Yes, but—*

*Yes, but I was more intelligent? More worldly and educated? Much good it did me. And I probably looked quite vulnerable when you saw me on the scaffold.*

Oh God. What can he say to this? He sees now that Beard is watching him, clearly wondering what's happening, why he's muttering to himself.

Anna, on the other hand, just chatters on in her oblivious way.

'As hunting and hawking are improper pastimes for ladies of rank in Cleves, I have never done either. But my brother William says that hunting and hawking are not at all popular with the English . . .'

*Not at all*, chortles Anne. *Henry never does either. Apart from all the time.*

'. . . and that our Cleves table manners are the same as theirs; that they lick their plates as a sign of appreciation, and belch as we do if the food has been especially excellent.'

*Oh my goodness!*

*Stop it, Anne*, Hans says. *The poor woman.*

And straight away she turns the tables on him again. *I was a poor woman, Hans. Don't forget. Alone, unjustly condemned. Facing a hideous death. And it* was *hideous, believe me.*

Hans closes his eyes. No one knows this better than he does. And no one wants revenge for it more. But can he send another woman to the same place, perhaps to the same fate?

Anna is flashing her brown smile at him. 'My brother William says that the English court is, like our Cleves court, a respectable place where the wine is locked away at nine of the clock. It will not be fond of music because it is an occasion of lightness for a lady to play on any instrument. This is why I have never learnt, nor do I sing.'

*Oh mon Dieu. Oh la la.* Anne is laughing.

*Listen to her*, Hans is almost pleading now. *Listen to how ignorant she is. How her brother lies to her and manipulates her.*

*But Hans, he will lie to and manipulate her even more if she stays here, I can promise you that. And he will be cruel to her because she will be a failure.*

He hasn't thought of this. But it's very probably true.

*No harm will come to her in England,* Anne promises in his ear. *A little embarrassment, but no actual harm. But if you miss this opportunity, no harm will come to Cromwell either. Have courage, Hans. Do you want to meddle of my cause or not? Do you really want to avenge me? Because if you do, this is your last and greatest chance.*

She fades after that; he can sense she is no longer there. Having delivered her ultimatum, she is gone.

Hans looks at the floor for a minute or two, then picks up his pen again.

# *Chapter Forty-Four*

Back in England, Beard does not accompany Hans to see Cromwell and the king. His excuse is that he's too ill from seasickness to make the journey on horseback to Grafton, the manor in Northamptonshire where Henry is on summer progress.

Hans suspects his companion's malady has nothing to do with the movement of the waves. He was fine on the way back, and the sea was, anyway, calm. While Beard has not confirmed this – he's not a diplomat for nothing – Hans guesses that what's making him feel sick is the finished portrait, the one in his pannier as he gallops up the road. Painted originally on parchment in fast-drying tempera, it's been mounted on canvas and carefully rolled for travel.

He has made the best of Anna, just as he made the worst of Christina. She does not look beautiful, but she certainly doesn't look ugly. She still looks like herself, only the best possible version. But will it be enough to convince the king?

Hans has never been north of London before. The trees and hedges are shaggy with high summer. Above rolling golden wheatfields stretches a bright blue sky. There are hundreds of shades of green, and the different colours of endless varieties of flowers. He would notice every detail normally, perhaps even stop, do quick sketches for future reference.

But today his every thought is bent on what will happen when he arrives. Whether Cromwell will be there as he is meant to be; whether the king himself is, or whether Henry has moved on, on a whim, as he often does.

Hans is tired; the travelling has been constant. He has barely even seen Jennet, stopping at Aldgate a mere couple of hours, just enough time to glue parchment to canvas. As his hands were stiff from travel, she helped him, smoothing the painting on the glue with careful fingers.

'She looks like a saint,' Jennet remarks of the portrait, and Hans realises that she's right. Even the altarpieces that all those years ago he grew so sick of painting have found their way into this image. Anna's face has the same flat, closed quality, the same passivity. How strange, after all he has done, all he has striven to achieve, to end up back there. For what he had once rejected to be the answer, the solution.

Grafton lies within a mellow village. It's a gracious red-brick mansion in the modern style, with evidence of building still going on. Hans wonders how many projects the king is engaged in at any one time, and why he can't seem to finish any of them.

As he waits in the entrance hall, Anna of Cleves in the bag beside him, a pretty girl runs giggling from one side to the other, pursued by a handsome boy.

'Charming creature, isn't she?' That familiar acid voice. He looks over and sees, in the lee of an archway, the watchful bug eyes of Jane Parker.

He shrugs. *I wouldn't know. I don't care.*

'Tut, tut, Hans. You *should* care. She's the alternative.'

'Alternative?'

A mirthless laugh. 'Oh, Hans, really. This is the court; there's always an alternative. In this case, to what you've got in that package there.'

How does she know what he has in his package?

'Everybody knows. We've all been waiting. How was the court of Cleves?'

The girl runs back, shrieking, the boy after her. 'Quite the tease, no?' Jane Parker observes. 'She's Norfolk's candidate for wife number four. Instrument of the old aristocracy and the religious conservatives. Although I have to admit she doesn't look it.'

Nor does she, this girl with her almost entirely exposed bosoms, wanton tumbling hair and air of untrammelled sexuality. Is Jane Parker serious?

'Who is she?' Hans can't resist asking.

'Ah, so now you're interested.' She sounds triumphant. 'Her name is Katherine Howard and she's sixteen, but with a mental age of ten. Cousin of our dear departed Anne, would you believe. Norfolk's niece. You have to hand it to the old snake.' She chuckles. 'If at first he doesn't succeed, he tries, tries, tries again.'

God, the woman is poison. Norfolk, too, with his endless scheming. Why can't things at court stay still for even a few days?

The acid voice cuts into his thoughts. 'I wouldn't worry. The Norfolk campaign has only just started; not sure Henry's even noticed the little Howard yet. The smart money's still on you and Cromwell. A glamorous German princess trumps a home-grown hoyden any day of the week, and Master Secretary's been singing Anna's praises ever since you left. With the result that our dread and sovereign lord is keenly awaiting your picture. And poised to fall wildly in love. Musicians are on standby to help the process along; Cromwell's brought them all the way from Italy, would you believe?'

No, he would not believe. He slides her a look from under his brows. 'Don't be ridiculous.'

'Ridiculous, *moi?*' The bug eyes stretch wide, mock-indignant. 'Hans. I'm like you, I only tell the truth. They're a family, the Bassanos. They have that special new instrument, the violin. Ready to strike up after the big reveal.'

Alarm swirls through him. He'd imagined a private meeting, himself and Cromwell. Himself, Cromwell and the king at the most. But she's suggesting he's to show the picture in front of everyone.

'Yes, I'd be nervous if I were you,' Jane Parker says lightly. 'The stakes are high. You don't want anything to go wrong.'

As she glides off, smiling, Hans tries to reassure himself. He's done it, he knows he has. Created the opportunity he and Wyatt have sought for three years. A silly sixteen-year-old and her scheming uncle cannot put him off his stroke. All that need happen now is for Henry to like the portrait. To want to marry it. After that, things will take care of themselves.

'Dear boy! Dear boy! You've arrived!' Cromwell is suddenly bustling into the hallway. 'Welcome back, welcome back. This way! We're all ready for you!'

Hans reaches for his bag, makes as if to open it. He wants Cromwell to see the portrait, to make sure.

'Oh no, no, dear boy,' Cromwell beams. 'The king insists on seeing it first. Far be it from me.'

Beard was right, Hans reflects as he gathers up his things. Cromwell's judgement is all over the place. The Master Secretary of former times would insist on examining every inch of the painting before Henry even knew it was in the building. Assessing the risk to himself.

And then another thought strikes him. Perhaps there is no risk to Cromwell. Perhaps Hans himself will take the blame if it's not a success. This is a new thought, and a terrifying one.

He thinks of what Jane Parker said. *I'd be nervous if I were you. The stakes are high. You don't want anything to go wrong.*

As he picks up the bag with Anna in it, his hands are sweating.

Master Secretary has always been a fast walker, but these days his small feet seem to be on wheels. Hans almost has to run after him down a wide passage and up imposing stone stairs, new-cut which twist back on themselves as they rise to a magnificent upper chamber with huge windows and great tapestries on every wall.

Here, courtiers are milling around. As Hans enters, a ripple goes through the crowd. Everyone stares, nudges, mutters. They all know what he's here for.

As he crosses the room, he glances swiftly round. Norfolk is there, all hooded eyes and long, mean face. Next to him, Katherine Howard pouts and tosses her hair. Some dark-eyed people in blue are holding instruments; the Italian musicians, presumably.

'Ah! Holborn!' The king's funny high-pitched voice.

Henry is across the room, throned under a great embroidered canopy. He looks even more enormous, his great padded shoulders now as big in real life as they are in Hans's portraits. That his stout bandaged leg is up on a stool explains the increase in weight. He looks grey, exhausted. But still there's that dangerous aura of power, that air of terrifying unpredictability.

'Brought the painting, have you?' The king's small eyes, tinier than ever now his face is so much fatter, glint with excitement. 'Come on, come on,' he urges. 'Let's have a look at it.'

Hans takes the picture out, unrolls it, holds it up with shaking hands.

All talking stops. All eyes are on the king, whose eyes are on Anna. Norfolk is watching. Katherine Howard is watching. Cromwell is watching. You can't see him swallow, because he doesn't have a neck. But you can see the sweat on his forehead.

Henry stares at Anna in silence. Hans can hear the royal breathing, wheezing through the royal nose. He can hear his own heartbeat, thumping in his ears. Does Henry like what he sees? What is he thinking? Will the mean little eyes suddenly fix on him? Will he be asked to explain himself, then bundled away in chains?

Henry glances at Cromwell, who raises his chin like an expectant dog. Norfolk, in the crowd of courtiers, clears his throat as a countermeasure. But the king does not look at him. He does not even look at Katherine Howard, who rams her elbows together to force her bosoms yet higher.

Henry puts his huge, fat head first on one side, then the other. Then his face relaxes, and he smiles. 'Ah, yes,' he says. 'A magnificent woman. A marvellous work.'

Cromwell, blazing with relief, nods at his Italian musicians, who begin to play. Courtiers crowd round the picture, gasping with admiration. 'Exquisite,' they say. 'Beautiful.'

'Isn't she just?' says Henry proudly, now blowing kisses to her. His ardour is growing by the second. Cromwell beams. Norfolk frowns. Katherine Howard looks deflated. Anna gazes back at them all serenely.

# *Chapter Forty-Five*

All is organised. Anna will arrive before Christmas begins and the wedding will take place before it ends on Twelfth Night. No expense is being spared for the double festivities, and Henry is full of enthusiasm for his beautiful new bride. Not the least of whose charms is how much the match is annoying his enemies.

'You know the emperor was actually planning to kidnap her?' Cromwell says to Hans. He's in Master Secretary's office to consult over the wedding decorations. Cromwell wants him to head a team of painters to transform Greenwich's great hall into 'a bower of love', as he calls it.

'Anna was going to sail from Calais,' he goes on. 'Travel overland from Cleves through the Netherlands, which of course is Imperial territory. He was going to grab her there.'

Hans's eyes widen. But he can believe it; Charles V has form in this respect. Not long ago, but before they were allies, he kidnapped the sons of the King of France. 'Seems like a risk, going through the Low Countries,' he observes.

'Her brother insisted, said a long sea voyage in winter would be bad for her skin. His solicitude is most touching; presumably she has a marvellous complexion.'

Hans says nothing, either about the solicitude or the complexion.

'She's still coming that way,' Cromwell goes on. 'In a gold chariot, would you believe.'

Hans frowns. 'But what about the emperor? The kidnap risk?'

A triumphant smile from Master Secretary. 'He has been persuaded not to, and has become most surprisingly cooperative. Issued passes for dear Anna left, right and centre. We may attribute that to the excellent skills of our man in Madrid.'

Hans looks down, grinning. Wyatt has no doubt told the emperor in glorious detail exactly why Anna must reach England. No doubt, too, the emperor's ally François keenly awaits the moment when Henry sets eyes on his new bride. Both rulers, he imagines, believe the Anglo-Cleves alliance will be of little worth after that.

He's glad to hear Wyatt is on manoeuvres, and relieved, too. While he has sent long descriptions of his Cleves adventures via Mistress Harris's laundry bag, nothing has come in response. He had half feared that his missives had gone astray, that the head washerwoman is distracted by her excitement over Jennet's swelling stomach. But it seems not.

Cromwell continues to go through the timetable. Anna – and her gold chariot, presumably – will arrive at Dover, to be met by the Duke and Duchess of Suffolk. After that, she will journey to Canterbury, where the mayor, citizens and fifty ladies in velvet bonnets will await her with flaming torches and a peal of guns. Archbishop Cranmer will give a speech. 'A treat if ever there was one,' he comments drily.

She will then journey to Sittingbourne and Rochester, at whose castle it's envisaged she will spend the New Year holiday. After that, she goes to Dartford, and meets her bridegroom-to-be at Blackheath on 3 January, the day before the wedding.

'And where is she now?' Hans asks.

'At Calais, awaiting a fair wind. Well, any suitable wind really.'

The various English representatives with her are apparently teaching her card games. 'Listen to this!' Cromwell exclaims happily, picking up a letter. It's from Admiral Fitzwilliam, head of the Calais receiving party. ' "I assure Your Majesty" – it's to the king, of course, not me, ha ha – "that she playeth as pleasantly and with as good a grace and countenance as ever in all my life I saw any noblewoman." '

Hans tries to look impressed and not as if he suspects this is damning with faint praise. Cromwell seizes and recites other reports that seem similarly careful in their phrasing. Words like 'good' and 'gentle' make frequent appearances.

Yet both Cromwell and Henry seem wildly encouraged by them; Henry in particular. Hans has seen him, heard him, roaring and limping around the palace like a caged lion with a heavily bandaged leg, burning with impatience to see the woman about whom he has heard so much, of whom he expects so much.

He writes to Wyatt. *It's all set up beautifully.*

The fair winds take their time in coming, however, and so impatient has the king become that by the time Anna lands, the day after Boxing Day, he has decided to ride to Rochester to greet her.

'He's very keen,' Cromwell tells Hans. The bower of love is almost finished and Master Secretary has come to inspect it. 'He's going to her in disguise,' he adds.

Hans stares. 'Why in disguise?'

Master Secretary looks amused. 'Oh, it's a thing with him. Always has been, particularly around New Year. About ten years ago, he did it to Wolsey, at his New Year dinner at York Place. Everyone was at table when there was a great noise of cannon fire from outside. Visitors in disguise then burst in and the cardinal had to guess which one was the king.'

'And did he?'

'Sadly not. He was as blind as a bat, mostly from working at the king's papers by candlelight.'

'Was the king angry?'

'Not after the cardinal gave him Hampton Court, which is what it took to get him back on side. But 1527 really wasn't the cardinal's year. His next dinner was ruined by news of the Sack of Rome, which meant all hope of a papal divorce was finished. As you'll remember, dear boy.' Cromwell shakes his head ruefully. 'I told him not to give any more dinners after that. They didn't seem to be going especially well.'

With the king gone, and Cromwell distracted, Hans takes the opportunity to slip home to Aldgate, where Jennet's pregnancy is well advanced. It's a foul night, hail rattling against the windows, but inside glows with candles and contentment. They are sitting by the fire, cracking nuts and discussing baby names, when a sudden banging at the door makes Jennet gasp and clutch her stomach and Hans leap from his chair.

Someone tall and wrapped in a cloak strides in. They're covered in a light dusting of snow and pursued by stinging slaps and scatters of hail.

'Merry Christmas!' the someone exclaims in a familiar aristocratic drawl. They throw off their cloak to reveal a familiar lanky figure. They push floppy dark hair back from their face with two long, inky-fingered hands.

'Wyatt!' exclaims Hans in delight. He positions him by the fire, helps him remove his boots and shoves a glass of jenever at him.

'God, I've missed this stuff,' Wyatt says, downing it in one. 'Sherry's not the same; bit too sweet and you need twice as much to knock you out.'

Grinning at them both, he stretches out his long, thin legs. His boots gently steam by the flames. 'Good to see the two of you. How are you, Jennet? Blooming, I hear. And you're to be a father, Holbein.'

'Looks like it,' Hans admits, red with pleasure.

'I can see it. You'll be good at it. Not like me, I was hopeless. Family life took a slight hit after my wife ran off with the butler.'

'What?' exclaims Jennet.

Wyatt sighs, raises his jenever. 'Story for another time. Well, here's to you both. Thomas if it's a boy, yes?'

Jennet strokes her belly and laughs. 'And Thomasina if it's a girl.'

Hans smiles at his old friend. There's a new energy in the room, a new excitement now that Wyatt is in it. 'So you're back from Madrid?' he asks. 'Cromwell never said you were coming.'

'Didn't know, dear boy. It's the emperor what's sent me, not that I'm telling Cromwell that. Charles is desperate for a first-hand account of the meeting of Europe's most legendary lovers.' He pauses, grins. 'And I have to say, he's not going to be disappointed.'

Hans looks at him closely. 'What do you mean?'

'Spent last night at Rochester Castle, didn't I? It's on the way here from Dover.'

'Yes, Lady Anna's due there. The king went to meet her . . . Oh.' Hans stops. He recognises Wyatt's expression; he's trying to contain his laughter.

'What's happened?' Jennet is leaning forward, her clear gaze intent on their visitor.

'It's more what hasn't happened.'

'What hasn't, then?'

'The king and Lady Anna, for one thing.'

'He doesn't like her?' Hans holds his breath.

Wyatt chortles. 'That, my dear Holbein, would be an understatement. He called her a Flanders mare.'

'The rude pig!'

Wyatt smiles at Jennet. 'Our pig, though, my dear. Suits our purposes.' He turns to Hans. 'Holbein, I so wish you'd been there. Embarrassing wasn't in it. She had absolutely no idea who he was.'

The king had gone in disguise, Hans remembers. 'She didn't recognise him?'

Jennet's fingers are over her face, the eyes looking through them wide with horror.

'You could say that. The whole thing was a complete disaster.' Wyatt raises his long arm, waves his glass in the air. 'Fill her up again, Holbein, and I'll tell you all about it.'

They listen agog as the replenished poet paints the scene.

'I'd only just got there myself. Must have been about halfway through the afternoon. Getting dark. Lady Anna was watching a bullfight when I arrived.'

'A bullfight? In Rochester?'

'I was surprised too. More the kind of thing we have in Madrid, I would have thought. Anyway, I flashed my diplomatic credentials, as you do, and went to greet her.' Wyatt stops, blows out a breath. 'It's hard to know what to say, really. Maybe it was the clogs. Maybe the headdress. But I could see there was a problem. And then, quite suddenly, it got a whole lot worse.'

He describes how the door suddenly burst open and six men in multicoloured cloaks bounded into the room. 'Poor Anna was quite shocked enough, but then one of them stepped forward, grabbed her and tried to kiss her. She shrieked and attempted to beat him off.'

'Oh no!' Jennet is still looking at Wyatt through her fingers. 'It was Henry, wasn't it?'

'Hate to say it, but yes. He didn't take it well. Especially as there were quite a few courtiers about the place, watching. He stormed out in a huff.'

'But how was Lady Anna to know it was him?' Jennet demands.

'It was so unfair. She'd never seen him before. She didn't have a picture, like he did.'

'Couldn't agree more,' says Wyatt lightly. 'But since when had fairness anything to do with Henry?'

'It wasn't her fault,' Jennet says hotly.

Hans steps in to support her. 'She was expecting someone young and handsome, anyway. That's what My Brother William told her.'

Wyatt laughs. 'Well, Henry *is* young and handsome—'

'No, he's not!' Jennet bursts out. 'He's fat and disgusting, with a stinking leg.'

'My dear, let me finish,' Wyatt chides with a grin. 'What I was going to say, before I was so rudely interrupted, was that Henry's young and handsome *in his own head*. He sees himself as a chivalric knight and was enacting a scene from some romance, appearing to his lady love in disguise.'

'Unbelievable.' Hans shakes his head. 'So what happened next?'

'Having stormed out, he stormed back in again. But this time in purple velvet, looking rather more kingly. The penny dropped then, and Lady Anna was very apologetic. But the damage was done. I heard him out in the courtyard, raging that she looked nothing like he'd been led to believe. He'll be back here now, I imagine. Cancelling the wedding. Tearing strips off Cromwell, which should take a while as there's plenty to tear off.'

Hans looks into the fire. He should feel triumphant, he knows; the plan is a complete success. But a cold fear churns his bowels all the same. 'You think,' he says as steadily as he can manage, 'that it will definitely be Cromwell who gets the blame?'

There's a gasp of alarm from Jennet. 'As opposed to whom? Not you, Hans, surely?'

But Wyatt is steadfastly shaking his tousled head. '"I marvel

that wise men would make such report of her as they have done."
Those were the king's very words. Reports, Holbein. Not paintings. I'd say you were off the hook.'

'And Cromwell?' This is Jennet.

'Ah, now I'd say he was very much on it.' Wyatt leans over, clinks the glass Hans is holding with his own. 'We've done it, Holbein. Defeated the bastard at last.'

## *Chapter Forty-Six*

Have they, though? Incredibly, despite everything, the wedding is going ahead.

'Cromwell's convinced Henry he has to marry her because of the alliance of the emperor and François,' Wyatt storms. 'Told him he needs Cleves and he'll just have to put up with Anna.'

But Henry doesn't sound to Hans as if he's happy to put up with her. No one who lives or works near the royal apartments can fail to hear the king yelling at Master Secretary.

'You got me into this marriage! Now get me out of it!'

There's a half-hearted effort to find evidence of Anna being pre-contracted to some French duke. This outrages the envoys from Cleves, dismays the bride and gets nowhere, just as Cromwell intended. He has staked everything on the Cleves alliance, and his enemies, Norfolk especially, are ever-circling. It's in his interests that the marriage takes place as soon as possible.

But still Henry resists. 'Do you think her so fair? Tell me the truth!'

Cromwell replies that he took her not for fair, but of a brown complexion. The man has audacity, for sure.

'He's got away with it!' Wyatt exclaims. 'I don't know how he does it. Just when you think you've cornered him, he escapes. Just when you think he's finally facing the block, he grows another head. Like one of those mythical monsters.'

Hans himself has given up hope many times. But this is the first time he's seen Wyatt do so. 'To stop this marriage now, the whole Franco-Imperial alliance would have to break apart,' the poet goes on, his lean, clever face full of frustration.

'Which is unlikely,' Hans has to admit. 'How would that happen?'

Wyatt's dark eyes, which have been despairing, look suddenly thoughtful.

The following day, he has left London.

'Where's Wyatt?' repeats Cromwell when Hans ventures to ask. 'I've sent him back to Madrid to shove this Cleves match right in the emperor and the King of France's bearded faces. Encourage them to bind together all the tighter.'

Not hard to guess why. The closer the alliance Charles and François build, the more reason there is for Henry to marry Anna. Is this what Wyatt is really doing? Hans remembers his friend's face the night before he left. How he'd looked like a man struck by a sudden thought. But perhaps he's now decided the fight is over.

It's certainly over for Henry. Hans is present at Anna and Henry's first official public encounter at Blackheath. Both wear cloth-of-gold and have armies of servants, a bit like the start of a battle.

Which might well be how Henry sees it. The king's face is a picture, his fiancée's a rich puce because of the cold. This does not enhance her appearance and he greets her with barely concealed resentment. They ride to Greenwich Palace through lines of velvet-clad courtiers who goggle as they pass and giggle once they've gone.

Later, there's more shouting from the Privy Chamber. Henry wants to delay it, postpone it, avoid it. Makes one last desperate effort to resist. 'Must I, against my will, put my neck in the yoke?' he roars at Cromwell.

'For the sake of England and the Cleves alliance, you must, sire. Do you want to drive the duke into the hands of the emperor?'

When the dispatches arrive from Madrid, Cromwell gleefully reads them out to Hans. '"The Emperor is obsessed with Cleves and Guelders." Excellent!'

Hans tries to look as if he agrees.

'"He minds more about Cleves and Guelders than he cares about Milan and the whole of Italy." Marvellous!'

He hurries off to relay the good news to the king, while Hans is left wondering what Wyatt is playing at.

On the morning of the wedding, it's the king who walks as if he's going to the Tower Hill scaffold.

He makes his way slowly to the Queen's Closet, where Cranmer waits with his old long face and new Church of England prayer book.

Even at this stage, Henry's trying to resist. 'If I'd known before what I know now,' he bleats, 'she would have never set foot in the country.'

Hans is following in the small group of courtiers, and while he can't hear Cromwell's reply, he can see from his businesslike carriage that he's quite unperturbed. Norfolk, next to Hans, meanwhile looks coldly furious. Katherine Howard is nowhere to be seen.

'I'm only doing this for England!' Henry wails as they enter the closet.

He's a vast square of cloth-of-gold, with arms and legs at the corners and a small, fat, angry head on top. Anna arrives in the same glinting fabric; they must between them have commandeered London's entire cloth-of-gold supply. Her hair, which released from the helmet turns out to be bright yellow and rather lank, hangs loosely down to where her waist would be if the design of the dress had allowed for one. But let's be thankful for small mercies, at least she's not wearing clogs.

She's wearing a gold coronet, which the jewellery designer in Hans looks at with interest. There's some sort of vegetation shoved into it; rosemary, he realises. For remembrance. As if anyone could ever forget all this.

Throughout the short service, Hans half expects, and Henry obviously fervently hopes for, an interruption. That it should go ahead in these circumstances seems impossible. But it is all too possible, and the king emerges from the closet a married man once again and Anna his fourth wife.

Shortly afterwards, Cromwell is made the Earl of Essex and Lord Great Chamberlain of England. Short of a dukedom, he can rise no higher, a fact that Norfolk is well aware of, to judge from his sour, malevolent face. Hans sends the bad news to Wyatt in Madrid.

*Far from weakening Cromwell over Anna, we have made him stronger than ever. These days, the king himself has to obey him.*

No one imagines the royal wedding night will go well, and it more than lives down to expectations. The king roars to Cromwell how he felt Anna's breasts and belly and was discouraged from going any further.

*Mon Dieu*, Anne says in Hans's ear. *Has the man no restraint? This is a delicate matter, not something for the whole palace to hear. Typical Henry. He has no class, never had.*

Jane Parker stops Hans in the corridor. In that insidious way of hers, she has somehow inserted herself into the train of the incoming queen. Anna will be the third she has served, if served is the word, and the second of that name.

'A funny thing,' she says, then proceeds to tell Hans how she's been charged by Cromwell to improve the queen's bedroom performance. 'Had to go and talk to the Flanders mare about the birds and the bees.'

Hans doesn't want to know, but Jane Parker is fixing him with her bug eyes. He senses she particularly wants to discuss sex with him; perhaps she always has. She comes closer. He backs into the wall.

'I asked her,' Jane breathes, 'if she were still a maid, and she said she was not.'

'Well then. Mission accomplished.'

'Except that it isn't. Do you know what else she said?'

'No. But I'm guessing you're about to tell me.'

'How can I be a maid,' Jane says, imitating a heavy German accent, 'and sleep every night with the king?' The bug eyes are close now, their lashes lowered, her nose almost touching his. 'Can you imagine, Hans? She thinks it's just a matter of *being in the same bed*! She says that Henry kisses her every night and in the morning. Asked me if that wasn't enough.'

She's tracing his jaw with her finger now, caressing his lips. The woman has a repulsive sensuality that stirs him despite himself. 'I said that no, it was not nearly enough,' she breathes. 'That there was a Good. Deal. More. To it. But it doesn't matter anyway, did the poor mare but know it.'

'*What* doesn't matter?'

A light giggle. '*It.* What we've just been talking about. The birds and the bees. Our dread and sovereign lord is looking elsewhere now for satisfaction.'

The bug eyes dance with teasing knowledge. The full, rather puffy lips stretch in a triumphant smile. 'Ah,' she says. 'Made you stare.'

'Where elsewhere is he looking?' Not at Jane Parker, surely.

She smiles slyly, and Hans has the sudden feeling he'll have to sleep with her to get the information. Never, ever. He starts to back away.

'He's been seen crossing the river in a little boat,' she says quickly. 'Often in broad daylight and sometimes even at midnight.'

'Boat going where?'

'Who can say?' she says, playfully touching the top of his upturned nose. 'But it might be the Dowager Duchess of Norfolk's house in Lambeth.'

'The king's getting satisfaction with the *Dowager Duchess of Norfolk?*' The woman must be seventy at least.

The corridor explodes with Jane Parker's laughter. 'Hardly,' she snorts. 'The duchess is Katherine Howard's grandmother. It's where *she* lives. Now do you understand?'

Hans transmits the news to Wyatt with all speed. But even this development, which plays directly into the hands of his enemies, doesn't seem to worry Cromwell. If he knows about this relationship, and surely he must, he shows no concern. On the contrary, the newly minted earl remains blithe, humming about his work, talking to Hans about the arrangements for Anna's coronation, currently slated for Whitsuntide.

And then, suddenly, just like that, everything changes. Hans arrives in Cromwell's office one morning to find him looking uncharacteristically shattered.

'What's the matter?'

The alliance, he discovers, is over. The emperor and the king have parted ways.

# *Chapter Forty-Seven*

The letter is waiting when he gets home. Jennet, who's sewing a baby dress by the fire, puts down her needle and hands it over. He rips off the familiar barnacle seal.

*Got to admit*, Wyatt writes, *it took some doing. I don't know whether you recall me mentioning a certain Robert Brancetour? Rich Englishman in the emperor's service, but better known to Cromwell and Henry as a one-time interpreter and guide to Cardinal Pole. Ask Jennet if you don't know who he is.*

Hans has heard Cromwell mention Pole. An enemy of the state, at large in Europe, where there have been several unsuccessful attempts to apprehend him. But he doesn't know much else. He asks Jennet.

'A sad story,' she tells him. 'They used to be close, Henry and Reginald – that's Pole's name.'

*'Reginald?'*

'Never mind that. Point is, when he was young, Pole was Henry's protégé. The king paid for his education. Reginald was very brilliant; there was an idea that he might one day be Archbishop of Canterbury. This was all before the split with Rome, obviously. Which is where it all went wrong. Henry expected Pole to support him, make arguments on his behalf to the Vatican and so on. But Reggie did the exact opposite. Actually said that the sooner

Henry was deposed, the better for England. You can imagine how that went down.'

Hans is not especially surprised that Jennet is this well informed; her knowledge of the court, he has discovered, is much wider and deeper than his own. What he is wondering, though, is how all this relates to what's just happened.

'Because,' Jennet says, 'Pole is a Plantagenet and . . .' for all they're in their own home, she lowers her voice to a whisper, 'has a better claim to the throne than the king. His family are part of the Norfolk faction. The old aristocrats, the religious conservatives. As an exile in France, which is what and where he is, he agitates for the invasion of England. There's a price on his head, obviously, but no one's got him yet. So that's the background.'

Hans nods, rather doubtfully, and resumes reading Wyatt's letter.

*So Brancetour, as Pole's aide and fixer, is just as much of a menace as Pole himself. In Cromwell and Henry's minds at least. It struck me that he might help us with our Cleves difficulties, and so I decided to find out where he was.*

He lowers the letter, really confused now. Why would an enemy of the state be of use to them with Anna?

*Paris, it turned out. Which was extremely useful, as the emperor was going there to visit his new best friend François. So I went with him and arrested Brancetour as an enemy of England. There was a bit of a fight and Brancetour refused to come with me. Said he was a subject of the emperor and not Henry and would submit to no other authority.*

Hans looks up, rubs his face. Jennet glances over, amused. 'Have you worked it out yet?'

He hasn't, obviously. He reads on.

*So back I went to the emperor and asked him to hand over Brancetour. He looked down his long Hapsburg jaw at me and said no. He added that he was very fond of Brancetour, and that he had been a good servant.*

*What was more, he would ask the King of France to release him from my custody.*

*This was going to really annoy François, because the emperor, for all his greatness elsewhere, had no authority in France. For him to demand this release was to countermand French sovereign power.*

*And this is where the really clever diplomatic bit comes in, Holbein. I told the emperor, in French obviously, that it would be disrespectful to King Henry to order the release of his enemy. Charles replied in a way that, depending how you interpreted it, suggested that he was superior to Henry and all other monarchs so respect didn't really come into it.*

He pauses and looks at Jennet. 'I'm guessing that's how they interpreted it.'

She nods, grinning.

*Obviously, we lost no time in sending the good news to our embassy in France, where they lost no time in informing François. He was outraged and offended to learn that he too was inferior to the Hapsburgs, and I fear that, very sadly, the great Franco-Imperial alliance is over as a result. And as a result of that result, there is no longer a need for an entente with Cleves. Or a marriage to its princess, come to that.*

Hans lets the letter drop to the floor. 'My God,' he says to Jennet. 'Wyatt has done it.'

After this, events move fast. Cromwell tries to move faster, keep ahead, cling to power the way he always has, by aggrandising his master. He scrambles to pass legislation that elevates the monarch to the status of a god. An Act of Proclamation, meaning that whatever Henry says is law. An Act of Attainder, meaning that anyone arrested can be condemned without the need for a trial. These laws, of course, have nothing to do with justice. But justice and Cromwell parted ways long ago. If, indeed, they were ever acquainted in the first place.

Cromwell must know he is finished. The machinery to divorce

Anna is in motion, and it was he who championed the match. He is alone, he has no support; the king is furious at being made to marry against his will, for what is now absolutely no reason. Master Secretary's enemies are crowding in. They can scent the blood in the water, and this is the blood they've long been waiting for.

Wyatt returns the morning Cromwell is arrested at the Council Board. They hear afterwards how Norfolk ripped his chain of office from his neck, and Admiral Southampton his Garter decoration. That Grisley was there too surprises Hans.

But not Wyatt. 'So what if Cromwell promoted him? There's no good turn goes unpunished.'

Cromwell has been taken to the Tower now, but quietly, slipping upriver in an unobtrusive barge. The first London knows of it is when the royal guards come to Austin Friars to inventory his goods. Hans pictures them being received by the many liveried servants, all perplexity.

There won't be a trial. Cromwell himself has obviated the need for this, with his Act of Attainder. He's legally dead already, the charges against him a fantastic, hastily scrambled mix of treason, heresy and something Hans has never heard of.

'What's *scandalum magnatum*?' he asks Wyatt.

'Being rude and oppressive to nobles,' is the reply. 'It's probably the only charge with any vestige of truth. But truth, as Cromwell has fatally taught Henry, is a lot less important than convenience.'

Convenience is keeping him alive for now, as with his formidable legal brain Cromwell is the only one who can unpick the Cleves marriage. The idea of Anna being pre-contracted is being returned to, with rather more vigour. She is putting up little objection. She is now acquainted with the fate of her predecessors and keen to be cooperative.

It's at the foot of one of Cromwell's missives about the divorce, addressed to Henry from the Tower, that he writes, *Most gracious prince, I cry for mercy, mercy, mercy.*

'The mercy he never granted anyone else,' Wyatt says when he hears about it. But he looks as sickened as Hans himself feels.

It's what they wanted, of course. Cromwell in his cell, racked with the same agonising fear as all his victims, but with the added layer of knowing he had caused their pain. Now he will meet the same end.

Perhaps that's why Anne has been quiet. Perhaps now she is satisfied. Her cause has been meddled with, justice has been done. Finally, the man who destroyed her is about to be destroyed himself.

# *Chapter Forty-Eight*

It's a hot day at the end of July and the sun beats down from a blue sky. The king is not present; when is he ever? As is often the case when one victim is being dispatched, he's taking his mind off it by marrying the next one. In this case it is Katherine Howard. It won't be long before it's her turn.

That's what they're saying, those lining the route to Tower Hill. Those at the front of the crowd, side by side like a line of soldiers. The line of Cromwell's victims.

The crowd behind them are wiping their brows, complaining of the heat. They don't see the ghosts, but Hans does. Thomas More is there, and his old friend Bishop John Fisher. They look calm, benevolent. Next to them, more restless, are the men co-accused with Anne: William Brereton, Francis Weston, Henry Norris. Poor Mark, too, and George Boleyn. He stands towards the end, nearest the scaffold, and next to him is his sister.

She's beautiful in her red dress, young again, almost as he first saw her. As she glances about her hair slides around her shoulders. Hans's heart lifts to hear that familiar giggle; she and George are laughing about something.

A roll of drums. A rumble through the crowd. Everyone looks down towards the river. From the gatehouse at the foot of the hill a small procession is emerging. Two lines of guards with halberds, and between them a familiar stocky figure.

*Who's that with him?* Hans hears Anne ask George.

*Some random nobleman who worked for Cromwell. Name of Hungerford. Wife-beating incestuous buggerer, they say.*

*Ew. Wish I hadn't asked.*

Cromwell stumps up the hill. All the terror and crying for mercy is over; his features are composed. But they have to be; he must think of his family now. Only those with no dependants and nothing to lose protest at the end. Or apportion blame, or complain. Thomas More even made a joke, moving his beard out of the way of the axe, saying it had done no harm.

'Cromwell's lucky really,' says someone from behind. Hans recognises the grinding voice of Norfolk. 'Background as low as his, he could have been burnt at the stake.'

Anne and George turn to look at him, and then shudder at each other. *Bad taste. But what else would you expect from Uncle Norfolk?*

Cromwell is now level with Thomas More, whose daughter Margaret ran from the crowd on just this spot to embrace him when he made this journey. No one runs to embrace Cromwell. Does he see More? He makes no sign if so. Possibly he does not see anything.

More watches him pass, his fine dark eyes sympathetic. Fisher shakes his head. However much you hate someone, you wouldn't wish this on them.

The other men might feel differently. Dispatched so quickly, they are clearly yet to come to terms with it. They watch Cromwell pass with burning eyes. Anne, for her part, observes him with a calm solemnity.

Only now, as he's about to pass Wyatt, does Cromwell react. 'Wyatt!' He smiles; seems surprised, delighted even. 'Pray for me,' he adds. Then he spots Hans. 'Dear boy!'

There's an awful pathos in his believing, at the end, that they remain his friends. But Hans doesn't begrudge him this small comfort. None of it is as he imagined. He had thought that watching Cromwell walk to the scaffold would be joyful and triumphant. The long struggle is over, the great adversary defeated. Instead, it feels flat, empty, even sad. They may have got rid of the man, but no one can erase the suffering he caused. And what now, anyway? It's dominated his life for so long, it's hard to think beyond it.

As Cromwell passes and moves up the hill, Hans stares at the back of his head.

Wyatt leans close. 'Strange how someone with so much brass neck had so little actual neck.'

Cromwell and Hungerford climb the scaffold. Hungerford is raving, and the drums beat over his words. He dies badly. Cromwell affects not to notice this, nor the blood coursing around his feet once it's over. He sets out his stall calmly: how he dies in the Catholic faith, how he prays for the king and commits his soul to God.

*Always supposing God wants it*, George Boleyn says tartly.

Cromwell's lack of neck is clearly a challenge for the axeman. It does indeed, as Wyatt and Hans once wanted, take several sickening hacks to get his head off. This fulfilment of their wishes is hard to watch; Hans turns away, while Wyatt covers his eyes. The ghosts, meanwhile, look on with an informed interest, exclaiming and making remarks. But even botched beheadings are soon over, and Cromwell's remains are bundled off the last of the many stages he commanded in his life.

# *Epilogue*

## Aldgate, London
## 1543

The rain has ceased. Spokes of late gold light pierce the gaps between the window shutters. The sick man in the bed opens wide-spaced blue eyes. They used to see so clearly, but now things are dim, confused.

Hans is ill; he is dying. Many years ago, in another country, the plague took his parents and brother. Now, finally, it has come for him. He knew it when he saw the smudges, watched them deepen to bruises and swell black and big as a fist. And then the racing pulse, the raging thirst. Then the headaches, the delirium he slips constantly in and out of.

It's like drowning, this plague fever. Like a river, but not the great ones he has known. The wide and fast-flowing Rhine, the leisurely silver Loire, the muddy and boat-packed Thames. They have meant life and freedom, escape and opportunity. But now his travelling is over, and this fever river is death.

The girl by the fire gets up, comes over. Is he dead yet? No, still going. Why doesn't he hurry up, this strange German? Plenty of others dying in this city. Plenty of families willing to pay her to see their loved ones out of this world so they don't have to.

After the German, she'll be on to the next. Another scurry, head shawled, through strangely silent streets, past men with covered mouths driving carts of corpses to plague pits. In at another door painted with another rough cross, to another someone gasping by a guttering candle. While, in the shadows, the same old Death stands waiting.

She's heard the German was a painter. She knows nothing about painting, but she knows about sheets, and his are good linen, not too worn. She might well take them; only be burnt otherwise when they clear the house. Nothing else worth having, just a few battered pewter plates and cracked drinking vessels. His wife – if that's what she was – and children have taken everything else they could cram in their covered cart. Now all that remains of them is the panicked footprints in the mud outside, the wheel ruts, the mass of hoof marks, the direction they eventually all lurched off in.

The girl returns to her chair, gives the dying fire an impatient poke. The flames rear up, glow in the dark room.

Hans, on his straw-stuffed mattress, feels sunshine warm his face. The air glitters, he smells that unmistakable Thames tang, hears the boatmen shout. He's at Greenwich, in the palace gardens by the river. With Jennet, whose lovely face is swollen with tears. No, he's not at Greenwich, he's here. She's clinging to him despite his sickness, despite the danger to herself. But he's trying to think ahead, form a plan.

'Leave,' he urges her. 'And when all this is over, go see the king. The next court painter should be you.'

She'll need to support herself somehow. He's not leaving her much, God knows. While, unlike Cromwell, he escaped with his life after Anna of Cleves, the failure of the whole business clung to him. He never regained his former pre-eminence, and royal commissions were far and few.

The German is saying something. The girl gets up again. Does he want a drink? There's some dragon water, useless stuff sold by those quacks who tell plague patients to eat onions and keep warm. She takes the cracked jug, approaches. The fingers that seize it are strong-looking, with short, square tips and neat nails. Not dirty and scarred like most she sees, broken and twisted, with fingers missing.

His eyes, too, are different; not the usual clouded eye-roll of the departing, but a focused, burning stare that seems to see right into her. He's smiling at her as if he knows her.

Does he know her? Hans is wondering. Dark hair, a sharp face. Is it Wyatt? How he misses his friend, dead since the previous autumn and courting trouble till the last, bailed out of his final scrape by none other than poor Queen Katherine Howard. Dead herself now, of course, beheaded like her cousin after a mere sixteen months and taking Jane Parker with her. Or perhaps it was the other way round; the knowing Parker encouraging the poor young woman in her folly.

The candle gutters. In the wax pooling beneath the wick, a pale and heavy face now seems to form. Those small, dangerous eyes – Henry, he thinks. Or Cromwell. Either way, there's a ruthlessness in the air now, a crushing, brutal power. He feels a cold terror. The left hand holding his brush shakes slightly.

But he is not holding a brush. He is not painting. Where is he? He knows there isn't much time left.

Bells are ringing, trumpets blaring, jewels flashing in the sun, the sound of hooves in sawdust-muffled streets. Anne's coronation procession. Her black hair cascades over her glittering silver cloak as she sways past on her shining golden litter. In the dim, incense-heavy Abbey, her tiny feet in their silver shoes slowly cross the mosaic pavement before the altar.

The girl watches him as he drinks greedily, his wasted throat convulsing, his strange, wide-spaced eyes locked on her all the while. '*Schauen Sie*,' he says, when the cup is empty. He can't remember any of his formerly excellent English now. *'Schauen Sie unter den Boden.' Look under the floor.* His shaking hand rises. A finger points downward, towards the wooden planks.

Gold? The girl dives excitedly down, peers, braced for rats. But in the gloom beneath the bed there's only dust, and what looks like a child's wooden doll, forgotten in the rush. She glances up, brow creased in anger.

That frown, it's Lady Alice, Hans thinks. So now he's at Chelsea, staying with Thomas More. He's just arrived in London, and drawing supplies are hard to find that far upriver. More's wife shouts at him for messing up her oven dishes making his charcoals. Alice shouts at More too, come to that. But not when Hans last saw her, when they came to take her husband to the Tower. She was weeping then.

He sinks back, his breath rasping, and tries again to summon the English. This time it comes. 'Board,' he says, slowly. 'Wood. Floor. Find. Pull up.'

The girl hastens to obey, her searching hands slapping the floorboards.

As she tugs out the plank, she's unaware that here is a secret only she shares. The others who lived here never knew what the floor was hiding. Or that when they were out and the house was quiet, he knelt and pulled up the board, exposed the shallow space, lifted out what lay there, swaddled in sacking.

The girl unwraps it eagerly, then her heart plummets. A small picture, that's all. A woman with black hair in a red dress.

'Give it to me,' he says to her, with what feels like the last of his strength.

Carelessly, she passes it over. It's no one she recognises, it's not worth taking. When he's dead, it can go on the bonfire with the rest.

He holds it in shaking hands, stares with fading eyes. He did this after Cromwell died, after it was all over, while he could still remember her as she was. Still draw and paint her, more to the point. With her dark eyes and her red dress and that touch of colour high on her cheeks, she's all brilliant, glowing life. And indeed, this small piece of oak is the only place Anne lives now. You won't find her anywhere else, look as you might. No other image of her survives.

*Ah no, Hans!* Her low voice laughs in his ear. *Remember, I am still there in our great picture. They didn't destroy that because they didn't know what it was. The idiots! We were too clever for them!*

*You were too clever always. And too beautiful, too merry, too witty, too honest, too interested, too French, too loyal, too loving, too good. Too everything.* He can tell her now, now that it's almost over.

*Flatterer! But our painting. As I said, you added the skull afterwards, without asking me.*

*And as I explained, it was because you weren't there. It was your story, and that was the way the story ended.*

*Our story will never end, Hans.*

He grins ruefully. *Now who's being the flatterer? Who's going to remember me?*

*The painter of truth? Who made people look even more real than they were? Of course they'll remember you.*

The irony, he thinks. He painted the truth, but missed so many lies. And he painted reality, but nothing in his life has felt real for seven years. Not since that sweet May morning in the Tower, all blue sky, blossom and birdsong. When the sword swung through Anne, it swung through him. But his body has remained alive; there's been a job to do.

A job that's now done.

*I avenged you*, he tells her silently. *I destroyed him.*

The black eyes sparkle. *Yes, I know.*

It's darkening around him. *Not long now*, he says.

*Not long.* She smiles her red smile.

THE END

*Hans was right. Henry's next court painter was indeed a woman: Levina Teerlinc (1510–1576). She received an annual salary of £40, £10 more than Hans.*

# *Acknowledgements*

Hans, with his efficiency and speed, would not have been impressed. *The Queen's Painter* has been a long time in the writing. Very possibly it's taken close to six decades because I can't remember when Holbein's portraits were not familiar and fascinating presences. This sounds grand but isn't. As a child in the 1970s I was fortunate to coincide with lots of improving heritage-focused television and was aided in my historical interests by a Tudor-crazed godmother.

The particular conceit of this book was the result of taking my children to the National Gallery a lot when they were small. We would make a beeline for the Holbeins and speculate about the circumstances of each painting. The sheer amount of clobber in *The Ambassadors*; why Erasmus had such filthy hands; why Christina of Milan, who was supposed to be so beautiful, looked so plain, at least in our view. Eventually a whole theory began to form, and then, very slowly, the story you've just read. I would like to thank my son Andrew McLeod and daughter Isabella McLeod for all this inspiration.

But it would never have made book form without my editor Jen Doyle and my agents Jonathan Lloyd and Lucy Morris. A huge thank you to them for all their patience, diligence, skill and experience in steering and shaping the good ship Hans.

Writing *The Queen's Painter* would not have been possible either without referring to a huge number of books. I am particularly indebted to the following:

*Hans Holbein* by Oskar Batschmann and Pascal Griener (Reaktion Books, 1997)
*Henry VIII and the Men Who Made Him* by Tracy Borman (Hodder & Stoughton, 2018)
*The Craftsman's Handbook* by Cennino d'Andrea Cennini (Dover Publications, 1960)
*Holbein in England* by Susan Foister (Tate Publishing, 2006)
*The Six Wives of Henry VIII* by Antonia Fraser (Weidenfeld & Nicolson, 1992)
*Holbein* by Elizabeth Goldring (Paul Mellon Centre, 2025)
*Thomas Cromwell* by Robert Hutchinson (Phoenix, 2007)
*The Life and Death of Anne Boleyn* by Eric Ives (Blackwell, 2004)
*Thomas Cromwell* by Diarmaid MacCulloch (Penguin, 2018)
*Holbein's Sir Thomas More* by Hilary Mantel and Xavier F. Salomon (The Frick Collection in association with D Giles Limited, 2018)
*In the Footsteps of Anne Boleyn* by Sarah Morris and Natalie Grueninger (Amberley Publishing, 2013)
*The King's Painter* by Franny Moyle (Head of Zeus, 2021)
*Graven With Diamonds* by Nicola Shulman (Short Books, 2011)
*Six Wives: The Queens of Henry VIII* by David Starkey (Vintage, 2003)
*Henry VIII: King and Court* by Alison Weir (Jonathan Cape, 2001)
*Hans Holbein: Portrait of an Unknown Man* by Derek Wilson (Pimlico Books, 2006)

Finally I would like to thank my husband Jon McLeod for his unfailing support and great good sense.

Wendy Holden
Derbyshire 2025

RAISING READERS

Books Build Bright Futures

Dear Reader,

We'd love your attention for one more page to tell you about the crisis in children's reading, and what we can all do.

Studies have shown that reading for fun is the **single biggest predictor of a child's future life chances** – more than family circumstance, parents' educational background or income. It improves academic results, mental health, wealth, communication skills, ambition and happiness.[1]

The number of children reading for fun is in rapid decline. Young people have a lot of competition for their time. In 2024, 1 in 10 children and young people in the UK aged 5 to 18 did not own a single book at home.[2]

Hachette works extensively with schools, libraries and literacy charities, but here are some ways we can all raise more readers:

- Reading to children for just 10 minutes a day makes a difference
- Don't give up if children aren't regular readers – there will be books for them!
- Visit bookshops and libraries to get recommendations
- Encourage them to listen to audiobooks
- Support school libraries
- Give books as gifts

There's a lot more information about how to encourage children to read on our website: **www.RaisingReaders.co.uk**

Thank you for reading.

hachette UK

---

[1] OECD, '21st-Century Readers: Developing Literacy Skills in a Digital World', 2021, https://www.oecd.org/en/publications/21st-century-readers_a83d84cb-en.html

[2] National Literacy Trust, 'Book Ownership in 2024', November 2024, https://literacytrust.org.uk/research-services/research-reports/book-ownership-in-2024